The Emperor meets The Three Sisters

THE
VIOLET FAIRY BOOK

Edited by

ANDREW LANG

With Numerous Illustrations
by H. J. Ford

DOVER PUBLICATIONS, INC.
NEW YORK

This Dover edition, first published in 1966, is an unabridged republication of the work originally published by Longmans, Green and Co., London, in 1901. Those illustrations that appeared in color in the original edition are here reproduced in black and white.

International Standard Book Number: 0-486-21675-6
Library of Congress Catalog Card Number: 66-24133

Manufactured in the United States of America
Dover Publications, Inc.
31 East 2nd Street
Mineola, N.Y. 11501

TO   VIOLET   MYERS

IS   DEDICATED

THE   VIOLET   FAIRY   BOOK

PREFACE

The Editor takes this opportunity to repeat what he has often said before, that he is not the author of the stories in the Fairy Books ; that he did not invent them ' out of his own head.' He is accustomed to being asked, by ladies, 'Have you written anything else except the Fairy Books?' He is then obliged to explain that he has *not* written the Fairy Books, but, save these, has written almost everything else, except hymns, sermons, and dramatic works.

The stories in this Violet Fairy Book, as in all the others of the series, have been translated out of the popular traditional tales in a number of different languages. These stories are as old as anything that men have invented. They are narrated by naked savage women to naked savage children. They have been inherited by our earliest civilised ancestors, who really believed that beasts and trees and stones can talk if they choose, and behave kindly or unkindly. The stories are full of the oldest ideas of ages when science did not exist, and magic took the place of science. Anybody who has the curiosity to read the ' Legendary Australian Tales,' which Mrs. Langloh Parker has collected from the lips of the Australian savages, will find that these tales are closely akin to our own. Who were the first authors of them nobody knows—probably the first men and women Eve may have told these tales to amuse Cain and Abel. As people grew more civilised and had kings and queens, princes and princesses, these exalted persons generally were chosen as heroes and heroines. But originally the characters were just ' a man,' and ' a woman,' and ' a boy,' and ' a girl,' with crowds of beasts, birds, and fishes, all behaving like human beings. When the nobles and other people became rich and educated, they forgot the old stories, but the country people did not, and handed them down, with changes at pleasure, from generation to generation. Then learned men collected and printed the country people's stories, and these we have translated, to amuse children. Their tastes remain like the tastes of their naked ancestors, thousands of years ago, and they seem to like fairy tales better than history, poetry, geography, or arithmetic, just as grown-up people like novels better than anything else.

This is the whole truth of the matter. I have said so before, and I say so again. But nothing will prevent children from thinking that I invented the stories, or some ladies from being of the same opinion. But who really invented the stories nobody knows; it is all so long ago, long before reading and writing were invented. The first of the stories actually written down, were written in Egyptian hieroglyphs, or on Babylonian cakes of clay, three or four thousand years before our time.

Of the stories in this book, Miss Blackley translated ' Dwarf Long Nose,' ' The Wonderful Beggars,' ' The Lute Player,' ' Two in a Sack,' and ' The Fish that swam in the Air.' Mr. W. A. Craigie translated from the Scandinavian, ' Jasper who herded the Hares.' Mrs. Lang did the rest.

Some of the most interesting are from the Roumanian, and three were previously published in the late Dr. Steere's ' Swahili Tales.' By the permission of his representatives these three African stories have here been abridged and simplified for children.

CONTENTS

	PAGE
A Tale of the Tontlawald	1
The finest Liar in the World	17
The Story of three Wonderful Beggars	23
Schippeitaro	36
The Three Princes and their Beasts	41
The Goat's Ears of the Emperor Trojan	52
The Nine Pea-hens and the Golden Apples	55
The Lute Player	70
The Grateful Prince	77
The Child who came from an Egg	98
Stan Bolovan	111
The Two Frogs	125
The Story of a Gazelle	127
How a Fish swam in the Air and a Hare in the Water .	148
Two in a Sack	153
The Envious Neighbour	160
The Fairy of the Dawn	165
The Enchanted Knife	199
Jesper who herded the Hares	205
The Underground Workers	217
The History of Dwarf Long Nose	226
The Nunda, Eater of People	249
The Story of Hassebu	263
The Maiden with the Wooden Helmet	270
The Monkey and the Jelly-fish	275
The Headless Dwarfs	281

x CONTENTS

PAGE

The young Man who would have his Eyes opened . . 294

The Boys with the Golden Stars 299

The Frog 311

The Princess who was hidden Underground 316

The Girl who pretended to be a Boy · 320

The Story of Halfman 345

The Prince who wanted to see the World 356

Virgilius the Sorcerer 364

Mogarzea and his Son 380

ILLUSTRATIONS

HALFTONE PLATES

[These illustrations appeared in color in the original edition.]

The Emperor meets the three Sisters . . .	*Frontispiece*	
The Tontlawald	*to face p.*	8
The Witch and the Prince	,,	50
The Gazelle	,,	146
The Whirlwind seizes the Wreath	,,	188
Morning Glory the Fairy of the Dawn . . .	,,	196
The Nunda, Eater of People	,,	254
The Girl with the Wooden Helmet	,,	272

FULL-PAGE PLATES

The Woodcutter in the Tontlawald	*to face p.*	2
How the Old Man disappeared after Dinner . .	,,	10
The Fairies catch the Baby	,,	24
The Beautiful Woman soothes the Serpent-King .	,,	30
The faithful Beasts wept round the dead Body of the Prince	,,	46
Under the Golden Apple Tree	,,	56
The Dragon flies off with the Empress . . .	,,	60
The Lute Player	,,	70
The Fairy and Dotterine pass unseen through the Camp of the Enemy	,,	104
The Gazelle brings the Diamond to the Sultan .	,,	130
Petru has to turn back	,,	170
The Battle with the Welwa in the Copper Wood .	,,	174
Among the Flowers were lovely Maidens calling to him with soft Voices	,,	184
The Princess at the Curtain	,,	200
The Underground Workers	,,	221
The Prince finds the Nunda	,,	258
The Monkey brought to Otohime	,,	276
A Dwarf was in the Bell	,,	282
Hans fights the Headless Dwarfs	,,	288
The Boys with the Golden Stars	,,	306

xii   *ILLUSTRATIONS*

The Princess charges the Lion   .   .   .   to face p. 326
Virgilius and the Evil Spirit   .   .   .   .   .   ,,   366
Febilla's Punishment   .   .   .   .   .   .   ,,   370
Virgilius the Sorcerer carries away the Princess of
    Babylon   .   .   .   .   ,,   376
Mogarzea and his Son return Home   .   .   .   ,,   384

IN TEXT

                                                                    PAGE
The Best Bee   19
Defeat of the Mountain-Spirit by the Youth and Schippei-
    taro   37
The Lion and the Fox come to the Rescue   43
The Prince meets a strange Man in the Wood   80
How the Black Cow was tricked   87
The Flight along the Hedge of Peas   92
Your Heart is heavy with two Sorrows   99
Stan Bolovan meets his Family   113
Stan Bolovan outwits the Dragon   116
The Dragon alarmed   123
The Gazelle brings Clothes to his Master   135
The Gazelle cuts off the Serpent's Heads   139
Two out of a Sack   154
In future leave the Stick alone   158
The Emperor whose right Eye laughed while his left Eye wept   166
Petru wakes the Giant up   193
The Enchanted Knife   203
A Hare for a Kiss   213
Jem follows the Old Woman   228
Hannah does not recognise Jem   233
The Goose finds the Magic Herb   247
Hassebu and the Serpent-King   267
The Impudent Young Men   272
What the Young Man saw in the Wood   297
The Stepmother digs a Grave for the Babies   .   .   .   302
The Punishment of the Stepmother   310
The Witches laughing   315
Fet-Fruners and Iliane escape from the Mother of the
    Genius   337
The Prince feeds the Baby from his Flask   357
For a moment the Dove's Head becomes that of a beautiful
    Girl   359
The Copper Horse .   .   .   .   .   ,   .   .   .   375
Where do you come from ?   381
The Boy pipes to the Elves   383

A TALE OF THE TONTLAWALD

LONG, long ago there stood in the midst of a country
covered with lakes a vast stretch of moorland called the
Tontlawald, on which no man ever dared set foot.
From time to time a few bold spirits had been drawn by
curiosity to its borders, and on their return had reported
that they had caught a glimpse of a ruined house in a
grove of thick trees, and round about it were a crowd of
beings resembling men, swarming over the grass like
bees. The men were as dirty and ragged as gipsies,
and there were besides a quantity of old women and half-
naked children.

One night a peasant who was returning home from a
feast wandered a little farther into the Tontlawald, and
came back with the same story. A countless number of
women and children were gathered round a huge fire,
and some were seated on the ground, while others danced
strange dances on the smooth grass. One old crone had
a broad iron ladle in her hand, with which every now
and then she stirred the fire, but the moment she touched
the glowing ashes the children rushed away, shrieking
like night owls, and it was a long while before they ven-
tured to steal back. And besides all this there had once
or twice been seen a little old man with a long beard
creeping out of the forest, carrying a sack bigger than
himself. The women and children ran by his side, weeping and trying to drag the sack from off his back, but he
shook them off, and went on his way. There was also a

tale of a magnificent black cat as large as a foal, but men could not believe all the wonders told by the peasant, and it was difficult to make out what was true and what was false in his story. However, the fact remained that strange things did happen there, and the King of Sweden, to whom this part of the country belonged, more than once gave orders to cut down the haunted wood, but there was no one with courage enough to obey his commands. At length one man, bolder than the rest, struck his axe into a tree, but his blow was followed by a stream of blood and shrieks as of a human creature in pain. The terrified woodcutter fled as fast as his legs would carry him, and after that neither orders nor threats would drive anybody to the enchanted moor.

A few miles from the Tontlawald was a large village, where dwelt a peasant who had recently married a young wife. As not uncommonly happens in such cases, she turned the whole house upside down, and the two quarrelled and fought all day long.

By his first wife the peasant had a daughter called Elsa, a good quiet girl, who only wanted to live in peace, but this her stepmother would not allow. She beat and cuffed the poor child from morning till night, but as the stepmother had the whip-hand of her husband there was no remedy.

For two years Elsa suffered all this ill-treatment, when one day she went out with the other village children to pluck strawberries. Carelessly they wandered on, till at last they reached the edge of the Tontlawald, where the finest strawberries grew, making the grass red with their colour. The children flung themselves down on the ground, and, after eating as many as they wanted, began to pile up their baskets, when suddenly a cry arose from one of the older boys :

' Run, run as fast as you can ! We are in the Tontlawald ! '

Quicker than lightning they sprang to their feet, and

THE WOODCUTTER IN THE TONTLAWALD

rushed madly away, all except Elsa, who had strayed farther than the rest, and had found a bed of the finest strawberries right under the trees. Like the others, she heard the boy's cry, but could not make up her mind to leave the strawberries.

'After all, what does it matter?' thought she. 'The dwellers in the Tontlawald cannot be worse than my stepmother'; and looking up she saw a little black dog with a silver bell on its neck come barking towards her, followed by a maiden clad all in silk.

'Be quiet,' said she; then turning to Elsa she added: 'I am so glad you did not run away with the other children. Stay here with me and be my friend, and we will play delightful games together, and every day we will go and gather strawberries. Nobody will dare to beat you if I tell them not. Come, let us go to my mother'; and taking Elsa's hand she led her deeper into the wood, the little black dog jumping up beside them and barking with pleasure.

Oh! what wonders and splendours unfolded themselves before Elsa's astonished eyes! She thought she really must be in Heaven. Fruit trees and bushes loaded with fruit stood before them, while birds gayer than the brightest butterfly sat in their branches and filled the air with their song. And the birds were not shy, but let the girls take them in their hands, and stroke their gold and silver feathers. In the centre of the garden was the dwelling-house, shining with glass and precious stones, and in the doorway sat a woman in rich garments, who turned to Elsa's companion and asked:

'What sort of a guest are you bringing to me?'

'I found her alone in the wood,' replied her daughter, 'and brought her back with me for a companion. You will let her stay?'

The mother laughed, but said nothing, only she looked Elsa up and down sharply. Then she told the girl to come near, and stroked her cheeks and spoke kindly to her, asking if her parents were alive, and if she really would like to stay with them.   Elsa stooped and kissed her hand, then, kneeling down, buried her face in the woman's lap, and sobbed out :

'My mother has lain for many years under the ground. My father is still alive, but I am nothing to him, and my stepmother beats me all the day long.   I can do nothing right, so let me, I pray you, stay with you.   I will look after the flocks or do any work you tell me ; I will obey your lightest word ; only do not, I entreat you, send me back to her.   She will half kill me for not having come back with the other children.'

And the woman smiled and answered, ' Well, we will see what we can do with you,' and, rising, went into the house.

Then the daughter said to Elsa, 'Fear nothing, my mother will be your friend.   I saw by the way she looked that she would grant your request when she had thought over it,' and, telling Elsa to wait, she entered the house to seek her mother.   Elsa meanwhile was tossed about between hope and fear, and felt as if the girl would never come.

At last Elsa saw her crossing the grass with a box in her hand.

'My mother says we may play together to-day, as she wants to make up her mind what to do about you.   But I hope you will stay here always, as I can't bear you to go away.   Have you ever been on the sea ? '

'The sea ? ' asked Elsa, staring ; ' what is that ?   I've never heard of such a thing ! '

'Oh, I'll soon show you,' answered the girl, taking the lid from the box, and at the very bottom lay a scrap of a cloak, a mussel shell, and two fish scales.   Two drops of water were glistening on the cloak, and these the girl shook on the ground.   In an instant the garden and lawn and everything else had vanished utterly, as if the earth had opened and swallowed them up, and as far as the eye could reach you could see nothing but water, which seemed at last to touch heaven itself. Only under their feet was a tiny dry spot. Then the girl placed the mussel shell on the water and took the fish scales in her hand. The mussel shell grew bigger and bigger, and turned into a pretty little boat, which would have held a dozen children. The girls stepped in, Elsa very cautiously, for which she was much laughed at by her friend, who used the fish scales for a rudder. The waves rocked the girls softly, as if they were lying in a cradle, and they floated on till they met other boats filled with men, singing and making merry.

'We must sing you a song in return,' said the girl, but as Elsa did not know any songs, she had to sing by herself. Elsa could not understand any of the men's songs, but one word, she noticed, came over and over again, and that was 'Kisika.' Elsa asked what it meant, and the girl replied that it was her name.

It was all so pleasant that they might have stayed there for ever had not a voice cried out to them, 'Children, it is time for you to come home!'

So Kisika took the little box out of her pocket, with the piece of cloth lying in it, and dipped the cloth in the water, and lo! they were standing close to a splendid house in the middle of the garden. Everything round them was dry and firm, and there was no water anywhere. The mussel shell and the fish scales were put back in the box, and the girls went in.

They entered a large hall, where four and twenty richly dressed women were sitting round a table, looking as if they were about to attend a wedding. At the head of the table sat the lady of the house in a golden chair.

Elsa did not know which way to look, for everything that met her eyes was more beautiful than she could have dreamed possible. But she sat down with the rest, and ate some delicious fruit, and thought she must be in heaven. The guests talked softly, but their speech was strange to Elsa, and she understood nothing of what was said. Then the hostess turned round and whispered something to a maid behind her chair, and the maid left the hall, and when she came back she brought a little old man with her, who had a beard longer than himself. He bowed low to the lady and then stood quietly near the door.

'Do you see this girl?' said the lady of the house, pointing to Elsa. 'I wish to adopt her for my daughter. Make me a copy of her, which we can send to her native village instead of herself.'

The old man looked Elsa all up and down, as if he was taking her measure, bowed again to the lady, and left the hall. After dinner the lady said kindly to Elsa, 'Kisika has begged me to let you stay with her, and you have told her you would like to live here. Is that so?'

At these words Elsa fell on her knees, and kissed the lady's hands and feet in gratitude for her escape from her cruel stepmother; but her hostess raised her from the ground and patted her head, saying, 'All will go well as long as you are a good, obedient child, and I will take care of you and see that you want for nothing till you are grown up and can look after yourself. My waiting-maid, who teaches Kisika all sorts of fine handiwork, shall teach you too.'

Not long after the old man came back with a mould full of clay on his shoulders, and a little covered basket in his left hand. He put down his mould and his basket on the ground, took up a handful of clay, and made a doll as large as life. When it was finished he bored a hole in the doll's breast and put a bit of bread inside; then, drawing a snake out of the basket, forced it to enter the hollow body.

'Now,' he said to the lady, 'all we want is a drop of the maiden's blood.'

When she heard this Elsa grew white with horror, for she thought she was selling her soul to the evil one.

'Do not be afraid!' the lady hastened to say; 'we do

The Tontlawald

not want your blood for any bad purpose, but rather to give you freedom and happiness.'

Then she took a tiny golden needle, pricked Elsa in the arm, and gave the needle to the old man, who stuck it into the heart of the doll. When this was done he placed the figure in the basket, promising that the next day they should all see what a beautiful piece of work he had finished.

When Elsa awoke the next morning in her silken bed, with its soft white pillows, she saw a beautiful dress lying over the back of a chair, ready for her to put on. A maid came in to comb out her long hair, and brought the finest linen for her use; but nothing gave Elsa so much joy as the little pair of embroidered shoes that she held in her hand, for the girl had hitherto been forced to run about barefoot by her cruel stepmother. In her excitement she never gave a thought to the rough clothes she had worn the day before, which had disappeared as if by magic during the night. Who could have taken them? Well, she was to know that by-and-by. But *we* can guess that the doll had been dressed in them, which was to go back to the village in her stead. By the time the sun rose the doll had attained her full size, and no one could have told one girl from the other. Elsa started back when she met herself as she looked only yesterday.

' You must not be frightened,' said the lady, when she noticed her terror ; ' this clay figure can do you no harm. It is for your stepmother, that she may beat it instead of you. Let her flog it as hard as she will, it can never feel any pain. And if the wicked woman does not come one day to a better mind your double will be able at last to give her the punishment she deserves.'

From this moment Elsa's life was that of the ordinary happy child, who has been rocked to sleep in her baby-hood in a lovely golden cradle. She had no cares or troubles of any sort, and every day her tasks became easier, and the years that had gone before seemed more and more like a bad dream. But the happier she grew the deeper was her wonder at everything around her, and the more firmly she was persuaded that some great unknown power must be at the bottom of it all.

In the courtyard stood a huge granite block about twenty steps from the house, and when meal times came round the old man with the long beard went to the block, drew out a small silver staff, and struck the stone with it three times, so that the sound could be heard a long way off. At the third blow, out sprang a large golden cock, and stood upon the stone. Whenever he crowed and flapped his wings the rock opened and something came out of it. First a long table covered with dishes ready laid for the number of persons who would be seated round it, and this flew into the house all by itself.

When the cock crowed for the second time, a number of chairs appeared, and flew after the table; then wine, apples, and other fruit, all without trouble to anybody. After everybody had had enough, the old man struck the rock again, the golden cock crowed afresh, and back went dishes, table, chairs, and plates into the middle of the block.

When, however, it came to the turn of the thirteenth dish, which nobody ever wanted to eat, a huge black cat ran up, and stood on the rock close to the cock, while the dish was on his other side. There they all remained, till they were joined by the old man.

He picked up the dish in one hand, tucked the cat under his arm, told the cock to get on his shoulder, and all four vanished into the rock. And this wonderful stone contained not only food, but clothes and everything you could possibly want in the house.

At first a language was often spoken at meals which was strange to Elsa, but by the help of the lady and her daughter she began slowly to understand it, though it was years before she was able to speak it herself.

One day she asked Kisika why the thirteenth dish

How the OLD MAN
Disappeared
after dinner

H J FORD

came daily to the table and was sent daily away untouched, but Kisika knew no more about it than she did. The girl must, however, have told her mother what Elsa had said, for a few days later she spoke to Elsa seriously :

'Do not worry yourself with useless wondering. You wish to know why we never eat of the thirteenth dish ? That, dear child, is the dish of hidden blessings, and we cannot taste of it without bringing our happy life here to an end. And the world would be a great deal better if men, in their greed, did not seek to snatch everything for themselves, instead of leaving something as a thankoffering to the giver of the blessings. Greed is man's worst fault.'

The years passed like the wind for Elsa, and she grew into a lovely woman, with a knowledge of many things that she would never have learned in her native village ; but Kisika was still the same young girl that she had been on the day of her first meeting with Elsa. Each morning they both worked for an hour at reading and writing, as they had always done, and Elsa was anxious to learn all she could, but Kisika much preferred childish games to anything else. If the humour seized her, she would fling aside her tasks, take her treasure box, and go off to play in the sea, where no harm ever came to her.

' What a pity,' she would often say to Elsa, ' that you have grown so big, you cannot play with me any more.'

Nine years slipped away in this manner, when one day the lady called Elsa into her room. Elsa was surprised at the summons, for it was unusual, and her heart sank, for she feared some evil threatened her. As she crossed the threshold, she saw that the lady's cheeks were flushed, and her eyes full of tears, which she dried hastily, as if she would conceal them from the girl. ' Dearest child,' she began, ' the time has come when we must part.'

' Part ? ' cried Elsa, burying her head in the lady's

lap. 'No, dear lady, that can never be till death parts us. You once opened your arms to me; you cannot thrust me away now.'

'Ah, be quiet, child,' replied the lady; 'you do not know what I would do to make you happy. Now you are a woman, and I have no right to keep you here. You must return to the world of men, where joy awaits you.'

'Dear lady,' entreated Elsa again. 'Do not, I beseech you, send me from you. I want no other happiness but to live and die beside you. Make me your waiting maid, or set me to any work you choose, but do not cast me forth into the world. It would have been better if you had left me with my stepmother, than first to have brought me to heaven and then send me back to a worse place.'

'Do not talk like that, dear child,' replied the lady; 'you do not know all that must be done to secure your happiness, however much it costs me. But it has to be. You are only a common mortal, who will have to die one day, and you cannot stay here any longer. Though we have the bodies of men, we are not men at all, though it is not easy for you to understand why. Some day or other you will find a husband who has been made expressly for you, and will live happily with him till death separates you. It will be very hard for me to part from you, but it has to be, and you must make up your mind to it.' Then she drew her golden comb gently through Elsa's hair, and bade her go to bed; but little sleep had the poor girl! Life seemed to stretch before her like a dark starless night.

Now let us look back a moment, and see what had been going on in Elsa's native village all these years, and how her double had fared. It is a well-known fact that a bad woman seldom becomes better as she grows older, and Elsa's stepmother was no exception to the rule; but as the figure that had taken the girl's place could feel no

pain, the blows that were showered on her night and day
made no difference. If the father ever tried to come to
his daughter's help, his wife turned upon him, and things
were rather worse than before.

One day the stepmother had given the girl a frightful
beating, and then threatened to kill her outright. Mad
with rage, she seized the figure by the throat with both
hands, when out came a black snake from her mouth and
stung the woman's tongue, and she fell dead without a
sound. At night, when the husband came home, he found
his wife lying dead upon the ground, her body all swollen
and disfigured, but the girl was nowhere to be seen.
His screams brought the neighbours from their cottages,
but they were unable to explain how it had all come
about. It was true, they said, that about mid-day they
had heard a great noise, but as that was a matter of daily
occurrence they did not think much of it. The rest of
the day all was still, but no one had seen anything of the
daughter. The body of the dead woman was then prepared
for burial, and her tired husband went to bed, rejoicing
in his heart that he had been delivered from the firebrand
who had made his home unpleasant. On the table he
saw a slice of bread lying, and, being hungry, he ate it
before going to sleep.

In the morning he too was found dead, and as
swollen as his wife, for the bread had been placed in the
body of the figure by the old man who made it. A few
days later he was placed in the grave beside his wife, but
nothing more was ever heard of their daughter.

All night long after her talk with the lady Elsa had
wept and wailed her hard fate in being cast out from her
home which she loved.

Next morning, when she got up, the lady placed a gold
seal ring on her finger, strung a little golden box on a
ribbon, and placed it round her neck ; then she called the
old man, and, forcing back her tears, took leave of Elsa.
The girl tried to speak, but before she could sob out her

thanks the old man had touched her softly on the head three times with his silver staff. In an instant Elsa knew that she was turning into a bird : wings sprang from beneath her arms ; her feet were the feet of eagles, with long claws ; her nose curved itself into a sharp beak, and feathers covered her body. Then she soared high in the air, and floated up towards the clouds, as if she had really been hatched an eagle.

For several days she flew steadily south, resting from time to time when her wings grew tired, for hunger she never felt. And so it happened that one day she was flying over a dense forest, and below hounds were barking fiercely, because, not having wings themselves, she was out of their reach. Suddenly a sharp pain quivered through her body, and she fell to the ground, pierced by an arrow.

When Elsa recovered her senses, she found herself lying under a bush in her own proper form. What had befallen her, and how she got there, lay behind her like a bad dream.

As she was wondering what she should do next the king's son came riding by, and, seeing Elsa, sprang from his horse, and took her by the hand, saying, ' Ah ! it was a happy chance that brought me here this morning. Every night, for half a year, have I dreamed, dear lady, that I should one day find you in this wood. And although I have passed through it hundreds of times in vain, I have never given up hope. To-day I was going in search of a large eagle that I had shot, and instead of the eagle I have found—you.' Then he took Elsa on his horse, and rode with her to the town, where the old king received her graciously.

A few days later the wedding took place, and as Elsa was arranging the veil upon her hair fifty carts arrived laden with beautiful things which the lady of the Tontlawald had sent to Elsa. And after the king's death Elsa became queen, and when she was old she told this story. But that was the last that was ever heard of the Tontlawald.

[From Ehstnische Märchen.]

THE FINEST LIAR IN THE WORLD

AT the edge of a wood there lived an old man who had only one son, and one day he called the boy to him and said he wanted some corn ground, but the youth must be sure never to enter any mill where the miller was beardless.

The boy took the corn and set out, and before he had gone very far he saw a large mill in front of him, with a beardless man standing in the doorway.

'Good greeting, beardless one!' cried he.

'Good greeting, sonny,' replied the man.

'Could I grind something here?'

'Yes, certainly! I will finish what I am doing and then you can grind as long as you like.'

But suddenly the boy remembered what his father had told him, and bade farewell to the man, and went further down the river, till he came to another mill, not knowing that as soon as his back was turned the beardless man had picked up a bag of corn and run hastily to the same mill before him. When the boy reached the second mill, and saw a second beardless man sitting there, he did not stop, and walked on till he came to a third mill. But this time also the beardless man had been too clever for him, and had arrived first by another road. When it happened a fourth time the boy grew cross, and said to himself, 'It is no good going on; there seems to be a beardless man in every mill'; and he took his sack from his back, and made up his mind to grind his corn where he was.

The beardless man finished grinding his own corn, and when he had done he said to the boy, who was beginning to grind his, 'Suppose, sonny, we make a cake of what you have there.'

Now the boy had been rather uneasy when he recollected his father's words, but he thought to himself, 'What is done cannot be undone,' and answered, 'Very well, so let it be.'

Then the beardless one got up, threw the flour into the tub, and made a hole in the middle, telling the boy to fetch some water from the river in his two hands, to mix the cake. When the cake was ready for baking they put it on the fire, and covered it with hot ashes, till it was cooked through. Then they leaned it up against the wall, for it was too big to go into a cupboard, and the beardless one said to the boy:

'Look here, sonny: if we share this cake we shall neither of us have enough. Let us see who can tell the biggest lie, and the one who lies the best shall have the whole cake.'

The boy, not knowing what else to do, answered, 'All right; you begin.'

So the beardless one began to lie with all his might, and when he was tired of inventing new lies the boy said to him, 'My good fellow, if *that* is all you can do it is not much! Listen to me, and I will tell you a true story.

'In my youth, when I was an old man, we had a quantity of beehives. Every morning when I got up I counted them over, and it was quite easy to number the bees, but I never could reckon the hives properly. One day, as I was counting the bees, I discovered that my best bee was missing, and without losing a moment I saddled a cock and went out to look for him. I traced him as far as the shore, and knew that he had crossed the sea, and that I must follow. When I had reached the other side I found a man had harnessed my bee to a plough, and with his help was sowing millet seed.

' " That is my bee ! " I shouted. " Where did you get
him from ? "

THE BEST BEE

' " Brother," replied the man, " if he is yours, take
him." And he not only gave me back my bee, but a sack

of millet seed into the bargain, because he had made use of my bee. Then I put the bag on my shoulders, took the saddle from the cock, and placed it on the back of the bee, which I mounted, leading the cock by a string, so that he should have a rest. As we were flying home over the sea one of the strings that held the bag of millet broke in two, and the sack dropped straight into the ocean. It was quite lost, of course, and there was no use thinking about it, and by the time we were safe back again night had come. I then got down from my bee, and let him loose, that he might get his supper, gave the cock some hay, and went to sleep myself. But when I awoke with the sun what a scene met my eyes! During the night wolves had come and had eaten my bee. And honey lay ankle-deep in the valley and knee-deep on the hills. Then I began to consider how I could best collect some, to take home with me.

'Now it happened that I had with me a small hatchet, and this I took to the wood, hoping to meet some animal which I could kill, whose skin I might turn into a bag. As I entered the forest I saw two roe-deer hopping on one foot, so I slew them with a single blow, and made three bags from their skins, all of which I filled with honey and placed on the back of the cock. At length I reached home, where I was told that my father had just been born, and that I must go at once to fetch some holy water to sprinkle him with. As I went I turned over in my mind if there was no way for me to get back my millet seed, which had dropped into the sea, and when I arrived at the place with the holy water I saw the seed had fallen on fruitful soil, and was growing before my eyes. And more than that, it was even cut by an invisible hand, and made into a cake.

'So I took the cake as well as the holy water, and was flying back with them over the sea, when there fell a great rain, and the sea was swollen, and swept away my millet

cake. Ah, how vexed I was at its loss when I was safe
on earth again.

'Suddenly I remembered that my hair was very long.
If I stood it touched the ground, although if I was sitting
it only reached my ears. I seized a knife and cut off a
large lock, which I plaited together, and when night came
tied it into a knot, and prepared to use it for a pillow.
But what was I to do for a fire? A tinder box I had, but
no wood. Then it occurred to me that I had stuck a
needle in my clothes, so I took the needle and split it
in pieces, and lit it, then laid myself down by the fire and
went to sleep. But ill-luck still pursued me. While I
was sleeping a spark from the fire lighted on the hair,
which was burnt up in a moment. In despair I threw
myself on the ground, and instantly sank in it as far as
my waist. I struggled to get out, but only fell in further;
so I ran to the house, seized a spade, dug myself out,
and took home the holy water. On the way I noticed
that the ripe fields were full of reapers, and suddenly the
air became so frightfully hot that the men dropped
down in a faint. Then I called to them, "Why don't
you bring out our mare, which is as tall as two days, and
as broad as half a day, and make a shade for yourselves?"
My father heard what I said and jumped quickly on the
mare, and the reapers worked with a will in the shadow,
while I snatched up a wooden pail to bring them some
water to drink. When I got to the well everything was
frozen hard, so in order to draw some water I had to
take off my head and break the ice with it. As I drew
near them, carrying the water, the reapers all cried out,
"Why, what has become of your head?" I put up my
hand and discovered that I really had no head, and that
I must have left it in the well. I ran back to look for it,
but found that meanwhile a fox which was passing by
had pulled my head out of the water, and was tearing at
my brains. I stole cautiously up to him, and gave him
such a kick that he uttered a loud scream, and let fall a

parchment on which was written, " The cake is mine, and the beardless one goes empty-handed." '

With these words the boy rose, took the cake, and went home, while the beardless one remained behind to swallow his disappointment.

[Volksmärchen der Serben.]

23

THE STORY OF THREE WONDERFUL BEGGARS

THERE once lived a merchant whose name was Mark, and whom people called 'Mark the Rich.' He was a very hard-hearted man, for he could not bear poor people, and if he caught sight of a beggar anywhere near his house, he would order the servants to drive him away, or would set the dogs at him.

One day three very poor old men came begging to the door, and just as he was going to let the fierce dogs loose on them, his little daughter, Anastasia, crept close up to him and said:

'Dear daddy, let the poor old men sleep here to-night, do —to please me.'

Her father could not bear to refuse her, and the three beggars were allowed to sleep in a loft, and at night, when everyone in the house was fast asleep, little Anastasia got up, climbed up to the loft, and peeped in.

The three old men stood in the middle of the loft, leaning on their sticks, with their long grey beards flowing down over their hands, and were talking together in low voices.

'What news is there?' asked the eldest.

In the next village the peasant Ivan has just had his seventh son. What shall we name him, and what fortune shall we give him?' said the second.

The third whispered, 'Call him Vassili, and give him all the property of the hard-hearted man in whose loft we stand, and who wanted to drive us from his door.'

After a little more talk the three made themselves ready and crept softly away.

Anastasia, who had heard every word, ran straight to her father, and told him all.

Mark was very much surprised; he thought, and thought, and in the morning he drove to the next village to try and find out if such a child really had been born. He went first to the priest, and asked him about the children in his parish.

' Yesterday,' said the priest, ' a boy was born in the poorest house in the village. I named the unlucky little thing " Vassili." He is the seventh son, and the eldest is only seven years old, and they hardly have a mouthful amongst them all. Who can be got to stand godfather to such a little beggar boy? '

The merchant's heart beat fast, and his mind was full of bad thoughts about that poor little baby. He would be godfather himself, he said, and he ordered a fine christening feast; so the child was brought and christened, and Mark was very friendly to its father. After the ceremony was over he took Ivan aside and said:

' Look here, my friend, you are a poor man. How can you afford to bring up the boy? Give him to me and I'll make something of him, and I'll give you a present of a thousand crowns. Is that a bargain? '

Ivan scratched his head, and thought, and thought, and then he agreed. Mark counted out the money, wrapped the baby up in a fox skin, laid it in the sledge beside him, and drove back towards home. When he had driven some miles he drew up, carried the child to the edge of a steep precipice and threw it over, muttering, ' There, now try to take my property! '

Very soon after this some foreign merchants travelled along that same road on the way to see Mark and to pay the twelve thousand crowns which they owed him.

THE FAIRIES CATCH THE BABY

As they were passing near the precipice they heard a sound of crying, and on looking over they saw a little green meadow wedged in between two great heaps of snow, and on the meadow lay a baby amongst the flowers.

The merchants picked up the child, wrapped it up carefully, and drove on. When they saw Mark they told him what a strange thing they had found. Mark guessed at once that the child must be his godson, asked to see him, and said :

' That's a nice little fellow ; I should like to keep him. If you will make him over to me, I will let you off your debt.'

The merchants were very pleased to make so good a bargain, left the child with Mark, and drove off.

At night Mark took the child, put it in a barrel, fastened the lid tight down, and threw it into the sea. The barrel floated away to a great distance, and at last it floated close up to a monastery. The monks were just spreading out their nets to dry on the shore, when they heard the sound of crying. It seemed to come from the barrel which was bobbing about near the water's edge. They drew it to land and opened it, and there was a little child ! When the abbot heard the news, he decided to bring up the boy, and named him ' Vassili.'

The boy lived on with the monks, and grew up to be a clever, gentle, and handsome young man. No one could read, write, or sing better than he, and he did everything so well that the abbot made him wardrobe keeper.

Now, it happened about this time that the merchant, Mark, came to the monastery in the course of a journey. The monks were very polite to him and showed him their house and church and all they had. When he went into the church the choir was singing, and one voice was so clear and beautiful, that he asked who it belonged to. Then the abbot told him of the wonderful way in which Vassili had come to them, and Mark saw clearly that this must be his godson whom he had twice tried to kill.

He said to the abbot : ' I can't tell you how much I enjoy that young man's singing. If he could only come to me I would make him overseer of all my business. As you say, he is so good and clever. Do spare him to me. I will make his fortune, and will present your monastery with twenty thousand crowns.'

The abbot hesitated a good deal, but he consulted all the other monks, and at last they decided that they ought not to stand in the way of Vassili's good fortune.

Then Mark wrote a letter to his wife and gave it to Vassili to take to her, and this was what was in the letter : ' When the bearer of this arrives, take him into the soap factory, and when you pass near the great boiler, push him in. If you don't obey my orders I shall be very angry, for this young man is a bad fellow who is sure to ruin us all if he lives.'

Vassili had a good voyage, and on landing set off on foot for Mark's home. On the way he met three beggars, who asked him : ' Where are you going, Vassili ? '

' I am going to the house of Mark the Merchant, and have a letter for his wife,' replied Vassili.

' Show us the letter.'

Vassili handed them the letter. They blew on it and gave it back to him, saying : ' Now go and give the letter to Mark's wife. You will not be forsaken.'

Vassili reached the house and gave the letter. When the mistress read it she could hardly believe her eyes and called for her daughter. In the letter was written, quite plainly : ' When you receive this letter, get ready for a wedding, and let the bearer be married next day to my daughter, Anastasia. If you don't obey my orders I shall be very angry.'

Anastasia saw the bearer of the letter and he pleased

her very much. They dressed Vassili in fine clothes and next day he was married to Anastasia.

In due time, Mark returned from his travels. His wife, daughter, and son-in-law all went out to meet him. When Mark saw Vassili he flew into a terrible rage with his wife. 'How dared you marry my daughter without my consent?' he asked.

'I only carried out your orders,' said she. 'Here is your letter.'

Mark read it. It certainly was his handwriting, but by no means his wishes.

'Well,' thought he, 'you've escaped me three times, but I think I shall get the better of you now.' And he waited a month and was very kind and pleasant to his daughter and her husband.

At the end of that time he said to Vassili one day, 'I want you to go for me to my friend the Serpent King, in his beautiful country at the world's end. Twelve years ago he built a castle on some land of mine. I want you to ask for the rent for those twelve years and also to find out from him what has become of my twelve ships which sailed for his country three years ago.'

Vassili dared not disobey. He said good-bye to his young wife, who cried bitterly at parting, hung a bag of biscuits over his shoulders, and set out.

I really cannot tell you whether the journey was long or short. As he tramped along he suddenly heard a voice saying: 'Vassili! where are you going?'

Vassili looked about him, and, seeing no one, called out: 'Who spoke to me?'

'I did; this old wide-spreading oak. Tell me where you are going.'

'I am going to the Serpent King to receive twelve years' rent from him.'

'When the time comes, remember me and ask the king: "Rotten to the roots, half dead but still green, stands the old oak. Is it to stand much longer on the earth ? " '

Vassili went on further. He came to a river and got into the ferryboat. The old ferryman asked : ' Are you going far, my friend ? '

' I am going to the Serpent King.'

' Then think of me and say to the king : " For thirty years the ferryman has rowed to and fro. Will the tired old man have to row much longer ? " '

' Very well,' said Vassili ; ' I'll ask him.'

And he walked on. In time he came to a narrow strait of the sea and across it lay a great whale over whose back people walked and drove as if it had been a bridge or a road. As he stepped on it the whale said, ' Do tell me where you are going.'

' I am going to the Serpent King.

And the whale begged : ' Think of me and say to the king : " The poor whale has been lying three years across the strait, and men and horses have nearly trampled his back into his ribs. Is he to lie there much longer ? " '

' I will remember,' said Vassili, and he went on.

He walked, and walked, and walked, till he came to a great green meadow. In the meadow stood a large and splendid castle. Its white marble walls sparkled in the light, the roof was covered with mother o' pearl, which shone like a rainbow, and the sun glowed like fire on the crystal windows. Vassili walked in, and went from one room to another astonished at all the splendour he saw.

When he reached the last room of all, he found a beautiful girl sitting on a bed.

As soon as she saw him she said : ' Oh, Vassili, what brings you to this accursed place ? '

Vassili told her why he had come, and all he had seen and heard on the way.

The girl said : ' You have not been sent here to collect rents, but for your own destruction, and that the serpent may devour you.'

THE BEAUTIFUL WOMAN SOOTHES THE SERPENT-KING

She had not time to say more, when the whole castle shook, and a rustling, hissing, groaning sound was heard. The girl quickly pushed Vassili into a chest under the bed, locked it and whispered : ' Listen to what the serpent and I talk about.'

Then she rose up to receive the Serpent King.

The monster rushed into the room, and threw itself panting on the bed, crying : ' I've flown half over the world. I'm tired, *very* tired, and want to sleep—scratch my head.'

The beautiful girl sat down near him, stroking his hideous head, and said in a sweet coaxing voice : ' You know everything in the world. After you left, I had such a wonderful dream. Will you tell me what it means ? '

' Out with it then, quick ! What was it ? '

' I dreamt I was walking on a wide road, and an oak tree said to me : " Ask the king this : Rotten at the roots, half dead, and yet green stands the old oak. Is it to stand much longer on the earth ? " '

' It must stand till some one comes and pushes it down with his foot. Then it will fall, and under its roots will be found more gold and silver than even Mark the Rich has got.'

' Then I dreamt I came to a river, and the old ferry-man said to me : " For thirty years the ferryman has rowed to and fro. Will the tired old man have to row much longer ? " '

' That depends on himself. If some one gets into the boat to be ferried across, the old man has only to push the boat off, and go his way without looking back. The man in the boat will then have to take his place.'

' And at last I dreamt that I was walking over a bridge made of a whale's back, and the living bridge spoke to me and said : " Here have I been stretched out these three years, and men and horses have trampled my back down into my ribs. Must I lie here much longer ? " '

'He will have to lie there till he has thrown up the twelve ships of Mark the Rich which he swallowed. Then he may plunge back into the sea and heal his back.'

And the Serpent King closed his eyes, turned round on his other side, and began to snore so loud that the windows rattled.

In all haste the lovely girl helped Vassili out of the chest, and showed him part of his way back. He thanked her very politely, and hurried off.

When he reached the strait the whale asked: 'Have you thought of me?'

'Yes, as soon as I am on the other side I will tell you what you want to know.'

When he was on the other side Vassili said to the whale: 'Throw up those twelve ships of Mark's which you swallowed three years ago.'

The great fish heaved itself up and threw up all the twelve ships and their crews. Then he shook himself for joy, and plunged into the sea.

Vassili went on further till he reached the ferry, where the old man asked: 'Did you think of me?'

'Yes, and as soon as you have ferried me across I will tell you what you want to know.'

When they had crossed over, Vassili said: 'Let the next man who comes stay in the boat, but do you step on shore, push the boat off, and you will be free, and the other man must take your place.'

Then Vassili went on further still, and soon came to the old oak tree, pushed it with his foot, and it fell over. There, at the roots, was more gold and silver than even Mark the Rich had.

And now the twelve ships which the whale had thrown up came sailing along and anchored close by. On the deck of the first ship stood the three beggars whom Vassili had met formerly, and they said: 'Heaven has blessed you, Vassili.' Then they vanished away and he never saw them again.

The sailors carried all the gold and silver into the ship, and then they set sail for home with Vassili on board.

Mark was more furious than ever. He had his horses harnessed and drove off himself to see the Serpent King and to complain of the way in which he had been betrayed. When he reached the river he sprang into the ferryboat. The ferryman, however, did not get in but pushed the boat off. . . .

Vassili led a good and happy life with his dear wife, and his kind mother-in-law lived with them. He helped the poor and fed and clothed the hungry and naked and all Mark's riches became his.

For many years Mark has been ferrying people across the river. His face is wrinkled, his hair and beard are snow white, and his eyes are dim ; but still he rows on.

[From the Serbian.]

SCHIPPEITARO

IT was the custom in old times that as soon as a Japanese
boy reached manhood he should leave his home and
roam through the land in search of adventures. Sometimes he would meet with a young man bent on the same
business as himself, and then they would fight in a
friendly manner, merely to prove which was the stronger,
but on other occasions the enemy would turn out to be a
robber, who had become the terror of the neighbourhood,
and then the battle was in deadly earnest.

One day a youth started off from his native village,
resolved never to come back till he had done some great
deed that would make his name famous. But adventures
did not seem very plentiful just then, and he wandered
about for a long time without meeting either with fierce
giants or distressed damsels. At last he saw in the
distance a wild mountain, half covered with a dense forest,
and thinking that this promised well at once took the
road that led to it. The difficulties he met with—huge
rocks to be climbed, deep rivers to be crossed, and
thorny tracts to be avoided—only served to make his
heart beat quicker, for he was really brave all through,
and not merely when he could not help himself, like a
great many people. But in spite of all his efforts he
could not find his way out of the forest, and he began to
think he should have to pass the night there. Once
more he strained his eyes to see if there was no place in
which he could take shelter, and this time he caught sight
of a small chapel in a little clearing. He hastened

quickly towards it, and curling himself up in a warm
corner soon fell asleep.

Not a sound was heard through the whole forest for
some hours, but at midnight there suddenly arose such a

DEFEAT OF THE MOUNTAIN-SPIRIT
BY THE YOUTH AND SCHIPPEITARO

clamour that the young man, tired as he was, started
broad awake in an instant. Peeping cautiously between
the wooden pillars of the chapel, he saw a troop of
hideous cats, dancing furiously, making the night horrible

with their yells. The full moon lighted up the weird scene, and the young warrior gazed with astonishment, taking great care to keep still, lest he should be discovered. After some time he thought that in the midst of all their shrieks he could make out the words, ' Do not tell Schippeitaro ! Keep it hidden and secret ! Do not tell Schippeitaro ! ' Then, the midnight hour having passed, they all vanished, and the youth was left alone. Exhausted by all that had been going on round him, he flung himself on the ground and slept till the sun rose.

The moment he woke he felt very hungry, and began to think how he could get something to eat. So he got up and walked on, and before he had gone very far was lucky enough to find a little side-path, where he could trace men's footsteps. He followed the track, and by-and-by came on some scattered huts, beyond which lay a village. Delighted at this discovery, he was about to hasten to the village when he heard a woman's voice weeping and lamenting, and calling on the men to take pity on her and help her. The sound of her distress made him forget he was hungry, and he strode into the hut to find out for himself what was wrong. But the men whom he asked only shook their heads and told him it was not a matter in which he could give any help, for all this sorrow was caused by the Spirit of the Mountain, to whom every year they were bound to furnish a maiden for him to eat.

' To-morrow night,' said they, ' the horrible creature will come for his dinner, and the cries you have heard were uttered by the girl before you, upon whom the lot has fallen.'

And when the young man asked if the girl was carried off straight from her home, they answered no, but that a large cask was set in the forest chapel, and into this she was fastened.

As he listened to this story, the young man was

filled with a great longing to rescue the maiden from her dreadful fate. The mention of the chapel set him thinking of the scene of the previous night, and he went over all the details again in his mind. 'Who is Schippeitaro?' he suddenly asked; 'can any of you tell me?'

'Schippeitaro is the great dog that belongs to the overseer of our prince,' said they; 'and he lives not far away.' And they began to laugh at the question, which seemed to them so odd and useless.

The young man did not laugh with them, but instead left the hut and went straight to the owner of the dog, whom he begged to lend him the animal just for one night. Schippeitaro's master was not at all willing to give him in charge to a man of whom he knew nothing, but in the end he consented, and the youth led the dog away, promising faithfully to return him next day to his master. He next hurried to the hut where the maiden lived, and entreated her parents to shut her up safely in a closet, after which he took Schippeitaro to the cask, and fastened him into it. In the evening he knew that the cask would be placed in the chapel, so he hid himself there and waited.

At midnight, when the full moon appeared above the top of the mountain, the cats again filled the chapel and shrieked and yelled and danced as before. But this time they had in their midst a huge black cat who seemed to be their king, and whom the young man guessed to be the Spirit of the Mountain. The monster looked eagerly about him, and his eyes sparkled with joy when he saw the cask. He bounded high into the air with delight and uttered cries of pleasure; then he drew near and undid the bolts. But instead of fastening his teeth in the neck of a beautiful maiden, Schippeitaro's teeth were fastened in *him*, and the youth ran up and cut off his head with his sword. The other cats were so astonished at the turn things had taken that they forgot to run away, and the young man and Schippeitaro between them killed several more before they thought of escaping.

At sunrise the brave dog was taken back to his master, and from that time the mountain girls were safe, and every year a feast was held in memory of the young warrior and the dog Schippeitaro.

[Japanische Märchen.]

THE THREE PRINCES AND THEIR BEASTS

(LITHUANIAN FAIRY TALE)

ONCE on a time there were three princes, who had a step-sister. One day they all set out hunting together. When they had gone some way through a thick wood they came on a great grey wolf with three cubs. Just as they were going to shoot, the wolf spoke and said, 'Do not shoot me, and I will give each of you one of my young ones. It will be a faithful friend to you.'

So the princes went on their way, and a little wolf followed each of them.

Soon after they came on a lioness with three cubs. And she too begged them not to shoot her, and she would give each of them a cub. And so it happened with a fox, a hare, a boar, and a bear, till each prince had quite a following of young beasts padding along behind him.

Towards evening they came to a clearing in the wood, where three birches grew at the crossing of three roads. The eldest prince took an arrow, and shot it into the trunk of one of the birch trees. Turning to his brothers he said:

'Let each of us mark one of these trees before we part on different ways. When any one of us comes back to this place, he must walk round the trees of the other two, and if he sees blood flowing from the mark in the tree he will know that that brother is dead, but if milk flows he will know that his brother is alive.'

So each of the princes did as the eldest brother had said, and when the three birches were marked by their

arrows they turned to their step-sister and asked her
with which of them she meant to live.

'With the eldest,' she answered. Then the brothers
separated from each other, and each of them set out down
a different road, followed by their beasts. And the step-
sister went with the eldest prince.

After they had gone a little way along the road they
came into a forest, and in one of the deepest glades they
suddenly found themselves opposite a castle in which
there lived a band of robbers. The prince walked up to
the door and knocked. The moment it was opened the
beasts rushed in, and each seized on a robber, killed him,
and dragged the body down to the cellar. Now, one of
the robbers was not really killed, only badly wounded,
but he lay quite still and pretended to be dead like the
others. Then the prince and his step-sister entered the
castle and took up their abode in it.

The next morning the prince went out hunting. Before
leaving he told his step-sister that she might go into every
room in the house except into the cave where the dead
robbers lay. But as soon as his back was turned she forgot
what he had said, and having wandered through all the
other rooms she went down to the cellar and opened the
door. As soon as she looked in the robber who had
only pretended to be dead sat up and said to her:

'Don't be afraid. Do what I tell you, and I will be
your friend. If you marry me you will be much happier
with me than with your brother. But you must first go
into the sitting-room and look in the cupboard. There
you will find three bottles. In one of them there is a
healing ointment which you must put on my chin to heal
the wound; then if I drink the contents of the second
bottle it will make me well, and the third bottle will
make me stronger than I ever was before. Then, when
your brother comes back from the wood with his beasts
you must go to him and say, " Brother, you are very strong.
If I were to fasten your thumbs behind your back with a

stout silk cord, could you wrench yourself free?" And
when you see that he cannot do it, call me.'

When the brother came home, the step-sister did as
the robber had told her, and fastened her brother's thumbs
behind his back. But with one wrench he set himself

THE LION & THE FOX COME TO THE RESCUE

free, and said to her, 'Sister, that cord is not strong
enough for me.'

The next day he went back to the wood with his
beasts, and the robber told her that she must take a much
stouter cord to bind his thumbs with. But again he freed
himself, though not so easily as the first time, and he
said to his sister :

' Even that cord is not strong enough.'

The third day, on his return from the wood he consented to have his strength tested for the last time. So she took a very strong cord of silk, which she had prepared by the robber's advice, and this time, though the prince pulled and tugged with all his might, he could not break the cord. So he called to her and said : ' Sister, this time the cord is so strong I cannot break it. Come and unfasten it for me.'

But instead of coming she called to the robber, who rushed into the room brandishing a knife, with which he prepared to attack the prince.

But the prince spoke and said :

' Have patience for one minute. I would like before I die to blow three blasts on my hunting horn—one in this room, one on the stairs, and one in the courtyard.'

So the robber consented, and the prince blew the horn. At the first blast, the fox, which was asleep in the cage in the courtyard, awoke, and knew that his master needed help. So he awoke the wolf by flicking him across the eyes with his brush. Then they awoke the lion, who sprang against the door of the cage with might and main, so that it fell in splinters on the ground, and the beasts were free. Rushing through the court to their master's aid, the fox gnawed the cord in two that bound the prince's thumbs behind his back, and the lion flung himself on the robber, and when he had killed him and torn him in pieces each of the beasts carried off a bone.

Then the prince turned to the step-sister and said :

' I will not kill you, but I will leave you here to repent.' And he fastened her with a chain to the wall, and put a great bowl in front of her and said, ' I will not see you again till you have filled this bowl with your tears.'

So saying, he called his beasts, and set out on his travels. When he had gone a little way he came to an inn. Everyone in the inn seemed so sad that he asked them what was the matter.

' Ah,' replied they, ' to-day our king's daughter is to die. She is to be handed over to a dreadful nine-headed dragon.'

Then the prince said : ' Why should she die ? I am very strong, I will save her.'

And he set out to the sea-shore, where the dragon was to meet the princess. And as he waited with his beasts round him a great procession came along, accompanying the unfortunate princess : and when the shore was reached all the people left her, and returned sadly to their houses. But the prince remained, and soon he saw a movement in the water a long way off. As it came nearer, he knew what it was, for skimming swiftly along the waters came a monster dragon with nine heads. Then the prince took counsel with his beasts, and as the dragon approached the shore the fox drew his brush through the water and blinded the dragon by scattering the salt water in his eyes, while the bear and the lion threw up more water with their paws, so that the monster was bewildered and could see nothing. Then the prince rushed forward with his sword and killed the dragon, and the beasts tore the body in pieces.

Then the princess turned to the prince and thanked him for delivering her from the dragon, and she said to him :

' Step into this carriage with me, and we will drive back to my father's palace.' And she gave him a ring and half of her handkerchief. But on the way back the coachman and footman spoke to one another and said :

' Why should we drive this stranger back to the palace ? Let us kill him, and then we can say to the king that we slew the dragon and saved the princess, and one of us shall marry her.'

So they killed the prince, and left him dead on the roadside. And the faithful beasts came round the dead body and wept, and wondered what they should do. Then suddenly the wolf had an idea, and he started off

into the wood, where he found an ox, which he straight-
way killed. Then he called the fox, and told him to
mount guard over the dead ox, and if a bird came past
and tried to peck at the flesh he was to catch it and bring
it to the lion. Soon after a crow flew past, and began to
peck at the dead ox. In a moment the fox had caught it
and brought it to the lion. Then the lion said to the
crow :

' We will not kill you if you will promise to fly to the
town where there are three wells of healing and to bring
back water from them in your beak to make this dead
man alive.'

So the crow flew away, and she filled her beak at the
well of healing, the well of strength, and the well of
swiftness, and she flew back to the dead prince and
dropped the water from her beak upon his lips, and he
was healed, and could sit up and walk.

Then he set out for the town, accompanied by his
faithful beasts. And when they reached the king's palace
they found that preparations for a great feast were being
made, for the princess was to marry the coachman.

So the prince walked into the palace, and went straight
up to the coachman and said : ' What token have you got
that you killed the dragon and won the hand of the
princess ? I have her token here—this ring and half her
handkerchief.'

And when the king saw these tokens he knew that the
prince was speaking the truth. So the coachman was
bound in chains and thrown into prison, and the prince
was married to the princess and rewarded with half the
kingdom.

One day, soon after his marriage, the prince was
walking through the woods in the evening, followed by
his faithful beasts. Darkness came on, and he lost his
way, and wandered about among the trees looking for the
path that would lead him back to the palace. As he
walked he saw the light of a fire, and making his way to

The faithful Beasts wept round the dead body of the Prince

it he found an old woman raking sticks and dried leaves together, and burning them in a glade of the wood.

As he was very tired, and the night was very dark, the prince determined not to wander further. So he asked the old woman if he might spend the night beside her fire.

'Of course you may,' she answered. 'But I am afraid of your beasts. Let me hit them with my rod, and then I shall not be afraid of them.'

'Very well,' said the prince, 'I don't mind'; and she stretched out her rod and hit the beasts, and in one moment they were turned into stone, and so was the prince.

Now soon after this the prince's youngest brother came to the cross-roads with the three birches, where the brothers had parted from each other when they set out on their wanderings. Remembering what they had agreed to do, he walked round the two trees, and when he saw that blood oozed from the cut in the eldest prince's tree he knew that his brother must be dead. So he set out, followed by his beasts, and came to the town over which his brother had ruled, and where the princess he had married lived. And when he came into the town all the people were in great sorrow because their prince had disappeared.

But when they saw his youngest brother, and the beasts following him, they thought it was their own prince, and they rejoiced greatly, and told him how they had sought him everywhere. Then they led him to the king, and he too thought that it was his son-in-law. But the princess knew that he was not her husband, and she begged him to go out into the woods with his beasts, and to look for his brother till he found him.

So the youngest prince set out to look for his brother, and he too lost his way in the wood and night overtook him. Then he came to the clearing among the trees, where the fire was burning and where the old woman was raking sticks and leaves into the flames. And he asked her if he might spend the night beside her fire, as it was too late and too dark to go back to the town.

And she answered : 'Certainly you may. But I am afraid of your beasts. May I give them a stroke with my rod, then I shall not be afraid of them.'

And he said she might, for he did not know that she was a wi'ch. So she stretched out her rod, and in a moment the beasts and their master were turned into stone.

It happened soon after that the second brother returned from his wanderings and came to the cross-roads where the three birches grew. As he went round the trees he saw that blood poured from the cuts in the bark of two of the trees. Then he wept and said :

'Alas ! both my brothers are dead.' And he too set out towards the town in which his brother had ruled, and his faithful beasts followed him. When he entered the town, all the people thought it was their own prince come back to them, and they gathered round him, as they had gathered round his youngest brother, and asked him where he had been and why he had not returned. And they led him to the king's palace, but the princess knew that he was not her husband. So when they were alone together she besought him to go and seek for his brother and bring him home. Calling his beasts round him, he set out and wandered through the woods. And he put his ear down to the earth, to listen if he could hear the sound of his brother's beasts. And it seemed to him as if he heard a faint sound far off, but he did not know from what direction it came. So he blew on his hunting horn and listened again. And again he heard the sound, and this time it seemed to come from the direction of a fire burning in the wood. So he went towards the fire, and there the old woman was raking sticks and leaves into the embers. And he asked her if he might spend the night beside her fire. But she told him she was afraid of his

The Witch and The Princes

beasts, and he must first allow her to give each of them a stroke with her rod.

But he answered her :

' Certainly not. I am their master, and no one shall strike them but I myself. Give me the rod ' ; and he touched the fox with it, and in a moment it was turned into stone. Then he knew that the old woman was a witch, and he turned to her and said :

' Unless you restore my brothers and their beasts back to life at once, my lion will tear you in pieces.'

Then the witch was terrified, and taking a young oak tree she burnt it into white ashes, and sprinkled the ashes on the stones that stood around. And in a moment the two princes stood before their brother, and their beasts stood round them.

Then the three princes set off together to the town. And the king did not know which was his son-in-law, but the princess knew which was her husband, and there were great rejoicings throughout the land.

THE GOAT'S EARS OF THE EMPEROR TROJAN

ONCE upon a time there lived an emperor whose name was Trojan, and he had ears like a goat. Every morning, when he was shaved, he asked if the man saw anything odd about him, and as each fresh barber always replied that the emperor had goat's ears, he was at once ordered to be put to death.

Now after this state of things had lasted a good while, there was hardly a barber left in the town that could shave the emperor, and it came to be the turn of the Master of the Company of Barbers to go up to the palace. But, unluckily, at the very moment that he should have set out, the master fell suddenly ill, and told one of his apprentices that he must go in his stead.

When the youth was taken to the emperor's bedroom, he was asked why he had come and not his master. The young man replied that the master was ill, and there was no one but himself who could be trusted with the honour. The emperor was satisfied with the answer, and sat down, and let a sheet of fine linen be put round him. Directly the young barber began his work, he, like the rest, remarked the goat's ears of the emperor, but when he had finished and the emperor asked his usual question as to whether the youth had noticed anything odd about him, the young man replied calmly, ' No, nothing at all.' This pleased the emperor so much that he gave him twelve ducats, and said, ' Henceforth you shall come every day to shave me.'

So when the apprentice returned home, and the master inquired how he had got on with the emperor, the young man answered, ' Oh, very well, and he says I am to shave him every day, and he has given me these twelve ducats ' ; but he said nothing about the goat's ears of the emperor.

From this time the apprentice went regularly up to the palace, receiving each morning twelve ducats in payment. But after a while, his secret, which he had carefully kept, burnt within him, and he longed to tell it to somebody. His master saw there was something on his mind, and asked what it was. The youth replied that he had been tormenting himself for some months, and should never feel easy until some one shared his secret.

' Well, trust me,' said the master, ' I will keep it to myself ; or, if you do not like to do that, confess it to your pastor, or go into some field outside the town and dig a hole, and, after you have dug it, kneel down and whisper your secret three times into the hole. Then put back the earth and come away.'

The apprentice thought that this seemed the best plan, and that very afternoon went to a meadow outside the town, dug a deep hole, then knelt and whispered to it three times over, ' The Emperor Trojan has goat's ears.' And as he said so a great burden seemed to roll off him, and he shovelled the earth carefully back and ran lightly home.

Weeks passed away, and there sprang up in the hole an elder tree which had three stems, all as straight as poplars. Some shepherds, tending their flocks near by, noticed the tree growing there, and one of them cut down a stem to make flutes of ; but, directly he began to play, the flute would do nothing but sing : ' The Emperor Trojan has goat's ears.' Of course, it was not long before the whole town knew of this wonderful flute and what it said ; and, at last, the news reached the emperor in his palace. He instantly sent for the apprentice and said to him :

'What have you been saying about me to all my people?'

The culprit tried to defend himself by saying that he had never told anyone what he had noticed; but the emperor, instead of listening, only drew his sword from its sheath, which so frightened the poor fellow that he confessed exactly what he had done, and how he had whispered the truth three times to the earth, and how in that very place an elder tree had sprung up, and flutes had been cut from it, which would only repeat the words he had said. Then the emperor commanded his coach to be made ready, and he took the youth with him, and they drove to the spot, for he wished to see for himself whether the young man's confession was true; but when they reached the place only one stem was left. So the emperor desired his attendants to cut him a flute from the remaining stem, and, when it was ready, he ordered his chamberlain to play on it. But no tune could the chamberlain play, though he was the best flute player about the court—nothing came but the words, 'The Emperor Trojan has goat's ears.' Then the emperor knew that even the earth gave up its secrets, and he granted the young man his life, but he never allowed him to be his barber any more.

[Völksmärchen der Serben.]

THE NINE PEA-HENS AND THE
GOLDEN APPLES

ONCE upon a time there stood before the palace of an
emperor a golden apple tree, which blossomed and bore
fruit each night. But every morning the fruit was gone,
and the boughs were bare of blossom, without anyone
being able to discover who was the thief.

At last the emperor said to his eldest son, ' If only I
could prevent those robbers from stealing my fruit, how
happy I should be ! '

And his son replied, ' I will sit up to-night and watch
the tree, and I shall soon see who it is ! '

So directly it grew dark the young man went and hid
himself near the apple tree to begin his watch, but the
apples had scarcely begun to ripen before he fell asleep,
and when he awoke at sunrise the apples were gone.
He felt very much ashamed of himself, and went with
lagging feet to tell his father !

Of course, though the eldest son had failed, the second
made sure that he would do better, and set out gaily at
nightfall to watch the apple tree. But no sooner had he
lain himself down than his eyes grew heavy, and when
the sunbeams roused him from his slumbers there was
not an apple left on the tree.

Next came the turn of the youngest son, who made
himself a comfortable bed under the apple tree, and prepared himself to sleep. Towards midnight he awoke, and
sat up to look at the tree. And behold ! the apples were
beginning to ripen, and lit up the whole palace with their

brightness. At the same moment nine golden pea-hens flew swiftly through the air, and while eight alighted upon the boughs laden with fruit, the ninth fluttered to the ground where the prince lay, and instantly was changed into a beautiful maiden, more beautiful far than any lady in the emperor's court. The prince at once fell in love with her, and they talked together for some time, till the maiden said her sisters had finished plucking the apples, and now they must all go home again. The prince, however, begged her so hard to leave him a little of the fruit that the maiden gave him two apples, one for himself and one for his father. Then she changed herself back into a pea-hen, and the whole nine flew away.

As soon as the sun rose the prince entered the palace, and held out the apple to his father, who was rejoiced to see it, and praised his youngest son heartily for his cleverness. That evening the prince returned to the apple tree, and everything passed as before, and so it happened for several nights. At length the other brothers grew angry at seeing that he never came back without bringing two golden apples with him, and they went to consult an old witch, who promised to spy after him, and discover how he managed to get the apples. So, when the evening came, the old woman hid herself under the tree and waited for the prince. Before long he arrived and laid down on his bed, and was soon fast asleep. Towards midnight there was a rush of wings, and the eight pea-hens settled on the tree, while the ninth became a maiden, and ran to greet the prince. Then the witch stretched out her hand, and cut off a lock of the maiden's hair, and in an instant the girl sprang up, a pea-hen once more, spread her wings and flew away, while her sisters, who were busily stripping the boughs, flew after her.

When he had recovered from his surprise at the unexpected disappearance of the maiden, the prince exclaimed, ' What can be the matter?' and, looking about him,

UNDER THE GOLDEN APPLE TREE

discovered the old witch hidden under the bed. He
dragged her out, and in his fury called his guards, and
ordered them to put her to death as fast as possible.
But that did no good as far as the pea-hens went. They
never came back any more, though the prince returned to
the tree every night, and wept his heart out for his lost
love. This went on for some time, till the prince could
bear it no longer, and made up his mind he would search
the world through for her. In vain his father tried to
persuade him that his task was hopeless, and that other
girls were to be found as beautiful as this one. The
prince would listen to nothing, and, accompanied by
only one servant, set out on his quest.

After travelling for many days, he arrived at length
before a large gate, and through the bars he could see the
streets of a town, and even the palace. The prince tried
to pass in, but the way was barred by the keeper of
the gate, who wanted to know who he was, why he was
there, and how he had learnt the way, and he was not
allowed to enter unless the empress herself came and
gave him leave. A message was sent to her, and when
she stood at the gate the prince thought he had lost his
wits, for there was the maiden he had left his home to
seek. And she hastened to him, and took his hand, and
drew him into the palace. In a few days they were
married, and the prince forgot his father and his brothers,
and made up his mind that he would live and die in the
castle.

One morning the empress told him that she was
going to take a walk by herself, and that she would leave
the keys of twelve cellars to his care. 'If you wish to
enter the first eleven cellars,' said she, 'you can; but
beware of even unlocking the door of the twelfth, or it
will be the worse for you.'

The prince, who was left alone in the castle, soon got
tired of being by himself, and began to look about for
something to amuse him.

'What *can* there be in that twelfth cellar,' he thought to himself, 'which I must not see?' And he went downstairs and unlocked the doors, one after the other. When he got to the twelfth he paused, but his curiosity was too much for him, and in another instant the key was turned and the cellar lay open before him. It was empty, save for a large cask, bound with iron hoops, and out of the cask a voice was saying entreatingly, 'For goodness' sake, brother, fetch me some water; I am dying of thirst!'

The prince, who was very tender-hearted, brought some water at once, and pushed it through a hole in the barrel; and as he did so one of the iron hoops burst.

He was turning away, when a voice cried the second time, 'Brother, for pity's sake fetch me some water; I'm dying of thirst!'

So the prince went back, and brought some more water, and again a hoop sprang.

And for the third time the voice still called for water; and when water was given it the last hoop was rent, the cask fell in pieces, and out flew a dragon, who snatched up the empress just as she was returning from her walk, and carried her off. Some servants who saw what had happened came rushing to the prince, and the poor young man went nearly mad when he heard the result of his own folly, and could only cry out that he would follow the dragon to the ends of the earth, until he got his wife again.

For months and months he wandered about, first in this direction and then in that, without finding any traces of the dragon or his captive. At last he came to a stream, and as he stopped for a moment to look at it he noticed a little fish lying on the bank, beating its tail convulsively, in a vain effort to get back into the water.

'Oh, for pity's sake, my brother,' shrieked the little creature, 'help me, and put me back into the river, and I will repay you some day. Take one of my scales, and

The Dragon flies off with the Empress.

when you are in danger twist it in your fingers, and I
will come ! '

The prince picked up the fish and threw it into the
water ; then he took off one of its scales, as he had been
told, and put it in his pocket, carefully wrapped in a
cloth. Then he went on his way till, some miles further
down the road, he found a fox caught in a trap.

' Oh ! be a brother to me ! ' called the fox, ' and free
me from this trap, and I will help you when you are in
need. Pull out one of my hairs, and when you are in
danger twist it in your fingers, and I will come.'

So the prince unfastened the trap, pulled out one of
the fox's hairs, and continued his journey. And as he
was going over the mountain he passed a wolf en-
tangled in a snare, who begged to be set at liberty.

' Only deliver me from death,' he said, ' and you will
never be sorry for it. Take a lock of my fur, and when
you need me twist it in your fingers.' And the prince
undid the snare and let the wolf go.

For a long time he walked on, without having any
more adventures, till at length he met a man travelling
on the same road.

' Oh, brother ! ' asked the prince, ' tell me, if you can,
where the dragon-emperor lives ? '

The man told him where he would find the palace,
and how long it would take him to get there, and the
prince thanked him, and followed his directions, till that
same evening he reached the town where the dragon-
emperor lived. When he entered the palace, to his great
joy he found his wife sitting alone in a vast hall, and
they began hastily to invent plans for her escape. There
was no time to waste, as the dragon might return directly,
so they took two horses out of the stable, and rode away
at lightning speed. Hardly were they out of sight of the
palace than the dragon came home and found that his
prisoner had flown. He sent at once for his talking
horse, and said to him :

'Give me your advice; what shall I do—have my supper as usual, or set out in pursuit of them?'

'Eat your supper with a free mind first,' answered the horse, 'and follow them afterwards.'

So the dragon ate till it was past mid-day, and when he could eat no more he mounted his horse and set out after the fugitives. In a short time he had come up with them, and as he snatched the empress out of her saddle he said to the prince:

'This time I will forgive you, because you brought me the water when I was in the cask; but beware how you return here, or you will pay for it with your life.'

Half mad with grief, the prince rode sadly on a little further, hardly knowing what he was doing. Then he could bear it no longer and turned back to the palace, in spite of the dragon's threats. Again the empress was sitting alone, and once more they began to think of a scheme by which they could escape the dragon's power.

'Ask the dragon when he comes home,' said the prince, 'where he got that wonderful horse from, and then you can tell me, and I will try to find another like it.'

Then, fearing to meet his enemy, he stole out of the castle.

Soon after the dragon came home, and the empress sat down near him, and began to coax and flatter him into a good humour, and at last she said:

'But tell me about that wonderful horse you were riding yesterday. There cannot be another like it in the whole world. Where *did* you get it from?'

And he answered:

'The way I got it is a way which no one else can take. On the top of a high mountain dwells an old woman, who has in her stables twelve horses, each one more beautiful than the other. And in one corner is a thin, wretched-looking animal whom no one would glance at a second time, but he is in reality the best of

the lot. He is twin brother to my own horse, and can
fly as high as the clouds themselves. But no one can
ever get this horse without first serving the old woman
for three whole days. And besides the horses she has a
foal and its mother, and the man who serves her must
look after them for three whole days, and if he does not
let them run away he will in the end get the choice of
any horse as a present from the old woman. But if he
fails to keep the foal and its mother safe on any one of
the three nights his head will pay.'

The next day the prince watched till the dragon left
the house, and then he crept in to the empress, who told
him all she had learnt from her gaoler. The prince at
once determined to seek the old woman on the top of the
mountain, and lost no time in setting out. It was a long
and steep climb, but at last he found her, and with a low
bow he began :

'Good greeting to you, little mother !'

'Good greeting to you, my son ! What are you doing
here ?'

'I wish to become your servant,' answered he.

'So you shall,' said the old woman. 'If you can take
care of my mare for three days I will give you a horse
for wages, but if you let her stray you will lose your
head '; and as she spoke she led him into a courtyard
surrounded with palings, and on every post a man's head
was stuck. One post only was empty, and as they passed
it cried out :

'Woman, give me the head I am waiting for !'

The old woman made no answer, but turned to the
prince and said :

'Look ! all those men took service with me, on the
same conditions as you, but not one was able to guard
the mare !'

But the prince did not waver, and declared he would
abide by his words.

When evening came he led the mare out of the stable

and mounted her, and the colt ran behind. He managed to keep his seat for a long time, in spite of all her efforts to throw him, but at length he grew so weary that he fell fast asleep, and when he woke he found himself sitting on a log, with the halter in his hands. He jumped up in terror, but the mare was nowhere to be seen, and he started with a beating heart in search of her. He had gone some way without a single trace to guide him, when he came to a little river. The sight of the water brought back to his mind the fish whom he had saved from death, and he hastily drew the scale from his pocket. It had hardly touched his fingers when the fish appeared in the stream beside him.

'What is it, my brother?' asked the fish anxiously.

'The old woman's mare strayed last night, and I don't know where to look for her.'

'Oh, I can tell you that: she has changed herself into a big fish, and her foal into a little one. But strike the water with the halter and say, "Come here, O mare of the mountain witch!" and she will come.'

The prince did as he was bid, and the mare and her foal stood before him. Then he put the halter round her neck, and rode her home, the foal always trotting behind them. The old woman was at the door to receive them, and gave the prince some food while she led the mare back to the stable.

'You should have gone among the fishes,' cried the old woman, striking the animal with a stick.

'I did go among the fishes,' replied the mare; 'but they are no friends of mine, for they betrayed me at once.'

'Well, go among the foxes this time,' said she, and returned to the house, not knowing that the prince had overheard her.

So when it began to grow dark the prince mounted the mare for the second time and rode into the meadows, and the foal trotted behind its mother. Again he managed to stick on till midnight : then a sleep overtook him that he could not battle against, and when he woke up he found himself, as before, sitting on the log, with the halter in his hands. He gave a shriek of dismay, and sprang up in search of the wanderers. As he went he suddenly remembered the words that the old woman had said to the mare, and he drew out the fox hair and twisted it in his fingers.

'What is it, my brother ? ' asked the fox, who instantly appeared before him.

'The old witch's mare has run away from me, and I do not know where to look for her.'

'She is with us,' replied the fox, 'and has changed herself into a big fox, and her foal into a little one, but strike the ground with a halter and say, " Come here, O mare of the mountain witch ! " '

The prince did so, and in a moment the fox became a mare and stood before him, with the little foal at her heels. He mounted and rode back, and the old woman placed food on the table, and led the mare back to the stable.

'You should have gone to the foxes, as I told you,' said she, striking the mare with a stick.

'I did go to the foxes,' replied the mare, 'but they are no friends of mine and betrayed me.'

'Well, this time you had better go to the wolves,' said she, not knowing that the prince had heard all she had been saying.

The third night the prince mounted the mare and rode her out to the meadows, with the foal trotting after. He tried hard to keep awake, but it was of no use, and in the morning there he was again on the log, grasping the halter. He started to his feet, and then stopped, for he remembered what the old woman had said, and pulled out the wolf's grey lock.

'What is it, my brother ? ' asked the wolf as it stood before him.

' The old witch's mare has run away from me,' replied the prince, ' and I don't know where to find her.'

' Oh, she is with us,' answered the wolf, ' and she has changed herself into a she-wolf, and the foal into a cub; but strike the earth here with the halter, and cry, " Come to me, O mare of the mountain witch." '

The prince did as he was bid, and as the hair touched his fingers the wolf changed back into a mare, with the foal beside her. And when he had mounted and ridden her home the old woman was on the steps to receive them, and she set some food before the prince, but led the mare back to her stable.

' You should have gone among the wolves,' said she, striking her with a stick.

' So I did,' replied the mare, ' but they are no friends of mine and betrayed me.'

The old woman made no answer, and left the stable, but the prince was at the door waiting for her.

' I have served you well,' said he, ' and now for my reward.'

' What I promised that will I perform,' answered she. ' Choose one of these twelve horses; you can have which you like.'

' Give me, instead, that half-starved creature in the corner,' asked the prince. ' I prefer him to all those beautiful animals.'

' You can't really mean what you say ? ' replied the woman.

' Yes, I do,' said the prince, and the old woman was forced to let him have his way. So he took leave of her, and put the halter round his horse's neck and led him into the forest, where he rubbed him down till his skin was shining like gold. Then he mounted, and they flew straight through the air to the dragon's palace. The empress had been looking for him night and day, and stole out to meet him, and he swung her on to his saddle, and the horse flew off again.

Not long after the dragon came home, and when he found the empress was missing he said to his horse, 'What shall we do ? Shall we eat and drink, or shall we follow the runaways ? ' and the horse replied, ' Whether you eat or don't eat, drink or don't drink, follow them or stay at home, matters nothing now, for you can never, never catch them.'

But the dragon made no reply to the horse's words, but sprang on his back and set off in chase of the fugitives. And when they saw him coming they were frightened, and urged the prince's horse faster and faster, till he said, ' Fear nothing ; no harm can happen to us,' and their hearts grew calm, for they trusted his wisdom.

Soon the dragon's horse was heard panting behind, and he cried out, ' Oh, my brother, do not go so fast! I shall sink to the earth if I try to keep up with you.'

And the prince's horse answered, ' Why do you serve a monster like that ? Kick him off, and let him break in pieces on the ground, and come and join us.'

And the dragon's horse plunged and reared, and the dragon fell on a rock, which broke him in pieces. Then the empress mounted his horse, and rode back with her husband to her kingdom, over which they ruled for many years.

[Volksmärchen der Serben.]

THE LUTE PLAYER

ONCE upon a time there was a king and queen who lived happily and comfortably together. They were very fond of each other and had nothing to worry them, but at last the king grew restless. He longed to go out into the world, to try his strength in battle against some enemy and to win all kinds of honour and glory.

So he called his army together and gave orders to start for a distant country where a heathen king ruled who ill-treated or tormented everyone he could lay his hands on. The king then gave his parting orders and wise advice to his ministers, took a tender leave of his wife, and set off with his army across the seas.

I cannot say whether the voyage was short or long; but at last he reached the country of the heathen king and marched on, defeating all who came in his way. But this did not last long, for in time he came to a mountain pass, where a large army was waiting for him, who put his soldiers to flight, and took the king himself prisoner.

He was carried off to the prison where the heathen king kept his captives, and now our poor friend had a very bad time indeed. All night long the prisoners were chained up, and in the morning they were yoked together like oxen and had to plough the land till it grew dark.

This state of things went on for three years before the king found any means of sending news of himself to his dear queen, but at last he contrived to send this letter: 'Sell all our castles and palaces, and put all our treasures

THE LUTE-PLAYER

in pawn and come and deliver me out of this horrible
prison.'

The queen received the letter, read it, and wept bitterly
as she said to herself, 'How can I deliver my dearest
husband? If I go myself and the heathen king sees me
he will just take me to be one of his wives. If I were to
send one of the ministers!—but I hardly know if I can
depend on them.'

She thought, and thought, and at last an idea came
into her head. She cut off all her beautiful long brown
hair and dressed herself in boy's clothes. Then she took
her lute and, without saying anything to anyone, she went
forth into the wide world.

She travelled through many lands and saw many cities,
and went through many hardships before she got to the
town where the heathen king lived. When she got there
she walked all round the palace and at the back she saw
the prison. Then she went into the great court in front
of the palace, and taking her lute in her hand, she began
to play so beautifully that one felt as though one could
never hear enough.

After she had played for some time she began to sing,
and her voice was sweeter than the lark's :

> ' I come from my own country far
>   Into this foreign land,
> Of all I own I take alone
>   My sweet lute in my hand.
>
> ' Oh! who will thank me for my song,
>   Reward my simple lay ?
> Like lover's sighs it still shall rise
>   To greet thee day by day.
>
> ' I sing of blooming flowers
>   Made sweet by sun and rain ;
> Of all the bliss of love's first kiss,
>   And parting's cruel pain.
>
> ' Of the sad captive's longing
>   Within his prison wall,
> Of hearts that sigh when none are nigh
>   To answer to their call.

' My song begs for your pity,
    And gifts from out your store,
And as I play my gentle lay
    I linger near your door.

' And if you hear my singing
    Within your palace, sire,
Oh ! give, I pray, this happy day,
    To me my heart's desire.'

No sooner had the heathen king heard this touching song sung by such a lovely voice, than he had the singer brought before him.

' Welcome, O lute player,' said he. ' Where do you come from ? '

' My country, sire, is far away across many seas. For years I have been wandering about the world and gaining my living by my music.'

' Stay here then a few days, and when you wish to leave I will give you what you ask for in your song— your heart's desire.'

So the lute player stayed on in the palace and sang and played almost all day long to the king, who could never tire of listening and almost forgot to eat or drink or to torment people. He cared for nothing but the music, and nodded his head as he declared, ' That's something like playing and singing. It makes me feel as if some gentle hand had lifted every care and sorrow from me.'

After three days the lute player came to take leave of the king.

' Well,' said the king, ' what do you desire as your reward ? '

' Sire, give me one of your prisoners. You have so many in your prison, and I should be glad of a companion on my journeys. When I hear his happy voice as I travel along I shall think of you and thank you.'

' Come along then,' said the king, ' choose whom you will.' And he took the lute player through the prison himself.

The queen walked about amongst the prisoners, and at length she picked out her husband and took him with her on her journey. They were long on their way, but he never found out who she was, and she led him nearer and nearer to his own country.

When they reached the frontier the prisoner said :

' Let me go now, kind lad ; I am no common prisoner, but the king of this country. Let me go free and ask what you will as your reward.'

' Do not speak of reward,' answered the luté player. ' Go in peace.'

' Then come with me, dear boy, and be my guest.'

' When the proper time comes I shall be at your palace,' was the reply, and so they parted.

The queen took a short way home, got there before the king and changed her dress.

An hour later all the people in the palace were running to and fro and crying out : ' Our king has come back ! Our king has returned to us.'

The king greeted every one very kindly, but he would not so much as look at the queen.

Then he called all his council and ministers together and said to them :

' See what sort of a wife I have. Here she is falling on my neck, but when I was pining in prison and sent her word of it she did nothing to help me.'

And his council answered with one voice, ' Sire, when news was brought from you the queen disappeared and no one knew where she went. She only returned to-day.'

Then the king was very angry and cried, ' Judge my faithless wife ! Never would you have seen your king again, if a young lute player had not delivered him. I shall remember him with love and gratitude as long as I live.'

Whilst the king was sitting with his council, the queen found time to disguise herself. She took her lute,

and slipping into the court in front of the palace she
sang, clear and sweet :

> ' I sing the captive's longing
>   Within his prison wall,
> Of hearts that sigh when none are nigh
>   To answer to their call.

> ' My song begs for your pity,
>   And gifts from out your store,
> And as I play my gentle lay
>   I linger near your door.

> ' And if you hear my singing
>   Within your palace, sire,
> Oh ! give, I pray, this happy day,
>   To me my heart's desire.'

As soon as the king heard this song he ran out to
meet the lute player, took him by the hand and led him
into the palace.

'Here,' he cried, 'is the boy who released me from
my prison. And now, my true friend, I will indeed give
you your heart's desire.'

'I am sure you will not be less generous than the
heathen king was, sire. I ask of you what I asked and
obtained from him. But this time I don't mean to give
up what I get. I want *you*—yourself ! '

And as she spoke she threw off her long cloak and
everyone saw it was the queen.

Who can tell how happy the king was ? In the joy of
his heart he gave a great feast to the whole world, and
the whole world came and rejoiced with him for a whole
week.

I was there too, and ate and drank many good things.
I sha'n't forget that feast as long as I live.

[From the Russian.]

THE GRATEFUL PRINCE

ONCE upon a time the king of the Goldland lost himself in a forest, and try as he would he could not find the way out. As he was wandering down one path which had looked at first more hopeful than the rest he saw a man coming towards him.

'What are you doing here, friend?' asked the stranger; 'darkness is falling fast, and soon the wild beasts will come from their lairs to seek for food.'

'I have lost myself,' answered the king, 'and am trying to get home.'

'Then promise me that you will give me the first thing that comes out of your house, and I will show you the way,' said the stranger.

The king did not answer directly, but after awhile he spoke : 'Why should I give away my *best* sporting dog. I can surely find my way out of the forest as well as this man.'

So the stranger left him, but the king followed path after path for three whole days, with no better success than before. He was almost in despair, when the stranger suddenly appeared, blocking up his way.

'Promise you will give me the first thing that comes out of your house to meet you?'

But still the king was stiff-necked and would promise nothing.

For some days longer he wandered up and down the forest, trying first one path, then another, but his courage at last gave way, and he sank wearily on the ground under a tree, feeling sure his last hour had come. Then for the third time the stranger stood before the king, and said:

'Why are you such a fool? What can a dog be to you, that you should give your life for him like this? Just promise me the reward I want, and I will guide you out of the forest.'

'Well, my life is worth more than a thousand dogs,' answered the king, 'the welfare of my kingdom depends on me. I accept your terms, so take me to my palace.' Scarcely had he uttered the words than he found himself at the edge of the wood, with the palace in the dim distance. He made all the haste he could, and just as he reached the great gates out came the nurse with the royal baby, who stretched out his arms to his father. The king shrank back, and ordered the nurse to take the baby away at once. Then his great boarhound bounded up to him, but his caresses were only answered by a violent push.

When the king's anger was spent, and he was able to think what was best to be done, he exchanged his baby, a beautiful boy, for the daughter of a peasant, and the prince lived roughly as the son of poor people, while the little girl slept in a golden cradle, under silken sheets. At the end of a year, the stranger arrived to claim his property, and took away the little girl, believing her to be the true child of the king. The king was so delighted with the success of his plan that he ordered a great feast to be got ready, and gave splendid presents to the foster parents of his son, so that he might lack nothing. But he did not dare to bring back the baby, lest the trick should be found out. The peasants were quite contented with this arrangement, which gave them food and money in abundance.

By-and-by the boy grew big and tall, and seemed to lead a happy life in the house of his foster parents. But a shadow hung over him which really poisoned most of his pleasure, and that was the thought of the poor innocent girl who had suffered in his stead, for his foster father had told him in secret, that he was the king's son. And the prince determined that when he grew old enough he would travel all over the world, and never rest till he had set her free. To become king at the cost of a maiden's life was too heavy a price to pay. So one day he put on the dress of a farm servant, threw a sack of peas on his back, and marched straight into the forest where eighteen years before his father had lost himself. After he had walked some way he began to cry loudly: 'Oh, how unlucky I am! Where can I be? Is there no one to show me the way out of the wood?'

Then appeared a strange man with a long grey beard, with a leather bag hanging from his girdle. He nodded cheerfully to the prince, and said: 'I know this place well, and can lead you out of it, if you will promise me a good reward.'

'What can a beggar such as I promise you?' answered the prince. 'I have nothing to give you save my life; even the coat on my back belongs to my master, whom I serve for my keep and my clothes.'

The stranger looked at the sack of peas, and said, 'But you must possess something; you are carrying this sack, which seems to be very heavy.'

'It is full of peas,' was the reply. 'My old aunt died last night, without leaving money enough to buy peas to give the watchers, as is the custom throughout the country. I have borrowed these peas from my master, and thought to take a short cut across the forest; but I have lost myself, as you see.'

'Then you are an orphan?' asked the stranger. 'Why should you not enter my service? I want a sharp fellow in the house, and you please me.'

'Why not, indeed, if we can strike a bargain?' said the other. 'I was born a peasant, and strange bread is always bitter, so it is the same to me whom I serve! What wages will you give me?'

' Every day fresh food, meat twice a week, butter and
vegetables, your summer and winter clothes, and a
portion of land for your own use.'

The Prince meets a strange man in the wood.

' I shall be satisfied with that,' said the youth. ' Somebody else will have to bury my aunt. I will go with you !'

Now this bargain seemed to please the old fellow so much that he spun round like a top, and sang so loud that the whole wood rang with his voice. Then he set out with his companion, and chattered so fast that he never noticed that his new servant kept dropping peas out of the sack. At night they slept under a fig tree, and when the sun rose started on their way. About noon they came to a large stone, and here the old fellow stopped, looked carefully round, gave a sharp whistle, and stamped three times on the ground with his left foot. Suddenly there appeared under the stone a secret door, which led to what looked like the mouth of a cave. The old fellow seized the youth by the arm, and said roughly, ' Follow me ! '

Thick darkness surrounded them, yet it seemed to the prince as if their path led into still deeper depths. After a long while he thought he saw a glimmer of light, but the light was neither that of the sun nor of the moon. He looked eagerly at it, but found it was only a kind of pale cloud, which was all the light this strange underworld could boast. Earth and water, trees and plants, birds and beasts, each was different from those he had seen before ; but what most struck terror into his heart was the absolute stillness that reigned everywhere. Not a rustle or a sound could be heard. Here and there he noticed a bird sitting on a branch, with head erect and swelling throat, but his ear caught nothing. The dogs opened their mouths as if to bark, the toiling oxen seemed about to bellow, but neither bark nor bellow reached the prince. The water flowed noiselessly over the pebbles, the wind bowed the tops of the trees, flies and chafers darted about, without breaking the silence. The old greybeard uttered no word, and when his companion tried to ask him the meaning of it all he felt that his voice died in his throat.

How long this fearful stillness lasted I do not know, but the prince gradually felt his heart turning to ice, his hair stood up like bristles, and a cold chill was creeping down his spine, when at last—oh, ecstasy!—a faint noise broke on his straining ears, and this life of shadows suddenly became real. It sounded as if a troop of horses were ploughing their way over a moor.

Then the greybeard opened his mouth, and said : ' The kettle is boiling ; we are expected at home.'

They walked on a little further, till the prince thought he heard the grinding of a saw-mill, as if dozens of saws were working together, but his guide observed, ' The grandmother is sleeping soundly ; listen how she snores.'

When they had climbed a hill which lay before them the prince saw in the distance the house of his master, but it was so surrounded with buildings of all kinds that the place looked more like a village or even a small town. They reached it at last, and found an empty kennel standing in front of the gate. ' Creep inside this,' said the master, ' and wait while I go in and see my grandmother. Like all very old people, she is very obstinate, and cannot bear fresh faces about her.'

The prince crept tremblingly into the kennel, and began to regret the daring which had brought him into this scrape.

By-and-by the master came back, and called him from his hiding-place. Something had put out his temper, for with a frown he said, ' Watch carefully our ways in the house, and beware of making any mistake, or it will go ill with you. Keep your eyes and ears open, and your mouth shut, obey without questions. Be grateful if you will, but never speak unless you are spoken to.'

When the prince stepped over the threshold he caught sight of a maiden of wonderful beauty, with brown eyes and fair curly hair. ' Well !' the young man said to himself, ' if the old fellow has many daughters like that I should not mind being his son-in-law. This one is just what I admire '; and he watched her lay the table, bring in the food, and take her seat by the fire as if she had never noticed that a strange man was present. Then she took out a needle and thread, and began to darn her stockings. The master sat at table alone, and invited neither his new servant nor the maid to eat with him. Neither was the old grandmother anywhere to be seen. His appetite was tremendous : he soon cleared all the dishes, and ate enough to satisfy a dozen men. When at last he could eat no more he said to the girl, ' Now you can pick up the pieces, and take what is left in the iron pot for your own dinner, but give the bones to the dog.'

The prince did not at all like the idea of dining off scraps, which he helped the girl to pick up, but, after all, he found that there was plenty to eat, and that the food was very good. During the meal he stole many glances at the maiden, and would even have spoken to her, but she gave him no encouragement. Every time he opened his mouth for the purpose she looked at him sternly, as if to say, ' Silence,' so he could only let his eyes speak for him. Besides, the master was stretched on a bench by the oven after his huge meal, and would have heard everything.

After supper that night, the old man said to the prince, ' For two days you may rest from the fatigues of the journey, and look about the house. But the day after to-morrow you must come with me, and I will point out the work you have to do. The maid will show you where you are to sleep.'

The prince thought, from this, he had leave to speak, but his master turned on him with a face of thunder and exclaimed :

' You dog of a servant ! If you disobey the laws of the house you will soon find yourself a head shorter ! Hold your tongue, and leave me in peace.'

The girl made a sign to him to follow her, and, throwing open a door, nodded to him to go in. He would have lingered a moment, for he thought she looked sad, but dared not do so, for fear of the old man's anger.

'It is impossible that she can be his daughter!' he said to himself, 'for she has a kind heart. I am quite sure she must be the same girl who was brought here instead of me, so I am bound to risk my head in this mad adventure.' He got into bed, but it was long before he fell asleep, and even then his dreams gave him no rest. He seemed to be surrounded by dangers, and it was only the power of the maiden who helped him through it all.

When he woke his first thoughts were for the girl, whom he found hard at work. He drew water from the well and carried it to the house for her, kindled the fire under the iron pot, and, in fact, did everything that came into his head that could be of any use to her. In the afternoon he went out, in order to learn something of his new home, and wondered greatly not to come across the old grandmother. In his rambles he came to the farm-yard, where a beautiful white horse had a stall to itself; in another was a black cow with two white-faced calves, while the clucking of geese, ducks, and hens reached him from a distance.

Breakfast, dinner, and supper were as savoury as before, and the prince would have been quite content with his quarters had it not been for the difficulty of keeping silence in the presence of the maiden. On the evening of the second day he went, as he had been told, to receive his orders for the following morning.

'I am going to set you something very easy to do to-morrow,' said the old man when his servant entered. 'Take this scythe and cut as much grass as the white horse will want for its day's feed, and clean out its stall. If I come back and find the manger empty it will go ill with you. So beware!'

The prince left the room, rejoicing in his heart, and saying to himself, 'Well, I shall soon get through that! If I have never yet handled either the plough or the scythe, at least I have often watched the country people work them, and know how easy it is.'

He was just going to open his door, when the maiden
glided softly past and whispered in his ear: 'What task
has he set you?'

'For to-morrow,' answered the prince, 'it is really
nothing at all! Just to cut hay for the horse, and to
clean out his stall!'

'Oh, luckless being!' sighed the girl; 'how will you
ever get through with it. The white horse, who is our
master's grandmother, is always hungry: it takes twenty
men always mowing to keep it in food for one day, and
another twenty to clean out its stall. How, then, do you
expect to do it all by yourself? But listen to me, and do
what I tell you. It is your only chance. When you
have filled the manger as full as it will hold you must
weave a strong plait of the rushes which grow among the
meadow hay, and cut a thick peg of stout wood, and be
sure that the horse sees what you are doing. Then it will
ask you what it is for, and you will say, ' With this plait
I intend to bind up your mouth so that you cannot eat
any more, and with this peg I am going to keep you still
in one spot, so that you cannot scatter your corn and
water all over the place!' After these words the
maiden went away as softly as she had come.

Early the next morning he set to work. His scythe
danced through the grass much more easily than he had
hoped, and soon he had enough to fill the manger. He
put it in the crib, and returned with a second supply,
when to his horror he found the crib empty. Then he
knew that without the maiden's advice he would
certainly have been lost, and began to put it into practice.
He took out the rushes which had somehow got mixed
up with the hay, and plaited them quickly.

'My son, what are you doing?' asked the horse
wonderingly.

'Oh, nothing!' replied he. 'Just weaving a chin
strap to bind your jaws together, in case you might wish
to eat any more!'

The white horse sighed deeply when it heard this, and made up its mind to be content with what it had eaten.

The youth next began to clean out the stall, and the horse knew it had found a master; and by mid-day there was still fodder in the manger, and the place was as clean as a new pin. He had barely finished when in walked the old man, who stood astonished at the door.

'Is it really you who have been clever enough to do that?' he asked. 'Or has some one else given you a hint?'

'Oh, I have had no help,' replied the prince, 'except what my poor weak head could give me.'

The old man frowned, and went away, and the prince rejoiced that everything had turned out so well.

In the evening his master said, 'To-morrow I have no special task to set you, but as the girl has a great deal to do in the house you must milk the black cow for her. But take care you milk her dry, or it may be the worse for you.'

'Well,' thought the prince as he went away, 'unless there is some trick behind, this does not sound very hard. I have never milked a cow before, but I have good strong fingers.'

He was very sleepy, and was just going toward his room, when the maiden came to him and asked: 'What is your task to-morrow?'

'I am to help you,' he answered, 'and have nothing to do all day, except to milk the black cow dry.'

'Oh, you *are* unlucky,' cried she. 'If you were to try from morning till night you couldn't do it. There is only one way of escaping the danger, and that is, when you go to milk her, take with you a pan of burning coals and a pair of tongs. Place the pan on the floor of the stall, and the tongs on the fire, and blow with all your might, till the coals burn brightly. The black cow will ask you what is the meaning of all this, and you must answer what I will whisper to you.' And she stood on tip-toe and whispered something in his ear, and then went away.

The dawn had scarcely reddened the sky when the prince jumped out of bed, and, with the pan of coals in one hand and the milk pail in the other, went straight to the cow's stall, and began to do exactly as the maiden had told him the evening before.

The black cow watched him with surprise for some time, and then said : 'What are you doing, sonny?'

HOW THE BLACK COW WAS TRICKED

'Oh, nothing,' answered he ; 'I am only heating a pair of tongs in case you may not feel inclined to give as much milk as I want.'

The cow sighed deeply, and looked at the milkman with fear, but he took no notice, and milked briskly into the pail, till the cow ran dry.

Just at that moment the old man entered the stable, and sat down to milk the cow himself, but not a drop of milk could he get. 'Have you really managed it all yourself, or did somebody help you?'

'I have nobody to help me,' answered the prince, 'but

my own poor head.' The old man got up from his seat and went away.

That night, when the prince went to his master to hear what his next day's work was to be, the old man said : ' I have a little hay-stack out in the meadow which must be brought in to dry. To-morrow you will have to stack it all in the shed, and, as you value your life, be careful not to leave the smallest strand behind.' The prince was overjoyed to hear he had nothing worse to do.

' To carry a little hay-rick requires no great skill,' thought he, ' and it will give me no trouble, for the horse will have to draw it in. I am certainly not going to spare the old grandmother.'

By-and-by the maiden stole up to ask what task he had for the next day.

The young man laughed, and said : ' It appears that I have got to learn all kinds of farmer's work. To-morrow I have to carry a hay-rick, and leave not a stalk in the meadow, and that is my whole day's work ! '

' Oh, you unlucky creature ! ' cried she ; ' and how do you think you are to do it. If you had all the men in the world to help you, you could not clear off this one little hay-rick in a week. The instant you have thrown down the hay at the top, it will take root again from below. But listen to what I say. You must steal out at day-break to-morrow and bring out the white horse and some good strong ropes. Then get on the hay-stack, put the ropes round it, and harness the horse to the ropes. When you are ready, climb up the hay-stack and begin to count one, two, three. The horse will ask you what you are counting, and you must be sure to answer what I whisper to you.'

So the maiden whispered something in his ear, and left the room. And the prince knew nothing better to do than to get into bed.

He slept soundly, and it was still almost dark when he

got up and proceeded to carry out the instructions given him by the girl. First he chose some stout ropes, and then he led the horse out of the stable and rode it to the hay-stack, which was made up of fifty cartloads, so that it could hardly be called ' a little one.' The prince did all that the maiden had told him, and when at last he was seated on top of the rick, and had counted up to twenty, he heard the horse ask in amazement : ' What are you counting up there, my son ? '

' Oh, nothing,' said he, ' I was just amusing myself with counting the packs of wolves in the forest, but there are really so many of them that I don't think I should ever be done.'

The word ' wolf ' was hardly out of his mouth than the white horse was off like the wind, so that in the twinkling of an eye it had reached the shed, dragging the hay-stack behind it. The master was dumb with surprise as he came in after breakfast and found his man's day's work quite done.

' Was it really you who were so clever ? ' asked he. ' Or did some one give you good advice ? '

' Oh, I have only myself to take counsel with,' said the prince, and the old man went away, shaking his head.

Late in the evening the prince went to his master to learn what he was to do next day.

' To-morrow,' said the old man, ' you must bring the white-headed calf to the meadow, and, as you value your life, take care it does not escape from you.'

The prince answered nothing, but thought, ' Well, most peasants of nineteen have got a whole herd to look after, so surely I can manage one.' And he went towards his room, where the maiden met him.

' To morrow I have got an idiot's work,' said he ; ' nothing but to take the white-headed calf to the meadow.'

' Oh, you unlucky being ! ' sighed she. ' Do you know

that this calf is so swift that in a single day he can run three times round the world? Take heed to what I tell you. Bind one end of this silk thread to the left fore-leg of the calf, and the other end to the little toe of your left foot, so that the calf will never be able to leave your side, whether you walk, stand, or lie.' After this the prince went to bed and slept soundly.

The next morning he did exactly what the maiden had told him, and led the calf with the silken thread to the meadow, where it stuck to his side like a faithful dog.

By sunset, it was back again in its stall, and then came the master and said, with a frown, ' Were you really so clever yourself, or did somebody tell you what to do? '

' Oh, I have only my own poor head,' answered the prince, and the old man went away growling, 'I don't believe a word of it! I am sure you have found some clever friend! '

In the evening he called the prince and said: ' To-morrow I have no work for you, but when I wake you must come before my bed, and give me your hand in greeting.'

The young man wondered at this strange freak, and went laughing in search of the maiden.

' Ah, it is no laughing matter,' sighed she. ' He means to eat you, and there is only one way in which I can help you. You must heat an iron shovel red hot, and hold it out to him instead of your hand.'

So next morning he wakened very early, and had heated the shovel before the old man was awake. At length he heard him calling, ' You lazy fellow, where are you? Come and wish me good morning.' But when the prince entered with the red-hot shovel his master only said, ' I am very ill to-day, and too weak even to touch your hand. You must return this evening, when I may be better.'

The prince loitered about all day, and in the evening went back to the old man's room. He was received in the most friendly manner, and, to his surprise, his master exclaimed, 'I am very well satisfied with you. Come to me at dawn and bring the maiden with you. I know you have long loved each other, and I wish to make you man and wife.'

The young man nearly jumped into the air for joy, but, remembering the rules of the house, he managed to keep still. When he told the maiden, he saw to his astonishment that she had become as white as a sheet, and she was quite dumb.

'The old man has found out who was your counsellor,' she said when she could speak, ' and he means to destroy us both.' We must escape somehow, or else we shall be lost. Take an axe, and cut off the head of the calf with one blow. With a second, split its head in two, and in its brain you will see a bright red ball. Bring that to me. Meanwhile, I will do what is needful here.

And the prince thought to himself, ' Better kill the calf than be killed ourselves. If we can once escape, we will go back home. The peas which I strewed about must have sprouted, so that we shall not miss the way.'

Then he went into the stall, and with one blow of the axe killed the calf, and with the second split its brain. In an instant the place was filled with light, as the red ball fell from the brain of the calf. The prince picked it up, and, wrapping it round with a thick cloth, hid it in his bosom. Mercifully, the cow slept through it all, or by her cries she would have awakened the master.

He looked round, and at the door stood the maiden, holding a little bundle in her arms.

' Where is the ball ? ' she asked.

' Here,' answered he.

' We must lose no time in escaping, she went on, and uncovered a tiny bit of the shining ball, to light them on their way.

As the prince had expected, the peas had taken root, and grown into a little hedge, so that they were sure they

would not lose the path.   As they fled, the girl told him
that she had overheard a conversation between the old
man and his grandmother, saying that she was a king's
daughter, whom the old fellow had obtained by cunning
from her parents.   The prince, who knew all about the
affair, was silent, though he was glad from his heart that

it had fallen to his lot to set her free.   So they went on
till the day began to dawn.

The old man slept very late that morning, and rubbed
his eyes till he was properly awake.   Then he remembered
that very soon the couple were to present themselves
before him.   After waiting and waiting till quite a long
time had passed, he said to himself, with a grin, ' Well,
they are not in much hurry to be married,' and waited again.

At last he grew a little uneasy, and cried loudly, 'Man and maid! what has become of you?'

After repeating this many times, he became quite frightened, but, call as he would, neither man nor maid appeared. At last he jumped angrily out of bed to go in search of the culprits, but only found an empty house, and beds that had never been slept in. Then he went straight to the stable, where the sight of the dead calf told him all. Swearing loudly, he opened the door of the third stall quickly, and cried to his goblin servants to go and chase the fugitives. 'Bring them to me, however you may find them, for have them I must!' he said. So spake the old man, and the servants fled like the wind.

The runaways were crossing a great plain, when the maiden stopped. 'Something has happened!' she said. 'The ball moves in my hand, and I'm sure we are being followed!' and behind them they saw a black cloud flying before the wind. Then the maiden turned the ball thrice in her hand, and cried,

> 'Listen to me, my ball, my ball.
> Be quick and change me into a brook,
> And my lover into a little fish.'

And in an instant there was a brook with a fish swimming in it. The goblins arrived just after, but, seeing nobody, waited for a little, then hurried home, leaving the brook and the fish undisturbed. When they were quite out of sight, the brook and the fish returned to their usual shapes and proceeded on their journey.

When the goblins, tired and with empty hands, returned, their master inquired what they had seen, and if nothing strange had befallen them.

'Nothing,' said they; 'the plain was quite empty, save for a brook and a fish swimming in it.'

'Idiots!' roared the master; 'of course it was they!' And dashing open the door of the fifth stall, he told the goblins inside that they must go and drink up the brook, and catch the fish.   And the goblins jumped up, and flew like the wind.

The young pair had almost reached the edge of the wood, when the maiden stopped again. 'Something has happened,' said she. 'The ball is moving in my hand,' and looking round she beheld a cloud flying towards them, large and blacker than the first, and striped with red. 'Those are our pursuers,' cried she, and turning the ball three times in her hand she spoke to it thus :

> 'Listen to me, my ball, my ball.
> Be quick and change us both.
> Me into a wild rose bush,
> And him into a rose on my stem.'

And in the twinkling of an eye it was done. Only just in time too, for the goblins were close at hand, and looked round eagerly for the stream and the fish. But neither stream nor fish was to be seen ; nothing but a rose bush. So they went sorrowing home, and when they were out of sight the rose bush and rose returned to their proper shapes and walked all the faster for the little rest they had had.

'Well, did you find them ? ' asked the old man when his goblins came back.

'No,' replied the leader of the goblins, ' we found neither brook nor fish in the desert.'

' And did you find nothing else at all ? '

' Oh, nothing but a rose tree on the edge of a wood, with a rose hanging on it.'

'Idiots ! ' cried he. ' Why, that was they.'   And he threw open the door of the seventh stall, where his mightiest goblins were locked in. ' Bring them to me, however you find them, dead or alive ! ' thundered he, ' for I will have them !   Tear up the rose tree and the roots too, and don't leave anything behind, however strange it may be ! '

The fugitives were resting in the shade of a wood, and

were refreshing themselves with food
and drink. Suddenly the maiden
looked up. 'Something has happened,' said she. 'The ball has
nearly jumped out of my bosom!
Some one is certainly following us,
and the danger is near, but the trees
hide our enemies from us.'

As she spoke she took the ball
in her hand, and said:

'Listen to me, my ball, my ball.
  Be quick and change me into a breeze,
  And make my lover into a midge.'

An instant,
and the girl
was dissolved
into thin air,
while the
prince darted

DANGERS FOLLOWING

about like a midge.   The next moment a crowd of goblins rushed up, and looked about in search of something strange, for neither a rose bush nor anything else was to be seen.   But they had hardly turned their backs to go home empty-handed when the prince and the maiden stood on the earth again.

'We must make all the haste we can,' said she, ' before the old man himself comes to seek us, for he will know us under any disguise.'

They ran on till they reached such a dark part of the forest that, if it had not been for the light shed by the ball, they could not have made their way at all.   Worn out and breathless, they came at length to a large stone, and here the ball began to move restlessly.   The maiden, seeing this, exclaimed :

> ' Listen to me, my ball, my ball.
> Roll the stone quickly to one side,
> That we may find a door.'

And in a moment the stone had rolled away, and they had passed through the door to the world again.

'Now we are safe,' cried she.   'Here the old wizard has no more power over us, and we can guard ourselves from his spells.   But, my friend, we have to part!   You will return to your parents, and I must go in search of mine.'

'No! no!' exclaimed the prince.   'I will never part from you.   You must come with me and be my wife. We have gone through many troubles together, and now we will share our joys.   The maiden resisted his words for some time, but at last she went with him.

In the forest they met a woodcutter, who told them that in the palace, as well as in all the land, there had been great sorrow over the loss of the prince, and many years had now passed away during which they had found no traces of him.   So, by the help of the magic ball, the maiden managed that he should put on the same clothes that he had been wearing at the time he had vanished, so that his father might know him more quickly. She herself stayed behind in a peasant's hut, so that father and son might meet alone.

But the father was no longer there, for the loss of his son had killed him ; and on his deathbed he confessed to his people how he had contrived that the old wizard should carry away a peasant's child instead of the prince, wherefore this punishment had fallen upon him.

The prince wept bitterly when he heard this news, for he had loved his father well, and for three days he ate and drank nothing. But on the fourth day he stood in the presence of his people as their new king, and, calling his councillors, he told them all the strange things that had befallen him, and how the maiden had borne him safe through all.

And the councillors cried with one voice, ' Let her be your wife, and our liege lady.'

And that is the end of the story.

[Ehstnische Märchen.]

THE CHILD WHO CAME FROM AN EGG

ONCE upon a time there lived a queen whose heart was sore because she had no children. She was sad enough when her husband was at home with her, but when he was away she would see nobody, but sat and wept all day long.

Now it happened that a war broke out with the king of a neighbouring country, and the queen was left in the palace alone. She was so unhappy that she felt as if the walls would stifle her, so she wandered out into the garden, and threw herself down on a grassy bank, under the shade of a lime tree. She had been there for some time, when a rustle among the leaves caused her to look up, and she saw an old woman limping on her crutches towards the stream that flowed through the grounds.

When she had quenched her thirst, she came straight up to the queen, and said to her: ' Do not take it evil, noble lady, that I dare to speak to you, and do not be afraid of me, for it may be that I shall bring you good luck.'

The queen looked at her doubtfully, and answered: ' You do not seem as if you had been very lucky your-self, or to have much good fortune to spare for anyone else.'

' Under rough bark lies smooth wood and sweet kernel,' replied the old woman. ' Let me see your hand, that I may read the future.'

The queen held out her hand, and the old woman examined its lines closely. Then she said, ' Your heart is

heavy with two sorrows, one old and one new. The new
sorrow is for your husband, who is fighting far away from
you; but, believe me, he is well, and will soon bring

you joyful news. But your other sorrow is much older
than this. Your happiness is spoilt because you have
no children.' At these words the queen became scarlet,

and tried to draw away her hand, but the old woman said :

'Have a little patience, for there are some things I want to see more clearly.'

'But who are you ?' asked the queen, 'for you seem to be able to read my heart.'

'Never mind my name,' answered she, 'but rejoice that it is permitted to me to show you a way to lessen your grief. You must, however, promise to do exactly what I tell you, if any good is to come of it.'

'Oh, I will obey you exactly,' cried the queen, 'and if you can help me you shall have in return anything you ask for.'

The old woman stood thinking for a little : then she drew something from the folds of her dress, and, undoing a number of wrappings, brought out a tiny basket made of birch-bark. She held it out to the queen, saying, 'In the basket you will find a bird's egg. This you must be careful to keep in a warm place for three months, when it will turn into a doll. Lay the doll in a basket lined with soft wool, and leave it alone, for it will not need any food, and by-and-by you will find it has grown to be the size of a baby. Then you will have a baby of your own, and you must put it by the side of the other child, and bring your husband to see his son and daughter. The boy you will bring up yourself, but you must en-trust the little girl to a nurse. When the time comes to have them christened you will invite me to be god-mother to the princess, and this is how you must send the invitation. Hidden in the cradle, you will find a goose's wing : throw this out of the window, and I will be with you directly ; but be sure you tell no one of all the things that have befallen you.'

The queen was about to reply, but the old woman was already limping away, and before she had gone two steps she had turned into a young girl, who moved so quickly that she seemed rather to fly than to walk. The queen, watching this transformation, could hardly believe her eyes, and would have taken it all for a dream, had it not been for the basket which she held in her hand. Feeling a different being from the poor sad woman who had wandered into the garden so short a time before, she hastened to her room, and felt carefully in the basket for the egg. There it was, a tiny thing of soft blue with little green spots, and she took it out and kept it in her bosom, which was the warmest place she could think of.

A fortnight after the old woman had paid her visit, the king came home, having conquered his enemies. At this proof that the old woman had spoken truth, the queen's heart bounded, for she now had fresh hopes that the rest of the prophecy might be fulfilled. She cherished the basket and the egg as her chiefest treasures, and had a golden case made for the basket, so that when the time came to lay the egg in it, it might not risk any harm.

Three months passed, and, as the old woman had bidden her, the queen took the egg from her bosom, and laid it snugly amidst the warm woollen folds. The next morning she went to look at it, and the first thing she saw was the broken eggshell, and a little doll lying among the pieces. Then she felt happy at last, and leaving the doll in peace to grow, waited, as she had been told, for a baby of her own to lay beside it.

In course of time, this came also, and the queen took the little girl out of the basket, and placed it with her son in a golden cradle which glittered with precious stones. Next she sent for the king, who nearly went mad with joy at the sight of the children.

Soon there came a day when the whole court was ordered to be present at the christening of the royal babies, and when all was ready the queen softly opened the window a little, and let the goose wing fly out. The guests were coming thick and fast, when suddenly there drove up a splendid coach drawn by six cream-coloured horses, and out of it stepped a young lady dressed in garments that shone like the sun. Her face could not be seen, for a veil covered her head, but as she came up to the place where the queen was standing with the babies she drew the veil aside, and everyone was dazzled with her beauty. She took the little girl in her arms, and holding it up before the assembled company announced that henceforward it would be known by the name of Dotterine—a name which no one understood but the queen, who knew that the baby had come from the yolk of an egg. The boy was called Willem.

After the feast was over and the guests were going away, the godmother laid the baby in the cradle, and said to the queen, 'Whenever the baby goes to sleep, be sure you lay the basket beside her, and leave the eggshells in it. As long as you do that, no evil can come to her; so guard this treasure as the apple of your eye, and teach your daughter to do so likewise.' Then, kissing the baby three times, she mounted her coach and drove away.

The children throve well, and Dotterine's nurse loved her as if she were the baby's real mother. Every day the little girl seemed to grow prettier, and people used to say she would soon be as beautiful as her godmother, but no one knew, except the nurse, that at night, when the child slept, a strange and lovely lady bent over her. At length she told the queen what she had seen, but they determined to keep it as a secret between them-selves.

The twins were by this time nearly two years old, when the queen was taken suddenly ill. All the best doctors in the country were sent for, but it was no use, for there is no cure for death. The queen knew she was dying, and sent for Dotterine and her nurse, who had now become her lady-in-waiting. To her, as her most faithful servant, she gave the lucky basket in charge, and besought her to treasure it carefully. 'When my daughter,' said the queen, 'is ten years old, you are to hand it over to her, but warn her solemnly that her whole future happiness depends on the way she guards it. About my son, I have no fears. He is the heir of the kingdom, and his father will look after him.' The lady-in-waiting promised to carry out the queen's directions, and above all to keep the affair a secret. And that same morning the queen died.

After some years the king married again, but he did not love his second wife as he had done his first, and had only married her for reasons of ambition. She hated her step-children, and the king, seeing this, kept them out of the way, under the care of Dotterine's old nurse. But if they ever strayed across the path of the queen, she would kick them out of her sight like dogs.

On Dotterine's tenth birthday her nurse handed her over the cradle, and repeated to her her mother's dying words; but the child was too young to understand the value of such a gift, and at first thought little about it.

Two more years slipped by, when one day during the king's absence the stepmother found Dotterine sitting under a lime tree. She fell as usual into a passion, and beat the child so badly that Dotterine went staggering to her own room. Her nurse was not there, but suddenly, as she stood weeping, her eyes fell upon the golden case in which lay the precious basket. She thought it might contain something to amuse her, and looked eagerly inside, but nothing was there save a handful of wool and two empty eggshells. Very much disappointed, she lifted the wool, and there lay the goose's wing. 'What old rubbish,' said the child to herself, and, turning, threw the wing out of the open window.

In a moment a beautiful lady stood beside her. 'Do not be afraid,' said the lady, stroking Dotterine's head. 'I am your godmother, and have come to pay you a visit. Your red eyes tell me that you are unhappy. I know that your stepmother is very unkind to you, but be brave and patient, and better days will come. She will have no power over you when you are grown up, and no one else can hurt you either, if only you are careful never to part from your basket, or to lose the eggshells that are in it. Make a silken case for the little basket, and hide it away in your dress night and day and you will be safe from your stepmother and anyone that tries to harm you. But if you should happen to find yourself in any difficulty, and cannot tell what to do, take the goose's wing from the basket, and throw it out of the window, and in a moment I will come to help you. Now come into the garden, that I may talk to you under the lime trees, where no one can hear us.'

They had so much to say to each other, that the sun was already setting when the godmother had ended all the good advice she wished to give the child, and saw it was time for her to be going. 'Hand me the basket,' said she, 'for you must have some supper. I cannot let you go hungry to bed.'

Then, bending over the basket, she whispered some magic words, and instantly a table covered with fruits and cakes stood on the ground before them. When they had finished eating, the godmother led the child back, and on the way taught her the words she must say to the basket when she wanted it to give her something.

In a few years more, Dotterine was a grown-up young lady, and those who saw her thought that the world did not contain so lovely a girl.

About this time a terrible war broke out, and the king and his army were beaten back and back, till at length they had to retire into the town, and make ready for a siege. It lasted so long that food began to fail, and even in the palace there was not enough to eat.

So one morning Dotterine, who had had neither supper nor breakfast, and was feeling very hungry, let her wing fly away. She was so weak and miserable,

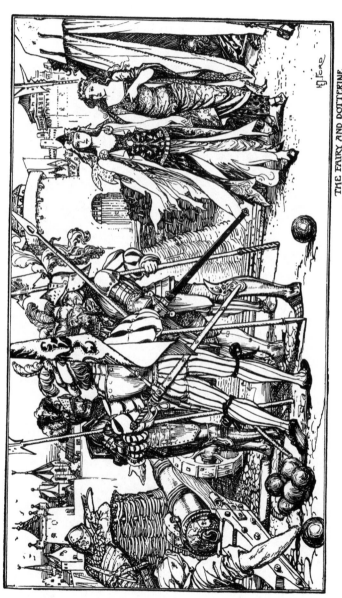

THE FAIRY AND DOTTERINE
PASS UNSEEN THROUGH
THE CAMP OF THE ENEMY

that directly her godmother appeared she burst into
tears, and could not speak for some time.

'Do not cry so, dear child,' said the godmother. ' I
will carry you away from all this, but the others I must
leave to take their chance.' Then, bidding Dotterine
follow her, she passed through the gates of the town, and
through the army outside, and nobody stopped them, or
seemed to see them.

The next day the town surrendered, and the king and
all his courtiers were taken prisoners, but in the confusion
his son managed to make his escape. The queen had
already met her death from a spear carelessly thrown.

As soon as Dotterine and her godmother were clear
of the enemy, Dotterine took off her own clothes, and put
on those of a peasant, and in order to disguise her better
her godmother changed her face completely. ' When
better times come,' her protectress said cheerfully, ' and
you want to look like yourself again, you have only to
whisper the words I have taught you into the basket,
and say you would like to have your own face once more,
and it will be all right in a moment. But you will have
to endure a little longer yet.' Then, warning her once
more to take care of the basket, the lady bade the girl
farewell.

For many days Dotterine wandered from one place to
another without finding shelter, and though the food
which she got from the basket prevented her from
starving, she was glad enough to take service in a
peasant's house till brighter days dawned. At first the
work she had to do seemed very difficult, but either she
was wonderfully quick in learning, or else the basket
may have secretly helped her. Anyhow at the end of
three days she could do everything as well as if she had
cleaned pots and swept rooms all her life.

One morning Dotterine was busy scouring a wooden
tub, when a noble lady happened to pass through the
village. The girl's bright face as she stood in the front

of the door with her tub attracted the lady, and she stopped and called the girl to come and speak to her.

'Would you not like to come and enter my service?' she asked.

'Very much,' replied Dotterine, 'if my present mistress will allow me.'

'Oh, I will settle that,' answered the lady; and so she did, and the same day they set out for the lady's house, Dotterine sitting beside the coachman.

Six months went by, and then came the joyful news that the king's son had collected an army and had defeated the usurper who had taken his father's place, but at the same moment Dotterine learned that the old king had died in captivity. The girl wept bitterly for his loss, but in secrecy, as she had told her mistress nothing about her past life.

At the end of a year of mourning, the young king let it be known that he intended to marry, and commanded all the maidens in the kingdom to come to a feast, so that he might choose a wife from among them. For weeks all the mothers and all the daughters in the land were busy preparing beautiful dresses and trying new ways of putting up their hair, and the three lovely daughters of Dotterine's mistress were as much excited as the rest. The girl was clever with her fingers, and was occupied all day with getting ready their smart clothes, but at night when she went to bed she always dreamed that her godmother bent over her and said, 'Dress your young ladies for the feast, and when they have started follow them yourself. Nobody will be so fine as you.'

When the great day came, Dotterine could hardly contain herself, and when she had dressed her young mistresses and seen them depart with their mother she flung herself on her bed, and burst into tears. Then she seemed to hear a voice whisper to her, 'Look in your basket, and you will find in it everything that you need.'

Dotterine did not want to be told twice! Up she jumped, seized her basket, and repeated the magic words, and behold! there lay a dress on the bed, shining as a star. She put it on with fingers that trembled with joy, and, looking in the glass, was struck dumb at her own beauty. She went downstairs, and in front of the door stood a fine carriage, into which she stepped and was driven away like the wind.

The king's palace was a long way off, yet it seemed only a few minutes before Dotterine drew up at the great gates. She was just going to alight, when she suddenly remembered she had left her basket behind her. What was she to do? Go back and fetch it, lest some ill-fortune should befall her, or enter the palace and trust to chance that nothing evil would happen? But before she could decide, a little swallow flew up with the basket in its beak, and the girl was happy again.

The feast was already at its height, and the hall was brilliant with youth and beauty, when the door was flung wide and Dotterine entered, making all the other maidens look pale and dim beside her. Their hopes faded as they gazed, but their mothers whispered together, saying, ' Surely this is our lost princess ! '

The young king did not know her again, but he never left her side nor took his eyes from her. And at midnight a strange thing happened. A thick cloud suddenly filled the hall, so that for a moment all was dark. Then the mist suddenly grew bright, and Dotterine's god-mother was seen standing there.

' This,' she said, turning to the king, ' is the girl whom you have always believed to be your sister, and who vanished during the siege. She is not your sister at all, but the daughter of the king of a neighbouring country, who was given to your mother to bring up, to save her from the hands of a wizard.'

Then she vanished, and was never seen again, nor the wonder-working basket either ; but now that Dotterine's troubles were over she could get on without them, and she and the young king lived happily together till the end of their days.

[Ehstnische Märchen.]

STAN BOLOVAN

ONCE upon a time what happened did happen, and if it had not happened this story would never have been told.

On the outskirts of a village just where the oxen were turned out to pasture, and the pigs roamed about burrowing with their noses among the roots of the trees, there stood a small house. In the house lived a man who had a wife, and the wife was sad all day long.

'Dear wife, what is wrong with you that you hang your head like a drooping rosebud?' asked her husband one morning. 'You have everything you want; why cannot you be merry like other women?'

'Leave me alone, and do not seek to know the reason,' replied she, bursting into tears, and the man thought that it was no time to question her, and went away to his work.

He could not, however, forget all about it, and a few days after he inquired again the reason of her sadness, but only got the same reply. At length he felt he could bear it no longer, and tried a third time, and then his wife turned and answered him.

'Good gracious!' cried she, 'why cannot you let things be as they are? If I were to tell you, you would become just as wretched as myself. If you would only believe, it is far better for you to know nothing.'

But no man yet was ever content with such an answer. The more you beg him not to inquire, the greater is his curiosity to learn the whole.

'Well, if you *must* know,' said the wife at last, 'I will tell you. There is no luck in this house—no luck at all!'

'Is not your cow the best milker in all the village? Are not your trees as full of fruit as your hives are full of bees? Has anyone cornfields like ours? Really you talk nonsense when you say things like that!'

'Yes, all that you say is true, but we have no children.'

Then Stan understood, and when a man once understands and has his eyes opened it is no longer well with him. From that day the little house in the outskirts contained an unhappy man as well as an unhappy woman. And at the sight of her husband's misery the woman became more wretched than ever.

And so matters went on for some time.

Some weeks had passed, and Stan thought he would consult a wise man who lived a day's journey from his own house. The wise man was sitting before his door when he came up, and Stan fell on his knees before him. 'Give me children, my lord, give me children.'

'Take care what you are asking,' replied the wise man. 'Will not children be a burden to you? Are you rich enough to feed and clothe them?'

'Only give them to me, my lord, and I will manage somehow!' and at a sign from the wise man Stan went his way.

He reached home that evening tired and dusty, but with hope in his heart. As he drew near his house a sound of voices struck upon his ear, and he looked up to see the whole place full of children. Children in the garden, children in the yard, children looking out of every window—it seemed to the man as if all the children in the world must be gathered there. And none was bigger than the other, but each was smaller than the other, and every one was more noisy and more impudent and more daring than the rest, and Stan gazed and grew cold with horror as he realised that they all belonged to him.

'Good gracious! how many there are! how many!' he muttered to himself.

'Oh, but not one too many,' smiled his wife, coming up with a crowd more children clinging to her skirts.

STAN BOLOVAN MEETS HIS FAMILY

But even she found that it was not so easy to look after a hundred children, and when a few days had passed and they had eaten up all the food there was in the house, they began to cry, 'Father! I am hungry—I am hungry,' till Stan scratched his head and wondered what he was to do next. It was not that he thought there were too many children, for his life had seemed more full of joy since they appeared, but now it came to the point he did not know how he was to feed them. The cow had ceased to give milk, and it was too early for the fruit trees to ripen.

'Do you know, old woman!' said he one day to his wife, 'I must go out into the world and try to bring back food somehow, though I cannot tell where it is to come from.'

To the hungry man any road is long, and then there was always the thought that he had to satisfy a hundred greedy children as well as himself.

Stan wandered, and wandered, and wandered, till he reached to the end of the world, where that which is, is mingled with that which is not, and there he saw, a little way off, a sheepfold, with seven sheep in it. In the shadow of some trees lay the rest of the flock.

Stan crept up, hoping that he might manage to decoy some of them away quietly, and drive them home for food for his family, but he soon found this could not be. For at midnight he heard a rushing noise, and through the air flew a dragon, who drove apart a ram, a sheep, and a lamb, and three fine cattle that were lying down close by. And besides these he took the milk of seventy-seven sheep, and carried it home to his old mother, that she might bathe in it and grow young again. And this happened every night.

The shepherd bewailed himself in vain : the dragon only laughed, and Stan saw that this was not the place to get food for his family.

But though he quite understood that it was almost hopeless to fight against such a powerful monster, yet the thought of the hungry children at home clung to him like a burr, and would not be shaken off, and at last he said to the shepherd, 'What will you give me if I rid you of the dragon ? '

'One of every three rams, one of every three sheep, one of every three lambs,' answered the herd.

'It is a bargain,' replied Stan, though at the moment he did not know how, supposing he *did* come off the victor, he would ever be able to drive so large a flock home.

However, that matter could be settled later. At present night was not far off, and he must consider how best to fight with the dragon.

Just at midnight, a horrible feeling that was new and strange to him came over Stan—a feeling that he could not put into words even to himself, but which almost forced him to give up the battle and take the shortest road home again. He half turned ; then he remembered the children, and turned back.

' You or I,' said Stan to himself, and took up his position on the edge of the flock.

'Stop ! ' he suddenly cried, as the air was filled with a rushing noise, and the dragon came dashing past.

' Dear me ! ' exclaimed the dragon, looking round. ' Who are you, and where do you come from ? '

' I am Stan Bolovan, who eats rocks all night, and in the day feeds on the flowers of the mountain ; and if you meddle with those sheep I will carve a cross on your back.'

When the dragon heard these words he stood quite still in the middle of the road, for he knew he had met with his match.

'But you will have to fight me first,' he said in a trembling voice, for when you faced him properly he was not brave at all.

' I fight you ? ' replied Stan, ' why I could slay you with one breath ! ' Then, stooping to pick up a large cheese which lay at his feet, he added, ' Go and get a stone like this out of the river, so that we may lose no time in seeing who is the best man.'

The dragon did as Stan bade him, and brought back a stone out of the brook.

' Can you get buttermilk out of your stone ? 'asked Stan.

The dragon picked up his stone with one hand, and squeezed it till it fell into powder, but no butter-

STAN BOLOVAN OUTWITS THE DRAGON

milk flowed from it. 'Of course I can't!' he said, half angrily.

'Well, if you can't, I can,' answered Stan, and he

pressed the cheese till buttermilk flowed through his fingers.

When the dragon saw that, he thought it was time he made the best of his way home again, but Stan stood in his path.

'We have still some accounts to settle,' said he, 'about what you have been doing here,' and the poor dragon was too frightened to stir, lest Stan should slay him at one breath and bury him among the flowers in the mountain pastures.

'Listen to me,' he said at last. 'I see you are a very useful person, and my mother has need of a fellow like you. Suppose you enter her service for three days, which are as long as one of your years, and she will pay you each day seven sacks full of ducats.'

Three times seven sacks full of ducats! The offer was very tempting, and Stan could not resist it. He did not waste words, but nodded to the dragon, and they started along the road.

It was a long, long way, but when they came to the end they found the dragon's mother, who was as old as time itself, expecting them. Stan saw her eyes shining like lamps from afar, and when they entered the house they beheld a huge kettle standing on the fire, filled with milk. When the old mother found that her son had arrived empty-handed she grew very angry, and fire and flame darted from her nostrils, but before she could speak the dragon turned to Stan.

'Stay here,' said he, 'and wait for me; I am going to explain things to my mother.'

Stan was already repenting bitterly that he had ever come to such a place, but, since he was there, there was nothing for it but to take everything quietly, and not show that he was afraid.

'Listen, mother,' said the dragon as soon as they were alone, 'I have brought this man in order to get rid of him. He is a terrific fellow who eats rocks, and can press buttermilk out of a stone,' and he told her all that had happened the night before.

' Oh, just leave him to me ! ' she said. ' I have never yet let a man slip through my fingers.' So Stan had to stay and do the old mother service.

The next day she told him that he and her son should try which was the strongest, and she took down a huge club, bound seven times with iron.

The dragon picked it up as if it had been a feather, and, after whirling it round his head, flung it lightly three miles away, telling Stan to beat that if he could.

They walked to the spot where the club lay. Stan stooped and felt it ; then a great fear came over him, for he knew that he and all his children together would never lift that club from the ground.

' What are you doing ? ' asked the dragon.

' I was thinking what a beautiful club it was, and what a pity it is that it should cause your death.'

' How do you mean—my death ? ' asked the dragon.

' Only that I am afraid that if I throw it you will never see another dawn. You don't know how strong I am ! '

' Oh, never mind that be quick and throw.'

' If you are really in earnest, let us go and feast for three days : that will at any rate give you three extra days of life.'

Stan spoke so calmly that this time the dragon began to get a little frightened, though he did not quite believe that things would be as bad as Stan said.

They returned to the house, took all the food that could be found in the old mother's larder, and carried it back to the place where the club was lying. Then Stan seated himself on the sack of provisions, and remained quietly watching the setting moon.

' What are you doing ? ' asked the dragon.

' Waiting till the moon gets out of my way.'

' What do you mean ? I don't understand.'

' Don't you see that the moon is exactly in my way ?
But of course, if you like, I will throw the club into the
moon.'

At these words the dragon grew uncomfortable for the
second time. He prized the club, which had been left
him by his grandfather, very highly, and had no desire
that it should be lost in the moon.

' I'll tell you what,' he said, after thinking a little.
' Don't throw the club at all. I will throw it a second
time, and that will do just as well.'

' No, certainly not ! ' replied Stan. ' Just wait till the
moon sets.'

But the dragon, in dread lest Stan should fulfil his
threats, tried what bribes could do, and in the end had
to promise Stan seven sacks of ducats before he was
suffered to throw back the club himself.

' Oh, dear me, that is indeed a strong man,' said the
dragon, turning to his mother. ' Would you believe that
I have had the greatest difficulty in preventing him from
throwing the club into the moon ? '

Then the old woman grew uncomfortable too ! Only
to think of it ! It was no joke to throw things into the
moon ! So no more was heard of the club, and the next
day they had all something else to think about.

' Go and fetch me water ! ' said the mother, when
the morning broke, and gave them twelve buffalo skins
with the order to keep filling them till night.

They set out at once for the brook, and in the
twinkling of an eye the dragon had filled the whole
twelve, carried them into the house, and brought them
back to Stan. Stan was tired : he could scarcely lift the
buckets when they were empty, and he shuddered to
think of what would happen when they were full. But
he only took an old knife out of his pocket and began to
scratch up the earth near the brook.

' What are you doing there ? How are you going to
carry the water into the house ? ' asked the dragon.

'How? Dear me, that is easy enough! I shall just take the brook!'

At these words the dragon's jaw dropped. This was the last thing that had ever entered his head, for the brook had been as it was since the days of his grandfather.

'I'll tell you what!' he said. 'Let me carry your skins for you.'

'Most certainly not,' answered Stan, going on with his digging, and the dragon, in dread lest he should fulfil his threat, tried what bribes would do, and in the end had again to promise seven sacks of ducats before Stan would agree to leave the brook alone and let him carry the water into the house.

On the third day the old mother sent Stan into the forest for wood, and, as usual, the dragon went with him.

Before you could count three he had pulled up more trees than Stan could have cut down in a lifetime, and had arranged them neatly in rows. When the dragon had finished, Stan began to look about him, and, choosing the biggest of the trees, he climbed up it, and, breaking off a long rope of wild vine, bound the top of the tree to the one next it. And so he did to a whole line of trees.

'What are you doing there?' asked the dragon.

'You can see for yourself,' answered Stan, going quietly on with his work.

'Why are you tying the trees together?'

'Not to give myself unnecessary work; when I pull up one, all the others will come up too.'

'But how will you carry them home?'

'Dear me! don't you understand that I am going to take the whole forest back with me?' said Stan, tying two other trees as he spoke.

'I'll tell you what,' cried the dragon, trembling with fear at the thought of such a thing; 'let me carry the wood for you, and you shall have seven times seven sacks full of ducats.'

' You are a good fellow, and I agree to your proposal,' answered Stan, and the dragon carried the wood.

Now the three days' service which were to be reckoned as a year were over, and the only thing that disturbed Stan was, how to get all those ducats back to his home !

In the evening the dragon and his mother had a long talk, but Stan heard every word through a crack in the ceiling.

' Woe be to us, mother,' said the dragon ; ' this man will soon get us into his power. Give him his money, and let us be rid of him.'

But the old mother was fond of money, and did not like this.

' Listen to me,' said she ; ' you must murder him this very night.'

' I am afraid,' answered he.

' There is nothing to fear,' replied the old mother. ' When he is asleep take the club, and hit him on the head with it. It is easily done.'

And so it would have been, had not Stan heard all about it. And when the dragon and his mother had put out their lights, he took the pigs' trough and filled it with earth, and placed it in his bed, and covered it with clothes. Then he hid himself underneath, and began to snore loudly.

Very soon the dragon stole softly into the room, and gave a tremendous blow on the spot where Stan's head should have been. Stan groaned loudly from under the bed, and the dragon went away as softly as he had come. Directly he had closed the door, Stan lifted out the pigs' trough, and lay down himself, after making everything clean and tidy, but he was wise enough not to shut his eyes that night.

The next morning he came into the room when the dragon and his mother were having their breakfast.

' Good morning,' said he.

'Good morning. How did you sleep?'

'Oh, very well, but I dreamed that a flea had bitten me, and I seem to feel it still.'

The dragon and his mother looked at each other. 'Do you hear that?' whispered he. 'He talks of a flea. I broke my club on his head.'

This time the mother grew as frightened as her son. There was nothing to be done with a man like this, and she made all haste to fill the sacks with ducats, so as to get rid of Stan as soon as possible. But on his side Stan was trembling like an aspen, as he could not lift even one sack from the ground. So he stood still and looked at them.

'What are you standing there for?' asked the dragon.

'Oh, I was standing here because it has just occurred to me that I should like to stay in your service for another year. I am ashamed that when I get home they should see I have brought back so little. I know that they will cry out, "Just look at Stan Bolovan, who in one year has grown as weak as a dragon."'

Here a shriek of dismay was heard both from the dragon and his mother, who declared they would give him seven or even seven times seven the number of sacks if he would only go away.

'I'll tell you what!' said Stan at last. 'I see you don't want me to stay, and I should be very sorry to make myself disagreeable. I will go at once, but only on condition that you shall carry the money home yourself, so that I may not be put to shame before my friends.'

The words were hardly out of his mouth before the dragon had snatched up the sacks and piled them on his back. Then he and Stan set forth.

The way, though really not far, was yet too long for Stan, but at length he heard his children's voices, and stopped short. He did not wish the dragon to know where he lived, lest some day he should come to take back his treasure. Was there nothing he could say to get rid of the monster? Suddenly an idea came into Stan's head, and he turned round.

'I hardly know what to do,' said he. 'I have a hundred children, and I am afraid they may do you

THE DRAGON ALARMED

harm, as they are always ready for a fight. However, I will do my best to protect you.'

A hundred children! That was indeed no joke! The dragon let fall the sacks from terror, and then picked them up again. But the children, who had had nothing to eat since their father had left them, came rushing towards him, waving knives in their right hands and forks in their left, and crying, ' Give us dragon's flesh ; we will have dragon's flesh.'

At this dreadful sight the dragon waited no longer : he flung down his sacks where he stood and took flight as fast as he could, so terrified at the fate that awaited him that from that day he has never dared to show his face in the world again.

[Adapted from Rumänische Märchen.]

THE TWO FROGS

ONCE upon a time in the country of Japan there lived two frogs, one of whom made his home in a ditch near the town of Osaka, on the sea coast, while the other dwelt in a clear little stream which ran through the city of Kioto. At such a great distance apart, they had never even heard of each other; but, funnily enough, the idea came into both their heads at once that they should like to see a little of the world, and the frog who lived at Kioto wanted to visit Osaka, and the frog who lived at Osaka wished to go to Kioto, where the great Mikado had his palace.

So one fine morning in the spring they both set out along the road that led from Kioto to Osaka, one from one end and the other from the other. The journey was more tiring than they expected, for they did not know much about travelling, and half way between the two towns there arose a mountain which had to be climbed. It took them a long time and a great many hops to reach the top, but there they were at last, and what was the surprise of each to see another frog before him! They looked at each other for a moment without speaking, and then fell into conversation, explaining the cause of their meeting so far from their homes. It was delightful to find that they both felt the same wish—to learn a little more of their native country—and as there was no sort of hurry they stretched themselves out in a cool, damp place, and agreed that they would have a good rest before they parted to go their ways.

'What a pity we are not bigger,' said the Osaka frog ;
' for then we could see both towns from here, and tell if
it is worth our while going on.'

'Oh, that is easily managed,' returned the Kioto frog.
' We have only got to stand up on our hind legs, and hold
on to each other, and then we can each look at the town
he is travelling to.'

This idea pleased the Osaka frog so much that he at
once jumped up and put his front paws on the shoulders
of his friend, who had risen also.   There they both stood,
stretching themselves as high as they could, and holding
each other tightly, so that they might not fall down.   The
Kioto frog turned his nose towards Osaka, and the Osaka
frog turned his nose towards Kioto ; but the foolish things
forgot that when they stood up their great eyes lay in the
backs of their heads, and that though their noses might
point to the places to which they wanted to go their eyes
beheld the places from which they had come.

'Dear me !' cried the Osaka frog, 'Kioto is exactly
like Osaka.   It is certainly not worth such a long
journey.   I shall go home !'

' If I had had any idea that Osaka was only a copy of
Kioto I should never have travelled all this way,' exclaimed the frog from Kioto, and as he spoke he took his
hands from his friend's shoulders, and they both fell down
on the grass.   Then they took a polite farewell of each
other, and set off for home again, and to the end of their
lives they believed that Osaka and Kioto, which are as
different to look at as two towns can be, were as like as
two peas.

[Japanische Märchen.]

THE STORY OF A GAZELLE

ONCE upon a time there lived a man who wasted all his
money, and grew so poor that his only food was a few
grains of corn, which he scratched like a fowl from out of
a dust-heap.

One day he was scratching as usual among a dust-heap
in the street, hoping to find something for breakfast, when
his eye fell upon a small silver coin, called an eighth,
which he greedily snatched up. 'Now I can have a
proper meal,' he thought, and after drinking some water
at a well he lay down and slept so long that it was sunrise before he woke again. Then he jumped up and
returned to the dust-heap. 'For who knows,' he said to
himself, 'whether I may not have some good luck again.'

As he was walking down the road, he saw a man
coming towards him, carrying a cage made of twigs.
'Hi! you fellow!' called he, 'what have you got inside
there?'

'Gazelles,' replied the man.

'Bring them here, for I should like to see them.'

As he spoke, some men who were standing by began
to laugh, saying to the man with the cage: 'You had
better take care how you bargain with him, for he has
nothing at all except what he picks up from a dust-heap,
and if he can't feed himself, will he be able to feed a
gazelle?'

But the man with the cage made answer: 'Since I
started from my home in the country, fifty people at the
least have called me to show them my gazelles, and was

there one among them who cared to buy? It is the custom for a trader in merchandise to be summoned hither and thither, and who knows where one may find a buyer?' And he took up his cage and went towards the scratcher of dust-heaps, and the men went with him.

'What do you ask for your gazelles?' said the beggar. 'Will you let me have one for an eighth?'

And the man with the cage took out a gazelle, and held it out, saying, 'Take this one, master!'

And the beggar took it and carried it to the dust-heap, where he scratched carefully till he found a few grains of corn, which he divided with his gazelle. This he did night and morning, till five days went by.

Then, as he slept, the gazelle woke him, saying, 'Master.'

And the man answered, 'How is it that I see a wonder?'

'What wonder?' asked the gazelle.

'Why, that you, a gazelle, should be able to speak, for, from the beginning, my father and mother and all the people that are in the world have never told me of a talking gazelle.'

'Never mind that,' said the gazelle, 'but listen to what I say! First, I took you for my master. Second, you gave for me all you had in the world. I cannot run away from you, but give me, I pray you, leave to go every morning and seek food for myself, and every evening I will come back to you. What you find in the dust-heaps is not enough for both of us.'

'Go, then,' answered the master; and the gazelle went.

When the sun had set, the gazelle came back, and the poor man was very glad, and they lay down and slept side by side.

In the morning it said to him, 'I am going away to feed.'

And the man replied, 'Go, my son,' but he felt very

lonely without his gazelle, and set out sooner than usual for the dust-heap where he generally found most corn. And glad he was when the evening came, and he could return home. He lay on the grass chewing tobacco, when the gazelle trotted up.

'Good evening, my master; how have you fared all day? I have been resting in the shade in a place where there is sweet grass when I am hungry, and fresh water when I am thirsty, and a soft breeze to fan me in the heat. It is far away in the forest, and no one knows of it but me, and to-morrow I shall go again.'

So for five days the gazelle set off at daybreak for this cool spot, but on the fifth day it came to a place where the grass was bitter, and it did not like it, and scratched, hoping to tear away the bad blades. But, instead, it saw something lying in the earth, which turned out to be a diamond, very large and bright. 'Oh, ho!' said the gazelle to itself, 'perhaps now I can do something for my master who bought me with all the money he had; but I must be careful or they will say he has stolen it. I had better take it myself to some great rich man, and see what it will do for me.'

Directly the gazelle had come to this conclusion, it picked up the diamond in its mouth, and went on and on and on through the forest, but found no place where a rich man was likely to dwell. For two more days it ran, from dawn to dark, till at last early one morning it caught sight of a large town, which gave it fresh courage.

The people were standing about the streets doing their marketing, when the gazelle bounded past, the diamond flashing as it ran. They called after it, but it took no notice till it reached the palace, where the sultan was sitting, enjoying the cool air. And the gazelle galloped up to him, and laid the diamond at his feet.

The sultan looked first at the diamond and next at the gazelle; then he ordered his attendants to bring cushions and a carpet, that the gazelle might rest itself after its long journey.   And he likewise ordered milk to be brought, and rice, that it might eat and drink and be refreshed.

And when the gazelle was rested, the sultan said to it: ' Give me the news you have come with.'

And the gazelle answered: ' I am come with this diamond, which is a pledge from my master the Sultan Darai.   He has heard you have a daughter, and sends you this small token, and begs you will give her to him to wife.'

And the sultan said : ' I am content.   The wife is his wife, the family is his family, the slave is his slave. Let him come to me empty-handed, I am content.'

When the sultan had ended, the gazelle rose, and said : ' Master, farewell; I go back to our town, and in eight days, or it may be in eleven days, we shall arrive as your guests.'

And the sultan answered : ' So let it be.'

All this time the poor man far away had been mourning and weeping for his gazelle, which he thought had run away from him for ever.   And when it came in at the door he rushed to embrace it with such joy that he would not allow it a chance to speak.

' Be still, master, and don't cry,' said the gazelle at last ; ' let us sleep now, and in the morning, when I go, follow me.'

With the first ray of dawn they got up and went into the forest, and on the fifth day, as they were resting near a stream, the gazelle gave its master a sound beating, and then bade him stay where he was till it returned. And the gazelle ran off, and about ten o'clock it came near the sultan's palace, where the road was all lined with soldiers who were there to do honour to Sultan Darai. And directly they caught sight of the gazelle in the distance one of the soldiers ran on and said, ' Sultan Darai is coming : I have seen the gazelle.'

Then the sultan rose up, and called his whole court to follow him, and went out to meet the gazelle, who, bound- ·

THE GAZELLE BRINGS THE DIAMOND TO THE SULTAN

ing up to him, gave him greeting. The sultan answered politely, and inquired where it had left its master, whom it had promised to bring back.

'Alas!' replied the gazelle, 'he is lying in the forest, for on our way here we were met by robbers, who, after beating and robbing him, took away all his clothes. And he is now hiding under a bush, lest a passing stranger might see him.'

The sultan, on hearing what had happened to his future son-in-law, turned his horse and rode to the palace, and bade a groom to harness the best horse in the stable and order a woman slave to bring a bag of clothes, such as a man might want, out of the chest; and he chose out a tunic and a turban and a sash for the waist, and fetched himself a gold-hilted sword, and a dagger and a pair of sandals, and a stick of sweet-smelling wood.

'Now,' said he to the gazelle, 'take these things with the soldiers to the sultan, that he may be able to come.'

And the gazelle answered: 'Can I take those soldiers to go and put my master to shame as he lies there naked? I am enough by myself, my lord.'

How will you be enough,' asked the sultan, 'to manage this horse and all these clothes?'

'Oh, that is easily done,' replied the gazelle. 'Fasten the horse to my neck and tie the clothes to the back of the horse, and be sure they are fixed firmly, as I shall go faster than he does.'

Everything was carried out as the gazelle had ordered, and when all was ready it said to the sultan: 'Farewell, my lord, I am going.'

'Farewell, gazelle,' answered the sultan; 'when shall we see you again?'

'To-morrow about five,' replied the gazelle, and, giving a tug to the horse's rein, they set off at a gallop.

The sultan watched them till they were out of sight:

then he said to his attendants, 'That gazelle comes from gentle hands, from the house of a sultan, and that is what makes it so different from other gazelles.' And in the eyes of the sultan the gazelle became a person of consequence.

Meanwhile the gazelle ran on till it came to the place where its master was seated, and his heart laughed when he saw the gazelle.

And the gazelle said to him, 'Get up, my master, and bathe in the stream!' and when the man had bathed it said again, 'Now rub yourself well with earth, and rub your teeth well with sand to make them bright and shining.' And when this was done it said, 'The sun has gone down behind the hills; it is time for us to go': so it went and brought the clothes from the back of the horse, and the man put them on and was well pleased.

'Master!' said the gazelle when the man was ready, 'be sure that where we are going you keep silence, except for giving greetings and asking for news. Leave all the talking to me. I have provided you with a wife, and have made her presents of clothes and turbans and rare and precious things, so it is needless for you to speak.'

'Very good, I will be silent,' replied the man as he mounted the horse. 'You have given all this; it is you who are the master, and I who am the slave, and I will obey you in all things.'

'So they went their way, and they went and went till the gazelle saw in the distance the palace of the sultan. Then it said, 'Master, that is the house we are going to, and you are not a poor man any longer: even your name is new.'

'What *is* my name, eh, my father?' asked the man.

'Sultan Darai,' said the gazelle.

Very soon some soldiers came to meet them, while others ran off to tell the sultan of their approach.

And the sultan set off at once, and the viziers and the emirs, and the judges, and the rich men of the city, all followed him.

THE·GAZELLE·BRINGS·CLOTHES·TO·HIS·MASTER

Directly the gazelle saw them coming, it said to its master : ' Your father-in-law is coming to meet you ; that is he in the middle, wearing a mantle of sky-blue. Get off your horse and go to greet him.'

And Sultan Darai leapt from his horse, and so did the other sultan, and they gave their hands to one another and kissed each other, and went together into the palace.

The next morning the gazelle went to the rooms of the sultan, and said to him : 'My lord, we want you to marry us our wife, for the soul of Sultan Darai is eager.'

'The wife is ready, so call the priest,' answered he, and when the ceremony was over a cannon was fired and music was played, and within the palace there was feasting.

'Master,' said the gazelle the following morning, 'I am setting out on a journey, and I shall not be back for seven days, and perhaps not then. But be careful not to leave the house till I come.'

And the master answered, 'I will not leave the house.'

And it went to the sultan of the country and said to him : 'My lord, Sultan Darai has sent me to his town to get the house in order. It will take me seven days, and if I am not back in seven days he will not leave the palace till I return.'

'Very good,' said the sultan.

And it went and it went through the forest and wilderness, till it arrived at a town full of fine houses. At the end of the chief road was a great house, beautiful exceedingly, built of sapphire and turquoise and marbles. 'That,' thought the gazelle, 'is the house for my master, and I will call up my courage and go and look at the people who are in it, if any people there are. For in this town have I as yet seen no people. If I die, I die, and if I live, I live. Here can I think of no plan, so if anything is to kill me, it will kill me.'

Then it knocked twice at the door, and cried 'Open,' but no one answered. And it cried again, and a voice replied :

' Who are you that are crying " Open " ? '

And the gazelle said, ' It is I, great mistress, your grandchild.'

' If you are my grandchild,' returned the voice, ' go back whence you came. Don't come and die here, and bring me to my death as well.'

' Open, mistress, I entreat, I have something to say to you.'

' Grandchild,' replied she, ' I fear to put your life in danger, and my own too.'

'Oh, mistress, my life will not be lost, nor yours either ; open, I pray you.' So she opened the door.

' What is the news where you come from, my grand-son,' asked she.

' Great lady, where I come from it is well, and with you it is well.'

' Ah, my son, here it is not well at all. If you seek a way to die, or if you have not yet seen death, then is to-day the day for you to know what dying is.'

' If I am to know it, I shall know it,' replied the gazelle ; ' but tell me, who is the lord of this house ? '

And she said : ' Ah, father ! in this house is much wealth, and much people, and much food, and many horses. And the lord of it all is an exceeding great and wonderful snake.'

' Oh ! ' cried the gazelle when he heard this ; ' tell me how I can get at the snake to kill him ? '

' My son,' returned the old woman, ' do not say words like these ; you risk both our lives. He has put me here all by myself, and I have to cook his food. When the great snake is coming there springs up a wind, and blows the dust about, and this goes on till the great snake glides into the courtyard and calls for his dinner, which must always be ready for him in those big pots. He eats till he has had enough, and then drinks a whole tankful of water. After that he goes away. Every second day he comes, when the sun is over the house. And he has seven heads. How then can you be a match for him, my son?'

'Mind your own business, mother,' answered the gazelle, 'and don't mind other people's! Has this snake a sword?'

'He has a sword, and a sharp one too. It cuts like a flash of lightning.'

'Give it to me, mother!' said the gazelle, and she unhooked the sword from the wall, as she was bidden. 'You must be quick,' she said, 'for he may be here at any moment. Hark! is not that the wind rising? He has come!'

They were silent, but the old woman peeped from behind a curtain, and saw the snake busy at the pots which she had placed ready for him in the courtyard. And after he had done eating and drinking he came to the door:

'You old body!' he cried; 'what smell is that I smell inside that is not the smell of every day?'

'Oh, master!' answered she, 'I am alone, as I always am! But to-day, after many days, I have sprinkled fresh scent all over me, and it is that which you smell. What else could it be, master?'

All this time the gazelle had been standing close to the door, holding the sword in one of its front paws. And as the snake put one of his heads through the hole that he had made so as to get in and out comfortably, it cut it off so clean that the snake really did not feel it. The second blow was not quite so straight, for the snake said to himself, 'Who is that who is trying to scratch me?' and stretched out his third head to see; but no sooner was the neck through the hole than the head went rolling to join the rest.

When six of his heads were gone the snake lashed his tail with such fury that the gazelle and the old woman could not see each other for the dust he made. And the gazelle said to him, 'You have climbed all sorts of

trees, but this you can't climb,' and as the seventh head
came darting through it went rolling to join the rest.

The Gazelle cuts
off the Serpent's
Heads

Then the sword fell rattling on the ground, for the
gazelle had fainted.

The old woman shrieked with delight when she saw her enemy was dead, and ran to bring water to the gazelle, and fanned it, and put it where the wind could blow on it, till it grew better and gave a sneeze. And the heart of the old woman was glad, and she gave it more water, till by-and-by the gazelle got up.

'Show me this house,' it said, 'from beginning to end, from top to bottom, from inside to out.'

So she arose and showed the gazelle rooms full of gold and precious things, and other rooms full of slaves. 'They are all yours, goods and slaves,' said she.

But the gazelle answered, 'You must keep them safe till I call my master.'

For two days it lay and rested in the house, and fed on milk and rice, and on the third day it bade the old woman farewell and started back to its master.

And when he heard that the gazelle was at the door he felt like a man who has found the time when all prayers are granted, and he rose and kissed it, saying : 'My father, you have been a long time ; you have left sorrow with me. I cannot eat, I cannot drink, I cannot laugh ; my heart felt no smile at anything, because of thinking of you.'

And the gazelle answered : 'I am well, and where I come from it is well, and I wish that after four days you would take your wife and go home.'

And he said : 'It is for you to speak. Where you go, I will follow.'

'Then I shall go to your father-in-law and tell him this news.'

'Go, my son.'

So the gazelle went to the father-in-law and said : 'I am sent by my master to come and tell you that after four days he will go away with his wife to his own home.'

'Must he really go so quickly? We have not yet sat much together, I and Sultan Darai, nor have we yet talked much together, nor have we yet ridden out together, nor have we eaten together; yet it is fourteen days since he came.'

But the gazelle replied: 'My lord, you cannot help it, for he wishes to go home, and nothing will stop him.'

'Very good,' said the sultan, and he called all the people who were in the town, and commanded that the day his daughter left the palace ladies and guards were to attend her on her way.

And at the end of four days a great company of ladies and slaves and horses went forth to escort the wife of Sultan Darai to her new home. They rode all day, and when the sun sank behind the hills they rested, and ate of the food the gazelle gave them, and lay down to sleep. And they journeyed on for many days, and they all, nobles and slaves, loved the gazelle with a great love— more than they loved the Sultan Darai.

At last one day signs of houses appeared, far, far off. And those who saw cried out, 'Gazelle!'

And it answered, 'Ah, my mistresses, that is the house of Sultan Darai.'

At this news the women rejoiced much, and the slaves rejoiced much, and in the space of two hours they came to the gates, and the gazelle bade them all stay behind, and it went on to the house with Sultan Darai.

When the old woman saw them coming through the courtyard she jumped and shouted for joy, and as the gazelle drew near she seized it in her arms, and kissed it. The gazelle did not like this, and said to her: 'Old woman, leave me alone; the one to be carried is my master, and the one to be kissed is my master.'

And she answered, 'Forgive me, my son. I did not know this was our master,' and she threw open all the doors so that the master might see everything that the rooms and storehouses contained. Sultan Darai looked about him, and at length he said:

'Unfasten those horses that are tied up, and let loose

those people that are bound. And let some sweep, and some spread the beds, and some cook, and some draw water, and some come out and receive the mistress.'

And when the sultana and her ladies and her slaves entered the house, and saw the rich stuffs it was hung with, and the beautiful rice that was prepared for them to eat, they cried : ' Ah, you gazelle, we have seen great houses, we have seen people, we have heard of things. But this house, and you, such as you are, we have never seen or heard of.'

After a few days, the ladies said they wished to go home again. The gazelle begged them hard to stay, but finding they would not, it brought many gifts, and gave some to the ladies and some to their slaves. And they all thought the gazelle greater a thousand times than its master, Sultan Darai.

The gazelle and its master remained in the house many weeks, and one day it said to the old woman, ' I came with my master to this place, and I have done many things for my master, good things, and till to-day he has never asked me : " Well, my gazelle, how did you get this house ? Who is the owner of it? And this town, were there no people in it ? "   All good things I have done for the master, and he has not one day done me any good thing. But people say, " If you want to do any one good, don't do him good only, do him evil also, and there will be peace between you." So, mother, I have done : I want to see the favours I have done to my master, that he may do me the like.'

' Good,' replied the old woman, and they went to bed.

In the morning, when light came, the gazelle was sick in its stomach and feverish, and its legs ached. And it said ' Mother ! '

And she answered, ' Here, my son ? '

And it said, ' Go and tell my master upstairs the gazelle is very ill.'

' Very good, my son ; and if he should ask me what is the matter, what am I to say ? '

' Tell him all my body aches badly ; I have no single part without pain.'

The old woman went upstairs, and she found the mistress and master sitting on a couch of marble spread with soft cushions, and they asked her, ' Well, old woman, what do you want ? '

' To tell the master the gazelle is ill,' said she.

' What is the matter ? ' asked the wife.

' All its body pains ; there is no part without pain.'

' Well, what can I do ? Make some gruel of red millet, and give to it.'

But his wife stared and said : ' Oh, master, do you tell her to make the gazelle gruel out of red millet, which a horse would not eat ? Eh, master, that is not well.'

But he answered, ' Oh, you are mad ! Rice is only kept for people.'

' Eh, master, this is not like a gazelle. It is the apple of your eye. If sand got into that, it would trouble you.'

' My wife, your tongue is long,' and he left the room.

The old woman saw she had spoken vainly, and went back weeping to the gazelle. And when the gazelle saw her it said, ' Mother, what is it, and why do you cry ? If it be good, give me the answer ; and if it be bad, give me the answer.'

But still the old woman would not speak, and the gazelle prayed her to let it know the words of the master. At last she said : ' I went upstairs and found the mistress and the master sitting on a couch, and he asked me what I wanted, and I told him that you, his slave, were ill. And his wife asked what was the matter, and I told her that there was not a part of your body without pain. And the master told me to take some red millet and make you gruel, but the mistress said, ' Eh, master, the gazelle is the apple of your eye ; you have no child, this gazelle is like your child; so this gazelle is not one to be done evil to. This is a gazelle in form, but not a gazelle in heart; he is in all things better than a gentleman, be he who he may.'

And he answered her, 'Silly chatterer, your words are many. I know its price; I bought it for an eighth. What loss will it be to me?'

The gazelle kept silence for a few moments. Then it said, 'The elders said, "One that does good like a mother," and I have done him good, and I have got this that the elders said. But go up again to the master, and tell him the gazelle is very ill, and it has not drunk the gruel of red millet.'

So the old woman returned, and found the master and the mistress drinking coffee. And when he heard what the gazelle had said, he cried: 'Hold your peace, old woman, and stay your feet and close your eyes, and stop your ears with wax; and if the gazelle bids you come to me, say your legs are bent, and you cannot walk; and if it begs you to listen, say your ears are stopped with wax; and if it wishes to talk, reply that your tongue has got a hook in it.'

The heart of the old woman wept as she heard such words, because she saw that when the gazelle first came to that town it was ready to sell its life to buy wealth for its master. Then it happened to get both life and wealth, but now it had no honour with its master.

And tears sprung likewise to the eyes of the sultan's wife, and she said, 'I am sorry for you, my husband, that you should deal so wickedly with that gazelle'; but he only answered, 'Old woman, pay no heed to the talk of the mistress: tell it to perish out of the way. I cannot sleep, I cannot eat, I cannot drink, for the worry of that gazelle. Shall a creature that I bought for an eighth trouble me from morning till night? Not so, old woman!'

The old woman went downstairs, and there lay the

gazelle, blood flowing from its nostrils. And she took it in her arms and said, ' My son, the good you did is lost ; there remains only patience.'

And it said, ' Mother, I shall die, for my soul is full of anger and bitterness. My face is ashamed, that I should have done good to my master, and that he should repay me with evil.' It paused for a moment, and then went on, ' Mother, of the goods that are in this house, what do I eat ? I might have every day half a basinful, and would my master be any the poorer ? But did not the elders say, " He that does good like a mother ! " '

And it said, ' Go and tell my master that the gazelle is nearer death than life.'

So she went, and spoke as the gazelle had bidden her ; but he answered, ' I have told you to trouble me no more.'

But his wife's heart was sore, and she said to him : ' Ah, master, what has the gazelle done to you ? How has he failed you ? The things you do to him are not good, and you will draw on yourself the hatred of the people. For this gazelle is loved by all, by small and great, by women and men. Ah, my husband ! I thought you had great wisdom, and you have not even a little ! '

But he answered, ' You are mad, my wife.'

The old woman stayed no longer, and went back to the gazelle, followed secretly by the mistress, who called a maidservant and bade her take some milk and rice and cook it for the gazelle.

' Take also this cloth,' she said, ' to cover it with, and this pillow for its head. And if the gazelle wants more, let it ask me, and not its master. And if it will, I will send it in a litter to my father, and he will nurse it till it is well.'

And the maidservant did as her mistress bade her, and said what her mistress had told her to say, but the gazelle made no answer, but turned over on its side and died quietly.

When the news spread abroad, there was much weeping among the people, and Sultan Darai arose in wrath, and cried, ' You weep for that gazelle as if you wept for me ! And, after all, what is it but a gazelle, that I bought for an eighth ? '

But his wife answered, ' Master, we looked upon that gazelle as we looked upon you. It was the gazelle who came to ask me of my father, it was the gazelle who brought me from my father, and I was given in charge to the gazelle by my father.'

And when the people heard her they lifted up their voices and spoke :

' We never saw you, we saw the gazelle. It was the gazelle who met with trouble here, it was the gazelle who met with rest here. So, then, when such an one departs from this world we weep for ourselves, we do not weep for the gazelle.'

And they said furthermore :

' The gazelle did you much good, and if anyone says he could have done more for you he is a liar ! Therefore, to us who have done you no good, what treatment will you give ? The gazelle has died from bitterness of soul, and you ordered your slaves to throw it into the well. Ah ! leave us alone that we may weep.'

But Sultan Darai would not heed their words, and the dead gazelle was thrown into the well.

When the mistress heard of it, she sent three slaves, mounted on donkeys, with a letter to her father the sultan, and when the sultan had read the letter he bowed his head and wept, like a man who had lost his mother. And he commanded horses to be saddled, and called the governor and the judges and all the rich men, and said :

' Come now with me ; let us go and bury it.'

Night and day they travelled, till the sultan came to the well where the gazelle had been thrown. And it was a large well, built round a rock, with room for many people ;

THE END

THE GAZELLE

and the sultan entered, and the judges and the rich men followed him. And when he saw the gazelle lying there he wept afresh, and took it in his arms and carried it away.

When the three slaves went and told their mistress what the sultan had done, and how all the people were weeping, she answered:

'I too have eaten no food, neither have I drunk water, since the day the gazelle died. I have not spoken, and I have not laughed.'

The sultan took the gazelle and buried it, and ordered the people to wear mourning for it, so there was great mourning throughout the city.

Now after the days of mourning were at an end, the wife was sleeping at her husband's side, and in her sleep she dreamed that she was once more in her father's house, and when she woke up it was no dream.

And the man dreamed that he was on the dust-heap, scratching. And when he woke, behold! that also was no dream, but the truth.

[Swahili Tales.]

HOW A FISH SWAM IN THE AIR AND A HARE IN THE WATER.

ONCE upon a time an old man and his wife lived together in a little village. They might have been happy if only the old woman had had the sense to hold her tongue at proper times. But anything which might happen indoors, or any bit of news which her husband might bring in when he had been anywhere, had to be told at once to the whole village, and these tales were repeated and altered till it often happened that much mischief was made, and the old man's back paid for it.

One day, he drove to the forest. When he reached the edge of it he got out of his cart and walked beside it. Suddenly he stepped on such a soft spot that his foot sank in the earth.

'What can this be?' thought he. 'I'll dig a bit and see.'

So he dug and dug, and at last he came on a little pot full of gold and silver.

'Oh, what luck! Now, if only I knew how I could take this treasure home with me——but I can never hope to hide it from my wife, and once she knows of it she'll tell all the world, and then I shall get into trouble.'

He sat down and thought over the matter a long time, and at last he made a plan. He covered up the pot again with earth and twigs, and drove on into the town, where he bought a live pike and a live hare in the market.

Then he drove back to the forest and hung the pike

up at the very top of a tree, and tied up the hare in a
fishing net and fastened it on the edge of a little stream,
not troubling himself to think how unpleasant such a wet
spot was likely to be to the hare.

Then he got into his cart and trotted merrily home.

'Wife!' cried he, the moment he got indoors. 'You
can't think what a piece of good luck has come our way.'

'What, what, dear husband? Do tell me all about it
at once.'

'No, no, you'll just go off and tell everyone.'

'No, indeed! How can you think such things! For
shame! If you like I will swear never to——'

'Oh, well! if you are really in earnest then, listen.'

And he whispered in her ear: 'I've found a pot full
of gold and silver in the forest! Hush!——'

'And why didn't you bring it back?'

'Because we'll drive there together and bring it carefully back between us.'

So the man and his wife drove to the forest.

As they were driving along the man said:

'What strange things one hears, wife! I was told
only the other day that fish will now live and thrive in
the tree tops and that some wild animals spend their
time in the water. Well! well! times are certainly
changed.'

'Why, you must be crazy, husband! Dear, dear,
what nonsense people do talk sometimes.'

'Nonsense, indeed! Why, just look. Bless my soul,
if there isn't a fish, a real pike I do believe, up in that
tree.'

'Gracious!' cried his wife. 'How did a pike get there?
It *is* a pike—you needn't attempt to say it's not. Can
people have said true——'

But the man only shook his head and shrugged his
shoulders and opened his mouth and gaped as if he really
could not believe his own eyes.

'What are you standing staring at there, stupid?' said

his wife. ' Climb up the tree quick and catch the pike, and we'll cook it for dinner.'

The man climbed up the tree and brought down the pike, and they drove on.

When they got near the stream he drew up.

' What are you staring at again ? ' asked his wife impatiently. ' Drive on, can't you ? '

' Why, I seem to see something moving in that net I set. I must just go and see what it is.'

He ran to it, and when he had looked in it he called to his wife : ' Just look ! Here is actually a four-footed creature caught in the net. I do believe it's a hare.'

' Good heavens ! ' cried his wife. ' How did the hare get into your net ? It *is* a hare, so you needn't say it isn't. After all, people must have said the truth——'

But her husband only shook his head and shrugged his shoulders as if he could not believe his own eyes.

' Now what are you standing there for, stupid ? ' cried his wife. ' Take up the hare. A nice fat hare is a dinner for a feast day.'

The old man caught up the hare, and they drove on to the place where the treasure was buried. They swept the twigs away, dug up the earth, took out the pot, and drove home again with it.

And now the old couple had plenty of money and were cheery and comfortable. But the wife was very foolish. Every day she asked a lot of people to dinner and feasted them, till her husband grew quite impatient. He tried to reason with her, but she would not listen.

' You've got no right to lecture me ! ' said she. ' We found the treasure together, and together we will spend it.'

Her husband took patience, but at length he said to her : ' You may do as you please, but I sha'n't give you another penny.'

The old woman was very angry. ' Oh, what a good-for-nothing fellow to want to spend all the money himself ! But just wait a bit and see what I shall do.'

Off she went to the governor to complain of her husband.

'Oh, my lord, protect me from my husband! Ever since he found the treasure there is no bearing him. He only eats and drinks, and won't work, and he keeps all the money to himself.'

The governor took pity on the woman, and ordered his chief secretary to look into the matter.

The secretary called the elders of the village together, and went with them to the man's house.

'The governor,' said he, 'desires you to give all that treasure you found into my care.'

The man shrugged his shoulders and said: 'What treasure? I know nothing about a treasure.'

'How? You know nothing? Why your wife has complained of you. Don't attempt to tell lies. If you don't hand over all the money at once you will be tried for daring to raise treasure without giving due notice to the governor about it.'

'Pardon me, your excellency, but what sort of treasure was it supposed to have been? My wife must have dreamt of it, and you gentlemen have listened to her nonsense.'

'Nonsense, indeed,' broke in his wife. 'A kettle full of gold and silver, do you call that nonsense?'

'You are not in your right mind, dear wife. Sir, I beg your pardon. Ask her how it all happened, and if she convinces you I'll pay for it with my life.'

'This is how it all happened, Mr. Secretary,' cried the wife. 'We were driving through the forest, and we saw a pike up in the top of a tree——'

'What, a *pike*?' shouted the secretary. 'Do you think you may joke with me, pray?'

'Indeed, I'm not joking, Mr. Secretary! I'm speaking the bare truth.'

'Now you see, gentlemen,' said her husband, 'how far you can trust her, when she chatters like this.'

' Chatter, indeed? I !! Perhaps you have forgotten, too, how we found a live hare in the river ? '

Everyone roared with laughter ; even the secretary smiled and stroked his beard, and the man said :

' Come, come, wife, everyone is laughing at you. You see for yourself, gentlemen, how far you can believe her.'

' Yes, indeed,' said the village elders, ' it is certainly the first time we have heard that hares thrive in the water or fish among the tree tops.'

The secretary could make nothing of it all, and drove back to the town. The old woman was so laughed at that she had to hold her tongue and obey her husband ever after, and the man bought wares with part of the treasure and moved into the town, where he opened a shop, and prospered, and spent the rest of his days in peace.

TWO IN A SACK

WHAT a life that poor man led with his wife, to be sure! Not a day passed without her scolding him and calling him names, and indeed sometimes she would take the broom from behind the stove and beat him with it. He had no peace or comfort at all, and really hardly knew how to bear it.

One day, when his wife had been particularly unkind and had beaten him black and blue, he strolled slowly into the fields, and as he could not endure to be idle he spread out his nets.

What kind of bird do you think he caught in his net? He caught a crane, and the crane said, 'Let me go free, and I'll show myself grateful.'

The man answered, 'No, my dear fellow. I shall take you home, and then perhaps my wife won't scold me so much.'

Said the crane : 'You had better come with me to my house,' and so they went to the crane's house.

When they got there, what do you think the crane took from the wall? He took down a sack, and he said :

'Two out of a sack!'

Instantly two pretty lads sprang out of the sack. They brought in oak tables, which they spread with silken covers, and placed all sorts of delicious dishes and refreshing drinks on them. The man had never seen anything so beautiful in his life, and he was delighted.

Then the crane said to him, 'Now take this sack to your wife.'

The man thanked him warmly, took the sack, and set out.

His home was a good long way off, and as it was growing dark, and he was feeling tired, he stopped to rest at his cousin's house by the way.

The cousin had three daughters, who laid out a

Two out of a Sack

tempting supper, but the man would eat nothing, and said to his cousin, 'Your supper is bad.'

'Oh, make the best of it,' said she, but the man only said : 'Clear away !' and taking out his sack he cried, as the crane had taught him :

'Two out of the sack ! '

And out came the two pretty boys, who quickly brought in the oak tables, spread the silken covers, and

laid out all sorts of delicious dishes and refreshing
drinks.

Never in their lives had the cousin and her daughters
seen such a supper, and they were delighted and
astonished at it.   But the cousin quietly made up her
mind to steal the sack, so she called to her daughters :
' Go quickly and heat the bathroom : I am sure our dear
guest would like to have a bath before he goes to bed.'

When the man was safe in the bathroom she told her
daughters to make a sack exactly like his, as quickly as
possible.   Then she changed the two sacks, and hid the
man's sack away.

The man enjoyed his bath, slept soundly, and set off
early next morning, taking what he believed to be the
sack the crane had given him.

All the way home he felt in such good spirits that he
sang and whistled as he walked through the wood, and
never noticed how the birds were twittering and laughing
at him.

As soon as he saw his house he began to shout from
a distance, ' Hallo ! old woman ! Come out and meet
me ! '

His wife screamed back : ' You come here, and I'll
give you a good thrashing with the poker ! '

The man walked into the house, hung his sack on a
nail, and said, as the crane had taught him :

' Two out of the sack ! '

But not a soul came out of the sack.

Then he said again, exactly as the crane had taught
him :

' Two out of the sack ! '

His wife, hearing him chattering goodness knows
what, took up her wet broom and swept the ground all
about him.

The man took flight and rushed off into the field, and
there he found the crane marching proudly about, and to
him he told his tale.

' Come back to my house,' said the crane, and so they went to the crane's house, and as soon as they got there, what did the crane take down from the wall? Why, he took down a sack, and he said :

' Two out of the sack ! '

And instantly two pretty lads sprang out of the sack, brought in oak tables, on which they laid silken covers, and spread all sorts of delicious dishes and refreshing drinks on them.

' Take this sack,' said the crane.

The man thanked him heartily, took the sack, and went. He had a long way to walk, and as he presently got hungry, he said to the sack, as the crane had taught him :

' Two out of the sack ! '

And instantly two rough men with thick sticks crept out of the bag and began to beat him well, crying as they did so :

> ' Don't boast to your cousins of what you have got,
>> One—two—
> Or you'll find you will catch it uncommonly hot,
>> One—two —'

And they beat on till the man panted out :

' Two into the sack.'

The words were hardly out of his mouth, when the two crept back into the sack.

Then the man shouldered the sack, and went off straight to his cousin's house. He hung the sack up on a nail, and said : ' Please have the bathroom heated, cousin.'

The cousin heated the bathroom, and the man went into it, but he neither washed nor rubbed himself, he just sat there and waited.

Meantime his cousin felt hungry, so she called her daughters, and all four sat down to table. Then the mother said :

' Two out of the sack.'

Instantly two rough men crept out of the sack, and began to beat the cousin as they cried :

'Greedy pack ! Thievish pack !
One—two—
Give the peasant back his sack !
One—two—'

And they went on beating till the woman called to her eldest daughter : ' Go and fetch your cousin from the bathroom. Tell him these two ruffians are beating me black and blue.'

' I've not finished rubbing myself yet,' said the peasant.

And the two ruffians kept on beating as they sang :

'Greedy pack ! Thievish pack !
One – two –
Give the peasant back his sack !
One—two—'

Then the woman sent her second daughter and said : ' Quick, quick, get him to come to me.'

' I'm just washing my head,' said the man.

Then she sent the youngest girl, and he said : ' I've not done drying myself.'

At last the woman could hold out no longer, and sent him the sack she had stolen.

Now he had quite finished his bath, and as he left the bathroom he cried :

' Two into the sack.'

And the two crept back at once into the sack.

Then the man took both sacks, the good and the bad one, and went away home.

When he was near the house he shouted : ' Hallo, old woman, come and meet me ! '

His wife only screamed out :

' You broomstick, come here ! Your back shall pay for this.'

The man went into the cottage, hung his sack on a nail, and said, as the crane had taught him :

' Two out of the sack.'

Instantly two pretty lads sprang out of the sack,

brought in oak tables, laid silken covers on them, and spread them with all sorts of delicious dishes and refreshing drinks.

The woman ate and drank, and praised her husband.

'Well, now, old man, I won't beat you any more,' said she.

When they had done eating, the man carried off the

IN·FVTVRE·LEAVE·THE·STICK·ALONE

TWO·OVT·OF·THE·SACK

good sack, and put it away in his store-room, but hung the bad sack up on the nail. Then he lounged up and down in the yard.

Meantime his wife became thirsty. She looked with longing eyes at the sack, and at last she said, as her husband had done:

'Two out of the sack.'

And at once the two rogues with their big sticks crept out of the sack, and began to belabour her as they sang:

> ' Would you beat your husband true?
> Don't cry so!
> Now we'll beat you black and blue!
> Oh! Oh!'

The woman screamed out: ' Old man, old man! Come here, quick! Here are two ruffians pommelling me fit to break my bones.'

Her husband only strolled up and down and laughed, as he said: ' Yes, they'll beat you well, old lady.'

And the two thumped away and sang again:

> ' Blows will hurt, remember, crone,
> We mean you well, we mean you well;
> In future leave the stick alone,
> For how it hurts, you now can tell,
> One—two—'

At last her husband took pity on her, and cried: ' Two into the sack.'

He had hardly said the words before they were back in the sack again.

From this time the man and his wife lived so happily together that it was a pleasure to see them, and so the story has an end.

[From Rüssiche Märchen.]

THE ENVIOUS NEIGHBOUR

LONG, long ago an old couple lived in a village, and, as they had no children to love and care for, they gave all their affection to a little dog. He was a pretty little creature, and instead of growing spoilt and disagreeable at not getting everything he wanted, as even children will do sometimes, the dog was grateful to them for their kindness, and never left their side, whether they were in the house or out of it.

One day the old man was working in his garden, with his dog, as usual, close by. The morning was hot, and at last he put down his spade and wiped his wet forehead, noticing, as he did so, that the animal was snuffling and scratching at a spot a little way off. There was nothing very strange in this, as all dogs are fond of scratching, and he went on quietly with his digging, when the dog ran up to his master, barking loudly, and back again to the place where he had been scratching. This he did several times, till the old man wondered what could be the matter, and, picking up the spade, followed where the dog led him. The dog was so delighted at his success that he jumped round, barking loudly, till the noise brought the old woman out of the house.

Curious to know if the dog had really found anything, the husband began to dig, and very soon the spade struck against something. He stooped down and pulled out a large box, filled quite full with shining gold pieces. The box was so heavy that the old woman had to help to carry

it home, and you may guess what a supper the dog had
that night ! Now that he had made them rich, they gave
him every day all that a dog likes best to eat, and the
cushions on which he lay were fit for a prince.

The story of the dog and his treasure soon became
known, and a neighbour whose garden was next the old
people's grew so envious of their good luck that he could
neither eat nor sleep. As the dog had discovered a
treasure once, this foolish man thought he must be able
to discover one always, and begged the old couple to lend
him their pet for a little while, so that he might be made
rich also.

' How can you ask such a thing ? ' answered the old
man indignantly. ' You know how much we love him,
and that he is never out of our sight for five minutes.'

But the envious neighbour would not heed his words,
and came daily with the same request, till at last the
old people, who could not bear to say no to anyone,
promised to lend the dog, just for a night or two. No
sooner did the man get hold of the dog than he turned
him into the garden, but the dog did nothing but race
about, and the man was forced to wait with what patience
he could.

The next morning the man opened the house door,
and the dog bounded joyfully into the garden, and, running up to the foot of a tree, began to scratch wildly.
The man called loudly to his wife to bring a spade, and
followed the dog, as he longed to catch the first glimpse
of the expected treasure. But when he had dug up the
ground, what did he find ? Why, nothing but a parcel of
old bones, which smelt so badly that he could not stay
there a moment longer. And his heart was filled with
rage against the dog who had played him this trick, and
he seized a pickaxe and killed it on the spot, before he
knew what he was doing. When he remembered that
he would have to go with his story to the old man and
his wife he was rather frightened, but there was nothing

to be gained by putting it off, so he pulled a very long face and went to his neighbour's garden.

'Your dog,' said he, pretending to weep, 'has suddenly fallen down dead, though I took every care of him, and gave him everything he could wish for. And I thought I had better come straight and tell you.'

Weeping bitterly, the old man went to fetch the body of his favourite, and brought it home and buried it under the fig-tree where he had found the treasure. From morning till night he and his wife mourned over their loss, and nothing could comfort them. At length, one night when he was asleep, he dreamt that the dog appeared to him and told him to cut down the fig-tree over his grave, and out of its wood to make a mortar. But when the old man woke and thought of his dream he did not feel at all inclined to cut down the tree, which bore well every year, and consulted his wife about it. The woman did not hesitate a moment, and said that after what had happened before, the dog's advice must certainly be obeyed, so the tree was felled, and a beautiful mortar made from it. And when the season came for the rice crop to be gathered the mortar was taken down from its shelf, and the grains placed in it for pounding, when, lo and behold! in a twinkling of an eye, they all turned into gold pieces. At the sight of all this gold the hearts of the old people were glad, and once more they blessed their faithful dog.

But it was not long before this story also came to the ears of their envious neighbour, and he lost no time in going to the old people and asking if they happened to have a mortar which they could lend him. The old man did not at all like parting with his precious treasure, but he never could say no, so the neighbour went off with the mortar under his arm.

The moment he got into his own house he took a great handful of rice, and began to shell off the husks, with the help of his wife. But, instead of the gold pieces for which they looked, the rice turned into berries with such a horrible smell that they were obliged to run away, after smashing the mortar in a rage and setting fire to the bits.

The old people next door were naturally very much put out when they learned the fate of their mortar, and were not at all comforted by the explanations and excuses made by their neighbour. But that night the dog again appeared in a dream to his master, and told him that he must go and collect the ashes of the burnt mortar and bring them home. Then, when he heard that the Daimio, or great lord to whom this part of the country belonged, was expected at the capital, he was to carry the ashes to the high road, through which the procession would have to pass. And as soon as it was in sight he was to climb up all the cherry-trees and sprinkle the ashes on them, and they would soon blossom as they had never blossomed before.

This time the old man did not wait to consult his wife as to whether he was to do what his dog had told him, but directly he got up he went to his neighbour's house and collected the ashes of the burnt mortar. He put them carefully in a china vase, and carried it to the high road, sitting down on a seat till the Daimio should pass. The cherry-trees were bare, for it was the season when small pots of them were sold to rich people, who kept them in hot places, so that they might blossom early and decorate their rooms. As to the trees in the open air, no one would ever think of looking for the tiniest bud for more than a month yet. The old man had not been waiting very long before he saw a cloud of dust in the far distance, and knew that it must be the procession of the Daimio. On they came, every man dressed in his finest clothes, and the crowd that was lining the road bowed their faces to the ground as they went by. Only the old man did not bow himself, and the great lord saw this, and bade one of his courtiers, in anger, go and inquire why he had disobeyed the ancient customs.   But before the messenger could reach him the old man had climbed the nearest tree and scattered his ashes far and wide, and in an instant the white flowers had flashed into life, and the heart of the Daimio rejoiced, and he gave rich presents to the old man, whom he sent for to his castle.

We may be sure that in a very little while the envious neighbour had heard this also, and his bosom was filled with hate.   He hastened to the place where he had burned the mortar, collected a few of the ashes which the old man had left behind, and took them to the road, hoping that his luck might be as good as the old man's, or perhaps even better.   His heart beat with pleasure when he caught the first glimpses of the Daimio's train, and he held himself ready for the right moment.   As the Daimio drew near he flung a great handful of ashes over the trees, but no buds or flowers followed the action: instead, the ashes were all blown back into the eyes of the Daimio and his warriors, till they cried out from pain.   Then the prince ordered the evil-doer to be seized and bound and thrown into prison, where he was kept for many months.   By the time he was set free everybody in his native village had found out his wickedness, and they would not let him live there any longer; and as he would not leave off his evil ways he soon went from bad to worse, and came to a miserable end.

[Japanische Märchen.]

THE FAIRY OF THE DAWN

Once upon a time what should happen *did* happen; and if it had not happened this tale would never have been told.

There was once an emperor, very great and mighty, and he ruled over an empire so large that no one knew where it began and where it ended. But if nobody could tell the exact extent of his sovereignty everybody was aware that the emperor's right eye laughed, while his left eye wept. One or two men of valour had the courage to go and ask him the reason of this strange fact, but he only laughed and said nothing; and the reason of the deadly enmity between his two eyes was a secret only known to the monarch himself.

And all the while the emperor's sons were growing up. And such sons! All three like the morning stars in the sky!

Florea, the eldest, was so tall and broad-shouldered that no man in the kingdom could approach him.

Costan, the second, was quite different. Small of stature, and slightly built, he had a strong arm and stronger wrist.

Petru, the third and youngest, was tall and thin, more like a girl than a boy. He spoke very little, but laughed and sang, sang and laughed, from morning till night. He was very seldom serious, but then he had a way when he was thinking of stroking his hair over his forehead, which made him look old enough to sit in his father's council!

' You are grown up, Florea,' said Petru one day to his eldest brother; ' do go and ask father why one eye laughs and the other weeps.'

the emperor whose right eye
laughed while his left eye wept

But Florea would not go. He had learnt by experience that this question always put the emperor in a rage.

Petru next went to Costan, but did not succeed any better with him.

'Well, well, as everyone else is afraid, I suppose I must do it myself,' observed Petru at length. No sooner said than done ; the boy went straight to his father and put his question.

'May you go blind !' exclaimed the emperor in wrath ; 'what business is it of yours?' and boxed Petru's ears soundly.

Petru returned to his brothers, and told them what had befallen him ; but not long after it struck him that his father's left eye seemed to weep less, and the right to laugh more.

'I wonder if it has anything to do with my question,' thought he. 'I'll try again ! After all, what do two boxes on the ear matter ? '

So he put his question for the second time, and had the same answer ; but the left eye only wept now and then, while the right eye looked ten years younger.

'It really *must* be true,' thought Petru. 'Now I know what I have to do. I shall have to go on putting that question, and getting boxes on the ear, till both eyes laugh together.'

No sooner said than done. Petru never, never forswore himself.

'Petru, my dear boy,' cried the emperor, both his eyes laughing together, 'I see you have got this on the brain. Well, I will let you into the secret. My right eye laughs when I look at my three sons, and see how strong and handsome you all are, and the other eye weeps because I fear that after I die you will not be able to keep the empire together, and to protect it from its enemies. But if you can bring me water from the spring of the Fairy of the Dawn, to bathe my eyes, then they will laugh for evermore ; for I shall know that my sons are brave enough to overcome any foe.'

Thus spoke the emperor, and Petru picked up his hat and went to find his brothers.

The three young men took counsel together, and talked the subject well over, as brothers should do. And the end of it was that Florea, as the eldest, went to the stables, chose the best and handsomest horse they contained, saddled him, and took leave of the court.

'I am starting at once,' said he to his brothers, 'and if after a year, a month, a week, and a day I have not returned with the water from the spring of the Fairy of the Dawn, you, Costan, had better come after me.' So saying he disappeared round a corner of the palace.

For three days and three nights he never drew rein. Like a spirit the horse flew over mountains and valleys till he came to the borders of the empire. Here was a deep, deep trench that girdled it the whole way round, and there was only a single bridge by which the trench could be crossed. Florea made instantly for the bridge, and there pulled up to look around him once more, to take leave of his native land Then he turned, but before him was standing a dragon—oh! *such* a dragon!—a dragon with three heads and three horrible faces, all with their mouths wide open, one jaw reaching to heaven and the other to earth.

At this awful sight Florea did not wait to give battle. He put spurs to his horse and dashed off, *where* he neither knew nor cared.

The dragon heaved a sigh and vanished without leaving a trace behind him.

A week went by. Florea did not return home. Two passed; and nothing was heard of him. After a month Costan began to haunt the stables and to look out a horse for himself. And the moment the year, the month, the week, and the day were over Costan mounted his horse and took leave of his youngest brother.

'If I fail, then you come,' said he, and followed the path that Florea had taken.

The dragon on the bridge was more fearful and his three heads more terrible than before, and the young hero rode away still faster than his brother had done.

Nothing more was heard either of him or Florea; and Petru remained alone.

'I must go after my brothers,' said Petru one day to his father.

'Go, then,' said his father, 'and may you have better luck than they'; and he bade farewell to Petru, who rode straight to the borders of the kingdom.

The dragon on the bridge was yet more dreadful than the one Florea and Costan had seen, for this one had seven heads instead of only three.

Petru stopped for a moment when he caught sight of this terrible creature. Then he found his voice.

'Get out of the way!' cried he. 'Get out of the way!' he repeated again, as the dragon did not move. 'Get out of the way!' and with this last summons he drew his sword and rushed upon him. In an instant the heavens seemed to darken round him and he was surrounded by fire—fire to right of him, fire to left of him, fire to front of him, fire to rear of him; nothing but fire whichever way he looked, for the dragon's seven heads were vomiting flame.

The horse neighed and reared at the horrible sight, and Petru could not use the sword he had in readiness.

'Be quiet! this won't do!' he said, dismounting hastily, but holding the bridle firmly in his left hand and grasping his sword in his right.

But even so he got on no better, for he could see nothing but fire and smoke.

'There is no help for it; I must go back and get a better horse,' said he, and mounted again and rode homewards.

At the gate of the palace his nurse, old Birscha, was waiting for him eagerly.

'Ah, Petru, my son, I knew you would have to come

back,' she cried. 'You did not set about the matter
properly.'

'How ought I to have set about it?' asked Petru, half
angrily, half sadly.

'Look here, my boy,' replied old Birscha. 'You
can never reach the spring of the Fairy of the Dawn
unless you ride the horse which your father, the emperor,
rode in his youth. Go and ask where it is to be found,
and then mount it and be off with you.'

Petru thanked her heartily for her advice, and went
at once to make inquiries about the horse.

'By the light of my eyes!' exclaimed the emperor
when Petru had put his question. 'Who has told you
anything about that? It must have been that old witch
of a Birscha? Have you lost your wits? Fifty years have
passed since I was young, and who knows where the
bones of my horse may be rotting, or whether a scrap of
his reins still lie in his stall? I have forgotten all about
him long ago.'

Petru turned away in anger, and went back to his
old nurse.

'Do not be cast down,' she said with a smile; 'if that
is how the affair stands all will go well. Go and fetch
the scrap of the reins; I shall soon know what must be
done.'

The place was full of saddles, bridles, and bits of
leather. Petru picked out the oldest, and blackest, and
most decayed pair of reins, and brought them to the old
woman, who murmured something over them and
sprinkled them with incense, and held them out to the
young man.

'Take the reins,' said she, 'and strike them violently
against the pillars of the house.'

Petru did what he was told, and scarcely had the
reins touched the pillars when something happened—
how I have no idea—that made Petru stare with surprise.
A horse stood before him—a horse whose equal in beauty

PETRU HAS TO TURN BACK

the world had never seen ; with a saddle on him of gold and precious stones, and with such a dazzling bridle you hardly dared to look at it, lest you should lose your sight. A splendid horse, a splendid saddle, and a splendid bridle, all ready for the splendid young prince !

'Jump on the back of the brown horse,' said the old woman, and she turned round and went into the house.

The moment Petru was seated on the horse he felt his arm three times as strong as before, and even his heart felt braver.

'Sit firmly in the saddle, my lord, for we have a long way to go and no time to waste,' said the brown horse, and Petru soon saw that they were riding as no man and horse had ever ridden before.

On the bridge stood a dragon, but not the same one as he had tried to fight with, for this dragon had twelve heads, each more hideous and shooting forth more terrible flames than the other. But, horrible though he was, he had met his match. Petru showed no fear, but rolled up his sleeves, that his arms might be free.

'Get out of the way !' he said when he had done, but the dragon's heads only breathed forth more flames and smoke. Petru wasted no more words, but drew his sword and prepared to throw himself on the bridge.

'Stop a moment; be careful, my lord,' put in the horse, 'and be sure you do what I tell you. Dig your spurs in my body up to the rowel, draw your sword, and keep yourself ready, for we shall have to leap over both bridge and dragon. When you see that we are right above the dragon cut off his biggest head, wipe the blood off the sword, and put it back clean in the sheath before we touch earth again.'

So Petru dug in his spurs, drew his sword, cut off the head, wiped the blood, and put the sword back in the sheath before the horse's hoofs touched the ground again.

And in this fashion they passed the bridge.

'But we have got to go further still,' said Petru, after he had taken a farewell glance at his native land.

'Yes, forwards,' answered the horse; 'but you must tell me, my lord, at what speed you wish to go. Like the wind? Like thought? Like desire? or like a curse?'

Petru looked about him, up at the heavens and down again to the earth. A desert lay spread out before him, whose aspect made his hair stand on end.

'We will ride at different speeds,' said he, 'not so fast as to grow tired nor so slow as to waste time.'

And so they rode, one day like the wind, the next like thought, the third and fourth like desire and like a curse, till they reached the borders of the desert.

'Now walk, so that I may look about, and see what I have never seen before,' said Petru, rubbing his eyes like one who wakes from sleep, or like him who beholds something so strange that it seems as if . . . Before Petru lay a wood made of copper, with copper trees and copper leaves, with bushes and flowers of copper also.

Petru stood and stared as a man does when he sees something that he has never seen, and of which he has never heard.

Then he rode right into the wood. On each side of the way the rows of flowers began to praise Petru, and to try and persuade him to pick some of them and make himself a wreath.

'Take me, for I am lovely, and can give strength to whoever plucks me,' said one.

'No, take me, for whoever wears me in his hat will be loved by the most beautiful woman in the world,' pleaded the second; and then one after another bestirred itself, each more charming than the last, all promising, in soft sweet voices, wonderful things to Petru, if only he would pick them.

Petru was not deaf to their persuasion, and was just stooping to pick one when the horse sprang to one side.

THE BATTLE WITH THE WELWA IN THE COPPER WOOD

'Why don't you stay still?' asked Petru roughly.

'Do not pick the flowers; it will bring you bad luck,' answered the horse.

'Why should it do that?'

'These flowers are under a curse. Whoever plucks them must fight the Welwa [1] of the woods.'

'What kind of a goblin is the Welwa?'

'Oh, do leave me in peace! But listen. Look at the flowers as much as you like, but pick none,' and the horse walked on slowly.

Petru knew by experience that he would do well to attend to the horse's advice, so he made a great effort and tore his mind away from the flowers.

But in vain! If a man is fated to be unlucky, unlucky he will be, whatever he may do!

The flowers went on beseeching him, and his heart grew ever weaker and weaker.

'What must come will come,' said Petru at length; 'at any rate I shall see the Welwa of the woods, what she is like, and which way I had best fight her. If she is ordained to be the cause of my death, well, then it will be so; but if not I shall conquer her though she were twelve hundred Welwas,' and once more he stooped down to gather the flowers.

'You have done very wrong,' said the horse sadly. 'But it can't be helped now. Get yourself ready for battle, for here is the Welwa!'

Hardly had he done speaking, scarcely had Petru twisted his wreath, when a soft breeze arose on all sides at once. Out of the breeze came a storm wind, and the storm wind swelled and swelled till everything around was blotted out in darkness, and darkness covered them as with a thick cloak, while the earth swayed and shook under their feet.

'Are you afraid?' asked the horse, shaking his mane.

'Not yet,' replied Petru stoutly, though cold shivers

[1] A goblin.

were running down his back. 'What must come will come, whatever it is.'

'Don't be afraid,' said the horse. 'I will help you. Take the bridle from my neck, and try to catch the Welwa with it.'

The words were hardly spoken, and Petru had no time even to unbuckle the bridle, when the Welwa herself stood before him; and Petru could not bear to look at her, so horrible was she.

She had not exactly a head, yet neither was she without one. She did not fly through the air, but neither did she walk upon the earth. She had a mane like a horse, horns like a deer, a face like a bear, eyes like a polecat; while her body had something of each. And that was the Welwa.

Petru planted himself firmly in his stirrups, and began to lay about him with his sword, but could feel nothing.

A day and a night went by, and the fight was still undecided, but at last the Welwa began to pant for breath.

'Let us wait a little and rest,' gasped she.

Petru stopped and lowered his sword.

'You must not stop an instant,' said the horse, and Petru gathered up all his strength, and laid about him harder than ever.

The Welwa gave a neigh like a horse and a howl like a wolf, and threw herself afresh on Petru. For another day and night the battle raged more furiously than before. And Petru grew so exhausted he could scarcely move his arm.

'Let us wait a little and rest,' cried the Welwa for the second time, 'for I see you are as weary as I am.'

'You must not stop an instant,' said the horse.

And Petru went on fighting, though he barely had strength to move his arm. But the Welwa had ceased to throw herself upon him, and began to deliver her blows cautiously, as if she had no longer power to strike.

And on the third day they were still fighting, but as the morning sky began to redden Petru somehow managed—how I cannot tell—to throw the bridle over the head of the tired Welwa. In a moment, from the Welwa sprang a horse—the most beautiful horse in the world.

'Sweet be your life, for you have delivered me from my enchantment,' said he, and began to rub his nose against his brother's. And he told Petru all his story, and how he had been bewitched for many years.

So Petru tied the Welwa to his own horse and rode on. Where did he ride ? That I cannot tell you, but he rode on fast till he got out of the copper wood.

'Stay still, and let me look about, and see what I never have seen before,' said Petru again to his horse. For in front of him stretched a forest that was far more wonderful, as it was made of glistening trees and shining flowers. It was the silver wood.

As before, the flowers began to beg the young man to gather them.

'Do not pluck them,' warned the Welwa, trotting beside him, ' for my brother is seven times stronger than I '; but though Petru knew by experience what this meant, it was no use, and after a moment's hesitation he began to gather the flowers, and to twist himself a wreath.

Then the storm wind howled louder, the earth trembled more violently, and the night grew darker, than the first time, and the Welwa of the silver wood came rushing on with seven times the speed of the other. For three days and three nights they fought, but at last Petru cast the bridle over the head of the second Welwa.

'Sweet be your life, for you have delivered me from enchantment,' said the second Welwa, and they all journeyed on as before.

But soon they came to a gold wood more lovely far

than the other two, and again Petru's companions pleaded with him to ride through it quickly, and to leave the flowers alone. But Petru turned a deaf ear to all they said, and before he had woven his golden crown he felt that something terrible, that he could not see, was coming near him right out of the earth. He drew his sword and made himself ready for the fight. 'I will die!' cried he, 'or he shall have my bridle over his head.'

He had hardly said the words when a thick fog wrapped itself around him, and so thick was it that he could not see his own hand, or hear the sound of his voice. For a day and a night he fought with his sword, without ever once seeing his enemy, then suddenly the fog began to lighten. By dawn of the second day it had vanished altogether, and the sun shone brightly in the heavens. It seemed to Petru that he had been born again.

And the Welwa? She had vanished.

'You had better take breath now you can, for the fight will have to begin all over again,' said the horse.

'What was it?' asked Petru.

'It was the Welwa,' replied the horse, 'changed into a fog! Listen! She is coming!'

And Petru had hardly drawn a long breath when he felt something approaching from the side, though *what* he could not tell. A river, yet not a river, for it seemed not to flow over the earth, but to go where it liked, and to leave no trace of its passage.

'Woe be to me!' cried Petru, frightened at last.

'Beware, and never stand still,' called the brown horse, and more he could not say, for the water was choking him.

The battle began anew. For a day and a night Petru fought on, without knowing at whom or what he struck. At dawn on the second, he felt that both his feet were lame.

'Now I am done for,' thought he, and his blows fell thicker and harder in his desperation. And the sun came

out and the water disappeared, without his knowing how
or when.

'Take breath,' said the horse, 'for you have no time
to lose. The Welwa will return in a moment.'

Petru made no reply, only wondered how, exhausted
as he was, he should ever be able to carry on the fight.
But he settled himself in his saddle, grasped his sword,
and waited.

And then something came to him—*what* I cannot tell
you. Perhaps, in his dreams, a man may see a creature
which has what it has not got, and has not got what it
has. At least, that was what the Welwa seemed like to
Petru. She flew with her feet, and walked with her
wings; her head was in her back, and her tail was on top
of her body; her eyes were in her neck, and her neck in
her forehead, and how to describe her further I do not
know.

Petru felt for a moment as if he was wrapped in a
garment of fear; then he shook himself and took heart,
and fought as he had never yet fought before.

As the day wore on, his strength began to fail, and
when darkness fell he could hardly keep his eyes open.
By midnight he knew he was no longer on his horse, but
standing on the ground, though he could not have told
how he got there. When the grey light of morning came,
he was past standing on his feet, but fought now upon his
knees.

'Make one more struggle; it is nearly over now,'
said the horse, seeing that Petru's strength was waning
fast.

Petru wiped the sweat from his brow with his
gauntlet, and with a desperate effort rose to his feet.

'Strike the Welwa on the mouth with the bridle,'
said the horse, and Petru did it.

The Welwa uttered a neigh so loud that Petru
thought he would be deaf for life, and then, though she
too was nearly spent, flung herself upon her enemy; but

Petru was on the watch and threw the bridle over her head, as she rushed on, so that when the day broke there were three horses trotting beside him.

'May your wife be the most beautiful of women,' said the Welwa, 'for you have delivered me from my enchantment.' So the four horses galloped fast, and by nightfall they were at the borders of the golden forest.

Then Petru began to think of the crowns that he wore, and what they had cost him.

'After all, what do I want with so many? I will keep the best,' he said to himself; and taking off first the copper crown and then the silver, he threw them away.

'Stay!' cried the horse, 'do not throw them away! Perhaps we shall find them of use. Get down and pick them up.' So Petru got down and picked them up, and they all went on.

In the evening, when the sun is getting low, and all the midges are beginning to bite, Peter saw a wide heath stretching before him.

At the same instant the horse stood still of itself.

'What is the matter?' asked Petru.

'I am afraid that something evil will happen to us,' answered the horse.

'But why should it?'

'We are going to enter the kingdom of the goddess Mittwoch,[1] and the further we ride into it the colder we shall get. But all along the road there are huge fires, and I dread lest you should stop and warm yourself at them.'

'And why should I not warm myself?'

'Something fearful will happen to you if you do,' replied the horse sadly.

'Well, forward!' cried Petru lightly, 'and if I have to bear cold, I must bear it!'

With every step they went into the kingdom of Mittwoch, the air grew colder and more icy, till even the

[1] In German 'Mittwoch,' the feminine form of Mercury.

marrow in their bones was frozen. But Petru was no coward; the fight he had gone through had strengthened his powers of endurance, and he stood the test bravely.

Along the road on each side were great fires, with men standing by them, who spoke pleasantly to Petru as he went by, and invited him to join them. The breath froze in his mouth, but he took no notice, only bade his horse ride on the faster.

How long Petru may have waged battle silently with the cold one cannot tell, for everybody knows that the kingdom of Mittwoch is not to be crossed in a day, but he struggled on, though the frozen rocks burst around, and though his teeth chattered, and even his eyelids were frozen.

At length they reached the dwelling of Mittwoch herself, and, jumping from his horse, Petru threw the reins over his horse's neck and entered the hut.

' Good-day, little mother ! ' said he.

' Very well, thank you, my frozen friend ! '

Petru laughed, and waited for her to speak.

'You have borne yourself bravely,' went on the goddess, tapping him on the shoulder. ' Now you shall have your reward,' and she opened an iron chest, out of which she took a little box.

' Look ! ' said she ; ' this little box has been lying here for ages, waiting for the man who could win his way through the Ice Kingdom. Take it, and treasure it, for some day it may help you. If you open it, it will tell you anything you want, and give you news of your fatherland.'

Petru thanked her gratefully for her gift, mounted his horse, and rode away.

When he was some distance from the hut, he opened the casket.

' What are your commands ? ' asked a voice inside.

' Give me news of my father,' he replied, rather nervously.

'He is sitting in council with his nobles,' answered the casket.

'Is he well?'

'Not particularly, for he is furiously angry.'

'What has angered him?'

'Your brothers Costan and Florea,' replied the casket. 'It seems to me they are trying to rule him and the kingdom as well, and the old man says they are not fit to do it.'

'Push on, good horse, for we have no time to lose!' cried Petru; then he shut up the box, and put it in his pocket.

They rushed on as fast as ghosts, as whirlwinds, as vampires when they hunt at midnight, and how long they rode no man can tell, for the way is far.

'Stop! I have some advice to give you,' said the horse at last.

'What is it?' asked Petru.

'You have known what it is to suffer cold; you will have to endure heat, such as you have never dreamed of. Be as brave now as you were then. Let no one tempt you to try to cool yourself, or evil will befall you.'

'Forwards!' answered Petru. 'Do not worry yourself. If I have escaped without being frozen, there is no chance of my melting.'

'Why not? This is a heat that will melt the marrow in your bones—a heat that is only to be felt in the kingdom of the Goddess of Thunder.'[1]

And it *was* hot. The very iron of the horse's shoes began to melt, but Petru gave no heed. The sweat ran down his face, but he dried it with his gauntlet. What heat could be he never knew before, and on the way, not a stone's throw from the road, lay the most delicious valleys, full of shady trees and bubbling streams. When Petru looked at them his heart burned within him, and

[1] In the German 'Donnerstag'—the day of the Thunder God, *i.e.* Jupiter.

Among the Flowers
were lovely maidens
calling to him with
~ soft voices ~

his mouth grew parched. And standing among the flowers were lovely maidens who called to him in soft voices, till he had to shut his eyes against their spells.

'Come, my hero, come and rest; the heat will kill you,' said they.

Petru shook his head and said nothing, for he had lost the power of speech.

Long he rode in this awful state, how long none can tell. Suddenly the heat seemed to become less, and, in the distance, he saw a little hut on a hill. This was the dwelling of the Goddess of Thunder, and when he drew rein at her door the goddess herself came out to meet him.

She welcomed him, and kindly invited him in, and bade him tell her all his adventures. So Petru told her all that had happened to him, and why he was there, and then took farewell of her, as he had no time to lose. 'For,' he said, 'who knows how far the Fairy of the Dawn may yet be?'

'Stay for one moment, for I have a word of advice to give you. You are about to enter the kingdom of Venus;[1] go and tell her, as a message from me, that I hope she will not tempt you to delay. On your way back, come to me again, and I will give you something that may be of use to you.'

So Petru mounted his horse, and had hardly ridden three steps when he found himself in a new country. Here it was neither hot nor cold, but the air was warm and soft like spring, though the way ran through a heath covered with sand and thistles.

'What can that be?' asked Petru, when he saw a long, long way off, at the very end of the heath, something resembling a house.

'That is the house of the goddess Venus,' replied the horse, 'and if we ride hard we may reach it before dark'; and he darted off like an arrow, so that as twilight fell

[1] 'Vineri' is Friday, and also 'Venus.'

they found themselves nearing the house. Petru's heart leaped at the sight, for all the way along he had been followed by a crowd of shadowy figures who danced about him from right to left, and from back to front, and Petru, though a brave man, felt now and then a thrill of fear.

'They won't hurt you,' said the horse; 'they are just the daughters of the whirlwind amusing themselves while they are waiting for the ogre of the moon.'

Then he stopped in front of the house, and Petru jumped off and went to the door.

'Do not be in such a hurry,' cried the horse. 'There are several things I must tell you first. You cannot enter the house of the goddess Venus like that. She is always watched and guarded by the whirlwind.'

'What am I to do then?'

'Take the copper wreath, and go with it to that little hill over there. When you reach it, say to yourself, " Were there ever such lovely maidens! such angels! such fairy souls ! " Then hold the wreath high in the air and cry, "Oh ! if I knew whether any one would accept this wreath from me . . . if I knew! if I knew! " and throw the wreath from you ! '

'And why should I do all this?' said Petru.

'Ask no questions, but go and do it,' replied the horse. And Petru did.

Scarcely had he flung away the copper wreath than the whirlwind flung himself upon it, and tore it in pieces.

Then Petru turned once more to the horse.

'Stop ! ' cried the horse again. 'I have other things to tell you. Take the silver wreath and knock at the windows of the goddess Venus. When she says, " Who is there ? " answer that you have come on foot and lost your way on the heath. She will then tell you to go your way back again; but take care not to stir from the spot. Instead, be sure you say to her, " No, indeed I shall

The Whirlwind Seizes the Wreath

do nothing of the sort, as from my childhood I have heard stories of the beauty of the goddess Venus, and it was not for nothing that I had shoes made of leather with soles of steel, and have travelled for nine years and nine months, and have won in battle the silver wreath, which I hope you may allow me to give you, and have done and suffered everything to be where I now am." This is what you must say. What happens after is your affair.'

Petru asked no more, but went towards the house.

By this time it was pitch dark, and there was only the ray of light that streamed through the windows to guide him, and at the sound of his footsteps two dogs began to bark loudly.

'Which of those dogs is barking? Is he tired of life?' asked the goddess Venus.

'It is I, O goddess!' replied Petru, rather timidly. 'I have lost my way on the heath, and do not know where I am to sleep this night.'

'Where did you leave your horse?' asked the goddess sharply.

Petru did not answer. He was not sure if he was to lie, or whether he had better tell the truth.

'Go away, my son, there is no place for you here,' replied she, drawing back from the window.

Then Petru repeated hastily what the horse had told him to say, and no sooner had he done so than the goddess opened the window, and in gentle tones she asked him:

'Let me see this wreath, my son,' and Petru held it out to her.

'Come into the house,' went on the goddess; 'do not fear the dogs, they always know my will.' And so they did, for as the young man passed they wagged their tails to him.

'Good evening,' said Petru as he entered the house, and, seating himself near the fire, listened comfortably to whatever the goddess might choose to talk about, which was for the most part the wickedness of men, with whom she was evidently very angry. But Petru agreed with her in everything, as he had been taught was only polite.

But was anybody ever so old as she ! I do not know why Petru devoured her so with his eyes, unless it was to count the wrinkles on her face ; but if so he would have had to live seven lives, and each life seven times the length of an ordinary one, before he could have reckoned them up.

But Venus was joyful in her heart when she saw Petru's eyes fixed upon her.

' Nothing was that is, and the world was not a world when I was born,' said she. ' When I grew up and the world came into being, everyone thought I was the most beautiful girl that ever was seen, though many hated me for it. But every hundred years there came a wrinkle on my face. And now I am old.' Then she went on to tell Petru that she was the daughter of an emperor, and their nearest neighbour was the Fairy of the Dawn, with whom she had a violent quarrel, and with that she broke out into loud abuse of her.

Petru did not know what to do. He listened in silence for the most part, but now and then he would say, ' Yes, yes, you must have been badly treated,' just for politeness' sake ; what more could he do ?

' I will give you a task to perform, for you are brave, and will carry it through,' continued Venus, when she had talked a long time, and both of them were getting sleepy. ' Close to the Fairy's house is a well, and whoever drinks from it will blossom again like a rose. Bring me a flagon of it, and I will do anything to prove my gratitude. It is not easy ! no one knows that better than I do ! The kingdom is guarded on every side by wild beasts and horrible dragons ; but I will tell you more about that, and I also have something to give you.'

Then she rose and lifted the lid of an iron-bound chest, and took out of it a very tiny flute.

'Do you see this?' she asked. 'An old man gave it to me when I was young: whoever listens to this flute goes to sleep, and nothing can wake him. Take it and play on it as long as you remain in the kingdom of the Fairy of the Dawn, and you will be safe.

At this, Petru told her that he had another task to fulfil at the well of the Fairy of the Dawn, and Venus was still better pleased when she heard his tale.

So Petru bade her good-night, put the flute in its case, and laid himself down in the lowest chamber to sleep.

Before the dawn he was awake again, and his first care was to give to each of his horses as much corn as he could eat, and then to lead them to the well to water. Then he dressed himself and made ready to start.

'Stop,' cried Venus from her window, 'I have still a piece of advice to give you. Leave one of your horses here, and only take three. Ride slowly till you get to the fairy's kingdom, then dismount and go on foot. When you return, see that all your three horses remain on the road, while you walk. But above all beware never to look the Fairy of the Dawn in the face, for she has eyes that will bewitch you, and glances that will befool you. She is hideous, more hideous than anything you can imagine, with owl's eyes, foxy face, and cat's claws. Do you hear? do you hear? Be sure you never look at her.'

Petru thanked her, and managed to get off at last.

Far, far away, where the heavens touch the earth, where the stars kiss the flowers, a soft red light was seen, such as the sky sometimes has in spring, only lovelier, more wonderful.

That light was behind the palace of the Fairy of the Dawn, and it took Petru two days and nights through flowery meadows to reach it. And besides, it was neither hot nor cold, bright nor dark, but something of them all, and Petru did not find the way a step too long.

After some time Petru saw something white rise up out of the red of the sky, and when he drew nearer he saw it was a castle, and so splendid that his eyes were dazzled when they looked at it. He did not know there was such a beautiful castle in the world.

But no time was to be lost, so he shook himself, jumped down from his horse, and, leaving him on the dewy grass, began to play on his flute as he walked along.

He had hardly gone many steps when he stumbled over a huge giant, who had been lulled to sleep by the music. This was one of the guards of the castle! As he lay there on his back, he seemed so big that in spite of Petru's haste he stopped to measure him.

The further went Petru, the more strange and terrible were the sights he saw—lions, tigers, dragons with seven heads, all stretched out in the sun fast asleep. It is needless to say what the dragons were like, for nowadays everyone knows, and dragons are not things to joke about. Petru ran through them like the wind. Was it haste or fear that spurred him on?

At last he came to a river, but let nobody think for a moment that this river was like other rivers? Instead of water, there flowed milk, and the bottom was of precious stones and pearls, instead of sand and pebbles. And it ran neither fast nor slow, but both fast and slow together. And the river flowed round the castle, and on its banks slept lions with iron teeth and claws; and beyond were gardens such as only the Fairy of the Dawn can have, and on the flowers slept a fairy! All this saw Petru from the other side.

But how was he to get over? To be sure there was a bridge, but, even if it had not been guarded by sleeping lions, it was plainly not meant for man to walk on. Who

could tell what it was made of? It looked like soft little
woolly clouds!

So he stood thinking what was to be done, for get
across he must. After a while, he determined to take the

PETRU WAKES THE GIANT UP

risk, and strode back to the sleeping giant. 'Wake up,
my brave man!' he cried, giving him a shake.

The giant woke and stretched out his hand to pick up
Petru, just as we should catch a fly. But Petru played

on his flute, and the giant fell back again. Petru tried this three times, and when he was satisfied that the giant was really in his power he took out a handkerchief, bound the two little fingers of the giant together, drew his sword, and cried for the fourth time, ' Wake up, my brave man.'

When the giant saw the trick which had been played on him he said to Petru, ' Do you call this a fair fight? Fight according to rules, if you really are a hero ! '

' I will by-and-by, but first I want to ask you a question ! Will you swear that you will carry me over the river if I fight honourably with you? ' And the giant swore.

When his hands were freed, the giant flung himself upon Petru, hoping to crush him by his weight. But he had met his match. It was not yesterday, nor the day before, that Petru had fought his first battle, and he bore himself bravely.

For three days and three nights the battle raged, and sometimes one had the upper hand, and sometimes the other, till at length they both lay struggling on the ground, but Petru was on top, with the point of his sword at the giant's throat.

' Let me go ! let me go ! ' shrieked he. ' I own that I am beaten ! '

' Will you take me over the river? ' asked Petru.

' I will,' gasped the giant.

' What shall I do to you if you break your word? '

' Kill me, any way you like ! But let me live now.'

' Very well,' said Petru, and he bound the giant's left hand to his right foot, tied one handkerchief round his mouth to prevent his crying out, and another round his eyes, and led him to the river.

Once they had reached the bank he stretched one leg over to the other side, and, catching up Petru in the palm of his hand, set him down on the further shore.

' That is all right,' said Petru. Then he played a few

notes on his flute, and the giant went to sleep again.
Even the fairies who had been bathing a little lower
down heard the music and fell asleep among the flowers
on the bank. Petru saw them as he passed, and thought,
' If they are so beautiful, why should the Fairy of the
Dawn be so ugly ? ' But he dared not linger, and pushed
on.

And now he was in the wonderful gardens, which
seemed more wonderful still than they had done from
afar. But Petru could see no faded flowers, nor any
birds, as he hastened through them to the castle. No
one was there to bar his way, for all were asleep. Even
the leaves had ceased to move.

He passed through the courtyard, and entered the castle
itself.

What he beheld there need not be told, for all the
world knows that the palace of the Fairy of the Dawn is
no ordinary place. Gold and precious stones were as
common as wood with us, and the stables where the
horses of the sun were kept were more splendid than
the palace of the greatest emperor in the world.

Petru went up the stairs and walked quickly through
eight-and-forty rooms, hung with silken stuffs, and all
empty. In the forty-ninth he found the Fairy of the
Dawn herself.

In the middle of this room, which was as large as a
church, Petru saw the celebrated well that he had come
so far to seek. It was a well just like other wells, and it
seemed strange that the Fairy of the Dawn should have
it in her own chamber ; yet anyone could tell it had been
there for hundreds of years. And by the well slept the
Fairy of the Dawn—the Fairy of the Dawn—herself !

And as Petru looked at her the magic flute dropped by
his side, and he held his breath.

Near the well was a table, on which stood bread
made with does' milk, and a flagon of wine. It was the
bread of strength and the wine of youth, and Petru

longed for them. He looked once at the bread and once at the wine, and then at the Fairy of the Dawn, still sleeping on her silken cushions.

As he looked a mist came over his senses. The fairy opened her eyes slowly and looked at Petru, who lost his head still further; but he just managed to remember his flute, and a few notes of it sent the Fairy to sleep again, and he kissed her thrice. Then he stooped and laid his golden wreath upon her forehead, ate a piece of the bread and drank a cupful of the wine of youth, and this he did three times over. Then he filled a flask with water from the well, and vanished swiftly.

As he passed through the garden it seemed quite different from what it was before. The flowers were lovelier, the streams ran quicker, the sunbeams shone brighter, and the fairies seemed gayer. And all this had been caused by the three kisses Petru had given the Fairy of the Dawn.

He passed everything safely by, and was soon seated in his saddle again. Faster than the wind, faster than thought, faster than longing, faster than hatred rode Petru. At length he dismounted, and, leaving his horses at the roadside, went on foot to the house of Venus.

The goddess Venus knew that he was coming, and went to meet him, bearing with her white bread and red wine.

' Welcome back, my prince,' said she.

' Good day, and many thanks,' replied the young man, holding out the flask containing the magic water. She received it with joy, and after a short rest Petru set forth, for he had no time to lose.

He stopped a few minutes, as he had promised, with the Goddess of Thunder, and was taking a hasty farewell of her, when she called him back.

' Stay, I have a warning to give you,' said she. ' Beware of your life; make friends with no man; do not ride fast, or let the water go out of your hand; believe

MORNING-GLORY THE FAIRY OF THE DAWN

no one, and flee flattering tongues. Go, and take care, for the way is long, the world is bad, and you hold something very precious. But I will give you this cloth to help you. It is not much to look at, but it is enchanted, and whoever carries it will never be struck by lightning, pierced by a lance, or smitten with a sword, and the arrows will glance off his body.'

Petru thanked her and rode off, and, taking out his treasure box, inquired how matters were going at home. Not well, it said. The emperor was blind altogether now, and Florea and Costan had besought him to give the government of the kingdom into their hands; but he would not, saying that he did not mean to resign the government till he had washed his eyes from the well of the Fairy of the Dawn. Then the brothers had gone to consult old Birscha, who told them that Petru was already on his way home bearing the water. They had set out to meet him, and would try to take the magic water from him, and then claim as their reward the government of the emperor.

'You are lying!' cried Petru angrily, throwing the box on the ground, where it broke into a thousand pieces.

It was not long before he began to catch glimpses of his native land, and he drew rein near a bridge, the better to look at it. He was still gazing, when he heard a sound in the distance as if some one was calling him by his name.

'You, Petru!' it said.

'On! on!' cried the horse; 'it will fare ill with you if you stop.'

'No, let us stop, and see who and what it is!' answered Petru, turning his horse round, and coming face to face with his two brothers. He had forgotten the warning given him by the Goddess of Thunder, and when Costan and Florea drew near with soft and flattering words he jumped straight off his horse, and rushed to embrace them.

He had a thousand questions to ask, and a thousand things to tell. But his brown horse stood sadly hanging his head.

'Petru, my dear brother,' at length said Florea, 'would it not be better if we carried the water for you? Some one might try to take it from you on the road, while no one would suspect us.'

'So it would,' added Costan. 'Florea speaks well.' But Petru shook his head, and told them what the Goddess of Thunder had said, and about the cloth she had given him. And both brothers understood there was only one way in which they could kill him.

At a stone's throw from where they stood ran a rushing stream, with clear deep pools.

'Don't you feel thirsty, Costan?' asked Florea, winking at him.

'Yes,' replied Costan, understanding directly what was wanted. 'Come, Petru, let us drink now we have the chance, and then we will set out on our way home. It is a good thing you have us with you, to protect you from harm.'

The horse neighed, and Petru knew what it meant, and did not go with his brothers.

No, he went home to his father, and cured his blindness; and as for his brothers, they never returned again.

[From Rümänische Märchen.]

THE ENCHANTED KNIFE

ONCE upon a time there lived a young man who vowed that he would never marry any girl who had not royal blood in her veins. One day he plucked up all his courage and went to the palace to ask the emperor for his daughter. The emperor was not much pleased at the thought of such a match for his only child, but being very polite, he only said :

' Very well, my son, if you can win the princess you shall have her, and the conditions are these. In eight days you must manage to tame and bring to me three horses that have never felt a master. The first is pure white, the second a foxy-red with a black head, the third coal black with a white head and feet. And besides that, you must also bring as a present to the empress, my wife, as much gold as the three horses can carry.'

The young man listened in dismay to these words, but with an effort he thanked the emperor for his kindness and left the palace, wondering how he was to fulfil the task allotted to him. Luckily for him, the emperor's daughter had overheard everything her father had said, and peeping through a curtain had seen the youth, and thought him handsomer than anyone she had ever beheld. So returning hastily to her own room, she wrote him a letter which she gave to a trusty servant to deliver, begging her wooer to come to her rooms early the next day, and to undertake nothing without her advice, if he ever wished her to be his wife.

That night, when her father was asleep, she crept

softly into his chamber and took out an enchanted knife
from the chest where he kept his treasures. and hid it
carefully in a safe place before she went to bed.

The sun had hardly risen the following morning when
the princess's nurse brought the young man to her apartments   Neither spoke for some minutes, but stood holding each other's hands for joy, till at last they both cried
out that nothing but death should part them.   Then the
maiden said :

'Take my horse, and ride straight through the wood
towards the sunset till you come to a hill with three
peaks.   When you get there, turn first to the right and
then to the left, and you will find yourself in a sun
meadow, where many horses are feeding.   Out of these
you must pick out the three described to you by my
father.   If they prove shy, and refuse to let you get near
them, draw out your knife, and let the sun shine on it so
that the whole meadow is lit up by its rays, and the
horses will then approach you of their own accord, and
will let you lead them away.   When you have them
safely, look about till you see a cypress tree, whose roots
are of brass, whose boughs are of silver, and whose leaves
are of gold.   Go to it, and cut away the roots with your
knife, and you will come to countless bags of gold.
Load the horses with all they can carry, and return to
my father, and tell him that you have done your task,
and can claim me for your wife.'

The princess had finished all she had to say, and now
it depended on the young man to do his part.   He hid
the knife in the folds of his girdle, mounted his horse,
and rode off in search of the meadow.   This he found
without much difficulty, but the horses were all so shy
that they galloped away directly he approached them.
Then he drew his knife, and held it up towards the sun,
and directly there shone such a glory that the whole
meadow was bathed in it.   From all sides the horses
rushed pressing round, and each one that passed him

The Princess at the Curtain

fell on its knees to do him honour. But he only chose
from them all the three that the emperor had described.
These he secured by a silken rope to his own horse, and

THE ENCHANTED KNIFE

then looked about for the cypress tree. It was standing
by itself in one corner, and in a moment he was beside
it, tearing away the earth with his knife. Deeper and

deeper he dug, till far down, below the roots of brass, his knife struck upon the buried treasure, which lay heaped up in bags all around.　With a great effort he lifted them from their hiding place, and laid them one by one on his horses' backs, and when they could carry no more he led them back to the emperor.　And when the emperor saw him, he wondered, but never guessed how it was the young man had been too clever for him, till the betrothal ceremony was over.　Then he asked his newly made son-in-law what dowry he would require with his bride.　To which the bridegroom made answer, 'Noble emperor! all I desire is that I may have your daughter for my wife, and enjoy for ever the use of your enchanted knife.'

[Volksmärchen der Serben.]

JESPER WHO HERDED THE HARES

THERE was once a king who ruled over a kingdom somewhere between sunrise and sunset. It was as small as
kingdoms usually were in old times, and when the king
went up to the roof of his palace and took a look round
he could see to the ends of it in every direction. But as
it was all his own, he was very proud of it, and often
wondered how it would get along without him. He had
only one child, and that was a daughter, so he foresaw
that she must be provided with a husband who would be
fit to be king after him. Where to find one rich enough
and clever enough to be a suitable match for the princess
was what troubled him, and often kept him awake at
night.

At last he devised a plan. He made a proclamation
over all his kingdom (and asked his nearest neighbours
to publish it in theirs as well) that whoever could bring
him a dozen of the finest pearls the king had ever seen,
and could perform certain tasks that would be set him,
should have his daughter in marriage and in due time
succeed to the throne. The pearls, he thought, could
only be brought by a very wealthy man, and the tasks
would require unusual talents to accomplish them.

There were plenty who tried to fulfil the terms which
the king proposed. Rich merchants and foreign princes
presented themselves one after the other, so that some
days the number of them was quite annoying ; but, though
they could all produce magnificent pearls, not one of
them could perform even the simplest of the tasks set

them. Some turned up, too, who were mere adventurers, and tried to deceive the old king with imitation pearls; but he was not to be taken in so easily, and they were soon sent about their business. At the end of several weeks the stream of suitors began to fall off, and still there was no prospect of a suitable son-in-law.

Now it so happened that in a little corner of the king's dominions, beside the sea, there lived a poor fisher, who had three sons, and their names were Peter, Paul, and Jesper. Peter and Paul were grown men, while Jesper was just coming to manhood. The two elder brothers were much bigger and stronger than the youngest, but Jesper was far the cleverest of the three, though neither Peter nor Paul would admit this. It was a fact, however, as we shall see in the course of our story.

One day the fisherman went out fishing, and among his catch for the day he brought home three dozen oysters. When these were opened, every shell was found to contain a large and beautiful pearl. Hereupon the three brothers, at one and the same moment, fell upon the idea of offering themselves as suitors for the princess. After some discussion, it was agreed that the pearls should be divided by lot, and that each should have his chance in the order of his age: of course, if the oldest was successful the other two would be saved the trouble of trying.

Next morning Peter put his pearls in a little basket, and set off for the king's palace. He had not gone far on his way when he came upon the King of the Ants and the King of the Beetles, who, with their armies behind them, were facing each other and preparing for battle.

'Come and help me,' said the King of the Ants; 'the beetles are too big for us. I may help you some day in return.'

'I have no time to waste on other people's affairs,' said Peter; 'just fight away as best you can;' and with that he walked off and left them.

A little further on the way he met an old woman.

'Good morning, young man,' said she ; 'you are early astir. What have you got in your basket ? '

'Cinders,' said Peter promptly, and walked on, adding to himself, 'Take that for being so inquisitive.'

'Very well, cinders be it,' the old woman called after him, but he pretended not to hear her.

Very soon he reached the palace, and was at once brought before the king. When he took the cover off the basket, the king and all his courtiers said with one voice that these were the finest pearls they had ever seen, and they could not take their eyes off them. But then a strange thing happened : the pearls began to lose their whiteness and grew quite dim in colour ; then they grew blacker and blacker till at last they were just like so many cinders. Peter was so amazed that he could say nothing for himself, but the king said quite enough for both, and Peter was glad to get away home again as fast as his legs would carry him. To his father and brothers, however, he gave no account of his attempt, except that it had been a failure.

Next day Paul set out to try his luck. He soon came upon the King of the Ants and the King of the Beetles, who with their armies had encamped on the field of battle all night, and were ready to begin the fight again.

'Come and help me,' said the King of the Ants ; 'we got the worst of it yesterday. I may help you some day in return.'

'I don't care though you get the worst of it to-day too,' said Paul. 'I have more important business on hand than mixing myself up in your quarrels.'

So he walked on, and presently the same old woman met him. 'Good morning,' said she ; 'what have *you* got in your basket ? '

'Cinders,' said Paul, who was quite as insolent as his brother, and quite as anxious to teach other people good manners.

'Very well, cinders be it,' the old woman shouted after him, but Paul neither looked back nor answered her. He thought more of what she said, however, after his pearls also turned to cinders before the eyes of king and court : then he lost no time in getting home again, and was very sulky when asked how he had succeeded.

The third day came, and with it came Jesper's turn to try his fortune. He got up and had his breakfast, while Peter and Paul lay in bed and made rude remarks, telling him that he would come back quicker than he went, for if they had failed it could not be supposed that he would succeed. Jesper made no reply, but put his pearls in the little basket and walked off.

The King of the Ants and the King of the Beetles were again marshalling their hosts, but the ants were greatly reduced in numbers, and had little hope of holding out that day.

'Come and help us,' said their king to Jesper, 'or we shall be completely defeated. I may help you some day in return.'

Now Jesper had always heard the ants spoken of as clever and industrious little creatures, while he never heard anyone say a good word for the beetles, so he agreed to give the wished-for help. At the first charge he made, the ranks of the beetles broke and fled in dismay, and those escaped best that were nearest a hole, and could get into it before Jesper's boots came down upon them. In a few minutes the ants had the field all to themselves ; and their king made quite an eloquent speech to Jesper, thanking him for the service he had done them, and promising to assist him in any difficulty.

'Just call on me when you want me,' he said, 'wherever you are. I'm never far away from anywhere, and if I can possibly help you, I shall not fail to do it.'

Jesper was inclined to laugh at this, but he kept a grave face, said he would remember the offer, and walked on. At a turn of the road he suddenly came upon the old woman. ' Good morning,' said she ; ' what have *you* got in your basket ? '

' Pearls,' said Jesper ; ' I'm going to the palace to win the princess with them.' And in case she might not believe him, he lifted the cover and let her see them.

' Beautiful,' said the old woman ; ' very beautiful indeed ; but they will go a very little way towards winning the princess, unless you can also perform the tasks that are set you. However,' she said, ' I see you have brought something with you to eat. Won't you give that to me : you are sure to get a good dinner at the palace.'

' Yes, of course,' said Jesper, ' I hadn't thought of that ' ; and he handed over the whole of his lunch to the old woman.

He had already taken a few steps on the way again, when the old woman called him back.

' Here,' she said ; ' take this whistle in return for your lunch. It isn't much to look at, but if you blow it, anything that you have lost or that has been taken from you will find its way back to you in a moment.'

Jesper thanked her for the whistle, though he did not see of what use it was to be to him just then, and held on his way to the palace.

When Jesper presented his pearls to the king there were exclamations of wonder and delight from everyone who saw them. It was not pleasant, however, to discover that Jesper was a mere fisher-lad ; that wasn't the kind of son-in-law that the king had expected, and he said so to the queen.

' Never mind,' said she, ' you can easily set him such tasks as he will never be able to perform : we shall soon get rid of him.'

' Yes, of course,' said the king ; ' really I forget things nowadays, with all the bustle we have had of late.'

That day Jesper dined with the king and queen and

their nobles, and at night was put into a bedroom grander than anything of the kind he had ever seen. It was all so new to him that he could not sleep a wink, especially as he was always wondering what kind of tasks would be set him to do, and whether he would be able to perform them. In spite of the softness of the bed, he was very glad when morning came at last.

After breakfast was over, the king said to Jesper, 'Just come with me, and I'll show you what you must do first.' He led him out to the barn, and there in the middle of the floor was a large pile of grain. 'Here,' said the king, ' you have a mixed heap of wheat, barley, oats, and rye, a sackful of each. By an hour before sunset you must have these sorted out into four heaps, and if a single grain is found to be in a wrong heap you have no further chance of marrying my daughter. I shall lock the door, so that no one can get in to assist you, and I shall return at the appointed time to see how you have succeeded.'

The king walked off, and Jesper looked in despair at the task before him. Then he sat down and tried what he could do at it, but it was soon very clear that single-handed he could never hope to accomplish it in the time. Assistance was out of the question—unless, he suddenly thought—unless the King of the Ants could help. On him he began to call, and before many minutes had passed that royal personage made his appearance. Jesper explained the trouble he was in.

' Is that all ? ' said the ant; 'we shall soon put that to rights.' He gave the royal signal, and in a minute or two a stream of ants came pouring into the barn, who under the king's orders set to work to separate the grain into the proper heaps.

Jesper watched them for a while, but through the continual movement of the little creatures, and his not having slept during the previous night, he soon fell sound asleep. When he woke again, the king had just come into the barn, and was amazed to find that not only was the task accomplished, but that Jesper had found time to take a nap as well.

'Wonderful,' said he; 'I couldn't have believed it possible. However, the hardest is yet to come, as you will see to-morrow.'

Jesper thought so too when the next day's task was set before him. The king's gamekeepers had caught a hundred live hares, which were to be let loose in a large meadow, and there Jesper must herd them all day, and bring them safely home in the evening: if even one were missing, he must give up all thought of marrying the princess. Before he had quite grasped the fact that this was an impossible task, the keepers had opened the sacks in which the hares were brought to the field, and, with a whisk of the short tail and a flap of the long ears, each one of the hundred flew in a different direction.

'Now,' said the king, 'as he walked away, 'let's see what your cleverness can do here.'

Jesper stared round him in bewilderment, and having nothing better to do with his hands, thrust them into his pockets, as he was in the habit of doing. Here he found something which turned out to be the whistle given to him by the old woman. He remembered what she had said about the virtues of the whistle, but was rather doubtful whether its powers would extend to a hundred hares, each of which had gone in a different direction and might be several miles distant by this time. However, he blew the whistle, and in a few minutes the hares came bounding through the hedge on all the four sides of the field, and before long were all sitting round him in a circle. After that, Jesper allowed them to run about as they pleased, so long as they stayed in the field.

The king had told one of the keepers to hang about for a little and see what became of Jesper, not doubting, however, that as soon as he saw the coast clear he would use his legs to the best advantage, and never show face at

the palace again. It was therefore with great surprise
and annoyance that he now learned of the mysterious
return of the hares and the likelihood of Jesper carrying
out his task with success.

'One of them must be got out of his hands by hook or
crook,' said he. 'I'll go and see the queen about it; she's
good at devising plans.'

A little later, a girl in a shabby dress came into the
field and walked up to Jesper.

'Do give me one of those hares,' she said; 'we have
just got visitors who are going to stay to dinner, and
there's nothing we can give them to eat.'

'I can't,' said Jesper. 'For one thing, they're not
mine; for another, a great deal depends on my having
them all here in the evening.'

But the girl (and she was a very pretty girl, though so
shabbily dressed) begged so hard for one of them that at
last he said :

'Very well; give me a kiss and you shall have one of
them.'

He could see that she didn't quite care for this, but
she consented to the bargain, and gave him the kiss, and
went away with a hare in her apron. Scarcely had she
got outside the field, however, when Jesper blew his
whistle, and immediately the hare wriggled out of its
prison like an eel, and went back to its master at the top
of its speed.

Not long after this the hare-herd had another visit.
This time it was a stout old woman in the dress of a
peasant, who also was after a hare to provide a dinner
for unexpected visitors. Jesper again refused, but the
old lady was so pressing, and would take no refusal, that
at last he said :

'Very well, you shall have a hare, and pay nothing for
it either, if you will only walk round me on tiptoe, look
up to the sky, and cackle like a hen.'

'Fie,' said she; 'what a ridiculous thing to ask anyone

to do ; just think what the neighbours would say if they
saw me. They would think I had taken leave of my
senses.'

A hare for a kiss

'Just as you like,' said Jesper ; 'you know best
whether you want the hare or not.'

There was no help for it, and a pretty figure the old lady made in carrying out her task; the cackling wasn't very well done, but Jesper said it would do, and gave her the hare. As soon as she had left the field, the whistle was sounded again, and back came long-legs-and-ears at a marvellous speed.

The next to appear on the same errand was a fat old fellow in the dress of a groom : it was the royal livery he wore, and he plainly thought a good deal of himself.

'Young man,' said he, 'I want one of those hares ; name your price, but I *must* have one of them.'

'All right,' said Jesper ; 'you can have one at an easy rate. Just stand on your head, whack your heels together, and cry "Hurrah," and the hare is yours.'

'Eh, what !' said the old fellow ; '*me* stand on my head ; what an idea !'

'Oh, very well,' said Jesper, 'you needn't unless you like, you know ; but then you won't get the hare.'

It went very much against the grain, one could see, but after some efforts the old fellow had his head on the grass and his heels in the air ; the whacking and the 'Hurrah' were rather feeble, but Jesper was not very exacting, and the hare was handed over. Of course, it wasn't long in coming back again, like the others.

Evening came, and home came Jesper with the hundred hares behind him. Great was the wonder over all the palace, and the king and queen seemed very much put out, but it was noticed that the princess actually smiled to Jesper.

'Well, well,' said the king ; 'you have done that very well indeed. If you are as successful with a little task which I shall give you to-morrow we shall consider the matter settled, and you shall marry the princess.'

Next day it was announced that the task would be performed in the great hall of the palace, and everyone was invited to come and witness it. The king and queen sat on their thrones, with the princess beside them, and the lords and ladies were all round the hall. At a sign from the king, two servants carried in a large empty tub, which they set down in the open space before the throne, and Jesper was told to stand beside it.

' Now,' said the king, ' you must tell us as many undoubted truths as will fill that tub, or you can't have the princess.'

' But how are we to know when the tub is full ? ' said Jesper.

' Don't you trouble about that,' said the king; ' that's my part of the business.'

This seemed to everybody present rather unfair, but no one liked to be the first to say so, and Jesper had to put the best face he could on the matter, and begin his story.

' Yesterday,' he said, ' when I was herding the hares, there came to me a girl, in a shabby dress, and begged me to give her one of them. She got the hare, but she had to give me a kiss for it ; *and that girl was the princess.* Isn't that true ? ' said he, looking at her.

The princess blushed and looked very uncomfortable, but had to admit that it was true.

'That hasn't filled much of the tub,' said the king. ' Go on again.'

' After that,' said Jesper, ' a stout old woman, in a peasant's dress, came and begged for a hare. Before she got it, she had to walk round me on tiptoe, turn up her eyes, and cackle like a hen ; *and that old woman was the queen.* Isn't that true, now ? '

The queen turned very red and hot, but couldn't deny it.

' H-m,' said the king ; ' that is something, but the tub isn't full yet.' To the queen he whispered, ' I didn't think you would be such a fool.'

' What did *you* do ? ' she whispered in return.

' Do you suppose I would do anything for *him* ? ' said the king, and then hurriedly ordered Jesper to go on.

' In the next place,' said Jesper, ' there came a fat old

fellow on the same errand. He was very proud and dignified, but in order to get the hare he actually stood on his head, whacked his heels together, and cried " Hurrah " ; *and that old fellow was the——*'

' Stop, stop,' shouted the king ; ' you needn't say another word ; the tub is full.' Then all the court applauded, and the king and queen accepted Jesper as their son-in-law, and the princess was very well pleased, for by this time she had quite fallen in love with him, because he was so handsome and so clever. When the old king got time to think over it, he was quite convinced that his kingdom would be safe in Jesper's hands if he looked after the people as well as he herded the hares.

[Scandinavian.]

THE UNDERGROUND WORKERS

ON a bitter night somewhere between Christmas and the
New Year, a man set out to walk to the neighbouring
village. It was not many miles off, but the snow was so
thick that there were no roads, or walls, or hedges left to
guide him, and very soon he lost his way altogether, and
was glad to get shelter from the wind behind a thick juniper
tree. Here he resolved to spend the night, thinking that
when the sun rose he would be able to see his path
again.

So he tucked his legs snugly under him like a hedge-
hog, rolled himself up in his sheepskin, and went to sleep.
How long he slept, I cannot tell you, but after awhile he
became aware that some one was gently shaking him,
while a stranger whispered, 'My good man, get up! If
you lie there any more, you will be buried in the snow,
and no one will ever know what became of you.'

The sleeper slowly raised his head from his furs, and
opened his heavy eyes. Near him stood a long thin man,
holding in his hand a young fir tree taller than himself.
'Come with me,' said the man, 'a little way off we have
made a large fire, and you will rest far better there than
out upon this moor.' The sleeper did not wait to be
asked twice, but rose at once and followed the stranger.
The snow was falling so fast that he could not see three
steps in front of him, till the stranger waved his staff,
when the drifts parted before them. Very soon they
reached a wood, and saw the friendly glow of a fire.

'What is your name?' asked the stranger, suddenly turning round.

'I am called Hans, the son of Long Hans,' said the peasant.

In front of the fire three men were sitting clothed in white, just as if it was summer, and for about thirty feet all round winter had been banished. The moss was dry and the plants green, while the grass seemed all alive with the hum of bees and cockchafers. But above the noise the son of Long Hans could hear the whistling of the wind and the crackling of the branches as they fell beneath the weight of the snow.

'Well! you son of Long Hans, isn't this more comfortable than your juniper bush?' laughed the stranger, and for answer Hans replied he could not thank his friend enough for having brought him here, and, throwing off his sheepskin, rolled it up as a pillow. Then, after a hot drink which warmed both their hearts, they lay down on the ground. The stranger talked for a little to the other men in a language Hans did not understand, and after listening for a short time he once more fell asleep.

When he awoke, neither wood nor fire was to be seen, and he did not know where he was. He rubbed his eyes, and began to recall the events of the night, thinking he must have been dreaming; but for all that, he could not make out how he came to be in this place.

Suddenly a loud noise struck on his ear, and he felt the earth tremble beneath his feet. Hans listened for a moment, then resolved to go towards the place where the sound came from, hoping he might come across some human being. He found himself at length at the mouth of a rocky cave in which a fire seemed burning. He entered, and saw a huge forge, and a crowd of men in front of it, blowing bellows and wielding hammers, and to each anvil were seven men, and a set of more comical smiths could not be found if you searched all the world

THE UNDERGROUND WORKERS

through! Their heads were bigger than their little bodies, and their hammers twice the size of themselves, but the strongest men on earth could not have handled their iron clubs more stoutly or given lustier blows.

The little blacksmiths were clad in leather aprons, which covered them from their necks to their feet in front, and left their backs naked. On a high stool against the wall sat the man with the pinewood staff, watching sharply the way the little fellows did their work, and near him stood a large can, from which every now and then the workers would come and take a drink. The master no longer wore the white garments of the day before, but a black jerkin, held in its place by a leathern girdle with huge clasps.

From time to time he would give his workmen a sign with his staff, for it was useless to speak amid such a noise.

If any of them had noticed that there was a stranger present they took no heed of him, but went on with what they were doing. After some hours' hard labour came the time for rest, and they all flung their hammers to the ground and trooped out of the cave.

Then the master got down from his seat and said to Hans:

'I saw you come in, but the work was pressing, and I could not stop to speak to you. To-day you must be my guest, and I will show you something of the way in which I live. Wait here for a moment, while I lay aside these dirty clothes.' With these words he unlocked a door in the cave, and bade Hans pass in before him.

Oh, what riches and treasures met Hans' astonished eyes! Gold and silver bars lay piled on the floor, and glittered so that you could not look at them! Hans thought he would count them for fun, and had already reached the five hundred and seventieth when his host returned and cried, laughing:

'Do not try to count them, it would take too long;

choose some of the bars from the heap, as I should like to make you a present of them.'

Hans did not wait to be asked twice, and stooped to pick up a bar of gold, but though he put forth all his strength he could not even move it with both hands, still less lift it off the ground.

' Why, you have no more power than a flea,' laughed the host ; ' you will have to content yourself with feasting your eyes upon them ! '

So he bade Hans follow him through other rooms, till they entered one bigger than a church, filled, like the rest, with gold and silver. Hans wondered to see these vast riches, which might have bought all the kingdoms of the world, and lay buried, useless, he thought, to anyone.

' What is the reason,' he asked of his guide, ' that you gather up these treasures here, where they can do good to nobody? If they fell into the hands of men, everyone would be rich, and none need work or suffer hunger.'

' And it is exactly for that reason,' answered he, ' that I must keep these riches out of their way. The whole world would sink to idleness if men were not forced to earn their daily bread. It is only through work and care that man can ever hope to be good for anything.'

Hans stared at these words, and at last he begged that his host would tell him what use it was to anybody that this gold and silver should lie mouldering there, and the owner of it be continually trying to increase his treasure, which already overflowed his store rooms.

' I am not really a man,' replied his guide, ' though I have the outward form of one, but one of those beings to whom is given the care of the world. It is my task and that of my workmen to prepare under the earth the gold and silver, a small portion of which finds its way every year to the upper world, but only just enough to help them carry on their business. To none comes wealth without trouble : we must first dig out the gold and mix the grains with earth, clay, and sand. Then, after long and hard seeking, it will be found in this state, by those who have good luck or much patience. But, my friend, the hour of dinner is at hand. If you wish to remain in this place, and feast your eyes on this gold, then stay till I call you.'

In his absence Hans wandered from one treasure chamber to another, sometimes trying to break off a little lump of gold, but never able to do it. After awhile his host came back, but so changed that Hans could not believe it was really he. His silken clothes were of the brightest flame colour, richly trimmed with gold fringes and lace ; a golden girdle was round his waist, while his head was encircled with a crown of gold, and precious stones twinkled about him like stars in a winter's night, and in place of his wooden stick he held a finely worked golden staff.

The lord of all this treasure locked the doors and put the keys in his pocket, then led Hans into another room, where dinner was laid for them. Table and seats were all of silver, while the dishes and plates were of solid gold. Directly they sat down, a dozen little servants appeared to wait on them, which they did so cleverly and so quickly that Hans could hardly believe they had no wings. As they did not reach as high as the table, they were often obliged to jump and hop right on to the top to get at the dishes. Everything was new to Hans, and though he was rather bewildered he enjoyed himself very much, especially when the man with the golden crown began to tell him many things he had never heard of before.

'Between Christmas and the New Year,' said he, 'I often amuse myself by wandering about the earth watching the doings of men and learning something about them. But as far as I have seen and heard I cannot speak well of them. The greater part of them are always quarrelling and complaining of each other's faults, while nobody thinks of his own.'

Hans tried to deny the truth of these words, but he could not do it, and sat silent, hardly listening to what his friend was saying. Then he went to sleep in his chair, and knew nothing of what was happening.

Wonderful dreams came to him during his sleep, where the bars of gold continually hovered before his eyes. He felt stronger than he had ever felt during his waking moments, and lifted two bars quite easily on to his back. He did this so often that at length his strength seemed exhausted, and he sank almost breathless on the ground. Then he heard the sound of cheerful voices, and the song of the blacksmiths as they blew their bellows—he even felt as if he saw the sparks flashing before his eyes. Stretching himself, he awoke slowly, and here he was in the green forest, and instead of the glow of the fire in the underworld the sun was streaming on him, and he sat up wondering why he felt so strange.

At length his memory came back to him, and as he called to mind all the wonderful things he had seen he tried in vain to make them agree with those that happen every day. After thinking it over till he was nearly mad, he tried at last to believe that one night between Christmas and the New Year he had met a stranger in the forest, and had slept all night in his company before a big fire ; the next day they had dined together, and had drunk a great deal more than was good for them—in short, he had spent two whole days revelling with another man. But here, with the full tide of summer around him, he could hardly accept his own explanation, and felt that he must have been the plaything or sport of some magician.

Near him, in the full sunlight, were the traces of a dead fire, and when he drew close to it he saw that what he had taken for ashes was really fine silver dust, and that the half burnt firewood was made of gold.

Oh, how lucky Hans thought himself ; but where

should he get a sack to carry his treasure home before anyone else found it ? But necessity is the mother of invention : Hans threw off his fur coat, gathered up the silver ashes so carefully in it that none remained behind, laid the gold sticks on top, and tied up the bag thus made with his girdle, so that nothing should fall out. The load was not, in point of fact, very heavy, although it seemed so to his imagination, and he moved slowly along till he found a safe hiding-place for it.

In this way Hans suddenly became rich—rich enough to buy a property of his own. But being a prudent man, he finally decided that it would be best for him to leave his old neighbourhood and look for a home in a distant part of the country, where nobody knew anything about him. It did not take him long to find what he wanted, and after he had paid for it there was plenty of money left over. When he was settled, he married a pretty girl who lived near by, and had some children, to whom on his death-bed he told the story of the lord of the underworld, and how he had made Hans rich.

[Ehstnische Märchen.]

THE HISTORY OF DWARF LONG NOSE

IT is a great mistake to think that fairies, witches, magicians, and such people lived only in Eastern countries and in such times as those of the Caliph Haroun Al-Raschid. Fairies and their like belong to every country and every age, and no doubt we should see plenty of them now—if we only knew how.

In a large town in Germany there lived, some couple of hundred years ago, a cobbler and his wife. They were poor and hard-working. The man sat all day in a little stall at the street corner and mended any shoes that were brought him. His wife sold the fruit and vegetables they grew in their garden in the Market Place, and as she was always neat and clean and her goods were temptingly spread out she had plenty of customers.

The couple had one boy called Jem. A handsome, pleasant-faced boy of twelve, and tall for his age. He used to sit by his mother in the market and would carry home what people bought from her, for which they often gave him a pretty flower, or a slice of cake, or even some small coin.

One day Jem and his mother sat as usual in the Market Place with plenty of nice herbs and vegetables spread out on the board, and in some smaller baskets early pears, apples, and apricots. Jem cried his wares at the top of his voice :

' This way, gentlemen ! See these lovely cabbages and these fresh herbs ! Early apples, ladies ; early pears and apricots, and all cheap. Come, buy, buy ! '

As he cried an old woman came across the Market Place. She looked very torn and ragged, and had a small sharp face, all wrinkled, with red eyes, and a thin hooked nose which nearly met her chin. She leant on a tall stick and limped and shuffled and stumbled along as if she were going to fall on her nose at any moment.

In this fashion she came along till she got to the stall where Jem and his mother were, and there she stopped.

'Are you Hannah the herb seller?' she asked in a croaky voice as her head shook to and fro.

'Yes, I am,' was the answer. 'Can I serve you?'

'We'll see; we'll see! Let me look at those herbs. I wonder if you've got what I want,' said the old woman as she thrust a pair of hideous brown hands into the herb basket, and began turning over all the neatly packed herbs with her skinny fingers, often holding them up to her nose and sniffing at them.

The cobbler's wife felt much disgusted at seeing her wares treated like this, but she dared not speak. When the old hag had turned over the whole basket she muttered, 'Bad stuff, bad stuff; much better fifty years ago—all bad.'

This made Jem very angry

'You are a very rude old woman,' he cried out. 'First you mess all our nice herbs about with your horrid brown fingers and sniff at them with your long nose till no one else will care to buy them, and then you say it's all bad stuff, though the duke's cook himself buys all his herbs from us.'

The old woman looked sharply at the saucy boy, laughed unpleasantly, and said:

'So you don't like my long nose, sonny? Well, you shall have one yourself, right down to your chin.'

As she spoke she shuffled towards the hamper of cabbages, took up one after another, squeezed them hard, and threw them back, muttering again, 'Bad stuff, bad stuff.'

'Don't waggle your head in that horrid way,' begged Jem anxiously. 'Your neck is as thin as a cabbage-stalk, and it might easily break and your head fall into the basket, and then who would buy anything?'

'Don't you like thin necks?' laughed the old woman. 'Then you sha'n't have any, but a head stuck close between your shoulders so that it may be quite sure not to fall off.'

JEM FOLLOWS THE OLD WOMAN

'Don't talk such nonsense to the child,' said the mother at last. 'If you wish to buy, please make haste, as you are keeping other customers away.'

'Very well, I will do as you ask,' said the old woman, with an angry look. 'I will buy these six cabbages, but, as you see, I can only walk with my stick and can carry nothing. Let your boy carry them home for me and I'll pay him for his trouble.'

The little fellow didn't like this, and began to cry, for

he was afraid of the old woman, but his mother ordered him to go, for she thought it wrong not to help such a weakly old creature; so, still crying, he gathered the cabbages into a basket and followed the old woman across the Market Place.

It took her more than half an hour to get to a distant part of the little town, but at last she stopped in front of a small tumble-down house. She drew a rusty old hook from her pocket and stuck it into a little hole in the door, which suddenly flew open. How surprised Jem was when they went in! The house was splendidly furnished, the walls and ceiling of marble, the furniture of ebony inlaid with gold and precious stones, the floor of such smooth slippery glass that the little fellow tumbled down more than once.

The old woman took out a silver whistle and blew it till the sound rang through the house. Immediately a lot of guinea pigs came running down the stairs, but Jem thought it rather odd that they all walked on their hind legs, wore nutshells for shoes, and men's clothes, whilst even their hats were put on in the newest fashion.

'Where are my slippers, lazy crew?' cried the old woman, and hit about with her stick. 'How long am I to stand waiting here?'

They rushed upstairs again and returned with a pair of cocoa nuts lined with leather, which she put on her feet. Now all limping and shuffling was at an end. She threw away her stick and walked briskly across the glass floor, drawing little Jem after her. At last she paused in a room which looked almost like a kitchen, it was so full of pots and pans, but the tables were of mahogany and the sofas and chairs covered with the richest stuffs.

'Sit down,' said the old woman pleasantly, and she pushed Jem into a corner of a sofa and put a table close in front of him. 'Sit down, you've had a long walk and a heavy load to carry, and I must give you something for your trouble. Wait a bit, and I'll give you some nice soup, which you'll remember as long as you live.'

So saying, she whistled again. First came in guinea pigs in men's clothing. They had tied on large kitchen aprons, and in their belts were stuck carving knives and sauce ladles and such things. After them hopped in a number of squirrels. They too walked on their hind legs, wore full Turkish trousers, and little green velvet caps on their heads. They seemed to be the scullions, for they clambered up the walls and brought down pots and pans, eggs, flour, butter, and herbs, which they carried to the stove. Here the old woman was bustling about, and Jem could see that she was cooking something very special for him. At last the broth began to bubble and boil, and she drew off the saucepan and poured its contents into a silver bowl, which she set before Jem.

'There, my boy,' said she, 'eat this soup and then you'll have everything which pleased you so much about me. And you shall be a clever cook too, but the real herb—no, the *real* herb you'll never find. Why had your mother not got it in her basket?'

The child could not think what she was talking about, but he quite understood the soup, which tasted most delicious. His mother had often given him nice things, but nothing had ever seemed so good as this. The smell of the herbs and spices rose from the bowl, and the soup tasted both sweet and sharp at the same time, and was very strong. As he was finishing it the guinea pigs lit some Arabian incense, which gradually filled the room with clouds of blue vapour. They grew thicker and thicker and the scent nearly overpowered the boy. He reminded himself that he must get back to his mother, but whenever he tried to rouse himself to go he sank back again drowsily, and at last he fell sound asleep in the corner of the sofa.

Strange dreams came to him. He thought the old woman took off all his clothes and wrapped him up in a squirrel skin, and that he went about with the other squirrels and guinea pigs, who were all very pleasant and well mannered, and waited on the old woman. First he learned to clean her cocoa-nut shoes with oil and to rub them up. Then he learnt to catch the little sun moths and rub them through the finest sieves, and the flour from them he made into soft bread for the toothless old woman.

In this way he passed from one kind of service to another, spending a year in each, till in the fourth year he was promoted to the kitchen. Here he worked his way up from under-scullion to head-pastrycook, and reached the greatest perfection. He could make all the most difficult dishes, and two hundred different kinds of patties, soup flavoured with every sort of herb—he had learnt it all, and learnt it well and quickly.

When he had lived seven years with the old woman she ordered him one day, as she was going out, to kill and pluck a chicken, stuff it with herbs, and have it very nicely roasted by the time she got back. He did this quite according to rule. He wrung the chicken's neck, plunged it into boiling water, carefully plucked out all the feathers, and rubbed the skin nice and smooth. Then he went to fetch the herbs to stuff it with. In the storeroom he noticed a half-opened cupboard which he did not remember having seen before. He peeped in and saw a lot of baskets from which came a strong and pleasant smell. He opened one and found a very uncommon herb in it. The stems and leaves were a bluish green, and above them was a little flower of a deep bright red, edged with yellow. He gazed at the flower, smelt it, and found it gave the same strong strange perfume which came from the soup the old woman had made him. But the smell was so sharp that he began to sneeze again and again, and at last—he woke up!

There he lay on the old woman's sofa and stared about him in surprise. ' Well, what odd dreams one does have to be sure!' he said to himself. 'Why, I could have sworn I had been a squirrel, a companion of guinea pigs and such creatures, and had become a great cook, too. How mother will laugh when I tell her! But won't she scold me, though, for sleeping away here in a strange house, instead of helping her at market!'

He jumped up and prepared to go: all his limbs still seemed quite stiff with his long sleep, especially his neck, for he could not move his head easily, and he laughed at his own stupidity at being still so drowsy that he kept knocking his nose against the wall or cupboards. The squirrels and guinea pigs ran whimpering after him, as though they would like to go too, and he begged them to come when he reached the door, but they all turned and ran quickly back into the house again.

The part of the town was out of the way, and Jem did not know the many narrow streets in it and was puzzled by their windings and by the crowd of people, who seemed excited about some show. From what he heard, he fancied they were going to see a dwarf, for he heard them call out: 'Just look at the ugly dwarf!' 'What a long nose he has, and see how his head is stuck in between his shoulders, and only look at his ugly brown hands!' If he had not been in such a hurry to get back to his mother, he would have gone too, for he loved shows with giants and dwarfs and the like.

He was quite puzzled when he reached the market-place. There sat his mother, with a good deal of fruit still in her baskets, so he felt he could not have slept so very long, but it struck him that she was sad, for she did not call to the passers-by, but sat with her head resting on her hand, and as he came nearer he thought she looked paler than usual.

He hesitated what to do, but at last he slipped behind her, laid a hand on her arm, and said: 'Mammy, what's the matter? Are you angry with me?'

She turned round quickly and jumped up with a cry
of horror.

'What do you want, you hideous dwarf?' she cried;
'get away; I can't bear such tricks.'

'But, mother dear, what's the matter with you?'

HANNAH DOES NOT RECOGNISE JEM

repeated Jem, quite frightened. 'You can't be well.
Why do you want to drive your son away?'

'I have said already, get away,' replied Hannah,
quite angrily. 'You won't get anything out of me by your
games, you monstrosity.'

'Oh dear, oh dear! she must be wandering in her mind,' murmured the lad to himself. 'How can I manage to get her home? Dearest mother, do look at me close. Can't you see I am your own son Jem?'

'Well, did you ever hear such impudence?' asked Hannah, turning to a neighbour. 'Just see that frightful dwarf—would you believe that he wants me to think he is my son Jem?'

Then all the market women came round and talked all together and scolded as hard as they could, and said what a shame it was to make game of Mrs. Hannah, who had never got over the loss of her beautiful boy, who had been stolen from her seven years ago, and they threatened to fall upon Jem and scratch him well if he did not go away at once.

Poor Jem did not know what to make of it all. He was sure he had gone to market with his mother only that morning, had helped to set out the stall, had gone to the old woman's house, where he had some soup and a little nap, and now, when he came back, they were all talking of seven years. And they called him a horrid dwarf! Why, what had happened to him? When he found that his mother would really have nothing to do with him he turned away with tears in his eyes, and went sadly down the street towards his father's stall.

'Now I'll see whether he will know me,' thought he. 'I'll stand by the door and talk to him.'

When he got to the stall he stood in the doorway and looked in. The cobbler was so busy at work that he did not see him for some time, but, happening to look up, he caught sight of his visitor, and letting shoes, thread, and everything fall to the ground, he cried with horror: 'Good heavens! what is that?'

'Good evening, master,' said the boy, as he stepped in. 'How do you do?'

'Very ill, little sir,' replied the father, to Jem's

surprise, for he did not seem to know him. 'Business does not go well. I am all alone, and am getting old, and a workman is costly.'

'But haven't you a son who could learn your trade by degrees?' asked Jem.

'I had one: he was called Jem, and would have been a tall sturdy lad of twenty by this time, and able to help me well. Why, when he was only twelve he was quite sharp and quick, and had learnt many little things, and a good-looking boy too, and pleasant, so that customers were taken by him. Well, well! so goes the world!'

'But where is your son?' asked Jem, with a trembling voice.

'Heaven only knows!' replied the man; 'seven years ago he was stolen from the market-place, and we have heard no more of him.'

'*Seven years ago!*' cried Jem, with horror.

'Yes, indeed, seven years ago, though it seems but yesterday that my wife came back howling and crying, and saying the child had not come back all day. I always thought and said that something of the kind would happen. Jem was a beautiful boy, and everyone made much of him, and my wife was so proud of him, and liked him to carry the vegetables and things to grand folks' houses, where he was petted and made much of. But I used to say, "Take care—the town is large, there are plenty of bad people in it—keep a sharp eye on Jem." And so it happened; for one day an old woman came and bought a lot of things—more than she could carry; so my wife, being a kindly soul, lent her the boy, and—we have never seen him since.'

'And that was seven years ago, you say?'

'Yes, seven years: we had him cried—we went from house to house. Many knew the pretty boy, and were fond of him, but it was all in vain. No one seemed to know the old woman who bought the vegetables either;

only one old woman, who is ninety years old, said it might have been the fairy Herbaline, who came into the town once in every fifty years to buy things.'

As his father spoke, things grew clearer to Jem's mind, and he saw now that he had not been dreaming, but had really served the old woman seven years in the shape of a squirrel. As he thought it over rage filled his heart. Seven years of his youth had been stolen from him, and what had he got in return? To learn to rub up cocoa nuts, and to polish glass floors, and to be taught cooking by guinea pigs! He stood there thinking, till at last his father asked him:

'Is there anything I can do for you, young gentleman? Shall I make you a pair of slippers, or perhaps'— with a smile—'a case for your nose?'

'What have you to do with my nose?' asked Jem. 'And why should I want a case for it?'

'Well, everyone to his taste,' replied the cobbler; 'but I must say if I had such a nose I would have a nice red leather cover made for it. Here is a nice piece; and think what a protection it would be to you. As it is, you must be constantly knocking up against things.'

The lad was dumb with fright. He felt his nose. It was thick, and quite two hands long. So, then, the old woman had changed his shape, and that was why his own mother did not know him, and called him a horrid dwarf!

'Master,' said he, 'have you got a glass that I could see myself in?'

'Young gentleman,' was the answer, 'your appearance is hardly one to be vain of, and there is no need to waste your time looking in a glass. Besides, I have none here, and if you must have one you had better ask Urban the barber, who lives over the way, to lend you his. Good morning.'

So saying, he gently pushed Jem into the street, shut the door, and went back to his work.

Jem stepped across to the barber, whom he had known in old days.

'Good morning, Urban,' said he; 'may I look at myself in your glass for a moment?'

'With pleasure,' said the barber, laughing, and all the people in his shop fell to laughing also. 'You are a pretty youth, with your swan-like neck and white hands and small nose. No wonder you are rather vain; but look as long as you like at yourself.'

So spoke the barber, and a titter ran round the room. Meantime Jem had stepped up to the mirror, and stood gazing sadly at his reflection. Tears came to his eyes.

'No wonder you did not know your child again, dear mother,' thought he; 'he wasn't like this when you were so proud of his looks.'

His eyes had grown quite small, like pigs' eyes, his nose was huge and hung down over his mouth and chin, his throat seemed to have disappeared altogether, and his head was fixed stiffly between his shoulders. He was no taller than he had been seven years ago, when he was not much more than twelve years old, but he made up in breadth, and his back and chest had grown into lumps like two great sacks. His legs were small and spindly, but his arms were as large as those of a well-grown man, with large brown hands, and long skinny fingers.

Then he remembered the morning when he had first seen the old woman, and her threats to him, and without saying a word he left the barber's shop.

He determined to go again to his mother, and found her still in the market-place. He begged her to listen quietly to him, and he reminded her of the day when he went away with the old woman, and of many things in his childhood, and told her how the fairy had bewitched him, and he had served her seven years. Hannah did not know what to think—the story was so strange; and it seemed impossible to think her pretty boy and this hideous dwarf were the same. At last she decided to go and talk to her husband about it. She gathered up her baskets, told Jem to follow her, and went straight to the cobbler's stall.

'Look here,' said she, 'this creature says he is our lost son. He has been telling me how he was stolen seven years ago, and bewitched by a fairy.'

'Indeed!' interrupted the cobbler angrily. 'Did he tell you this? Wait a minute, you rascal! Why I told him all about it myself only an hour ago, and then he goes off to humbug you. So you were bewitched, my son were you? Wait a bit, and I'll bewitch you!'

So saying, he caught up a bundle of straps, and hit out at Jem so hard that he ran off crying.

The poor little dwarf roamed about all the rest of the day without food or drink, and at night was glad to lie down and sleep on the steps of a church. He woke next morning with the first rays of light, and began to think what he could do to earn a living. Suddenly he remembered that he was an excellent cook, and he determined to look out for a place.

As soon as it was quite daylight he set out for the palace, for he knew that the grand duke who reigned over the country was fond of good things.

When he reached the palace all the servants crowded about him, and made fun of him, and at last their shouts and laughter grew so loud that the head steward rushed out, crying, 'For goodness sake, be quiet, can't you. Don't you know his highness is still asleep?'

Some of the servants ran off at once, and others pointed out Jem. Indeed, the steward found it hard to keep himself from laughing at the comic sight, but he ordered the servants off and led the dwarf into his own room.

When he heard him ask for a place as cook, he said: 'You make some mistake, my lad. I think you want to be the grand duke's dwarf, don't you?'

'No, sir,' replied Jem. 'I am an experienced cook,

and if you will kindly take me to the head cook he may find me of some use.'

' Well, as you will ; but believe me, you would have an easier place as the grand ducal dwarf.'

So saying, the head steward led him to the head cook's room.

' Sir,' asked Jem, as he bowed till his nose nearly touched the floor, ' do you want an experienced cook ? '

The head cook looked him over from head to foot, and burst out laughing.

' You a cook ! Do you suppose our cooking stoves are so low that you can look into any saucepan on them ? Oh, my dear little fellow, whoever sent you to me wanted to make fun of you.'

But the dwarf was not to be put off.

' What matters an extra egg or two, or a little butter or flour and spice more or less, in such a house as this ? ' said he. ' Name any dish you wish to have cooked, and give me the materials I ask for, and you shall see.'

He said much more, and at last persuaded the head cook to give him a trial.

They went into the kitchen—a huge place with at least twenty fireplaces, always alight. A little stream of clear water ran through the room, and live fish were kept at one end of it. Everything in the kitchen was of the best and most beautiful kind, and swarms of cooks and scullions were busy preparing dishes.

When the head cook came in with Jem everyone stood quite still.

' What has his highness ordered for luncheon ? ' asked the head cook.

' Sir, his highness has graciously ordered a Danish soup and red Hamburg dumplings.'

' Good,' said the head cook. ' Have you heard, and do you feel equal to making these dishes ? Not that you will be able to make the dumplings, for they are a secret receipt.'

'Is that all!' said Jem, who had often made both dishes. 'Nothing easier. Let me have some eggs, a piece of wild boar, and such and such roots and herbs for the soup; and as for the dumplings,' he added in a low voice to the head cook, 'I shall want four different kinds of meat, some wine, a duck's marrow, some ginger, and a herb called heal-well.'

'Why,' cried the astonished cook, 'where did you learn cooking? Yes, those are the exact materials, but we never used the herb heal-well, which, I am sure, must be an improvement.'

And now Jem was allowed to try his hand. He could not nearly reach up to the kitchen range, but by putting a wide plank on two chairs he managed very well. All the cooks stood round to look on, and could not help admiring the quick, clever way in which he set to work. At last, when all was ready, Jem ordered the two dishes to be put on the fire till he gave the word. Then he began to count: 'One, two, three,' till he got to five hundred when he cried, 'Now!' The saucepans were taken off, and he invited the head cook to taste.

The first cook took a golden spoon, washed and wiped it, and handed it to the head cook, who solemnly approached, tasted the dishes, and smacked his lips over them. 'First rate, indeed!' he exclaimed. 'You certainly are a master of the art, little fellow, and the herb heal-well gives a particular relish.'

As he was speaking, the duke's valet came to say that his highness was ready for luncheon, and it was served at once in silver dishes. The head cook took Jem to his own room, but had hardly had time to question him before he was ordered to go at once to the grand duke. He hurried on his best clothes and followed the messenger.

The grand duke was looking much pleased. He had emptied the dishes, and was wiping his mouth as the head cook came in. 'Who cooked my luncheon to-day?' asked he. 'I must say your dumplings are always very good ; but I don't think I ever tasted anything so delicious as they were to-day. Who made them ? '

' It is a strange story, your highness,' said the cook, and told him the whole matter, which surprised the duke so much that he sent for the dwarf and asked him many questions. Of course, Jem could not say he had been turned into a squirrel, but he said he was without parents and had been taught cooking by an old woman.

' If you will stay with me,' said the grand duke, ' you shall have fifty ducats a year, besides a new coat and a couple of pairs of trousers. You must undertake to cook my luncheon yourself and to direct what I shall have for dinner, and you shall be called assistant head cook.'

Jem bowed to the ground, and promised to obey his new master in all things.

He lost no time in setting to work, and everyone rejoiced at having him in the kitchen, for the duke was not a patient man, and had been known to throw plates and dishes at his cooks and servants if the things served were not quite to his taste. Now all was changed. He never even grumbled at anything, had five meals instead of three, thought everything delicious, and grew fatter daily.

And so Jem lived on for two years, much respected and considered, and only saddened when he thought of his parents. One day passed much like another till the following incident happened.

Dwarf Long Nose—as he was always called—made a practice of doing his marketing as much as possible himself, and whenever time allowed went to the market to buy his poultry and fruit. One morning he was in the goose market, looking for some nice fat geese. No one thought of laughing at his appearance now; he was known as the duke's special body cook, and every goose-woman felt honoured if his nose turned her way.

He noticed one woman sitting apart with a number of geese, but not crying or praising them like the rest. He went up to her, felt and weighed her geese, and, finding them very good, bought three and the cage to put them in, hoisted them on his broad shoulders, and set off on his way back.

As he went, it struck him that two of the geese were gobbling and screaming as geese do, but the third sat quite still, only heaving a deep sigh now and then, like a human being. 'That goose is ill,' said he ; 'I must make haste to kill and dress her.'

But the goose answered him quite distinctly :

> 'Squeeze too tight
> And I'll bite,
> If my neck a twist you gave
> I'd bring you to an early grave.'

Quite frightened, the dwarf set down the cage, and the goose gazed at him with sad wise-looking eyes and sighed again.

'Good gracious!' said Long Nose. 'So you can speak, Mistress Goose. I never should have thought it! Well, don't be anxious. I know better than to hurt so rare a bird. But I could bet you were not always in this plumage—wasn't I a squirrel myself for a time?'

'You are right,' said the goose, 'in supposing I was not born in this horrid shape. Ah! no one ever thought that Mimi, the daughter of the great Weatherbold, would be killed for the ducal table.'

'Be quite easy, Mistress Mimi,' comforted Jem. 'As sure as I'm an honest man and assistant head cook to his highness, no one shall harm you. I will make a hutch for you in my own rooms, and you shall be well fed, and I'll come and talk to you as much as I can. I'll tell all the other cooks that I am fattening up a goose on very special food for the grand duke, and at the first good opportunity I will set you free.'

The goose thanked him with tears in her eyes, and the dwarf kept his word. He killed the other two geese for dinner, but built a little shed for Mimi in one of his rooms, under the pretence of fattening her under his own eye. He spent all his spare time talking to her and comforting her, and fed her on all the daintiest dishes. They confided their histories to each other, and Jem learnt that the goose was the daughter of the wizard Weatherbold, who lived on the island of Gothland. He fell out with an old fairy, who got the better of him by cunning and treachery, and to revenge herself turned his daughter into a goose and carried her off to this distant place. When Long Nose told her his story she said :

' I know a little of these matters, and what you say shows me that you are under a herb enchantment—that is to say, that if you can find the herb whose smell woke you up the spell would be broken.'

This was but small comfort for Jem, for how and where was he to find the herb ?

About this time the grand duke had a visit from a neighbouring prince, a friend of his. He sent for Long Nose and said to him :

' Now is the time to show what you can really do. This prince who is staying with me has better dinners than any one except myself, and is a great judge of cooking. As long as he is here you must take care that my table shall be served in a manner to surprise him constantly. At the same time, on pain of my displeasure, take care that no dish shall appear twice. Get everything you wish and spare nothing. If you want to melt down gold and precious stones, do so. I would rather be a poor man than have to blush before him.'

The dwarf bowed and answered :

' Your highness shall be obeyed. I will do all in my power to please you and the prince.'

From this time the little cook was hardly seen except in the kitchen, where, surrounded by his helpers, he gave orders, baked, stewed, flavoured and dished up all manner of dishes.

The prince had been a fortnight with the grand duke, and enjoyed himself mightily. They ate five times a day, and the duke had every reason to be content with the dwarf's talents, for he saw how pleased his guest looked. On the fifteenth day the duke sent for the dwarf and presented him to the prince.

'You are a wonderful cook,' said the prince, 'and you certainly know what is good. All the time I have been here you have never repeated a dish, and all were excellent. But tell me why you have never served the queen of all dishes, a Suzeraine Pasty?'

The dwarf felt frightened, for he had never heard of this Queen of Pasties before. But he did not lose his presence of mind, and replied :

'I have waited, hoping that your highness' visit here would last some time, for I proposed to celebrate the last day of your stay with this truly royal dish.'

'Indeed,' laughed the grand duke; 'then I suppose you would have waited for the day of my death to treat me to it, for you have never sent it up to me yet. However, you will have to invent some other farewell dish, for the pasty must be on my table to-morrow.'

'As your highness pleases,' said the dwarf, and took leave.

But it did not please *him* at all. The moment of disgrace seemed at hand, for he had no idea how to make this pasty. He went to his rooms very sad. As he sat there lost in thought the goose Mimi, who was left free to walk about, came up to him and asked what was the matter? When she heard she said:

'Cheer up, my friend. I know the dish quite well : we often had it at home, and I can guess pretty well how it was made.' Then she told him what to put in, adding : 'I think that will be all right, and if some trifle is left out perhaps they won't find it out.'

Sure enough, next day a magnificent pasty all wreathed round with flowers was placed on the table. Jem himself put on his best clothes and went into the dining hall. As he entered the head carver was in the act of cutting up the pie and helping the duke and his guests. The grand duke took a large mouthful and threw up his eyes as he swallowed it.

'Oh! oh! this may well be called the Queen of Pasties, and at the same time my dwarf must be called the king of cooks. Don't you think so, dear friend?'

The prince took several small pieces, tasted and examined carefully, and then said with a mysterious and sarcastic smile:

'The dish is very nicely made, but the Suzeraine is not quite complete—as I expected.'

The grand duke flew into a rage.

'Dog of a cook,' he shouted; 'how dare you serve me so? I've a good mind to chop off your great head as a punishment.'

'For mercy's sake, don't, your highness! I made the pasty according to the best rules; nothing has been left out. Ask the prince what else I should have put in.'

The prince laughed. 'I was sure you could not make this dish as well as my cook, friend Long Nose. Know, then, that a herb is wanting called Relish, which is not known in this country, but which gives the pasty its peculiar flavour, and without which your master will never taste it to perfection.'

The grand duke was more furious than ever.

'But I *will* taste it to perfection,' he roared. 'Either the pasty must be made properly to-morrow or this rascal's head shall come off. Go, scoundrel, I give you twenty-four hours respite.'

The poor dwarf hurried back to his room, and poured out his grief to the goose.

'Oh, is that all,' said she, 'then I can help you, for my father taught me to know all plants and herbs.

Luckily this is a new moon just now, for the herb only
springs up at such times. But tell me, are there chestnut
trees near the palace?'

'Oh, yes!' cried Long Nose, much relieved; 'near
the lake—only a couple of hundred yards from the palace
—is a large clump of them. But why do you ask?'

'Because the herb only grows near the roots of chestnut
trees,' replied Mimi; 'so let us lose no time in finding it.
Take me under your arm and put me down out of doors,
and I'll hunt for it.'

He did as she bade, and as soon as they were in the
garden put her on the ground, when she waddled off as
fast as she could towards the lake, Jem hurrying after
her with an anxious heart, for he knew that his life depended on her success. The goose hunted everywhere,
but in vain. She searched under each chestnut tree,
turning every blade of grass with her bill—nothing to be
seen, and evening was drawing on!

Suddenly the dwarf noticed a big old tree standing
alone on the other side of the lake. 'Look,' cried he, 'let
us try our luck there.'

The goose fluttered and skipped in front, and he ran
after as fast as his little legs could carry him. The tree
cast a wide shadow, and it was almost dark beneath it,
but suddenly the goose stood still, flapped her wings with
joy, and plucked something, which she held out to her
astonished friend, saying: 'There it is, and there is more
growing here, so you will have no lack of it.'

The dwarf stood gazing at the plant. It gave out a
strong sweet scent, which reminded him of the day of his
enchantment. The stems and leaves were a bluish green,
and it bore a dark, bright red flower with a yellow edge.

'What a wonder!' cried Long Nose. 'I do believe
this is the very herb which changed me from a squirrel
into my present miserable form. Shall I try an experi-
ment?'

'Not yet,' said the goose. 'Take a good handful of

the herb with you, and let us go to your rooms. We will collect all your money and clothes together, and then we will test the powers of the herb.'

THE GOOSE FINDS THE MAGIC HERB

So they went back to Jem's rooms, and here he gathered together some fifty ducats he had saved, his clothes and shoes, and tied them all up in a bundle. Then he plunged his face into the bunch of herbs, and drew in their perfume.

As he did so, all his limbs began to crack and stretch; he felt his head rising above his shoulders; he glanced down at his nose, and saw it grow smaller and smaller; his chest and back grew flat, and his legs grew long.

The goose looked on in amazement. ' Oh, how big and how beautiful you are ! ' she cried. ' Thank heaven, you are quite changed.'

Jem folded his hands in thanks, as his heart swelled with gratitude. But his joy did not make him forget all he owed to his friend Mimi.

' I owe you my life and my release,' he said, ' for without you I should never have regained my natural shape, and, indeed, would soon have been beheaded. I will now take you back to your father, who will certainly know how to disenchant you.'

The goose accepted his offer with joy, and they managed to slip out of the palace unnoticed by anyone.

They got through the journey without accident, and the wizard soon released his daughter, and loaded Jem with thanks and valuable presents. He lost no time in hastening back to his native town, and his parents were very ready to recognise the handsome, well-made young man as their long-lost son. With the money given him by the wizard he opened a shop, which prospered well, and he lived long and happily.

I must not forget to mention that much disturbance was caused in the palace by Jem's sudden disappearance, for when the grand duke sent orders next day to behead the dwarf, if he had not found the necessary herbs, the dwarf was not to be found. The prince hinted that the duke had allowed his cook to escape, and had therefore broken his word. The matter ended in a great war between the two princes, which was known in history as the ' Herb War.' After many battles and much loss of life, a peace was at last concluded, and this peace became known as the ' Pasty Peace,' because at the banquet given in its honour the prince's cook dished up the Queen of Pasties—the Suzeraine—and the grand duke declared it to be quite excellent.

THE NUNDA, EATER OF PEOPLE

ONCE upon a time there lived a sultan who loved his garden dearly, and planted it with trees and flowers and fruits from all parts of the world. He went to see them three times every day: first at seven o'clock, when he got up, then at three, and lastly at half-past five. There was no plant and no vegetable which escaped his eye, but he lingered longest of all before his one date tree.

Now the sultan had seven sons. Six of them he was proud of, for they were strong and manly, but the youngest he disliked, for he spent all his time among the women of the house. The sultan had talked to him, and he paid no heed; and he had beaten him, and he paid no heed; and he had tied him up, and he paid no heed, till at last his father grew tired of trying to make him change his ways, and let him alone.

Time passed, and one day the sultan, to his great joy, saw signs of fruit on his date tree. And he told his vizir, ' My date tree is bearing; ' and he told the officers, ' My date tree is bearing; ' and he told the judges, ' My date tree is bearing; ' and he told all the rich men of the town.

He waited patiently for some days till the dates were nearly ripe, and then he called his six sons, and said: ' One of you must watch the date tree till the dates are ripe, for if it is not watched the slaves will steal them, and I shall not have any for another year.'

And the eldest son answered, ' I will go, father,' and he went.

The first thing the youth did was to summon his slaves, and bid them beat drums all night under the date tree, for he feared to fall asleep. So the slaves beat the drums, and the young man danced till four o'clock, and then it grew so cold he could dance no longer, and one of the slaves said to him : ' It is getting light ; the tree is safe ; lie down, master, and go to sleep.'

So he lay down and slept, and his slaves slept likewise.

A few minutes went by, and a bird flew down from a neighbouring thicket, and ate all the dates, without leaving a single one. And when the tree was stripped bare, the bird went as it had come. Soon after, one of the slaves woke up and looked for the dates, but there were no dates to see. Then he ran to the young man and shook him, saying :

' Your father set you to watch the tree, and you have not watched, and the dates have all been eaten by a bird.'

The lad jumped up and ran to the tree to see for himself, but there was not a date anywhere. And he cried aloud, ' What am I to say to my father ? Shall I tell him that the dates have been stolen, or that a great rain fell and a great storm blew ? But he will send me to gather them up and bring them to him, and there are none to bring ! Shall I tell him that Bedouins drove me away, and when I returned there were no dates ? And he will answer, " You had slaves, did they not fight with the Bedouins ? " It is the truth that will be best, and that will I tell him.'

Then he went straight to his father, and found him sitting in his verandah with his five sons round him ; and the lad bowed his head.

' Give me the news from the garden,' said the sultan.

And the youth answered, ' The dates have all been eaten by some bird : there is not one left.'

The sultan was silent for a moment: then he asked, 'Where were you when the bird came ?'

The lad answered : 'I watched the date tree till the cocks were crowing and it was getting light; then I lay down for a little, and I slept. When I woke a slave was standing over me, and he said, "There is not one date left on the tree !" And I went to the date tree, and saw it was true ; and that is what I have to tell you.'

And the sultan replied, 'A son like you is only good for eating and sleeping. I have no use for you. Go your way, and when my date tree bears again, I will send another son ; perhaps he will watch better.'

So he waited many months, till the tree was covered with more dates than any tree had ever borne before. When they were near ripening he sent one of his sons to the garden : saying, 'My son, I am longing to taste those dates : go and watch over them, for to-day's sun will bring them to perfection.'

And the lad answered : 'My father, I am going now, and to-morrow, when the sun has passed the hour of seven, bid a slave come and gather the dates.'

'Good,' said the sultan.

The youth went to the tree, and lay down and slept. And about midnight he arose to look at the tree, and the dates were all there—beautiful dates, swinging in bunches.

'Ah, my father will have a feast, indeed,' thought he. 'What a fool my brother was not to take more heed ! Now he is in disgrace, and we know him no more. Well, I will watch till the bird comes. I should like to see what manner of bird it is.'

And he sat and read till the cocks crew and it grew light, and the dates were still on the tree.

'Oh my father will have his dates; they are all safe now,' he thought to himself. 'I will make myself comfortable against this tree,' and he leaned against the trunk, and sleep came on him, and the bird flew down and ate all the dates.

When the sun rose, the head-man came and looked for the dates, and there were no dates. And he woke the young man, and said to him, ' Look at the tree.'

And the young man looked, and there were no dates. And his ears were stopped, and his legs trembled, and his tongue grew heavy at the thought of the sultan. His slave became frightened as he looked at him, and asked, ' My master, what is it? '

He answered, ' I have no pain anywhere, but I am ill everywhere. My whole body is well, and my whole body is sick   I fear my father, for did I not say to him, " To-morrow at seven you shall taste the dates " ?   And he will drive me away, as he drove away my brother !   I will go away myself, before he sends me.'

Then he got up and took a road that led straight past the palace, but he had not walked many steps before he met a man carrying a large silver dish, covered with a white cloth to cover the dates. And the young man said, ' The dates are not ripe yet; you must return to-morrow.'

And the slave went with him to the palace, where the sultan was sitting with his four sons.

' Good greeting, master ! ' said the youth.

And the sultan answered, ' Have you seen the man I sent ? '

' I have, master ; but the dates are not yet ripe.'

But the sultan did not believe his words, and said : ' This second year I have eaten no dates, because of my sons.   Go your ways, you are my son no longer ! '

And the sultan looked at the four sons that were left him, and promised rich gifts to whichever of them would bring him the dates from the tree. But year by year passed, and he never got them. One son tried to keep himself awake with playing cards ; another mounted a horse and rode round and round the tree, while the two others, whom their father as a last hope sent together, lit bonfires. But whatever they did, the result was always the same. Towards dawn they fell asleep, and the bird ate the dates on the tree.

The sixth year had come, and the dates on the tree were thicker than ever. And the head-man went to the palace and told the sultan what he had seen. But the sultan only shook his head, and said sadly, ' What is that to me ? I have had seven sons, yet for five years a bird has devoured my dates ; and this year it will be the same as ever.'

Now the youngest son was sitting in the kitchen, as was his custom, when he heard his father say those words. And he rose up, and went to his father, and knelt before him. ' Father, this year you shall eat dates,' cried he. ' And on the tree are five great bunches, and each bunch I will give to a separate nation, for the nations in the town are five. This time, I will watch the date tree myself.' But his father and his mother laughed heartily, and thought his words idle talk.

One day, news was brought to the sultan that the dates were ripe, and he ordered one of his men to go and watch the tree. His son, who happened to be standing by, heard the order, and he said :

' How is it that you have bidden a man to watch the tree, when I, your son, am left ? '

And his father answered, ' Ah, six were of no use, and where they failed, will you succeed ? '

But the boy replied : ' Have patience to-day, and let me go, and to-morrow you shall see whether I bring you dates or not.'

' Let the child go, Master,' said his wife ; ' perhaps we shall eat the dates—or perhaps we shall not—but let him go.'

And the sultan answered : ' I do not refuse to let him go, but my heart distrusts him. His brothers all promised fair, and what did they do ? '

But the boy entreated, saying, ' Father, if you and I and mother be alive to-morrow, you shall eat the dates.'

' Go then,' said his father.

When the boy reached the garden, he told the slaves to leave him, and to return home themselves and sleep. When he was alone, he laid himself down and slept fast till one o'clock, when he arose, and sat opposite the date tree. Then he took some Indian corn out of one fold of his dress, and some sandy grit out of another. And he chewed the corn till he felt he was growing sleepy, and then he put some grit into his mouth, and that kept him awake till the bird came.

It looked about at first without seeing him, and whispering to itself, ' There is no one here,' fluttered lightly on to the tree and stretched out his beak for the dates. Then the boy stole softly up, and caught it by the wing.

The bird turned and flew quickly away, but the boy never let go, not even when they soared high into the air.

' Son of Adam,' the bird said when the tops of the mountains looked small below them, ' if you fall, you will be dead long before you reach the ground, so go your way, and let me go mine.'

But the boy answered, ' Wherever you go, I will go with you. You cannot get rid of me.'

' I did not eat your dates,' persisted the bird, ' and the day is dawning. Leave me to go my way.'

But again the boy answered him : ' My six brothers are hateful to my father because you came and stole the dates, and to-day my father shall see you, and my brothers shall see you, and all the people of the town, great and small, shall see you. And my father's heart will rejoice.'

' Well, if you will not leave me, I will throw you off,' said the bird.

So it flew up higher still—so high that the earth shone like one of the other stars.

' How much of you will be left if you fall from here ? ' asked the bird.

'If I die, I die,' said the boy, 'but I will not leave you.'

And the bird saw it was no use talking, and went down to the earth again.

'Here you are at home, so let me go my way,' it begged once more ; 'or at least make a covenant with me.'

'What covenant?' said the boy.

'Save me from the sun,' replied the bird, 'and I will save you from rain.'

'How can you do that, and how can I tell if I can trust you?'

'Pull a feather from my tail, and put it in the fire, and if you want me I will come to you, wherever I am.'

And the boy answered, 'Well, I agree ; go your way.'

'Farewell, my friend. When you call me, if it is from the depths of the sea, I will come.'

The lad watched the bird out of sight ; then he went straight to the date tree. And when he saw the dates his heart was glad, and his body felt stronger and his eyes brighter than before. And he laughed out loud with joy, and said to himself, 'This is *my* luck, mine, Sit-in-the-kitchen ! Farewell, date tree, I am going to lie down. What ate you will eat you no more.'

The sun was high in the sky before the head-man, whose business it was, came to look at the date tree, expecting to find it stripped of all its fruit, but when he saw the dates so thick that they almost hid the leaves he ran back to his house, and beat a big drum till everybody came running, and even the little children wanted to know what had happened.

'What is it ? What is it, head-man?' cried they.

'Ah, it is not a son that the master has, but a lion ! This day Sit-in-the-kitchen has uncovered his face before his father ! '

'But how, head-man ? '

'To-day the people may eat the dates.

'Is it true, head-man?'

'Oh yes, it is true, but let him sleep till each man has brought forth a present. He who has fowls, let him take fowls; he who has a goat, let him take a goat; he who has rice, let him take rice.' And the people did as he had said.

Then they took the drum, and went to the tree where the boy lay sleeping.

And they picked him up, and carried him away, with horns and clarionets and drums, with clappings of hands and shrieks of joy, straight to his father's house.

When his father heard the noise and saw the baskets made of green leaves, brimming over with dates, and his son borne high on the necks of slaves, his heart leaped, and he said to himself 'To-day at last I shall eat dates.' And he called his wife to see what her son had done, and ordered his soldiers to take the boy and bring him to his father.

'What news, my son?' said he.

'News? I have no news, except that if you will open your mouth you shall see what dates taste like.' And he plucked a date, and put it into his father's mouth.

'Ah! You are indeed my son,' cried the sultan. 'You do not take after those fools, those good-for-nothings. But, tell me, what did you do with the bird, for it was you, and you only who watched for it?'

'Yes, it was I who watched for it and who saw it. And it will not come again, neither for its life, nor for your life, nor for the lives of your children.'

'Oh, once I had six sons, and now I have only one. It is you, whom I called a fool, who have given me the dates: as for the others, I want none of them.

But his wife rose up and went to him, and said, 'Master, do not, I pray you, reject them,' and she entreated long, till the sultan granted her prayer, for she loved the six elder ones more than her last one.

So they all lived quietly at home, till the sultan's cat went and caught a calf. And the owner of the calf went and told the sultan, but he answered, 'The cat is mine, and the calf mine,' and the man dared not complain further.

Two days after, the cat caught a cow, and the sultan was told, ' Master, the cat has caught a cow,' but he only said, ' It was my cow and my cat.'

And the cat waited a few days, and then it caught a donkey, and they told the sultan, ' Master, the cat has caught a donkey,' and he said, ' My cat and my donkey.' Next it was a horse, and after that a camel, and when the sultan was told he said, ' You don't like this cat, and want me to kill it. And I shall not kill it. Let it eat the camel : let it even eat a man.'

And it waited till the next day, and caught some one's child. And the sultan was told, ' The cat has caught a child.' And he said, ' The cat is mine and the child mine.' Then it caught a grown-up man.

After that the cat left the town and took up its abode in a thicket near the road. So if any one passed, going for water, it devoured him. If it saw a cow going to feed, it devoured him. If it saw a goat, it devoured him. Whatever went along that road the cat caught and ate.

Then the people went to the sultan in a body, and told him of all the misdeeds of that cat. But he answered as before, ' The cat is mine and the people are mine.' And no man dared kill the cat, which grew bolder and bolder, and at last came into the town to look for its prey.

One day, the sultan said to his six sons, ' I am going into the country, to see how the wheat is growing, and you shall come with me.' They went on merrily along the road, till they came to a thicket, when out sprang the cat, and killed three of the sons.

' The cat ! The cat ! ' shrieked the soldiers who were with him. And this time the sultan said :

' Seek for it and kill it. It is no longer a cat, but a demon ! '

And the soldiers answered him, 'Did we not tell you, master, what the cat was doing, and did you not say, " My cat and my people " ? '

And he answered : ' True, I said it.'

Now the youngest son had not gone with the rest, but had stayed at home with his mother ; and when he heard that his brothers had been killed by the cat he said, ' Let me go, that it may slay me also.' His mother entreated him not to leave her, but he would not listen, and he took his sword and a spear and some rice cakes, and went after the cat, which by this time had run off to a great distance.

The lad spent many days hunting the cat, which now bore the name of ' The Nunda, eater of people,' but though he killed many wild animals he saw no trace of the enemy he was hunting for. There was no beast, however fierce, that he was afraid of, till at last his father and mother begged him to give up the chase after the Nunda.

But he answered : ' What I have said, I cannot take back. If I am to die, then I die, but every day I must go and seek for the Nunda.'

And again his father offered him what he would, even the crown itself, but the boy would hear nothing, and went on his way.

Many times his slaves came and told him, ' We have seen footprints, and to-day we shall behold the Nunda.' But the footprints never turned out to be those of the Nunda. They wandered far through deserts and through forests, and at length came to the foot of a great hill. And something in the boy's soul whispered that here was the end of all their seeking, and to-day they would find the Nunda.

But before they began to climb the mountain the boy ordered his slaves to cook some rice, and they rubbed the stick to make a fire, and when the fire was kindled they cooked the rice and ate it. Then they began their climb.

THE PRINCE FINDS THE NUNDA

Suddenly, when they had almost reached the top, a slave who was on in front cried :

'Master ! Master ! ' And the boy pushed on to where the slave stood, and the slave said :

' Cast your eyes down to the foot of the mountain.' And the boy looked, and his soul told him it was the Nunda.

And he crept down with his spear in his hand, and then he stopped and gazed below him.

'This *must* be the real Nunda,' thought he. ' My mother told me its ears were small, and this one's are small. She told me it was broad and not long, and this is broad and not long. She told me it had spots like a civet-cat, and this has spots like a civet-cat.'

Then he left the Nunda lying asleep at the foot of the mountain, and went back to his slaves.

' We will feast to-day,' he said ; ' make cakes of batter, and bring water,' and they ate and drank. And when they had finished he bade them hide the rest of the food in the thicket, that if they slew the Nunda they might return and eat and sleep before going back to the town. And the slaves did as he bade them.

It was now afternoon, and the lad said : ' It is time we went after the Nunda.' And they went till they reached the bottom and came to a great forest which lay between them and the Nunda.

Here the lad stopped, and ordered every slave that wore two cloths to cast one away and tuck up the other between his legs. ' For,' said he, ' the wood is not a little one. Perhaps we may be caught by the thorns, or perhaps we may have to run before the Nunda, and the cloth might bind our legs, and cause us to fall before it.'

And they answered, ' Good, master,' and did as he bade them. Then they crawled on their hands and knees to where the Nunda lay asleep.

Noiselessly they crept along till they were quite close to it ; then, at a sign from the boy, they threw their spears. The Nunda did not stir: the spears had done their work, but a great fear seized them all, and they ran away and climbed the mountain.

The sun was setting when they reached the top, and glad they were to take out the fruit and the cakes and the water which they had hidden away, and sit down and rest themselves. And after they had eaten and were filled, they lay down and slept till morning.

When the dawn broke they rose up and cooked more rice, and drank more water. After that they walked all round the back of the mountain to the place where they had left the Nunda, and they saw it stretched out where they had found it, stiff and dead. And they took it up and carried it back to the town, singing as they went, ' He has killed the Nunda, the eater of people.'

And when his father heard the news, and that his son was come, and was bringing the Nunda with him, he felt that the man did not dwell on the earth whose joy was greater than his. And the people bowed down to the boy and gave him presents, and loved him, because he had delivered them from the bondage of fear, and had slain the Nunda

[Adapted from Swahili Tales.]

THE STORY OF HASSEBU

ONCE upon a time there lived a poor woman who had only one child, and he was a little boy called Hassebu. When he ceased to be a baby, and his mother thought it was time for him to learn to read, she sent him to school. And, after he had done with school, he was put into a shop to learn how to make clothes, and did not learn; and he was put to do silversmith's work, and did not learn; and whatsoever he was taught, he did not learn it. His mother never wished him to do anything he did not like, so she said: ' Well, stay at home, my son.' And he stayed at home, eating and sleeping.

One day the boy said to his mother : ' What was my father's business ? '

' He was a very learned doctor,' answered she.

' Where, then, are his books ? ' asked Hassebu.

' Many days have passed, and I have thought nothing of them. But look inside and see if they are there.' So Hassebu looked, and saw they were eaten by insects, all but one book, which he took away and read

He was sitting at home one morning poring over the medicine book, when some neighbours came by and said to his mother : ' Give us this boy, that we may go together to cut wood.' For wood-cutting was their trade, and they loaded several donkeys with the wood, and sold it in the town.

And his mother answered, ' Very well ; to-morrow I will buy him a donkey, and you can all go together.'

So the donkey was bought, and the neighbours came,

and they worked hard all day, and in the evening they brought the wood back into the town, and sold it for a good sum of money. And for six days they went and did the like, but on the seventh it rained, and the wood-cutters ran and hid in the rocks, all but Hassebu, who did not mind wetting, and stayed where he was.

While he was sitting in the place where the wood-cutters had left him, he took up a stone that lay near him, and idly dropped it on the ground. It rang with a hollow sound, and he called to his companions, and said, ' Come here and listen ; the ground seems hollow ! '

' Knock again ! ' cried they. And he knocked and listened.

' Let us dig,' said the boy. And they dug, and found a large pit like a well, filled with honey up to the brim.

' This is better than firewood,' said they ; ' it will bring us more money. And as you have found it, Hassebu, it is you who must go inside and dip out the honey and give to us, and we will take it to the town and sell it, and will divide the money with you.'

The following day each man brought every bowl and vessel he could find at home, and Hassebu filled them all with honey. And this he did every day for three months.

At the end of that time the honey was very nearly finished, and there was only a little left, quite at the bottom, and that was very deep down, so deep that it seemed as if it must be right in the middle of the earth. Seeing this, the men said to Hassebu, ' We will put a rope under your arms, and let you down, so that you may scrape up all the honey that is left, and when you have done we will lower the rope again, and you shall make it fast, and we will draw you up.'

' Very well,' answered the boy, and he went down, and he scraped and scraped till there was not so much honey left as would cover the point of a needle. ' Now I am ready ! ' he cried ; but they consulted together and said, ' Let us leave him there inside the pit, and take his share of the money, and we will tell his mother, " Your son was caught by a lion and carried off into the forest, and we tried to follow him, but could not." '

Then they arose and went into the town and told his mother as they had agreed, and she wept much and made her mourning for many months. And when the men were dividing the money, one said, ' Let us send a little to our friend's mother,' and they sent some to her ; and every day one took her rice, and one oil ; one took her meat, and one took her cloth, every day.

It did not take long for Hassebu to find out that his companions had left him to die in the pit, but he had a brave heart, and hoped that he might be able to find a way out for himself. So he at once began to explore the pit and found it ran back a long way underground. And by night he slept, and by day he took a little of the honey he had gathered and ate it ; and so many days passed by.

One morning, while he was sitting on a rock having his breakfast, a large scorpion dropped down at his feet, and he took a stone and killed it, fearing it would sting him. Then suddenly the thought darted into his head, ' This scorpion must have come from somewhere ! Perhaps there is a hole. I will go and look for it,' and he felt all round the walls of the pit till he found a very little hole in the roof of the pit, with a tiny glimmer of light at the far end of it. Then his heart felt glad, and he took out his knife and dug and dug, till the little hole became a big one, and he could wriggle himself through. And when he had got outside, he saw a large open space in front of him, and a path leading out of it.

He went along the path, on and on, till he reached a large house, with a golden door standing open. Inside was a great hall, and in the middle of the hall a throne set with precious stones and a sofa spread with the softest cushions. And he went in and lay down on it, and fell fast asleep, for he had wandered far.

By-and-by there was a sound of people coming through the courtyard, and the measured tramp of soldiers. This was the King of the Snakes coming in state to his palace.

They entered the hall, but all stopped in surprise at finding a man lying on the king's own bed. The soldiers wished to kill him at once, but the king said, 'Leave him alone, put me on a chair,' and the soldiers who were carrying him knelt on the floor, and he slid from their shoulders on to a chair. When he was comfortably seated, he turned to his soldiers, and bade them wake the stranger gently. And they woke him, and he sat up and saw many snakes all round him, and one of them very beautiful, decked in royal robes.

'Who are you?' asked Hassebu.

'I am the King of the Snakes,' was the reply, 'and this is my palace. And will you tell me who you are, and where you come from?'

'My name is Hassebu, but whence I come I know not, nor whither I go.'

'Then stay for a little with me,' said the king, and he bade his soldiers bring water from the spring and fruits from the forest, and to set them before the guest.

For some days Hassebu rested and feasted in the palace of the King of the Snakes, and then he began to long for his mother and his own country. So he said to the King of the Snakes, 'Send me home, I pray.'

But the King of the Snakes answered, 'When you go home, you will do me evil!'

'I will do you no evil,' replied Hassebu; 'send me home, I pray.'

But the king said, 'I know it. If I send you home, you will come back, and kill me. I dare not do it.' But Hassebu begged so hard that at last the king said, 'Swear that when you get home you will not go to

bathe where many people are gathered.' And Hassebu
swore, and the king ordered his soldiers to take Hassebu

Hassebu & the Serpent-King

in sight of his native city. Then he went straight to his
mother's house, and the heart of his mother was glad.

Now the Sultan of the city was very ill, and all the

wise men said that the only thing to cure him was the flesh of the King of the Snakes, and that the only man who could get it was a man with a strange mark on his chest. So the Vizir had set people to watch at the public baths, to see if such a man came there.

For three days Hassebu remembered his promise to the King of the Snakes, and did not go near the baths ; then came a morning so hot he could hardly breathe, and he forgot all about it.

The moment he had slipped off his robe he was taken before the Vizir, who said to him, ' Lead us to the place where the King of the Snakes lives.'

' I do not know it ! ' answered he, but the Vizir did not believe him, and had him bound and beaten till his back was all torn.

Then Hassebu cried, ' Loose me, that I may take you.'

They went together a long, long way, till they reached the palace of the King of the Snakes.

And Hassebu said to the King : ' It was not I : look at my back and you will see how they drove me to it.'

' Who has beaten you like this ? ' asked the King.

' It was the Vizir,' replied Hassebu.

' Then I am already dead,' said the King sadly, ' but you must carry me there yourself.'

So Hassebu carried him. And on the way the King said, ' When I arrive, I shall be killed, and my flesh will be cooked. But take some of the water that I am boiled in, and put it in a bottle and lay it on one side. The Vizir will tell you to drink it, but be careful not to do so. Then take some more of the water, and drink it, and you will become a great physician, and the third supply you will give to the Sultan. And when the Vizir comes to you and asks, " Did you drink what I gave you ? " you must answer, " I did, and this is for you," and he will drink it and die, and your soul will rest.'

And they went their way into the town, and all happened as the King of the Snakes had said.

And the Sultan loved Hassebu, who became a great physician, and cured many sick people. But he was always sorry for the poor King of the Snakes.

[Adapted from Swahili Tales.]

THE MAIDEN WITH THE WOODEN HELMET

In a little village in the country of Japan there lived long, long ago a man and his wife. For many years they were happy and prosperous, but bad times came, and at last nothing was left them but their daughter, who was as beautiful as the morning. The neighbours were very kind, and would have done anything they could to help their poor friends, but the old couple felt that since everything had changed they would rather go elsewhere, so one day they set off to bury themselves in the country, taking their daughter with them.

Now the mother and daughter had plenty to do in keeping the house clean and looking after the garden, but the man would sit for hours together gazing straight in front of him, and thinking of the riches that once were his. Each day he grew more and more wretched, till at length he took to his bed and never got up again.

His wife and daughter wept bitterly for his loss, and it was many months before they could take pleasure in anything. Then one morning the mother suddenly looked at the girl, and found that she had grown still more lovely than before. Once her heart would have been glad at the sight, but now that they two were alone in the world she feared some harm might come of it. So, like a good mother, she tried to teach her daughter all she knew, and to bring her up to be always busy, so that she would never have time to think about herself. And the girl was a good girl, and listened to all her mother's lessons, and so the years passed away.

At last one wet spring the mother caught cold, and though in the beginning she did not pay much attention to it, she gradually grew more and more ill, and knew that she had not long to live. Then she called her daughter and told her that very soon she would be alone in the world; that she must take care of herself, as there would be no one to take care of her. And because it was more difficult for beautiful women to pass unheeded than for others, she bade her fetch a wooden helmet out of the next room, and put it on her head, and pull it low down over her brows, so that nearly the whole of her face should lie in its shadow. The girl did as she was bid, and her beauty was so hidden beneath the wooden cap, which covered up all her hair, that she might have gone through any crowd, and no one would have looked twice at her. And when she saw this the heart of the mother was at rest, and she lay back in her bed and died.

The girl wept for many days, but by-and-by she felt that, being alone in the world, she must go and get work, for she had only herself to depend upon. There was none to be got by staying where she was, so she made her clothes into a bundle, and walked over the hills till she reached the house of the man who owned the fields in that part of the country. And she took service with him and laboured for him early and late, and every night when she went to bed she was at peace, for she had not forgotten one thing that she had promised her mother ; and, however hot the sun might be, she always kept the wooden helmet on her head, and the people gave her the nickname of Hatschihime.

In spite, however, of all her care the fame of her beauty spread abroad : many of the impudent young men that are always to be found in the world stole softly up behind her while she was at work, and tried to lift off the wooden helmet. But the girl would have nothing to say to them, and only bade them be off; then they began to talk to her, but she never answered them, and went on with what she was doing, though her wages were low and food not very plentiful. Still she could manage to live, and that was enough.

THE IMPVDENT YOVNG MEN

One day her master happened to pass through the field where she was working, and was struck by her industry and stopped to watch her. After a while he put one or two questions to her, and then led her into

THE GIRL WITH THE WOODEN HELMET

his house, and told her that henceforward her only duty should be to tend his sick wife. From this time the girl felt as if all her troubles were ended, but the worst of them was yet to come.

Not very long after Hatschihime had become maid to the sick woman, the eldest son of the house returned home from Kioto, where he had been studying all sorts of things. He was tired of the splendours of the town and its pleasures, and was glad enough to be back in the green country, among the peach-blossoms and sweet flowers. Strolling about in the early morning, he caught sight of the girl with the odd wooden helmet on her head, and immediately he went to his mother to ask who she was, and where she came from, and why she wore that strange thing over her face. His mother answered that it was a whim, and nobody could persuade her to lay it aside; whereat the young man laughed, but kept his thoughts to himself.

One hot day, however, he happened to be going towards home when he caught sight of his mother's waiting maid kneeling by a little stream that flowed through the garden, splashing some water over her face. The helmet was pushed on one side, and as the youth stood watching from behind a tree he had a glimpse of the girl's great beauty; and he determined that no one else should be his wife. But when he told his family of his resolve to marry her they were very angry, and made up all sorts of wicked stories about her. However, they might have spared themselves the trouble, as he knew it was only idle talk. 'I have merely to remain firm,' thought he, 'and they will have to give in.' It was such a good match for the girl that it never occurred to anyone that she would refuse the young man, but so it was. It would not be right, she felt, to make a quarrel in the house, and though in secret she wept bitterly, for a long while, nothing would make her change her mind. At length one night her mother appeared to her in a dream, and bade her marry the young man. So the next time he asked her—as he did nearly every day—to his surprise and joy she consented. The parents then saw they had better make the best of a bad business, and set about making the grand preparations suitable to the occasion. Of course the neighbours said a great many ill-natured things about the wooden helmet, but the bridegroom was too happy to care, and only laughed at them.

When everything was ready for the feast, and the bride was dressed in the most beautiful embroidered dress to be found in Japan, the maids took hold of the helmet to lift it off her head, so that they might do her hair in the latest fashion. But the helmet would not come, and the harder they pulled, the faster it seemed to be, till the poor girl yelled with pain. Hearing her cries the bridegroom ran in and soothed her, and declared that she should be married in the helmet, as she could not be married without. Then the ceremonies began, and the bridal pair sat together, and the cup of wine was brought them, out of which they had to drink. And when they had drunk it all, and the cup was empty, a wonderful thing happened. The helmet suddenly burst with a loud noise, and fell in pieces on the ground; and as they all turned to look they found the floor covered with precious stones which had fallen out of it. But the guests were less astonished at the brilliancy of the diamonds than at the beauty of the bride, which was beyond anything they had ever seen or heard of. The night was passed in singing and dancing, and then the bride and bridegroom went to their own house, where they lived till they died, and had many children, who were famous throughout Japan for their goodness and beauty.

[Japanische Märchen.]

THE MONKEY AND THE JELLY-FISH

CHILDREN must often have wondered why jelly-fishes have no shells, like so many of the creatures that are washed up every day on the beach. In old times this was not so; the jelly-fish had as hard a shell as any of them, but he lost it through his own fault, as may be seen in this story.

The sea-queen Otohime, whom you read of in the story of Uraschimatoro, grew suddenly very ill. The swiftest messengers were sent hurrying to fetch the best doctors from every country under the sea, but it was all of no use ; the queen grew rapidly worse instead of better. Every-one had almost given up hope, when one day a doctor arrived who was cleverer than the rest, and said that the only thing that would cure her was the liver of an ape. Now apes do not dwell under the sea, so a council of the wisest heads in the nation was called to consider the question how a liver could be obtained. At length it was decided that the turtle, whose prudence was well known, should swim to land and contrive to catch a living ape and bring him safely to the ocean kingdom.

It was easy enough for the council to entrust this mission to the turtle, but not at all so easy for him to fulfil it. However he swam to a part of the coast that was covered with tall trees, where he thought the apes were likely to be ; for he was old, and had seen many things. It was some time before he caught sight of any monkeys, and he often grew tired with watching for them, so that one hot day he fell fast asleep, in spite of all his efforts to keep awake. By-and-by some apes, who had been peeping at him from the tops of the trees, where they had been carefully hidden from the turtle's eyes, stole noiselessly down, and stood round staring at him, for they had never seen a turtle before, and did not know what to make of it. At last one young monkey, bolder than the rest, stooped down and stroked the shining shell that the strange new creature wore on its back. The movement, gentle though it was, woke the turtle. With one sweep he seized the monkey's hand in his mouth, and held it tight, in spite of every effort to pull it away. The other apes, seeing that the turtle was not to be trifled with, ran off, leaving their young brother to his fate.

Then the turtle said to the monkey, 'If you will be quiet, and do what I tell you, I won't hurt you. But you must get on my back and come with me.'

The monkey, seeing there was no help for it, did as he was bid; indeed he could not have resisted, as his hand was still in the turtle's mouth.

Delighted at having secured his prize, the turtle hastened back to the shore and plunged quickly into the water. He swam faster than he had ever done before, and soon reached the royal palace. Shouts of joy broke forth from the attendants when he was seen approaching, and some of them ran to tell the queen that the monkey was there, and that before long she would be as well as ever she was. In fact, so great was their relief that they gave the monkey such a kind welcome, and were so anxious to make him happy and comfortable, that he soon forgot all the fears that had beset him as to his fate, and was generally quite at his ease, though every now and then a fit of home-sickness would come over him, and he would hide himself in some dark corner till it had passed away.

It was during one of these attacks of sadness that a jelly-fish happened to swim by. At that time jelly-fishes

THE MONKEY BROUGHT TO OTOHIME

had shells. At the sight of the gay and lively monkey crouching under a tall rock, with his eyes closed and his head bent, the jelly-fish was filled with pity, and stopped, saying, 'Ah, poor fellow, no wonder you weep ; a few days more, and they will come and kill you and give your liver to the queen to eat.'

The monkey shrank back horrified at these words and asked the jelly-fish what crime he had committed that deserved death.

' Oh, none at all,' replied the jelly-fish, ' but your liver is the only thing that will cure our queen, and how can we get at it without killing you ? You had better submit to your fate, and make no noise about it, for though I pity you from my heart there is no way of helping you.' Then he went away, leaving the ape cold with horror.

At first he felt as if his liver was already being taken from his body, but soon he began to wonder if there was no means of escaping this terrible death, and at length he invented a plan which he thought would do. For a few days he pretended to be gay and happy as before, but when the sun went in, and rain fell in torrents, he wept and howled from dawn to dark, till the turtle, who was his head keeper, heard him, and came to see what was the matter. Then the monkey told him that before he left home he had hung his liver out on a bush to dry, and if it was always going to rain like this it would become quite useless. And the rogue made such a fuss and moaning that he would have melted a heart of stone, and nothing would content him but that somebody should carry him back to land and let him fetch his liver again.

The queen's councillors were not the wisest of people, and they decided between them that the turtle should take the monkey back to his native land and allow him to get his liver off the bush, but desired the turtle not to lose sight of his charge for a single moment. The monkey knew this, but trusted to his power of beguiling the turtle when the time came, and mounted on his back with feelings of joy, which he was, however, careful to conceal. They set out, and in a few hours were wandering about the forest where the ape had first been caught, and when the monkey saw his family peering out from the tree tops, he swung himself up by the nearest branch, just managing to save his hind leg from being seized by the turtle. He told them all the dreadful things that had happened to him, and gave a war cry which brought the rest of the tribe from the neighbouring hills. At a word from him they rushed in a body to the unfortunate turtle, threw him on his back, and tore off the shield that covered his body. Then with mocking words they hunted him to the shore, and into the sea, which he was only too thankful to reach alive. Faint and exhausted he entered the queen's palace, for the cold of the water struck upon his naked body, and made him feel ill and miserable. But wretched though he was, he had to appear before the queen's advisers and tell them all that had befallen him, and how he had suffered the monkey to escape. But, as sometimes happens, the turtle was allowed to go scot-free, and had his shell given back to him, and all the punishment fell on the poor jelly-fish, who was condemned by the queen to go shieldless for ever after.

[Japanische Märchen.]

THE HEADLESS DWARFS

THERE was once a minister who spent his whole time in trying to find a servant who would undertake to ring the church bells at midnight, in addition to all his other duties.

Of course it was not everyone who cared to get up in the middle of the night, when he had been working hard all day; still, a good many had agreed to do it. But the strange thing was that no sooner had the servant set forth to perform his task than he disappeared, as if the earth had swallowed him up. No bells were rung, and no ringer ever came back. The minister did his best to keep the matter secret, but it leaked out for all that, and the end of it was that no one would enter his service. Indeed, there were even those who whispered that the minister himself had murdered the missing men !

It was to no purpose that Sunday after Sunday the minister gave out from his pulpit that double wages would be paid to anyone that would fulfil the sacred duty of ringing the bells of the church.' No one took the slightest notice of any offer he might make, and the poor man was in despair, when one day, as he was standing at his house door, a youth known in the village as Clever Hans came up to him. ' I am tired of living with a miser who will not give me enough to eat and drink,' said he, ' and I am ready to do all you want.' ' Very good, my son,' replied the minister, ' you shall have the chance of proving your courage this very night. To-morrow we will settle what your wages are to be.'

Hans was quite content with this proposal, and went straight into the kitchen to begin his work, not knowing that his new master was quite as stingy as his old one. In the hope that his presence might be a restraint upon them, the minister used to sit at the table during his servants' meals, and would exhort them to drink much and often, thinking that they would not be able to eat as well, and beef was dearer than beer. But in Hans he had met his match, and the minister soon found to his cost that in his case at any rate a full cup did not mean an empty plate.

About an hour before midnight, Hans entered the church and locked the door behind him, but what was his surprise when, in place of the darkness and silence he expected, he found the church brilliantly lighted, and a crowd of people sitting round a table playing cards. Hans felt no fear at this strange sight, or was prudent enough to hide it if he did, and, going up to the table, sat down amongst the players. One of them looked up and asked, ' My friend, what are you doing here ? ' and Hans gazed at him for a moment, then laughed and answered, ' Well, if anybody has a right to put that question, it is I ! And if *I* do not put it, it will certainly be wiser for you not to do so ! '

Then he picked up some cards, and played with the unknown men as if he had known them all his life. The luck was on his side, and soon the money of the other gamblers found its way from their pockets into his. On the stroke of midnight the cock crew, and in an instant lights, table, cards, and people all had vanished, and Hans was left alone.

He groped about for some time, till he found the staircase in the tower, and then began to feel his way up the steps.

On the first landing a glimmer of light came through a slit in the wall, and he saw a tiny man sitting there, without a head. ' Ho ! ho ! my little fellow, what are

A DWARF WAS IN THE BELL

H. J. FORD

you doing there? ' asked Hans, and, without waiting for an answer, gave him a kick which sent him flying down the stairs. Then he climbed higher still, and finding as he went dumb watchers sitting on every landing, treated them as he had done the first.

At last he reached the top, and as he paused for a moment to look round him he saw another headless man cowering in the very bell itself, waiting till Hans should seize the bell-pull in order to strike him a blow with the clapper, which would soon have made an end of him.

' Stop, my little friend! ' cried Hans. ' That is not part of the bargain! Perhaps you saw how your comrades walked down stairs, and you are going after them. But as you are in the highest place you shall make a more dignified exit, and follow them through the window! '

With these words he began to climb the ladder, in order to take the little man from the bell and carry out his threat.

At this the dwarf cried out imploringly, ' Oh, brother! spare my life, and I promise that neither I nor my comrades will ever trouble you any more. I am small and weak, but who knows whether some day I shall not be able to reward you.'

' You wretched little shrimp,' replied Hans, ' a great deal of good your gratitude is likely to do me! But as I happen to be feeling in a cheerful mood to-night I will let you have your life. But take care how you come across me again, or you may not escape so easily! '

The headless man thanked him humbly, slid hastily down the bell rope, and ran down the steps of the tower as if he had left a fire behind him. Then Hans began to ring lustily.

When the minister heard the sound of the midnight bells he wondered greatly, but rejoiced that he had at last found some one to whom he could trust this duty.

Hans rang the bells for some time, then went to the hay-
loft, and fell fast asleep.

Now it was the custom of the minister to get up very
early, and to go round to make sure that the men were
all at their work. This morning everyone was in his
place except Hans, and no one knew anything about him.
Nine o'clock came, and no Hans, but when eleven struck
the minister began to fear that he had vanished like the
ringers who had gone before him. When, however, the
servants all gathered round the table for dinner, Hans at
last made his appearance stretching himself and yawning.

'Where have you been all this time?' asked the
minister.

'Asleep,' said Hans.

'Asleep!' exclaimed the minister in astonishment.
'You don't mean to tell me that you can go on sleeping
till mid-day?'

'That is exactly what I do mean,' replied Hans. 'If
one works in the night one must sleep in the day, just
as if one works in the day one sleeps in the night. If
you can find somebody else to ring the bells at midnight
I am ready to begin work at dawn; but if you want me
to ring them I must go on sleeping till noon at the very
earliest.'

The minister tried to argue the point with him, but
at length the following agreement was come to. Hans
was to give up the ringing, and was to work like the rest
from sunrise to sunset, with the exception of an hour
after breakfast and an hour after dinner, when he might go
to sleep. 'But, of course,' added the minister carelessly,
'it may happen now and then, especially in winter, when
the days are short, that you will have to work a little
longer, to get something finished.'

'Not at all!' answered Hans. 'Unless I were to leave
off work earlier in summer, I will not do a stroke more
than I have promised, and that is from dawn to dark; so
you know what you have to expect.'

A few weeks later the minister was asked to attend a christening in the neighbouring town. He bade Hans come with him, but, as the town was only a few hours' ride from where he lived, the minister was much surprised to see Hans come forth laden with a bag containing food.

'What are you taking that for?' asked the minister. 'We shall be there before dark.'

'Who knows?' replied Hans. 'Many things may happen to delay our journey, and I need not remind you of our contract that the moment the sun sets I cease to be your servant. If we don't reach the town while it is still daylight I shall leave you to shift for yourself.'

The minister thought he was joking, and made no further remark. But when they had left the village behind them, and had ridden a few miles, they found that snow had fallen during the night, and had been blown by the wind into drifts. This hindered their progress, and by the time they had entered the thick wood which lay between them and their destination the sun was already touching the tops of the trees. The horses ploughed their way slowly through the deep soft snow and as they went Hans kept turning to look at the sun, which lay at their backs.

'Is there anything behind you?' asked the minister. 'Or what is it you are always turning round for?'

'I turn round because I have no eyes in the back of my neck,' said Hans.

'Cease talking nonsense,' replied the minister, 'and give all your mind to getting us to the town before nightfall.'

Hans did not answer, but rode on steadily, though every now and then he cast a glance over his shoulder.

When they arrived in the middle of the wood the sun sank altogether. Then Hans reined up his horse, took his knapsack, and jumped out of the sledge.

'What are you doing? Are you mad?' asked the

minister, but Hans answered quietly, ' The sun is set and my work is over, and I am going to camp here for the night.'

In vain the master prayed and threatened, and promised Hans a large reward if he would only drive him on. The young man was not to be moved.

' Are you not ashamed to urge me to break my word?' said he. ' If you want to reach the town to-night you must go alone. The hour of my freedom has struck, and I cannot go with you.'

' My good Hans,' entreated the minister, ' I really ought not to leave you here. Consider what danger you would be in! Yonder, as you see, a gallows is set up, and two evil-doers are hanging on it. You could not possibly sleep with such ghastly neighbours.'

' Why not?' asked Hans. ' Those gallows birds hang high in the air, and my camp will be on the ground; we shall have nothing to do with each other.' As he spoke, he turned his back on the minister, and went his way.

There was no help for it, and the minister had to push on by himself, if he expected to arrive in time for the christening. His friends were much surprised to see him drive up without a coachman, and thought some accident had happened. But when he told them of his conversation with Hans they did not know which was the most foolish, master or man.

It would have mattered little to Hans had he known what they were saying or thinking of him. He satisfied his hunger with the food he had in his knapsack, lit his pipe, pitched his tent under the boughs of a tree, wrapped himself in his furs, and went sound asleep. After some hours, he was awakened by a sudden noise, and sat up and looked about him. The moon was shining brightly above his head, and close by stood two headless dwarfs, talking angrily. At the sight of Hans the little dwarfs cried out:

' It is he! It is he!' and one of them stepping nearer

Hans·fights·the·headless·dwarfs

exclaimed, ' Ah, my old friend ! it is a lucky chance that
has brought us here. My bones still ache from my fall
down the steps of the tower. I dare say you have not
forgotten that night ! Now it is the turn of your bones.
Hi ! comrades, make haste ! make haste ! '

Like a swarm of midges, a host of tiny headless
creatures seemed to spring straight out of the ground,
and every one was armed with a club. Although they
were so small, yet there were such numbers of them and
they struck so hard that even a strong man could do
nothing against them. Hans thought his last hour was
come, when just as the fight was at the hottest another
little dwarf arrived on the scene.

' Hold, comrades ! ' he shouted, turning to the attacking
party. ' This man once did me a service, and I am his
debtor. When I was in his power he granted me my
life. And even if he did throw you downstairs, well, a
warm bath soon cured your bruises, so you must just
forgive him and go quietly home.'

The headless dwarfs listened to his words and disappeared as suddenly as they had come. As soon as
Hans recovered himself a little he looked at his rescuer,
and saw he was the dwarf he had found seated in the
church bell.

' Ah ! ' said the dwarf, seating himself quietly under
the tree. ' You laughed at me when I told you that some
day I might do you a good turn. Now you see I was
right, and perhaps you will learn for the future not to
despise any creature, however small.'

' I thank you from my heart,' answered Hans. ' My
bones are still sore from their blows, and had it not been
for you I should indeed have fared badly.'

' I have almost paid my debt,' went on the little man,
' but as you have suffered already, I will do more, and
give you a piece of information. You need not remain
any longer in the service of that stingy minister, but when
you get home to-morrow go at once to the north corner

of the church, and there you will find a large stone built into the wall, but not cemented like the rest. The day after to-morrow the moon is full, and at midnight you must go to the spot and get the stone out of the wall with a pickaxe. Under the stone lies a great treasure, which has been hidden there in time of war. Besides church plate, you will find bags of money, which have been lying in this place for over a hundred years, and no one knows to whom it all belongs. A third of this money you must give to the poor, but the rest you may keep for yourself.' As he finished, the cocks in the village crowed, and the little man was nowhere to be seen. Hans found that his limbs no longer pained him, and lay for some time thinking of the hidden treasure. Towards morning he fell asleep.

The sun was high in the heavens when his master returned from the town.

'Hans,' said he, 'what a fool you were not to come with me yesterday! I was well feasted and entertained, and I have money in my pocket into the bargain,' he went on, rattling some coins while he spoke, to make Hans understand how much he had lost.

'Ah, sir,' replied Hans calmly, 'in order to have gained so much money you must have lain awake all night, but I have earned a hundred times that amount while I was sleeping soundly.'

'How did you manage that?' asked the minister eagerly, but Hans answered, 'It is only fools who boast of their farthings; wise men take care to hide their crowns.'

They drove home, and Hans neglected none of his duties, but put up the horses and gave them their food before going to the church corner, where he found the loose stone, exactly in the place described by the dwarf. Then he returned to his work.

The first night of the full moon, when the whole village was asleep, he stole out, armed with a pickaxe, and with much difficulty succeeded in dislodging the stone from its place. Sure enough, there was the hole, and in the hole lay the treasure, exactly as the little man had said.

The following Sunday he handed over the third part to the village poor, and informed the minister that he wished to break his bond of service. As, however, he did not claim any wages, the minister made no objections, but allowed him to do as he wished. So Hans went his way, bought himself a large house, and married a young wife, and lived happily and prosperously to the end of his days.

[Ehstnische Märchen.]

THE YOUNG MAN WHO WOULD HAVE
HIS EYES OPENED

ONCE upon a time there lived a youth who was never happy unless he was prying into something that other people knew nothing about. After he had learned to understand the language of birds and beasts, he discovered accidentally that a great deal took place under cover of night which mortal eyes never saw. From that moment he felt he could not rest till these hidden secrets were laid bare to him, and he spent his whole time wandering from one wizard to another, begging them to open his eyes, but found none to help him. At length he reached an old magician called Mana, whose learning was greater than that of the rest, and who could tell him all he wanted to know. But when the old man had listened attentively to him, he said, warningly:

'My son, do not follow after empty knowledge, which will not bring you happiness, but rather evil. Much is hidden from the eyes of men, because did they know everything their hearts would no longer be at peace. Knowledge kills joy, therefore think well what you are doing, or some day you will repent. But if you will not take my advice, then truly I can show you the secrets of the night. Only you will need more than a man's courage to bear the sight.'

He stopped and looked at the young man, who nodded his head, and then the wizard continued, 'To-morrow night you must go to the place where, once in seven years, the serpent-king gives a great feast to his whole court. In front of him stands a golden bowl filled with goats' milk, and if you can manage to dip a piece of bread in this milk, and eat it before you are obliged to fly, you will understand all the secrets of the night that are hidden from other men. It is lucky for you that the serpent-king's feast happens to fall this year, otherwise you would have had long to wait for it. But take care to be quick and bold, or it will be the worse for you.'

The young man thanked the wizard for his counsel, and went his way firmly resolved to carry out his purpose, even if he paid for it with his life ; and when night came he set out for a wide, lonely moor, where the serpent-king held his feast. With sharpened eyes, he looked eagerly all round him, but could see nothing but a multitude of small hillocks, that lay motionless under the moonlight. He crouched behind a bush for some time, till he felt that midnight could not be far off, when suddenly there arose in the middle of the moor a brilliant glow, as if a star was shining over one of the hillocks. At the same moment all the hillocks began to writhe and to crawl, and from each one came hundreds of serpents and made straight for the glow, where they knew they should find their king. When they reached the hillock where he dwelt, which was higher and broader than the rest, and had a bright light hanging over the top, they coiled themselves up and waited. The whirr and confusion from all the serpent-houses were so great that the youth did not dare to advance one step, but remained where he was, watching intently all that went on ; but at last he began to take courage, and moved on softly step by step.

What he saw was creepier than creepy, and surpassed all he had ever dreamt of. Thousands of snakes, big and little and of every colour, were gathered together in one great cluster round a huge serpent, whose body was as thick as a beam, and which had on its head a golden crown, from which the light sprang. Their hissings and darting tongues so terrified the young man that his heart sank, and he felt he should never have courage to push on to certain death, when suddenly he caught sight of the golden bowl in front of the serpent-king, and knew that if he lost this chance it would never come back. So, with his hair standing on end and his blood frozen in his veins, he crept forwards. Oh ! what a noise and a whirr rose afresh among the serpents. Thousands of heads were reared, and tongues were stretched out to sting the intruder to death, but happily for him their bodies were so closely entwined one in the other that they could not disentangle themselves quickly. Like lightning he seized a bit of bread, dipped it in the bowl, and put it in his mouth, then dashed away as if fire was pursuing him. On he flew as if a whole army of foes were at his heels, and he seemed to hear the noise of their approach growing nearer and nearer. At length his breath failed him, and he threw himself almost senseless on the turf. While he lay there dreadful dreams haunted him. He thought that the serpent-king with the fiery crown had twined himself round him, and was crushing out his life. With a loud shriek he sprang up to do battle with his enemy, when he saw that it was rays of the sun which had wakened him. He rubbed his eyes and looked all round, but nothing could he see of the foes of the past night, and the moor where he had run into such danger must be at least a mile away. But it was no dream that he had run hard and far, or that he had drunk of the magic goats' milk. And when he felt his limbs, and found them whole, his joy was great that he had come through such perils with a sound skin.

After the fatigues and terrors of the night, he lay still till mid-day, but he made up his mind he would go that very evening into the forest to try what the goats' milk could really do for him, and if he would now be able to understand all that had been a mystery to him. And once in the forest his doubts were set at rest, for he saw what no mortal eyes had ever seen before.   Beneath the

What the Young Man Saw in the Wood

trees were golden pavilions, with flags of silver all brightly lighted up.   He was still wondering why the pavilions were there, when a noise was heard among the trees,

as if the wind had suddenly got up, and on all sides
beautiful maidens stepped from the trees into the bright
light of the moon.   These were the wood-nymphs,
daughters of the earth-mother, who came every night to
hold their dances, in the forest.   The young man, watching from his hiding place, wished he had a hundred eyes
in his head, for two were not nearly enough for the sight
before him, the dances lasting till the first streaks of
dawn.   Then a silvery veil seemed to be drawn over the
ladies, and they vanished from sight.   But the young
man remained where he was till the sun was high in the
heavens, and then went home.

He felt that day to be endless, and counted the minutes till night should come, and he might return to the
forest.   But when at last he got there he found neither
pavilions nor nymphs, and though he went back many nights
after he never saw them again.   Still, he thought about
them night and day, and ceased to care about anything
else in the world, and was sick to the end of his life with
longing for that beautiful vision.   And that was the way
he learned that the wizard had spoken truly when he
said, ' Blindness is man's highest good.'

[Ehstnische Märchen.]

THE BOYS WITH THE GOLDEN STARS

ONCE upon a time what happened did happen : and if it had not happened, you would never have heard this story.

Well, once upon a time there lived an emperor who had half a world all to himself to rule over, and in this world dwelt an old herd and his wife and their three daughters, Anna, Stana, and Laptitza.

Anna, the eldest, was so beautiful that when she took the sheep to pasture they forgot to eat as long as she was walking with them. Stana, the second, was so beautiful that when she was driving the flock the wolves protected the sheep. But Laptitza, the youngest, with a skin as white as the foam on the milk, and with hair as soft as the finest lamb's wool, was as beautiful as both her sisters put together—as beautiful as she alone could be.

One summer day, when the rays of the sun were pouring down on the earth, the three sisters went to the wood on the outskirts of the mountain to pick strawberries. As they were looking about to find where the largest berries grew they heard the tramp of horses approaching, so loud that you would have thought a whole army was riding by. But it was only the emperor going to hunt with his friends and attendants.

They were all fine handsome young men, who sat their horses as if they were part of them, but the finest and handsomest of all was the young emperor himself.

As they drew near the three sisters, and marked their beauty, they checked their horses and rode slowly by.

'Listen, sisters!' said Anna, as they passed on. 'If one of those young men should make me his wife, I would bake him a loaf of bread which should keep him young and brave for ever.'

'And if I,' said Stana, 'should be the one chosen, I would weave my husband a shirt which will keep him unscathed when he fights with dragons; when he goes through water he will never even be wet; or if through fire, it will not scorch him.'

'And I,' said Laptitza, 'will give the man who chooses me two boys, twins, each with a golden star on his forehead, as bright as those in the sky.'

And though they spoke low the young men heard, and turned their horses' heads.

'I take you at your word, and mine shall you be, most lovely of empresses!' cried the emperor, and swung Laptitza and her strawberries on the horse before him.

'And I will have you,' 'And I you,' exclaimed two of his friends, and they all rode back to the palace together.

The following morning the marriage ceremony took place, and for three days and three nights there was nothing but feasting over the whole kingdom. And when the rejoicings were over the news was in everybody's mouth that Anna had sent for corn, and had made the loaf of which she had spoken at the strawberry beds. And then more days and nights passed, and this rumour was succeeded by another one—that Stana had procured some flax, and had dried it, and combed it, and spun it into linen, and sewed it herself into the shirt of which she had spoken over the strawberry beds.

Now the emperor had a stepmother, and she had a daughter by her first husband, who lived with her in the palace. The girl's mother had always believed that her daughter would be empress, and not the 'Milkwhite Maiden,' the child of a mere shepherd. So she hated the girl with all her heart, and only bided her time to do her ill.

But she could do nothing as long as the emperor remained with his wife night and day, and she began to wonder what she could do to get him away from her.

At last, when everything else had failed, she managed to make her brother, who was king of the neighbouring country, declare war against the emperor, and besiege some of the frontier towns with a large army. This time her scheme was successful. The young emperor sprang up in wrath the moment he heard the news, and vowed that nothing, not even his wife, should hinder his giving them battle. And hastily assembling whatever soldiers happened to be at hand he set off at once to meet the enemy. The other king had not reckoned on the swiftness of his movements, and was not ready to receive him. The emperor fell on him when he was off his guard, and routed his army completely. Then when victory was won, and the terms of peace hastily drawn up, he rode home as fast as his horse would carry him, and reached the palace on the third day.

But early that morning, when the stars were growing pale in the sky, two little boys with golden hair and stars on their foreheads were born to Laptitza. And the stepmother, who was watching, took them away, and dug a hole in the corner of the palace, under the windows of the emperor, and put them in it, while in their stead she placed two little puppies.

The emperor came into the palace, and when they told him the news he went straight to Laptitza's room. No words were needed; he saw with his own eyes that Laptitza had not kept the promise she had made at the strawberry beds, and, though it nearly broke his heart, he must give orders for her punishment.

So he went out sadly and told his guards that the empress was to be buried in the earth up to her neck, so that everyone might know what would happen to those who dared to deceive the emperor.

The Stepmother digs a Grave for the Babies

Not many days after, the stepmother's wish was fulfilled. The emperor took her daughter to wife, and again the rejoicings lasted for three days and three nights.

Let us now see what happened to the two little boys.

The poor little babies had found no rest even in their graves. In the place where they had been buried there sprang up two beautiful young aspens, and the step-mother, who hated the sight of the trees, which reminded her of her crime, gave orders that they should be up-rooted. But the emperor heard of it, and forbade the trees to be touched, saying, 'Let them alone; I like to see them there! They are the finest aspens I have ever beheld!'

And the aspens grew as no aspens had ever grown before. In each day they added a year's growth, and each night they added a year's growth, and at dawn, when the stars faded out of the sky, they grew three years' growth in the twinkling of an eye, and their boughs swept across the palace windows. And when the wind moved them softly, the emperor would sit and listen to them all the day long.

The stepmother knew what it all meant, and her mind never ceased from trying to invent some way of destroying the trees. It was not an easy thing, but a woman's will can press milk out of a stone, and her cunning will overcome heroes. What craft will not do soft words may attain, and if these do not succeed there still remains the resource of tears.

One morning the empress sat on the edge of her husband's bed, and began to coax him with all sorts of pretty ways.

It was some time before the bait took, but at length— even emperors are only men!

'Well, well,' he said at last, 'have your way and cut down the trees; but out of one they shall make a bed for me, and out of the other, one for you!'

And with this the empress was forced to be content. The aspens were cut down next morning, and before night the new bed had been placed in the emperor's room.

Now when the emperor lay down in it he seemed as

if he had grown a hundred times heavier than usual, yet he felt a kind of calm that was quite new to him. But the empress felt as if she was lying on thorns and nettles, and could not close her eyes.

When the emperor was fast asleep, the bed began to crack loudly, and to the empress each crack had a meaning. She felt as if she were listening to a language which no one but herself could understand.

'Is it too heavy for you, little brother?' asked one of the beds.

'Oh, no, it is not heavy at all,' answered the bed in which the emperor was sleeping. 'I feel nothing but joy now that my beloved father rests over me.'

'It is very heavy for me!' said the other bed, 'for on me lies an evil soul.'

And so they talked on till the morning, the empress listening all the while.

By daybreak the empress had determined how to get rid of the beds. She would have two others made exactly like them, and when the emperor had gone hunting they should be placed in his room. This was done, and the aspen beds were burnt in a large fire, till only a little heap of ashes was left.

Yet while they were burning the empress seemed to hear the same words, which she alone could understand.

Then she stooped and gathered up the ashes, and scattered them to the four winds, so that they might blow over fresh lands and fresh seas, and nothing remain of them.

But she had not seen that where the fire burnt brightest two sparks flew up, and, after floating in the air for a few moments, fell down into the great river that flows through the heart of the country. Here the sparks had turned into two little fishes with golden scales, and one was so exactly like the other that everyone could tell at the first glance that they must be twins. Early one

morning the emperor's fishermen went down to the river
to get some fish for their master's breakfast, and cast
their nets into the stream. As the last star twinkled out
of the sky they drew them in, and among the multitude
of fishes lay two with scales of gold, such as no man had
ever looked on.

They all gathered round and wondered, and after
some talk they decided that they would take the little
fishes alive as they were, and give them as a present to
the emperor.

'Do not take us there, for that is whence we came,
and yonder lies our destruction,' said one of the fishes.

'But what are we to do with you?' asked the
fisherman.

'Go and collect all the dew that lies on the leaves,
and let us swim in it. Then lay us in the sun, and do
not come near us till the sun's rays shall have dried off
the dew,' answered the other fish.

The fisherman did as they told him—gathered the
dew from the leaves and let them swim in it, then put
them to lie in the sun till the dew should be all dried
up.

And when he came back, what do you think he saw?
Why, two boys, two beautiful young princes, with hair as
golden as the stars on their foreheads, and each so like
the other, that at the first glance every one would have
known them for twins.

The boys grew fast. In every day they grew a year's
growth, and in every night another year's growth, but
at dawn, when the stars were fading, they grew three
years' growth in the twinkling of an eye. And they grew
in other things besides height, too. Thrice in age, and
thrice in wisdom, and thrice in knowledge. And when
three days and three nights had passed they were twelve
years in age, twenty-four in strength, and thirty-six in
wisdom.

'Now take us to our father,' said they. So the fisherman gave them each a lambskin cap which half covered their faces, and completely hid their golden hair and the stars on their foreheads, and led them to the court.

By the time they arrived there it was midday, and the fisherman and his charges went up to an official who was standing about. 'We wish to speak with the emperor,' said one of the boys.

'You must wait until he has finished his dinner,' replied the porter.

'No, while he is eating it,' said the second boy, stepping across the threshold.

The attendants all ran forward to thrust such impudent youngsters outside the palace, but the boys slipped through their fingers like quicksilver, and entered a large hall, where the emperor was dining, surrounded by his whole court.

'We desire to enter,' said one of the princes sharply to a servant who stood near the door.

'That is quite impossible,' replied the servant.

'Is it? let us see!' said the second prince, pushing the servants to right and left.

But the servants were many, and the princes only two. There was the noise of a struggle, which reached the emperor's ears.

'What is the matter?' asked he angrily.

The princes stopped at the sound of their father's voice.

'Two boys who want to force their way in,' replied one of the servants, approaching the emperor.

'To *force* their way in? Who dares to use force in my palace? What boys are they?' said the emperor all in one breath.

'We know not, O mighty emperor,' answered the servant, 'but they must surely be akin to you, for they have the strength of lions, and have scattered the guards at the gate. And they are as proud as they are strong, for they will not take their caps from their heads.'

THE BOYS WITH THE GOLDEN STARS

The emperor, as he listened, grew red with anger.

'Thrust them out,' cried he. 'Set the dogs after them.'

'Leave us alone, and we will go quietly,' said the princes, and stepped backwards, weeping silently at the harsh words. They had almost reached the gates when a servant ran up to them.

'The emperor commands you to return,' panted he: 'the empress wishes to see you.'

The princes thought a moment: then they went back the way they had come, and walked straight up to the emperor, their caps still on their heads.

He sat at the top of a long table covered with flowers and filled with guests. And beside him sat the empress, supported by twelve cushions. When the princes entered one of the cushions fell down, and there remained only eleven.

'Take off your caps,' said one of the courtiers.

'A covered head is among men a sign of honour. We wish to seem what we are.'

'Never mind,' said the emperor, whose anger had dropped before the silvery tones of the boy's voice. 'Stay as you are, but tell me *who* you are! Where do you come from, and what do you want?'

'We are twins, two shoots from one stem, which has been broken, and half lies in the ground and half sits at the head of this table. We have travelled a long way; we have spoken in the rustle of the wind, have whispered in the wood, we have sung in the waters, but now we wish to tell you a story which you know without knowing it, in the speech of men.'

And a second cushion fell down.

'Let them take their silliness home,' said the empress.

'Oh, no, let them go on,' said the emperor. 'You wished to see them, but I wish to hear them. Go on, boys, sing me the story.'

The empress was silent, but the princes began to sing the story of their lives.

'There was once an emperor,' began they, and the third cushion fell down.

When they reached the warlike expedition of the emperor three of the cushions fell down at once.

And when the tale was finished there were no more cushions under the empress, but the moment that they lifted their caps, and showed their golden hair and the golden stars, the eyes of the emperor and of all his guests were bent on them, and they could hardly bear the power of so many glances.

And there happened in the end what should have happened in the beginning. Laptitza sat next her husband at the top of the table. The stepmother's daughter became the meanest sewing maid in the palace, the stepmother was tied to a wild horse, and every one knew and has never forgotten that whoever has a mind turned to wickedness is sure to end badly.

[Rumänische Märchen.]

THE FROG

ONCE upon a time there was a woman who had three
sons. Though they were peasants they were well off,
for the soil on which they lived was fruitful, and yielded
rich crops. One day they all three told their mother
they meant to get married. To which their mother
replied : ' Do as you like, but see that you choose good
housewives, who will look carefully after your affairs ;
and, to make certain of this, take with you these three
skeins of flax, and give it to them to spin. Whoever
spins the best will be my favourite daughter-in-law.'

Now the two eldest sons had already chosen their
wives ; so they took the flax from their mother, and
carried it off with them, to have it spun as she had said.
But the youngest son was puzzled what to do with his
skein, as he knew no girl (never having spoken to any) to
whom he could give it to be spun. He wandered hither
and thither, asking the girls that he met if they would
undertake the task for him, but at the sight of the flax
they laughed in his face and mocked at him. Then in
despair he left their villages, and went out into the
country, and, seating himself on the bank of a pond
began to cry bitterly.

Suddenly there was a noise close beside him, and a
frog jumped out of the water on to the bank and asked
him why he was crying. The youth told her of his
trouble, and how his brothers would bring home linen
spun for them by their promised wives, but that no one
would spin his thread.

Then the frog answered: 'Do not weep on that account; give me the thread, and I will spin it for you.' And, having said this, she took it out of his hand, and flopped back into the water, and the youth went back, not knowing what would happen next.

In a short time the two elder brothers came home, and their mother asked to see the linen which had been woven out of the skeins of flax she had given them. They all three left the room; and in a few minutes the two eldest returned, bringing with them the linen that had been spun by their chosen wives. But the youngest brother was greatly troubled, for he had nothing to show for the skein of flax that had been given to him. Sadly he betook himself to the pond, and sitting down on the bank, began to weep.

Flop! and the frog appeared out of the water close beside him.

'Take this,' she said; 'here is the linen that I have spun for you.'

You may imagine how delighted the youth was. She put the linen into his hands, and he took it straight back to his mother, who was so pleased with it that she declared she had never seen linen so beautifully spun, and that it was far finer and whiter than the webs that the two elder brothers had brought home.

Then she turned to her sons and said: 'But this is not enough, my sons, I must have another proof as to what sort of wives you have chosen. In the house there are three puppies. Each of you take one, and give it to the woman whom you mean to bring home as your wife. She must train it and bring it up. Whichever dog turns out the best, its mistress will be my favourite daughter-in-law.'

So the young men set out on their different ways, each taking a puppy with him. The youngest, not knowing where to go, returned to the pond, sat down once more on the bank, and began to weep.

Flop ! and close beside him, he saw the frog. ' Why are you weeping?' she said. Then he told her his difficulty, and that he did not know to whom he should take the puppy.

' Give it to me,' she said, ' and I will bring it tor you.' And, seeing that the youth hesitated, she took the little creature out of his arms, and disappeared with it into the pond.

The weeks and months passed, till one day the mother said she would like to see how the dogs had been trained by her future daughters-in-law. The two eldest sons departed, and returned shortly, leading with them two great mastiffs, who growled so fiercely, and looked so savage, that the mere sight of them made the mother tremble with fear.

The youngest son, as was his custom, went to the pond, and called on the frog to come to his rescue.

In a minute she was at his side, bringing with her the most lovely little dog, which she put into his arms. It sat up and begged with its paws, and went through the prettiest tricks, and was almost human in the way it understood and did what it was told.

In high spirits the youth carried it off to his mother. As soon as she saw it, she exclaimed : ' This is the most beautiful little dog I have ever seen. You are indeed fortunate, my son ; you have won a pearl of a wife.'

Then, turning to the others, she said : ' Here are three shirts ; take them to your chosen wives. Whoever sews the best will be my favourite daughter-in-law.'

So the young men set out once more ; and again, this time, the work of the frog was much the best and the neatest.

This time the mother said : ' Now that I am content with the tests I gave, I want you to go and fetch home your brides, and I will prepare the wedding-feast.'

You may imagine what the youngest brother felt on hearing these words. Whence was he to fetch a bride? Would the frog be able to help him in this new difficulty? With bowed head, and feeling very sad, he sat down on the edge of the pond.

Flop! and once more the faithful frog was beside him.

'What is troubling you so much?' she asked him, and then the youth told her everything.

'Will you take me for a wife?' she asked.

'What should I do with you as a wife,' he replied, wondering at her strange proposal.

'Once more, will you have me or will you not?' she said.

'I will neither have you, nor will I refuse you,' said he.

At this the frog disappeared; and the next minute the youth beheld a lovely little chariot, drawn by two tiny ponies, standing on the road. The frog was holding the carriage door open for him to step in.

'Come with me,' she said. And he got up and followed her into the chariot.

As they drove along the road they met three witches; the first of them was blind, the second was hunchbacked, and the third had a large thorn in her throat. When the three witches beheld the chariot, with the frog seated pompously among the cushions, they broke into such fits of laughter that the eyelids of the blind one burst open, and she recovered her sight; the hunchback rolled about on the ground in merriment till her back became straight, and in a roar of laughter the thorn fell out of the throat of the third witch. Their first thought was to reward the frog, who had unconsciously been the means of curing them of their misfortunes. The first witch waved her magic wand over the frog, and changed her into the loveliest girl that had ever been seen. The second witch waved the wand over the tiny chariot and ponies, and they were turned into a beautiful large carriage with prancing horses, and a coachman on the seat. The

third witch gave the girl a magic purse, filled with
money. Having done this, the witches disappeared,
and the youth with his lovely bride drove to his
mother's home. Great was the delight of the mother at

THE WITCHES LAUGHING

her youngest son's good fortune. A beautiful house was
built for them; she was the favourite daughter-in-law;
everything went well with them, and they lived happily
ever after.

[From the Italian.]

THE PRINCESS WHO WAS HIDDEN UNDERGROUND

ONCE there was a king who had great riches, which, when he died, he divided among his three sons. The two eldest of these lived in rioting and feasting, and thus wasted and squandered their father's wealth till nothing remained, and they found themselves in want and misery. The youngest of the three sons, on the contrary, made good use of his portion. He married a wife and soon they had a most beautiful daughter, for whom, when she was grown up, he caused a great palace to be built underground, and then killed the architect who had built it. Next he shut up his daughter inside, and then sent heralds all over the world to make known that he who should find the king's daughter should have her to wife. If he were not capable of finding her then he must die. Many young men sought to discover her, but all perished in the attempt.

After many had met their death thus, there came a young man, beautiful to behold, and as clever as he was beautiful, who had a great desire to attempt the enterprise. First he went to a herdsman, and begged him to hide him in a sheepskin, which had a golden fleece, and in this disguise to take him to the king. The shepherd let himself be persuaded so to do, took a skin having a golden fleece, sewed the young man in it, putting in also food and drink, and so brought him before the king.

When the latter saw the golden lamb, he asked the herd: ' Will you sell me this lamb ? '

But the herd answered : ' No, oh king ; I will not sell it ; but if you find pleasure therein, I will be willing to oblige you, and I will lend it to you, free of charge, for three days, after that you must give it back to me.'

This the king agreed to do, and he arose and took the lamb to his daughter. When he had led it into her palace, and through many rooms, he came to a shut door. Then he called ' Open, Sartara Martara of the earth ! ' and the door opened of itself. After that they went through many more rooms, and came to another closed door. Again the king called out : ' Open, Sartara Martara of the earth ! ' and this door opened like the other, and they came into the apartment where the princess dwelt, the floor, walls, and roof of which were all of silver.

When the king had embraced the princess, he gave her the lamb, to her great joy. She stroked it, caressed it, and played with it.

After a while the lamb got loose, which, when the princess saw, she said : ' See, father, the lamb is free.'

But the king answered : ' It is only a lamb, why should it not be free ? '

Then he left the lamb with the princess, and went his way.

In the night, however, the young man threw off the skin. When the princess saw how beautiful he was, she fell in love with him, and asked him : ' Why did you come here disguised in a sheepskin like that ? '

Then he answered : ' When I saw how many people sought you, and could not find you, and lost their lives in so doing, I invented this trick, and so I am come safely to you.'

The princess exclaimed : ' You have done well so to do ; but you must know that your wager is not yet won, for my father will change me and my maidens into ducks, and will ask you, " Which of these ducks is the princess ? " Then I will turn my head back, and with my bill will clean my wings, so that you may know me.'

When they had spent three days together, chatting and caressing one another, the herd came back to the king, and demanded his lamb. Then the king went to his daughter to bring it away, which troubled the princess very much, for she said they had played so nicely together.

But the king said: 'I cannot leave it with you, my daughter, for it is only lent to me.' So he took it away with him, and gave it back to the shepherd.

Then the young man threw the skin from off him, and went to the king, saying: 'Sire, I am persuaded I can find your daughter.'

When the king saw how handsome he was, he said: 'My lad, I have pity on your youth. This enterprise has already cost the lives of many, and will certainly be your death as well.'

But the young man answered, 'I accept your conditions, oh king; I will either find her or lose my head.'

Thereupon he went before the king, who followed after him, till they came to the great door. Then the young man said to the king: 'Speak the words that it may open.'

And the king answered: 'What are the words? Shall I say something like this: "Shut; shut; shut"?'

'No,' said he; 'say· "Open, Sartara Martara of the earth."'

When the king had so said, the door opened of itself, and they went in, while the king gnawed his moustache in anger. Then they came to the second door, where the same thing happened as at the first, and they went in and found the princess.

Then spoke the king and said: 'Yes, truly, you have found the princess. Now I will turn her as well as all her maidens into ducks, and if you can guess which of these ducks is my daughter, then you shall have her to wife.'

And immediately the king changed all the maidens into ducks, and he drove them before the young man, and said : 'Now show me which is my daughter.'

Then the princess, according to their understanding, began to clean her wings with her bill, and the lad said : 'She who cleans her wings is the princess.'

Now the king could do nothing more but give her to the young man to wife, and they lived together in great joy and happiness.

[From the German.]

THE GIRL WHO PRETENDED TO BE
A BOY

ONCE upon a time there lived an emperor who was a
great conqueror, and reigned over more countries than
anyone in the world. And whenever he subdued a fresh
kingdom, he only granted peace on condition that the
king should deliver him one of his sons for ten years'
service.

Now on the borders of his kingdom lay a country
whose emperor was as brave as his neighbour, and as
long as he was young he was the victor in every war.
But as years passed away, his head grew weary of making
plans of campaign, and his people wanted to stay at
home and till their fields, and at last he too felt that he
must do homage to the other emperor.

One thing, however, held him back from this step
which day by day he saw more clearly was the only one
possible. His new overlord would demand the service of
one of his sons. And the old emperor had no son; only
three daughters.

Look on which side he would, nothing but ruin
seemed to lie before him, and he became so gloomy, that
his daughters were frightened, and did everything they
could think of to cheer him up, but all to no purpose.

At length one day when they were at dinner, the
eldest of the three summoned up all her courage and said
to her father :

'What secret grief is troubling you? Are your
subjects discontented? or have we given you cause for

displeasure ? To smooth away your wrinkles, we would gladly shed our blood, for our lives are bound up in yours; and this you know.'

'My daughter,' answered the emperor, 'what you say is true. Never have you given me one moment's pain. Yet now you cannot help me. Ah! why is not one of you a boy!'

'I don't understand,' she answered in surprise. 'Tell us what is wrong: and though we are not boys, we are not quite useless!'

'But what can you do, my dear children ? Spin, sew, and weave—that is all your learning. Only a warrior can deliver me now, a young giant who is strong to wield the battle-axe: whose sword deals deadly blows.'

'But *why* do you need a son so much at present ? Tell us all about it! It will not make matters worse if we know!'

'Listen then, my daughters, and learn the reason of my sorrow. You have heard that as long as I was young no man ever brought an army against me without it costing him dear. But the years have chilled my blood and drunk my strength. And now the deer can roam the forest, my arrows will never pierce his heart; strange soldiers will set fire to my houses and water their horses at my wells, and my arm cannot hinder them. No, my day is past, and the time has come when I too must bow my head under the yoke of my foe! But who is to give him the ten years' service that is part of the price which the vanquished must pay?'

'*I* will,' cried the eldest girl, springing to her feet. But her father only shook his head sadly.

'Never will I bring shame upon you,' urged the girl. 'Let me go. Am I not a princess, and the daughter of an emperor?'

'Go then!' he said.

The brave girl's heart almost stopped beating from

joy, as she set about her preparations. She was not still for a single moment, but danced about the house, turning chests and wardrobes upside down. She set aside enough things for a whole year—dresses embroidered with gold and precious stones, and a great store of provisions. And she chose the most spirited horse in the stable, with eyes of flame, and a coat of shining silver.

When her father saw her mounted and curvetting about the court, he gave her much wise advice, as to how she was to behave like the young man she appeared to be, and also how to behave as the girl she really was. Then he gave her his blessing, and she touched her horse with the spur.

The silver armour of herself and her steed dazzled the eyes of the people as she darted past. She was soon out of sight, and if after a few miles she had not pulled up to allow her escort to join her, the rest of the journey would have been performed alone.

But though none of his daughters were aware of the fact, the old emperor was a magician, and had laid his plans accordingly. He managed, unseen, to overtake his daughter, and throw a bridge of copper over a stream which she would have to cross. Then, changing himself into a wolf, he lay down under one of the arches, and waited.

He had chosen his time well, and in about half an hour the sound of a horse's hoofs was heard. His feet were almost on the bridge, when a big grey wolf with grinning teeth appeared before the princess. With a deep growl that froze the blood, he drew himself up, and prepared to spring.

The appearance of the wolf was so sudden and so unexpected, that the girl was almost paralysed, and never even dreamt cf flight, till the horse leaped violently to one side. Then she turned him round, and urging him to his fullest speed, never drew rein till she saw the gates of the palace rising before her.

The old emperor, who had got back long since, came to the door to meet her, and touching her shining armour, he said, 'Did I not tell you, my child, that flies do not make honey?'

The days passed on, and one morning the second princess implored her father to allow her to try the adventure in which her sister had made such a failure. He listened unwillingly, feeling sure it was no use, but she begged so hard that in the end he consented, and having chosen her arms, she rode away.

But though, unlike her sister, she was quite prepared for the appearance of the wolf when she reached the copper bridge, she showed no greater courage, and galloped home as fast as her horse could carry her. On the steps of the castle her father was standing, and as still trembling with fright she knelt at his feet, he said gently, 'Did I not tell you, my child, that every bird is not caught in a net?'

The three girls stayed quietly in the palace for a little while, embroidering, spinning, weaving, and tending their birds and flowers, when early one morning, the youngest princess entered the door of the emperor's private apartments. 'My father, it is my turn now. Perhaps I shall get the better of that wolf!'

'What, do you think you are braver than your sisters, vain little one? You who have hardly left your long clothes behind you!' but she did not mind being laughed at, and answered,

'For your sake, father, I would cut the devil himself into small bits, or even become a devil myself. I think I shall succeed, but if I fail, I shall come home without more shame than my sisters.'

Still the emperor hesitated, but the girl petted and coaxed him till at last he said,

'Well, well, if you must go, you must. It remains to

be seen what I shall get by it, except perhaps a good laugh when I see you come back with your head bent and your eyes on the ground.'

'He laughs best who laughs last,' said the princess.

Happy at having got her way, the princess decided that the first thing to be done was to find some old white-haired boyard, whose advice she could trust, and then to be very careful in choosing her horse. So she went straight to the stables where the most beautiful horses in the empire were feeding in the stalls, but none of them seemed quite what she wanted. Almost in despair she reached the last box of all, which was occupied by her father's ancient war-horse, old and worn like himself, stretched sadly out on the straw.

The girl's eyes filled with tears, and she stood gazing at him. The horse lifted his head, gave a little neigh, and said softly, 'You look gentle and pitiful, but I know it is your love for your father which makes you tender to me. Ah, what a warrior he was, and what good times we shared together! But now I too have grown old, and my master has forgotten me, and there is no reason to care whether my coat is dull or shining. Yet, it is not too late, and if I were properly tended, in a week I could vie with any horse in the stables!'

'And how should you be tended?' asked the girl.

'I must be rubbed down morning and evening with rain water, my barley must be boiled in milk, because of my bad teeth, and my feet must be washed in oil.'

'I should like to try the treatment, as you might help me in carrying out my scheme.'

'Try it then, mistress, and I promise you will never repent.'

So in a week's time the horse woke up one morning with a sudden shiver through all his limbs ; and when it had passed away, he found his skin shining like a mirror,

his body as fat as a water melon, his movement light as
a chamois.'

Then looking at the princess who had come early to
the stable, he said joyfully,

'May success await on the steps of my master's
daughter, for she has given me back my life. Tell me
what I can do for you, princess, and I will do it.'

'I want to go to the emperor who is our over-lord,
and I have no one to advise me. Which of all the
white-headed boyards shall I choose as counsellor?'

'If you have me, you need no one else: I will serve
you as I served your father, if you will only listen to
what I say.'

'I will listen to everything. Can you start in three
days?'

'This moment, if you like,' said the horse.

The preparations of the emperor's youngest daughter
were much fewer and simpler than those of her sisters.
They only consisted of some boy's clothes, a small
quantity of linen and food, and a little money in case of
necessity. Then she bade farewell to her father, and
rode away.

A day's journey from the palace, she reached the
copper bridge, but before they came in sight of it, the
horse, who was a magician, had warned her of the means
her father would take to prove her courage.

Still in spite of his warning she trembled all over
when a huge wolf, as thin as if he had fasted for a month,
with claws like saws, and mouth as wide as an oven,
bounded howling towards her. For a moment her heart
failed her, but the next, touching the horse lightly with
her spur, she drew her sword from its sheath, ready
to separate the wolf's head from its body at a single
blow.

The beast saw the sword, and shrank back, which

was the best thing it could do, as now the girl's blood was up, and the light of battle in her eyes. Then without looking round, she rode across the bridge.

The emperor, proud of this first victory, took a short cut, and waited for her at the end of another day's journey, close to a river, over which he threw a bridge of silver. And this time he took the shape of a lion.

But the horse guessed this new danger and told the princess how to escape it. But it is one thing to receive advice when we feel safe and comfortable, and quite another to be able to carry it out when some awful peril is threatening us. And if the wolf had made the girl quake with terror, it seemed like a lamb beside this dreadful lion.

At the sound of his roar the very trees quivered and his claws were so large that every one of them looked like a cutlass.

The breath of the princess came and went, and her feet rattled in the stirrups. Suddenly the remembrance flashed across her of the wolf whom she had put to flight, and waving her sword, she rushed so violently on the lion that he had barely time to spring on one side, so as to avoid the blow. Then, like a flash, she crossed this bridge also.

Now during her whole life, the princess had been so carefully brought up, that she had never left the gardens of the palace, so that the sight of the hills and valleys and tinkling streams, and the song of the larks and blackbirds, made her almost beside herself with wonder and delight. She longed to get down and bathe her face in the clear pools, and pick the brilliant flowers, but the horse said ' No,' and quickened his pace, neither turning to the right or the left.

' Warriors,' he told her, ' only rest when they have won the victory. You have still another battle to fight, and it is the hardest of all.'

This time it was neither a wolf nor a lion that was

THE PRINCESS CHARGES THE LION

waiting for her at the end of the third day's journey, but a dragon with twelve heads, and a golden bridge behind it.

The princess rode up without seeing anything to frighten her, when a sudden puff of smoke and flame from beneath her feet, caused her to look down, and there was the horrible creature twisted and writhing, its twelve heads reared up as if to seize her between them.

The bridle fell from her hand : and the sword which she had just grasped slid back into its sheath, but the horse bade her fear nothing, and with a mighty effort she sat upright and spurred straight on the dragon.

The fight lasted an hour and the dragon pressed her hard. But in the end, by a well-directed side blow, she cut off one of the heads, and with a roar that seemed to rend the heavens in two, the dragon fell back on the ground, and rose as a man before her.

Although the horse had informed the princess the dragon was really her own father, the girl had hardly believed him, and stared in amazement at the transformation. But he flung his arms round her and pressed her to his heart saying, ' Now I see that you are as brave as the bravest, and as wise as the wisest. You have chosen the right horse, for without his help you would have returned with a bent head and downcast eyes. You have filled me with the hope that you may carry out the task you have undertaken, but be careful to forget none of my counsels, and above all to listen to those of your horse.'

When he had done speaking, the princess knelt down to receive his blessing, and they went their different ways.

The princess rode on and on, till at last she came to the mountains which hold up the roof of the world. There she met two Genii who had been fighting fiercely for two years, without one having got the least advantage over the other. Seeing what they took to be a young man seeking adventures, one of the combatants called out? 'Fet-Fruners! deliver me from my enemy, and I will give you the horn that can be heard the distance of a three days' journey;' while the other cried, 'Fet-Fruners! help me to conquer this pagan thief, and you shall have my horse, Sunlight.'

Before answering, the princess consulted her own horse as to which offer she should accept, and he advised her to side with the genius who was master of Sunlight, his own younger brother, and still more active than himself.

So the girl at once attacked the other genius, and soon clove his skull; then the one who was left victor begged her to come back with him to his house and he would hand her over Sunlight, as he had promised.

The mother of the genius was rejoiced to see her son return safe and sound, and prepared her best room for the princess, who, after so much fatigue, needed rest badly. But the girl declared that she must first make her horse comfortable in his stable; but this was really only an excuse, as she wanted to ask his advice on several matters.

But the old woman had suspected from the very first that the boy who had come to the rescue of her son was a girl in disguise, and told the genius that she was exactly the wife he needed. The genius scoffed, and inquired what female hand could ever wield a sabre like that; but, in spite of his sneers, his mother persisted, and as a proof of what she said, laid at night on each of their pillows a handful of magic flowers, that fade at the touch of man, but remain eternally fresh in the fingers of a woman.

It was very clever of her, but unluckily the horse had warned the princess what to expect, and when the house was silent, she stole very softly to the genius's room, and exchanged his faded flowers for those she held. Then she crept back to her own bed and fell fast asleep.

At break of day, the old woman ran to see her son, and found, as she knew she would, a bunch of dead flowers in his hand. She next passed on to the bedside of the princess, who still lay asleep grasping the withered flowers. But she did not believe any the more that her guest was a man, and so she told her son. So they put their heads together and laid another trap for her.

After breakfast the genius gave his arm to his guest, and asked her to come with him into the garden. For some time they walked about looking at the flowers, the genius all the while pressing her to pick any she fancied. But the princess, suspecting a trap, inquired roughly why they were wasting the precious hours in the garden, when, as men, they should be in the stables looking after their horses. Then the genius told his mother that she was quite wrong, and his deliverer was certainly a man. But the old woman was not convinced for all that.

She would try once more she said, and her son must lead his visitor into the armoury, where hung every kind of weapon used all over the world—some plain and bare, others ornamented with precious stones—and beg her to make choice of one of them. The princess looked at them closely, and felt the edges and points of their blades, then she hung at her belt an old sword with a curved blade, that would have done credit to an ancient warrior. After this she informed the genius that she would start early next day and take Sunlight with her.

And there was nothing for the mother to do but to submit, though she still stuck to her own opinion.

The princess mounted Sunlight, and touched him with her spur, when the old horse, who was galloping at her side, suddenly said :

' Up to this time, mistress, you have obeyed my counsels and all has gone well. Listen to me once more, and do what I tell you. I am old, and—now that there is someone to take my place, I will confess it—I am afraid that my strength is not equal to the task that lies before me. Give me leave, therefore, to return home, and do you continue your journey under the care of my brother. Put your faith in him as you put it in me, and you will never repent. Wisdom has come early to Sunlight.'

'Yes, my old comrade, you have served me well; and it is only through your help that up to now I have been victorious. So grieved though I am to say farewell, I will obey you yet once more, and will listen to your brother as I would to yourself. Only, I must have a proof that he loves me as well as you do.'

'How should I not love you?' answered Sunlight; 'how should I not be proud to serve a warrior such as you? Trust me, mistress, and you shall never regret the absence of my brother. I know there will be difficulties in our path, but we will face them together.'

Then, with tears in her eyes, the princess took leave of her old horse, who galloped back to her father.

She had ridden only a few miles further, when she saw a golden curl lying on the road before her. Checking her horse, she asked whether it would be better to take it or let it lie.

'If you take it,' said Sunlight, 'you will repent, and if you don't, you will repent too: so take it.' On this the girl dismounted, and picking up the curl, wound it round her neck for safety.

They passed by hills, they passed by mountains, they passed through valleys, leaving behind them thick forests, and fields covered with flowers; and at length they reached the court of the over-lord.

He was sitting on his throne, surrounded by the sons of the other emperors, who served him as pages. These youths came forward to greet their new companion, and wondered why they felt so attracted towards him.

However, there was no time for talking and concealing her fright. The princess was led straight up to the throne, and explained, in a low voice, the reason of her coming. The emperor received her kindly, and declared himself fortunate at finding a vassal so brave and so charming, and begged the princess to remain in attendance on his person.

She was, however, very careful in her behaviour towards the other pages, whose way of life did not please her. One day, however, she had been amusing herself by making sweetmeats, when two of the young princes looked in to pay her a visit. She offered them some of the food which was already on the table, and they thought it so delicious that they even licked their fingers so as not to lose a morsel. Of course they did not keep the news of their discovery to themselves, but told all their companions that they had just been enjoying the best supper they had had since they were born. And from that moment the princess was left no peace, till she had promised to cook them all a dinner.

Now it happened that, on the very day fixed, all the cooks in the palace became intoxicated, and there was no one to make up the fire.

When the pages heard of this shocking state of things, they went to their companion and implored her to come to the rescue.

The princess was fond of cooking, and was, besides, very good-natured ; so she put on an apron and went down to the kitchen without delay. When the dinner was placed before the emperor he found it so nice that he ate much more than was good for him. The next morning, as soon as he woke, he sent for his head cook, and told him to send up the same dishes as before. The cook, seized with fright at this command, which he knew he could not fulfil, fell on his knees, and confessed the truth.

The emperor was so astonished that he forgot to scold, and while he was thinking over the matter, some of his pages came in and said that their new companion had been heard to boast that he knew where Iliane was to be found—the celebrated Iliane of the song which begins:

> ' Golden Hair
> The fields are green,'

and that to their certain knowledge he had a curl of her hair in his possession.

When he heard that, the emperor desired the page to be brought before him, and, as soon as the princess obeyed his summons, he said to her abruptly:

' Fet-Fruners, you have hidden from me the fact that you knew the golden-haired Iliane! Why did you do this? for I have treated you more kindly than all my other pages.'

Then, after making the princess show him the golden curl which she wore round her neck, he added: ' Listen to me; unless by some means or other you bring me the owner of this lock, I will have your head cut off in the place where you stand. Now go!'

In vain the poor girl tried to explain how the lock of hair came into her possession; the emperor would listen to nothing, and, bowing low, she left his presence and went to consult Sunlight what she was to do.

At his first words she brightened up. ' Do not be afraid, mistress; only last night my brother appeared to me in a dream and told me that a genius had carried off Iliane, whose hair you picked up on the road. But Iliane declares that, before she marries her captor, he must bring her, as a present, the whole stud of mares which belong to her. The genius, half crazy with love, thinks of nothing night and day but how this can be done, and meanwhile she is quite safe in the island swamps of the sea. Go back to the emperor and ask him for twenty ships filled with precious merchandise. The rest you shall know by-and-by.'

On hearing this advice, the princess went at once into the emperor's presence.

' May a long life be yours, O Sovereign all mighty ! '
said she. ' I have come to tell you that I can do as you
command if you will give me twenty ships, and load
them with the most precious wares in your kingdom.'

' You shall have all that I possess if you will bring
me the golden-haired Iliane,' said the emperor.

The ships were soon ready, and the princess entered
the largest and finest, with Sunlight at her side. Then
the sails were spread and the voyage began.

For seven weeks the wind blew them straight towards
the west, and early one morning they caught sight of the
island swamps of the sea.

They cast anchor in a little bay, and the princess
made haste to disembark with Sunlight, but, before leaving the ship, she tied to her belt a pair of tiny gold
slippers, adorned with precious stones. Then mounting
Sunlight, she rode about till she came to several palaces,
built on hinges, so that they could always turn towards
the sun.

The most splendid of these was guarded by three
slaves, whose greedy eyes were caught by the glistening
gold of the slippers. They hastened up to the owner
of these treasures, and inquired who he was. ' A
merchant,' replied the princess, ' who had somehow missed
his road, and lost himself among the island swamps of
the sea.'

Not knowing if it was proper to receive him or not,
the slaves returned to their mistress and told her all they
had seen, but not before she had caught sight of the
merchant from the roof of her palace. Luckily her
gaoler was away, always trying to catch the stud of
mares, so for the moment she was free and alone.

The slaves told their tale so well that their mistress
insisted on going down to the shore and seeing the
beautiful slippers for herself. They were even lovelier
than she expected, and when the merchant besought her

to come on board, and inspect some that he thought were finer still, her curiosity was too great to refuse, and she went.

Once on board ship, she was so busy turning over all the precious things stored there, that she never knew that the sails were spread, and that they were flying along with the wind behind them; and when she did know, she rejoiced in her heart, though she pretended to weep and lament at being carried captive a second time. Thus they arrived at the court of the emperor.

They were just about to land, when the mother of the genius stood before them. She had learnt that Iliane had fled from her prison in company with a merchant, and, as her son was absent, had come herself in pursuit. Striding over the blue waters, hopping from wave to wave, one foot reaching to heaven, and the other planted in the foam, she was close at their heels, breathing fire and flame, when they stepped on shore from the ship. One glance told Iliane who the horrible old woman was, and she whispered hastily to her companion. Without saying a word, the princess swung her into Sunlight's saddle, and leaping up behind her, they were off like a flash.

It was not till they drew near the town that the princess stooped and asked Sunlight what they should do. 'Put your hand into my left ear,' said he, 'and take out a sharp stone, which you must throw behind you.'

The princess did as she was told, and a huge mountain sprang up behind them. The mother of the genius began to climb up it, and though they galloped quickly, she was quicker still.

They heard her coming, faster, faster; and again the princess stooped to ask what was to be done now. 'Put your hand into my right ear,' said the horse, 'and throw the brush you will find there behind you.' The princess did so, and a great forest sprang up behind them, and, so thick were its leaves, that even a wren could not get through. But the old woman seized hold of the branches and flung herself like a monkey from one to the others, and always she drew nearer—always, always—till their hair was singed by the flames of her mouth.

FETFRUNERS & ILIANE
eSCaPe FRom
the Mother of the Genius

Then, in despair, the princess again bent down and asked if there was nothing more to be done, and Sunlight replied ' Quick, quick, take off the betrothal ring on the finger of Iliane and throw it behind you.'

This time there sprang up a great tower of stone, smooth as ivory, hard as steel, which reached up to heaven itself. And the mother of the genius gave a howl of rage, knowing that she could neither climb it nor get through it. But she was not beaten yet, and gathering herself together, she made a prodigious leap, which landed her on the top of the tower, right in the middle of Iliane's ring which lay there, and held her tight. Only her claws could be seen grasping the battlements.

All that could be done the old witch did; but the fire that poured from her mouth never reached the fugitives, though it laid waste the country a hundred miles round the tower, like the flames of a volcano. Then, with one last effort to free herself, her hands gave way, and, falling down to the bottom of the tower, she was broken in pieces.

When the flying princess saw what had happened she rode back to the spot, as Sunlight counselled her, and placed her finger on the top of the tower, which was gradually shrinking into the earth. In an instant the tower had vanished as if it had never been, and in its place was the finger of the princess with a ring round it.

The emperor received Iliane with all the respect that was due to her, and fell in love at first sight besides.

But this did not seem to please Iliane, whose face was sad as she walked about the palace or gardens, wondering how it was that, while other girls did as they liked, she was always in the power of someone whom she hated.

So when the emperor asked her to share his throne, Iliane answered:

'Noble Sovereign, I may not think of marriage till my stud of horses has been brought me, with their trappings all complete.'

When he heard this, the emperor once more sent for Fet-Fruners, and said:

Fet-Fruners, fetch me instantly the stud of mares, with their trappings all complete. If not, your head shall pay the forfeit.'

' Mighty Emperor, I kiss your hands! I have but just returned from doing your bidding, and, behold, you send me on another mission, and stake my head on its fulfil-ment, when your court is full of valiant young men, pining to win their spurs. They say you are a just man ; then why not entrust this quest to one of them? Where am I to seek these mares that I am to bring you?'

' How do I know? They may be anywhere in heaven or earth ; but, wherever they are, you will have to find them.'

The princess bowed and went to consult Sunlight. He listened while she told her tale, and then said :

' Fetch quickly nine buffalo skins ; smear them well with tar, and lay them on my back. Do not fear ; you will succeed in this also ; but, in the end, the emperor's desires will be his undoing.'

The buffalo skins ·were soon got, and the princess started off with Sunlight. The way was long and difficult, but at length they reached the place where the mares were grazing. Here the genius who had carried off Iliane was wandering about, trying to discover how to capture them, all the while believing that Iliane was safe in the palace where he had left her.

As soon as she caught sight of him, the princess went up and told him that Iliane had escaped, and that his mother, in her efforts to recapture her, had died of rage. At this news a blind fury took possession of the genius, and he rushed madly upon the princess, who awaited his onslaught with perfect calmness. As he came on, with his sabre lifted high in the air, Sunlight bounded right over his head, so that the sword fell harmless. And when in her turn the princess prepared to strike, the horse sank upon his knees, so that the blade pierced the genius's thigh.

The fight was so fierce that it seemed as if the earth would give way under them, and for twenty miles round the beasts in the forests fled to their caves for shelter

At last, when her strength was almost gone, the genius lowered his sword for an instant. The princess saw her chance, and, with one swoop of her arm, severed her enemy's head from his body. Still trembling from the long struggle, she turned away, and went to the meadow where the stud were feeding.

By the advice of Sunlight, she took care not to let them see her, and climbed a thick tree, where she could see and hear without being seen herself. Then he neighed, and the mares came galloping up, eager to see the new comer—all but one horse, who did not like strangers, and thought they were very well as they were. As Sunlight stood his ground, well pleased with the attention paid him, this sulky creature suddenly advanced to the charge, and bit so violently that had it not been for the nine buffalo skins Sunlight's last moment would have come. When the fight was ended, the buffalo skins were in ribbons, and the beaten animal writhing with pain on the grass.

Nothing now remained to be done but to drive the whole stud to the emperor's court. So the princess came down from the tree and mounted Sunlight, while the stud followed meekly after, the wounded horse bringing up the rear. On reaching the palace, she drove them into a yard, and went to inform the emperor of her arrival.

The news was told at once to Iliane, who ran down directly and called them to her one by one, each mare by its name. And at the first sight of her the wounded animal shook itself quickly, and in a moment its wounds were healed, and there was not even a mark on its glossy skin.

By this time the emperor, on hearing where she was, joined her in the yard, and at her request ordered the mares to be milked, so that both he and she might bathe in the milk and keep young for ever. But they would suffer no one to come near them, and the princess was commanded to perform this service also.

At this, the heart of the girl swelled within her. The hardest tasks were always given to her, and long before the two years were up, she would be worn out and useless. But while these thoughts passed through her mind, a fearful rain fell, such as no man remembered before, and rose till the mares were standing up to their knees in water. Then as suddenly it stopped, and, behold! the water was ice, which held the animals firmly in its grasp. And the princess's heart grew light again, and she sat down gaily to milk them, as if she had done it every morning of her life.

The love of the emperor for Iliane waxed greater day by day, but she paid no heed to him, and always had an excuse ready to put off their marriage. At length, when she had come to the end of everything she could think of, she said to him one day : ' Grant me, Sire, just one request more, and then I will really marry you ; for you have waited patiently this long time.'

' My beautiful dove,' replied the emperor, ' both I and all I possess are yours, so ask your will, and you shall have it.'

' Get me, then,' she said, ' a flask of the holy water that is kept in a little church beyond the river Jordan, and I will be your wife.'

Then the emperor ordered Fet-Fruners to ride without delay to the river Jordan, and to bring back, at whatever cost, the holy water for Iliane.

' This, my mistress,' said Sunlight, when she was saddling him, ' is the last and most difficult of your tasks. But fear nothing, for the hour of the emperor has struck.'

So they started ; and the horse, who was not a wizard for nothing, told the princess exactly where she was to look for the holy water.

' It stands,' he said, ' on the altar of a little church, and is guarded by a troop of nuns. They never sleep, night or day, but every now and then a hermit comes to visit them, and from him they learn certain things it is needful for them to know. When this happens, only one of the nuns remains on guard at a time, and if we are lucky enough to hit upon this moment, we may get hold of the vase at once ; if not, we shall have to wait the arrival of the hermit, however long it may be ; for there is no other means of obtaining the holy water.'

They came in sight of the church beyond the Jordan, and, to their great joy, beheld the hermit just arriving at the door. They could hear him calling the nuns around him, and saw them settle themselves under a tree, with the hermit in their midst—all but one, who remained on guard, as was the custom.

The hermit had a great deal to say, and the day was very hot, so the nun, tired of sitting by herself, lay down right across the threshold, and fell sound asleep.

Then Sunlight told the princess what she was to do, and the girl stepped softly over the sleeping nun, and crept like a cat along the dark aisle, feeling the wall with her fingers, lest she should fall over something and ruin it all by a noise. But she reached the altar in safety, and found the vase of holy water standing on it. This she thrust into her dress, and went back with the same care as she came. With a bound she was in the saddle, and seizing the reins bade Sunlight take her home as fast as his legs could carry him.

The sound of the flying hoofs aroused the nun, who understood instantly that the precious treasure was stolen, and her shrieks were so loud and piercing that all the rest came flying to see what was the matter. The hermit followed at their heels, but seeing it was impossible to overtake the thief, he fell on his knees and called his most deadly curse down on her head, praying that if the thief was a man, he might become a woman ; and if she was a woman, that she might become a man. In either case he thought that the punishment would be severe.

But punishments are things about which people do not always agree, and when the princess suddenly felt she was really the man she had pretended to be, she was delighted, and if the hermit had only been within reach she would have thanked him from her heart.

By the time she reached the emperor's court, Fet-Fruners looked a young man all over in the eyes of everyone; and even the mother of the genius would now have had her doubts set at rest. He drew forth the vase from his tunic and held it up to the emperor, saying: ' Mighty Sovereign, all hail ! I have fulfilled this task also, and I hope it is the last you have for me ; let another now take his turn.'

' I am content, Fet-Fruners,' replied the emperor, ' and when I am dead it is you who will sit upon my throne ; for I have yet no son to come after me. But if one is given me, and my dearest wish is accomplished, then you shall be his right hand, and guide him with your counsels.'

But though the emperor was satisfied, Iliane was not, and she determined to revenge herself on the emperor for the dangers which he had caused Fet-Fruners to run. And as for the vase of holy water, she thought that, in common politeness, her suitor ought to have fetched it himself, which he could have done without any risk at all.

So she ordered the great bath to be filled with the milk of her mares, and begged the emperor to clothe himself in white robes, and enter the bath with her, an invitation he accepted with joy. Then, when both were standing with the milk reaching to their necks, she sent for the horse which had fought Sunlight, and made a secret sign to him. The horse understood what he was to do, and from one nostril he breathed fresh air over Iliane, and from the other, he snorted a burning wind which shrivelled up the emperor where he stood, leaving only a little heap of ashes.

His strange death, which no one could explain, made a great sensation throughout the country, and the funeral his people gave him was the most splendid ever known. When it was over, Iliane summoned Fet-Fruners before her, and addressed him thus :

' Fet-Fruners ! it is you who brought me and have saved my life, and obeyed my wishes. It is you who gave me back my stud ; you who killed the genius, and the old witch his mother ; you who brought me the holy water. And you, and none other, shall be my husband.'

' Yes, I will marry you,' said the young man, with a voice almost as soft as when he was a princess. ' But know that in *our* house, it will be the cock who sings and not the hen ! '

[From *Sept Contes Roumains,* Jules Brun and Leo Bachelin.]

THE STORY OF HALFMAN

In a certain town there lived a judge who was married but had no children. One day he was standing lost in thought before his house, when an old man passed by.

' What is the matter, sir, said he; ' you look troubled ? '

' Oh, leave me alone, my good man ! '

' But what is it ? ' persisted the other.

' Well, I am successful in my profession and a person of importance, but I care nothing for it all, as I have no children.'

Then the old man said, ' Here are twelve apples. If your wife eats them, she will have twelve sons.'

The judge thanked him joyfully as he took the apples, and went to seek his wife. ' Eat these apples at once,' he cried, ' and you will have twelve sons.'

So she sat down and ate eleven of them, but just as she was in the middle of the twelfth her sister came in, and she gave her the half that was left.

The eleven sons came into the world, strong and handsome boys; but when the twelfth was born, there was only half of him.

By-and-by they all grew into men, and one day they told their father it was high time he found wives for them. ' I have a brother,' he answered, ' who lives away in the East, and he has twelve daughters ; go and marry them.' So the twelve sons saddled their horses and rode for twelve days, till they met an old woman.

' Good greeting to you, young men ! ' said she, ' we have

waited long for you, your uncle and I. The girls have become women, and are sought in marriage by many, but I knew you would come one day, and I have kept them for you. Follow me into my house.'

And the twelve brothers followed her gladly, and their father's brother stood at the door, and gave them meat and drink. But at night, when every one was asleep, Halfman crept softly to his brothers, and said to them, ' Listen, all of you! This man is no uncle of ours, but an ogre.'

' Nonsense ; of course he is our uncle,' answered they.

' Well, this very night you will see ! ' said Halfman. And he did not go to bed, but hid himself and watched.

Now in a little while he saw the wife of the ogre steal into the room on tiptoe and spread a red cloth over the brothers and then go and cover her daughters with a white cloth. After that she lay down and was soon snoring loudly. When Halfman was quite sure she was sound asleep, he took the red cloth from his brothers and put it on the girls, and laid their white cloth over his brothers. Next he drew their scarlet caps from their heads and exchanged them for the veils which the ogre's daughters were wearing. This was hardly done when he heard steps coming along the floor, so he hid himself quickly in the folds of a curtain. There was only half of him !

The ogress came slowly and gently along, stretching out her hands before her, so that she might not fall against anything unawares, for she had only a tiny lantern slung at her waist, which did not give much light. And when she reached the place where the sisters were lying, she stooped down and held a corner of the cloth up to the lantern. Yes! it certainly was red ! Still, to make sure that there was no mistake, she passed her hands lightly over their heads, and felt the caps that covered them. Then she was quite certain the brothers lay sleeping before her, and began to kill them one by one. And Halfman whispered to his brothers, 'Get up and run for your lives, as the ogress is killing her daughters.' The brothers needed no second bidding, and in a moment were out of the house.

By this time the ogress had slain all her daughters but one, who awoke suddenly and saw what had happened. 'Mother, what are you doing?' cried she. 'Do you know that you have killed my sisters?'

'Oh, woe is me!' wailed the ogress. 'Halfman has outwitted me after all!' And she turned to wreak vengeance on him, but he and his brothers were far away.

They rode all day till they got to the town where their real uncle lived, and inquired the way to his house.

'Why have you been so long in coming?' asked he, when they had found him.

'Oh, dear uncle, we were very nearly not coming at all!' replied they. 'We fell in with an ogress who took us home and would have killed us if it had not been for Halfman. He knew what was in her mind and saved us, and here we are. Now give us each a daughter to wife, and let us return whence we came.'

'Take them!' said the uncle; 'the eldest for the eldest, the second for the second, and so on to the youngest.'

But the wife of Halfman was the prettiest of them all, and the other brothers were jealous and said to each other: 'What, is he who is only half a man to get the best? Let us put him to death and give his wife to our eldest brother!' And they waited for a chance.

After they had all ridden, in company with their brides, for some distance, they arrived at a brook, and one of them asked, 'Now, who will go and fetch water from the brook?'

'Halfman is the youngest,' said the elder brother, 'he must go.'

So Halfman got down and filled a skin with water, and they drew it up by a rope and drank. When they had done drinking, Halfman, who was standing in the middle of the stream, called out: 'Throw me the rope and draw me up, for I cannot get out alone.' And the brothers threw him a rope to draw him up the steep bank; but when he was half-way up they cut the rope, and he fell back into the stream. Then the brothers rode away as fast as they could, with his bride.

Halfman sank down under the water from the force of the fall, but before he touched the bottom a fish came and said to him, 'Fear nothing, Halfman; I will help you.' And the fish guided him to a shallow place, so that he scrambled out. On the way it said to him, 'Do you understand what your brothers, whom you saved from death, have done to you?'

'Yes; but what am I to do?' asked Halfman.

'Take one of my scales,' said the fish, 'and when you find yourself in danger, throw it in the fire. Then I will appear before you.'

'Thank you,' said Halfman, and went his way, while the fish swam back to its home.

The country was strange to Halfman, and he wandered about without knowing where he was going, till he suddenly found the ogress standing before him. 'Ah, Halfman, have I got you at last? You killed my daughters and helped your brothers to escape. What do you think I shall do with you?'

'Whatever you like!' said Halfman.

'Come into my house, then,' said the ogress, and he followed her. 'Look here!' she called to her husband, 'I have got hold of Halfman. I am going to roast him, so be quick and make up the fire!'

So the ogre brought wood, and heaped it up till the flames roared up the chimney. Then he turned to his wife and said: 'It is all ready, let us put him on!'

'What is the hurry, my good ogre?' asked Halfman. 'You have me in your power, and I cannot escape. I am so thin now, I shall hardly make one mouthful. Better fatten me up; you will enjoy me much more.'

'That is a very sensible remark,' replied the ogre ;
' but what fattens you quickest ? '

' Butter, meat, and red wine,' answered Halfman.

' Very good ; we will lock you into this room, and here
you shall stay till you are ready for eating.'

So Halfman was locked into the room, and the ogre
and his wife brought him his food. At the end of three
months he said to his gaolers : ' Now I have got quite fat ;
take me out, and kill me.'

' Get out, then ! ' said the ogre.

' But,' went on Halfman, ' you and your wife had better
go to invite your friends to the feast, and your daughter
can stay in the house and look after me ! '

' Yes, that is a good idea,' answered they.

' You had better bring the wood in here,' continued
Halfman, ' and I will split it up small, so that there may
be no delay in cooking me.'

So the ogress gave Halfman a pile of wood and an axe,
and then set out with her husband, leaving Halfman and
her daughter busy in the house.

After he had chopped for a little while he called to the
girl, ' Come and help me, or else I shan't have it all
ready when your mother gets back.'

' All right,' said she, and held a billet of wood for him
to chop. But he raised his axe and cut off her head,
and ran away like the wind. By-and-by the ogre and
his wife returned and found their daughter lying without
her head, and they began to cry and sob, saying, ' This is
Halfman's work, why did we listen to him ? ' But Halfman was far away.

When he escaped from the house he ran on straight
before him for some time, looking for a safe shelter, as
he knew that the ogre's legs were much longer than his,
and that it was his only chance. At last he saw an iron
tower which he climbed up. Soon the ogre appeared,
looking right and left lest his prey should be sheltering
behind a rock or tree, but he did not know Halfman

was so near till he heard his voice calling, 'Come up! come up! you will find me here!'

'But how can I come up?' said the ogre, 'I see no door, and I could not possibly climb that tower.'

'Oh, there is no door,' replied Halfman.

'Then how did you climb up?'

'A fish carried me on his back.'

'And what am I to do?'

'You must go and fetch all your relations, and tell them to bring plenty of sticks; then you must light a fire, and let it burn till the tower becomes red hot. After that you can easily throw it down.'

'Very good,' said the ogre, and he went round to every relation he had, and told them to collect wood and bring it to the tower where Halfman was. The men did as they were ordered, and soon the tower was glowing like coral, but when they flung themselves against it to overthrow it, they caught themselves on fire and were burnt to death. And overhead sat Halfman, laughing heartily. But the ogre's wife was still alive, for she had taken no part in kindling the fire.

'Oh,' she shrieked with rage, 'you have killed my daughters and my husband, and all the men belonging to me; how can I get at you to avenge myself?'

'Oh, that is easy enough,' said Halfman. 'I will let down a rope, and if you tie it tightly round you, I will draw it up.'

'All right,' returned the ogress, fastening the rope which Halfman let down. 'Now pull me up.'

'Are you sure it is secure?'

'Yes, quite sure.'

'Don't be afraid.'

'Oh, I am not afraid at all!'

So Halfman slowly drew her up, and when she was near the top he let go the rope, and she fell down and broke her neck. Then Halfman heaved a great sigh and said, 'That was hard work; the rope has hurt my hands badly, but now I am rid of her for ever.'

So Halfman came down from the tower, and went on, till he got to a desert place, and as he was very tired, he lay down to sleep. While it was still dark, an ogress passed by, and she woke him and said, 'Halfman, to-morrow your brother is to marry your wife.'

'Oh, how can I stop it?' asked he. 'Will you help me?'

'Yes, I will,' replied the ogress.

'Thank you, thank you!' cried Halfman, kissing her on the forehead. 'My wife is dearer to me than anything else in the world, and it is not my brother's fault that I am not dead long ago.'

'Very well, I will rid you of him,' said the ogress, 'but only on one condition. If a boy is born to you, you must give him to me!'

'Oh, anything,' answered Halfman, 'as long as you deliver me from my brother, and get me my wife.'

'Mount on my back, then, and in a quarter of an hour we shall be there.'

The ogress was as good as her word, and in a few minutes they arrived at the outskirts of the town where Halfman and his brothers lived. Here she left him, while she went into the town itself, and found the wedding guests just leaving the brother's house. Unnoticed by anyone, the ogress crept into a curtain, changing herself into a scorpion, and when the brother was going to get into bed, she stung him behind the ear, so that he fell dead where he stood. Then she returned to Halfman and told him to go and claim his bride. He jumped up hastily from his seat, and took the road to his father's house. As he drew near he heard sounds of weeping and lamentations, and he said to a man he met: 'What is the matter?'

'The judge's eldest son was married yesterday, and died suddenly before night.'

'Well,' thought Halfman, 'my conscience is clear anyway, for it is quite plain he coveted my wife, and that is why he tried to drown me.' He went at once to his father's room, and found him sitting in tears on the floor. 'Dear father,' said Halfman, 'are you not glad to see me? You weep for my brother, but I am your son too, and he stole my bride from me and tried to drown me in the brook. If he is dead, I at least am alive.'

'No, no, he was better than you!' moaned the father.

'Why, dear father?'

'He told me you had behaved very ill,' said he.

'Well, call my brothers,' answered Halfman, 'as I have a story to tell them.' So the father called them all into his presence. Then Halfman began: 'After we were twelve days' journey from home, we met an ogress, who gave us greeting and said, "Why have you been so long coming? The daughters of your uncle have waited for you in vain," and she bade us follow her to the house, saying, "Now there need be no more delay; you can marry your cousins as soon as you please, and take them with you to your own home." But I warned my brothers that the man was not our uncle, but an ogre.

'When we lay down to sleep, she spread a red cloth over us, and covered her daughters with a white one; but I changed the cloths, and when the ogress came back in the middle of the night, and looked at the cloths, she mistook her own daughters for my brothers, and killed them one by one, all but the youngest. Then I woke my brothers, and we all stole softly from the house, and we rode like the wind to our real uncle.

'And when he saw us, he bade us welcome, and married us to his twelve daughters, the eldest to the eldest, and so on to me, whose bride was the youngest of all and also the prettiest. And my brothers were filled with envy, and left me to drown in a brook, but I was saved by a fish who showed me how to get out. Now, you are a judge! Who did well, and who did evil—I or my brothers?'

'Is this story true?' said the father, turning to his sons.

'It is true, my father,' answered they. 'It is even as Halfman has said, and the girl belongs to him.'

Then the judge embraced Halfman and said to him : 'You have done well, my son. Take your bride, and may you both live long and happily together!'

At the end of the year Halfman's wife had a son, and not long after she came one day hastily into the room. and found her husband weeping. 'What is the matter?' she asked.

'The matter?' said he.

'Yes, why are you weeping?'

'Because,' replied Halfman, 'the baby is not really ours, but belongs to an ogress.'

'Are you mad?' cried the wife. 'What do you mean by talking like that?'

'I promised,' said Halfman, 'when she undertook to kill my brother and to give you to me, that the first son we had should be hers.'

'And will she take him from us now?' said the poor woman.

'No, not quite yet,' replied Halfman; 'when he is bigger.'

'And is she to have all our children?' asked she.

'No, only this one,' returned Halfman.

Day by day the boy grew bigger, and one day as he was playing in the street with the other children, the ogress came by. 'Go to your father,' she said, 'and repeat this speech to him : " I want my forfeit ; when am I to have it?"'

'All right,' replied the child, but when he went home forgot all about it. The next day the ogress came again, and asked the boy what answer the father had given. 'I forgot all about it,' said he.

'Well, put this ring on your finger, and then you won't forget.'

'Very well,' replied the boy, and went home.

The next morning, as he was at breakfast, his mother said to him, ' Child, where did you get that ring ? '

'A woman gave it to me yesterday, and she told me, father, to tell you that she wanted her forfeit, and when was she to have it ? '

Then his father burst into tears and said, ' If she comes again you must say to her that your parents bid her take her forfeit at once, and depart.'

At this they both began to weep afresh, and his mother kissed him, and put on his new clothes and said, ' If the woman bids you to follow her, you must go,' but the boy did not heed her grief, he was so pleased with his new clothes. And when he went out, he said to his play-fellows, ' Look how smart I am ; I am going away with my aunt to foreign lands.'

At that moment the ogress came up and asked him, ' Did you give my message to your father and mother ? '

' Yes, dear aunt, I did.'

' And what did they say ? '

' Take it away at once ! '

So she took him.

But when dinner-time came, and the boy did not return, his father and mother knew that he would never come back, and they sat down and wept all day. At last Halfman rose up and said to his wife, ' Be comforted ; we will wait a year, and then I will go to the ogress and see the boy, and how he is cared for.'

' Yes, that will be the best,' said she.

The year passed away, then Halfman saddled his horse, and rode to the place where the ogress had found him sleeping. She was not there, but not knowing what to do next, he got off his horse and waited. About midnight she suddenly stood before him.

' Halfman, why did you come here ? ' said she.

' I have a question I want to ask you.'

' Well, ask it ; but I know quite well what it is. Your wife wishes you to ask whether I shall carry off your second son as I did the first.'

' Yes, that is it,' replied Halfman. Then he seized her hand and said, ' Oh, let me see my son, and how he looks, and what he is doing.'

The ogress was silent, but stuck her staff hard in the earth, and the earth opened, and the boy appeared and said, ' Dear father, have you come too ? ' And his father clasped him in his arms, and began to cry. But the boy struggled to be free, saying ' Dear father, put me down. I have got a new mother, who is better than the old one ; and a new father, who is better than you.'

Then his father sat him down and said, ' Go in peace, my boy, but listen first to me. Tell your father the ogre and your mother the ogress, that never more shall they have any children of mine.'

' All right,' replied the boy, and called ' Mother ! '

' What is it ? '

' You are never to take away any more of my father and mother's children ! '

' Now that I have got you, I don't want any more,' answered she.

Then the boy turned to his father and said, ' Go in peace, dear father, and give my mother greeting and tell her not to be anxious any more, for she can keep all her children.'

And Halfman mounted his horse and rode home, and told his wife all he had seen, and the message sent by Mohammed—Mohammed the son of Halfman, the son of the judge.

[*Märchen und Gedichte aus der Stadt Tripolis.* Hans von Stumme.]

THE PRINCE WHO WANTED TO SEE
THE WORLD

THERE was once a king who had only one son, and this young man tormented his father from morning till night to allow him to travel in far countries. For a long time the king refused to give him leave ; but at last, wearied out, he granted permission, and ordered his treasurer to produce a large sum of money for the prince's expenses. The youth was overjoyed at the thought that he was really going to see the world, and after tenderly embracing his father he set forth.

He rode on for some weeks without meeting with any adventures ; but one night when he was resting at an inn, he came across another traveller, with whom he fell into conversation, in the course of which the stranger inquired if he never played cards. The young man replied that he was very fond of doing so. Cards were brought, and in a very short time the prince had lost every penny he possessed to his new acquaintance. When there was absolutely nothing left at the bottom of the bag, the stranger proposed that they should have just one more game, and that if the prince won he should have the money restored to him, but in case he lost, should remain in the inn for three years, and besides that should be his servant for another three. The prince agreed to those terms, played, and lost ; so the stranger took rooms for him, and furnished him with bread and water every day for three years.

The prince lamented his lot, but it was no use ; and at the end of three years he was released and had to go to the house of the stranger, who was really the king

of a neighbouring country, and be his servant. Before
he had gone very far he met a woman carrying a child,
which was crying from hunger. The prince took it from

The Prince feeds the baby
from his flask.

her, and fed it with his last crust of bread and last drop of
water, and then gave it back to its mother. The woman
thanked him gratefully, and said:

'Listen, my lord. You must walk straight on till you notice a very strong scent, which comes from a garden by the side of the road. Go in and hide yourself close to a tank, where three doves will come to bathe. As the last one flies past you, catch hold of its robe of feathers, and refuse to give it back till the dove has promised you three things.'

The young man did as he was told, and everything happened as the woman had said. He took the robe of feathers from the dove, who gave him in exchange for it a ring, a collar, and one of its own plumes, saying: 'When you are in any trouble, cry "Come to my aid, O dove!" I am the daughter of the king you are going to serve, who hates your father and made you gamble in order to cause your ruin.'

Thus the prince went on his way, and in course of time he arrived at the king's palace. As soon as his master knew he was there, the young man was sent for into his presence, and three bags were handed to him with these words:

'Take this wheat, this millet, and this barley, and sow them at once, so that I may have loaves of them all to-morrow.'

The prince stood speechless at this command, but the king did not condescend to give any further explanation, and when he was dismissed the young man flew to the room which had been set aside for him, and pulling out his feather, he cried: 'Dove, dove! be quick and come.'

'What is it?' said the dove, flying in through the open window, and the prince told her of the task before him, and of his despair at being unable to accomplish it. 'Fear nothing; it will be all right,' replied the dove, as she flew away again.

The next morning when the prince awoke he saw the three loaves standing beside his bed. He jumped up and dressed, and he was scarcely ready when a page arrived with the message that he was to go at once into the king's chamber. Taking the loaves in his arm he followed the boy, and, bowing low, laid them down before the king. The monarch looked at the loaves for a moment without speaking, then he said :

'Good. The man who can do this can also find the ring which my eldest daughter dropped into the sea.'

FOR A MOMENT THE DOVE'S HEAD BECOMES THAT OF A GIRL

The prince hastened back to his room and summoned the dove, and when she heard this new command she said : 'Now listen. To-morrow take a knife and a basin and go down to the shore and get into a boat you will find there.'

The young man did not know what he was to do when he was in the boat or where he was to go, but as the dove had come to his rescue before, he was ready to obey her blindly.

When he reached the boat he found the dove perched on one of the masts, and at a signal from her he put to sea ; the wind was behind them and they soon lost sight of land.   The dove then spoke for the first time and said, ' Take that knife and cut off my head, but be careful that not a single drop of blood falls to the ground.   Afterwards you must throw it into the sea.'

Wondering at this strange order, the prince picked up his knife and severed the dove's head from her body at one stroke.   A little while after a dove rose from the water with a ring in its beak, and laying it in the prince's hand, dabbled itself with the blood that was in the basin, when its head became that of a beautiful girl.   Another moment and it had vanished completely, and the prince took the ring and made his way back to the palace.

The king stared with surprise at the sight of the ring, but he thought of another way of getting rid of the young man which was surer even than the other two.

' This evening you will mount my colt and ride him to the field, and break him in properly.'

The prince received this command as silently as he had received the rest, but no sooner was he in his room than he called for the dove, who said : 'Attend to me. My father longs to see you dead, and thinks he will kill you by this means.   He himself is the colt, my mother is the saddle, my two sisters are the stirrups, and I am the bridle.   Do not forget to take a good club, to help you in dealing with such a crew.'

So the prince mounted the colt, and gave him such a beating that when he came to the palace to announce that the animal was now so meek that it could be ridden by the smallest child, he found the king so bruised that he had to be wrapped in cloths dipped in vinegar, the mother was too stiff to move, and several of the daughters' ribs were broken.   The youngest, however, was quite unharmed. That night she came to the prince and whispered to him :

'Now that they are all in too much pain to move, we had better seize our chance and run away. Go to the stable and saddle the leanest horse you can find there.' But the prince was foolish enough to choose the fattest : and when they had started and the princess saw what he had done, she was very sorry, for though this horse ran like the wind, the other flashed like thought. However, it was dangerous to go back, and they rode on as fast as the horse would go.

In the night the king sent for his youngest daughter, and as she did not come he sent again ; but she did not come any the more for that. The queen, who was a witch, discovered that her daughter had gone off with the prince, and told her husband he must leave his bed and go after them. The king got slowly up, groaning with pain, and dragged himself to the stables, where he saw the lean horse still in his stall.

Leaping on his back he shook the reins, and his daughter, who knew what to expect and had her eyes open, saw the horse start forward, and in the twinkling of an eye changed her own steed into a cell, the prince into a hermit, and herself into a nun.

When the king reached the chapel, he pulled up his horse and asked if a girl and a young man had passed that way. The hermit raised his eyes, which were bent on the ground, and said that he had not seen a living creature. The king, much disgusted at this news, and not knowing what to do, returned home and told his wife that, though he had ridden for miles, he had come across nothing but a hermit and a nun in a cell.

'Why those were the runaways, of course,' she cried, flying into a passion, 'and if you had only brought a scrap of the nun's dress, or a bit of stone from the wall, I should have had them in my power.'

At these words the king hastened back to the stable, and

brought out the lean horse who travelled quicker than thought. But his daughter saw him coming, and changed her horse into a plot of ground, herself into a rose-tree covered with roses, and the prince into a gardener. As the king rode up, the gardener looked up from the tree which he was trimming and asked if anything was the matter. 'Have you seen a young man and a girl go by?' said the king, and the gardener shook his head and replied that no one had passed that way since he had been working there. So the king turned his steps homewards and told his wife.

'Idiot!' cried she, 'if you had only brought me one of the roses, or a handful of earth, I should have had them in my power. But there is no time to waste. I shall have to go with you myself.'

The girl saw them from afar, and a great fear fell on her, for she knew her mother's skill in magic of all kinds. However, she determined to fight to the end, and changed the horse into a deep pool, herself into an eel, and the prince into a turtle. But it was no use. Her mother recognised them all, and, pulling up, asked her daughter if she did not repent and would not like to come home again. The eel wagged 'No' with her tail, and the queen told her husband to put a drop of water from the pool into a bottle, because it was only by that means that she could seize hold of her daughter. The king did as he was bid, and was just in the act of drawing the bottle out of the water after he had filled it, when the turtle knocked against and spilt it all. The king then filled it a second time, but again the turtle was too quick for him.

The queen saw that she was beaten, and called down a curse on her daughter that the prince should forget all about her. After having relieved her feelings in this manner, she and the king went back to the palace.

The others resumed their proper shapes and continued their journey, but the princess was so silent that at last the prince asked her what was the matter. 'It is because I know you will soon forget all about me,' said she, and though he laughed at her and told her it was impossible, she did not cease to believe it.

They rode on and on and on, till they reached the end of the world, where the prince lived, and leaving the girl in an inn he went himself to the palace to ask leave of his father to present her to him as his bride ; but in his joy at seeing his family once more he forgot all about her, and even listened when the king spoke of arranging a marriage for him.

When the poor girl heard this she wept bitterly, and cried out, ' Come to me, my sisters, for I need you badly ! '

In a moment they stood beside her, and the elder one said, ' Do not be sad, all will go well,' and they told the innkeeper that if any of the king's servants wanted any birds for their master they were to be sent up to them, as they had three doves for sale.

And so it fell out, and as the doves were very beautiful the servant bought them for the king, who admired them so much that he called his son to look at them. The prince was much pleased with the doves and was coaxing them to come to him, when one fluttered on to the top of the window and said, ' If you could only hear us speak, you would admire us still more.'

And another perched on a table and added, ' Talk away, it might help him to remember ! '

And the third flew on his shoulder and whispered to him, ' Put on this ring, prince, and see if it fits you.'

And it did. Then they hung a collar round his neck, and held a feather on which was written the name of the dove. And at last his memory came back to him, and he declared he would marry the princess and nobody else. So the next day the wedding took place, and they lived happy till they died.

[From the Portuguese.]

VIRGILIUS THE SORCERER

LONG, long ago there was born to a Roman knight and his wife Maja a little boy called Virgilius. While he was still quite little, his father died, and the kinsmen, instead of being a help and protection to the child and his mother, robbed them of their lands and money, and the widow, fearing that they might take the boy's life also, sent him away to Spain, that he might study in the great University of Toledo.

Virgilius was fond of books, and pored over them all day long. But one afternoon, when the boys were given a holiday, he took a long walk, and found himself in a place where he had never been before. In front of him was a cave, and, as no boy ever sees a cave without entering it, he went in. The cave was so deep that it seemed to Virgilius as if it must run far into the heart of the mountain, and he thought he would like to see if it came out anywhere on the other side. For some time he walked on in pitch darkness, but he went steadily on, and by-and-by a glimmer of light shot across the floor, and he heard a voice calling, ' Virgilius ! Virgilius ! '

' Who calls ? ' he asked, stopping and looking round.

' Virgilius ! ' answered the voice, ' do you mark upon the ground where you are standing a slide or bolt ? '

' I do,' replied Virgilius.

' Then,' said the voice, ' draw back that bolt, and set me free.'

' But who are you ? ' asked Virgilius, who never did anything in a hurry.

' I am an evil spirit,' said the voice, ' shut up here till Doomsday, unless a man sets me free. If you will let me out I will give you some magic books, which will make you wiser than any other man.'

Now Virgilius loved wisdom, and was tempted by these promises, but again his prudence came to his aid, and he demanded that the books should be handed over to him first, and that he should be told how to use them. The evil spirit, unable to help itself, did as Virgilius bade him, and then the bolt was drawn back. Underneath was a small hole, and out of this the evil spirit gradually wriggled himself; but it took some time, for when at last he stood upon the ground he proved to be about three times as large as Virgilius himself, and coal black besides.

' Why, you can't have been as big as that when you were in the hole ! ' cried Virgilius.

' But I was ! ' replied the spirit.

' I don't believe it ! ' answered Virgilius.

' Well, I'll just get in and show you,' said the spirit, and after turning and twisting, and curling himself up, then he lay neatly packed into the hole. Then Virgilius drew the bolt, and, picking the books up under his arm, he left the cave.

For the next few weeks Virgilius hardly ate or slept, so busy was he in learning the magic the books contained. But at the end of that time a messenger from his mother arrived in Toledo, begging him to come at once to Rome, as she had been ill, and could look after their affairs no longer.

Though sorry to leave Toledo, where he was much thought of as showing promise of great learning, Virgilius would willingly have set out at once, but there were many things he had first to see to. So he entrusted to the messenger four pack-horses laden with precious things, and a white palfrey on which she was to ride out every day. Then he set about his own preparations, and, followed by a large train of scholars, he at length started for Rome, from which he had been absent twelve years.

His mother welcomed him back with tears in her eyes, and his poor kinsmen pressed round him, but the rich ones kept away, for they feared that they would no longer be able to rob their kinsman as they had done for many years past. Of course, Virgilius paid no attention to this behaviour, though he noticed they looked with envy on the rich presents he bestowed on the poorer relations and on anyone who had been kind to his mother.

Soon after this had happened the season of tax-gathering came round, and everyone who owned land was bound to present himself before the emperor. Like the rest, Virgilius went to court, and demanded justice from the emperor against the men who had robbed him. But as these were kinsmen to the emperor he gained nothing, as the emperor told him he would think over the matter for the next four years, and then give judgment. This reply naturally did not satisfy Virgilius, and, turning on his heel, he went back to his own home, and, gathering in his harvest, he stored it up in his various houses.

When the enemies of Virgilius heard of this, they assembled together and laid siege to his castle. But Virgilius was a match for them. Coming forth from the castle so as to meet them face to face, he cast a spell over them of such power that they could not move, and then bade them defiance. After which he lifted the spell, and the invading army slunk back to Rome, and reported what Virgilius had said to the emperor.

Now the emperor was accustomed to have his lightest word obeyed, almost before it was uttered, and he hardly knew how to believe his ears. But he got together another army, and marched straight off to the castle. But directly they took up their position Virgilius girded them about with a great river, so that they could neither move hand nor foot, then, hailing the emperor, he offered

VIRGILIVS AND THE EVIL SPIRIT

H J FORD

him peace, and asked for his friendship. The emperor, however, was too angry to listen to anything, so Virgilius, whose patience was exhausted, feasted his own followers in the presence of the starving host, who could not stir hand or foot.

Things seemed getting desperate, when a magician arrived in the camp and offered to sell his services to the emperor. His proposals were gladly accepted, and in a moment the whole of the garrison sank down as if they were dead, and Virgilius himself had much ado to keep awake. He did not know how to fight the magician, but with a great effort struggled to open his Black Book, which told him what spells to use. In an instant all his foes seemed turned to stone, and where each man was there he stayed. Some were half way up the ladders, some had one foot over the wall, but wherever they might chance to be there every man remained, even the emperor and his sorcerer. All day they stayed there like flies upon the wall, but during the night Virgilius stole softly to the emperor, and offered him his freedom, as long as he would do him justice. The emperor, who by this time was thoroughly frightened, said he would agree to anything Virgilius desired. So Virgilius took off his spells, and, after feasting the army and bestowing on every man a gift, bade them return to Rome. And more than that, he built a square tower for the emperor, and in each corner all that was said in that quarter of the city might be heard, while if you stood in the centre every whisper throughout Rome would reach your ears.

Having settled his affairs with the emperor and his enemies, Virgilius had time to think of other things, and his first act was to fall in love! The lady's name was Febilla, and her family was noble, and her face fairer than any in Rome, but she only mocked Virgilius, and was always playing tricks upon him. To this end, she bade him one day come to visit her in the tower where she lived, promising to let down a basket to draw him up as far as the roof. Virgilius was enchanted at this quite unexpected favour, and stepped with glee into the basket. It was drawn up very slowly, and by-and-by came altogether to a standstill, while from above rang the voice of Febilla crying, ' Rogue of a sorcerer, there shalt thou hang ! ' And there he hung over the market-place, which was soon thronged with people, who made fun of him till he was mad with rage. At last the emperor, hearing of his plight, commanded Febilla to release him, and Virgilius went home vowing vengeance.

The next morning every fire in Rome went out, and as there were no matches in those days this was a very serious matter. The emperor, guessing that this was the work of Virgilius, besought him to break the spell. Then Virgilius ordered a scaffold to be erected in the market-place, and Febilla to be brought clothed in a single white garment. And further, he bade every one to snatch fire from the maiden, and to suffer no neighbour to kindle it. And when the maiden appeared, clad in her white smock, flames of fire curled about her, and the Romans brought some torches, and some straw, and some shavings, and fires were kindled in Rome again.

For three days she stood there, till every hearth in Rome was alight, and then she was suffered to go where she would.

But the emperor was wroth at the vengeance of Virgilius, and threw him into prison, vowing that he should be put to death. And when everything was ready he was led out to the Viminal Hill, where he was to die.

He went quietly with his guards, but the day was hot, and on reaching his place of execution he begged for some water. A pail was brought, and he, crying ' Emperor, all hail ! seek for me in Sicily,' jumped headlong into the pail, and vanished from their sight.

For some time we hear no more of Virgilius, or how he made his peace with the emperor, but the next event in his history was his being sent for to the palace to give the emperor advice how to guard Rome from foes within

FEBILLA'S PUNISHMENT

as well as foes without. Virgilius spent many days in
deep thought, and at length invented a plan which was
known to all as the ' Preservation of Rome.'

On the roof of the Capitol, which was the most famous
public building in the city, he set up statues representing
the gods worshipped by every nation subject to Rome,
and in the middle stood the god of Rome herself. Each
of the conquered gods held in its hand a bell, and if there
was even a thought of treason in any of the countries
its god turned its back upon the god of Rome and rang its
bell furiously, and the senators came hurrying to see who
was rebelling against the majesty of the empire. Then
they made ready their armies, and marched against the foe.

Now there was a country which had long felt bitter
jealousy of Rome, and was anxious for some way of
bringing about its destruction. So the people chose three
men who could be trusted, and, loading them with money,
sent them to Rome, bidding them to pretend that they
were diviners of dreams. No sooner had the messengers
reached the city than they stole out at night and buried a
pot of gold far down in the earth, and let down another into
the bed of the Tiber, just where a bridge spans the river.

Next day they went to the senate house, where the
laws were made, and, bowing low, they said, ' Oh, noble
lords, last night we dreamed that beneath the foot of a
hill there lies buried a pot of gold. Have we your leave
to dig for it?' And leave having been given, the messengers took workmen and dug up the gold and made
merry with it.

A few days later the diviners again appeared before
the senate, and said, ' Oh, noble lords, grant us leave to
seek out another treasure, which has been revealed to us
in a dream as lying under the bridge over the river.'

And the senators gave leave, and the messengers hired
boats and men, and let down ropes with hooks, and at
length drew up the pot of gold, some of which they gave
as presents to the senators.

A week or two passed by, and once more they appeared in the senate house.

'O, noble lords!' said they, 'last night in a vision we beheld twelve casks of gold lying under the foundation stone of the Capitol, on which stands the statue of the Preservation of Rome. Now, seeing that by your goodness we have been greatly enriched by our former dreams, we wish, in gratitude, to bestow this third treasure on you for your own profit; so give us workers, and we will begin to dig without delay.'

And receiving permission they began to dig, and when the messengers had almost undermined the Capitol they stole away as secretly as they had come.

And next morning the stone gave way, and the sacred statue fell on its face and was broken. And the senators knew that their greed had been their ruin.

From that day things went from bad to worse, and every morning crowds presented themselves before the emperor, complaining of the robberies, murders, and other crimes that were committed nightly in the streets.

The emperor, desiring nothing so much as the safety of his subjects, took counsel with Virgilius how this violence could be put down.

Virgilius thought hard for a long time, and then he spoke:

'Great prince,' said he, 'cause a copper horse and rider to be made, and stationed in front of the Capitol. Then make a proclamation that at ten o'clock a bell will toll, and every man is to enter his house, and not leave it again.'

The emperor did as Virgilius advised, but thieves and murderers laughed at the horse, and went about their misdeeds as usual.

But at the last stroke of the bell the horse set off at full gallop through the streets of Rome, and by daylight men counted over two hundred corpses that it had trodden down. The rest of the thieves—and there were still many remaining—instead of being

frightened into honesty, as Virgilius had hoped, prepared
rope ladders with hooks to them, and when they heard
the sound of the horse's hoofs they stuck their ladders

· THE · COPPER · HORSE ·

into the walls, and climbed up above the reach of the
horse and its rider.

Then the emperor commanded two copper dogs to
be made that would run after the horse, and when the

thieves, hanging from the walls, mocked and jeered at
Virgilius and the emperor, the dogs leaped high after them
and pulled them to the ground, and bit them to death.

Thus did Virgilius restore peace and order to the city.

Now about this time there came to be noised abroad
the fame of the daughter of the sultan who ruled over the
province of Babylon, and indeed she was said to be the
most beautiful princess in the world.

Virgilius, like the rest, listened to the stories that were
told of her, and fell so violently in love with all he heard
that he built a bridge in the air, which stretched all the way
between Rome and Babylon. He then passed over it to visit
the princess, who, though somewhat surprised to see him,
gave him welcome, and after some conversation became
in her turn anxious to see the distant country where this
stranger lived, and he promised that he would carry her
there himself, without wetting the soles of his feet.

The princess spent some days in the palace of Virgilius, looking at wonders of which she had never dreamed,
though she declined to accept the presents he longed
to heap on her. The hours passed as if they were
minutes, till the princess said that she could be no
longer absent from her father. Then Virgilius conducted
her himself over the airy bridge, and laid her gently down
on her own bed, where she was found next morning by
her father.

She told him all that had happened to her, and he pretended to be very much interested, and begged that the
next time Virgilius came he might be introduced to him.

Soon after, the sultan received a message from his
daughter that the stranger was there, and he commanded
that a feast should be made ready, and, sending for the
princess delivered into her hands a cup, which he said
she was to present to Virgilius herself, in order to do him
honour.

When they were all seated at the feast the princess
rose and presented the cup to Virgilius, who directly he
had drunk fell into a deep sleep.

VIRGILIVS THE SORCERER
· CARRIES AWAY ·
THE PRINCESS OF BABYLON

Then the sultan ordered his guards to bind him, and left him there till the following day.

Directly the sultan was up he summoned his lords and nobles into his great hall, and commanded that the cords which bound Virgilius should be taken off, and the prisoner brought before him. The moment he appeared the sultan's passion broke forth, and he accused his captive of the crime of conveying the princess into distant lands without his leave.

Virgilius replied that if he had taken her away he had also brought her back, when he might have kept her, and that if they would set him free to return to his own land he would come hither no more.

'Not so!' cried the sultan, 'but a shameful death you shall die!' And the princess fell on her knees, and begged she might die with him.

'You are out in your reckoning, Sir Sultan!' said Virgilius, whose patience was at an end, and he cast a spell over the sultan and his lords, so that they believed that the great river of Babylon was flowing through the hall, and that they must swim for their lives. So, leaving them to plunge and leap like frogs and fishes, Virgilius took the princess in his arms, and carried her over the airy bridge back to Rome.

Now Virgilius did not think that either his palace, or even Rome itself, was good enough to contain such a pearl as the princess, so he built her a city whose foundations stood upon eggs, buried far away down in the depths of the sea. And in the city was a square tower, and on the roof of the tower was a rod of iron, and across the rod he laid a bottle, and on the bottle he placed an egg, and from the egg there hung chained an apple, which hangs there to this day. And when the egg shakes the city quakes, and when the egg shall be broken the city shall be destroyed. And the city Virgilius filled full of wonders, such as never were seen before, and he called its name Naples.

[Adapted from ' Virgilius the Sorcerer.']

MOGARZEA AND HIS SON

THERE was once a little boy, whose father and mother, when they were dying, left him to the care of a guardian. But the guardian whom they chose turned out to be a wicked man, and spent all the money, so the boy determined to go away and strike out a path for himself.

So one day he set off, and walked and walked through woods and meadows till when evening came he was very tired, and did not know where to sleep. He climbed a hill and looked about him to see if there was no light shining from a window. At first all seemed dark, but at length he noticed a tiny spark far, far off, and, plucking up his spirits, he at once went in search of it.

The night was nearly half over before he reached the spark, which turned out to be a big fire, and by the fire a man was sleeping who was so tall he might have been a giant. The boy hesitated for a moment what he should do; then he crept close up to the man, and lay down by his legs.

When the man awoke in the morning he was much surprised to find the boy nestling up close to him.

'Dear me! where do you come from?' said he.

'I am your son, born in the night,' replied the boy.

'If that is true,' said the man, 'you shall take care of my sheep, and I will give you food. But take care you never cross the border of my land, or you will repent it.' Then he pointed out where the border of his land lay, and bade the boy begin his work at once.

The young shepherd led his flock out to the richest

meadows and stayed with them till evening, when he brought them back, and helped the man to milk them. When this was done, they both sat down to supper, and while they were eating the boy asked the big man:

What is your name, father?'

MOGARZEA ⚬ & ⚬ HIS ⚬ SON ⚬   " WHERE DO YOU COME FROM ?"

'Mogarzea,' answered he.

'I wonder you are not tired of living by yourself in this lonely place.'

'There is no reason you should wonder! Don't you know that there was never a bear yet who danced of his own free will?'

'Yes, that is true,' replied the boy. 'But why is it you are always so sad? Tell me your history, father.'

'What is the use of my telling you things that would only make you sad too?'

'Oh, never mind that! I should like to hear. Are you not my father, and am I not your son?'

'Well, if you really want to know my story, this is it: As I told you, my name is Mogarzea, and my father is an emperor. I was on my way to the Sweet Milk Lake, which lies not far from here, to marry one of the three fairies who have made the lake their home. But on the road three wicked elves fell on me, and robbed me of my soul, so that ever since I have stayed in this spot watching my sheep without wishing for anything different, without having felt one moment's joy, or ever once being able to laugh. And the horrible elves are so ill-natured that if anyone sets one foot on their land he is instantly punished. That is why I warn you to be careful, lest you should share my fate.'

'All right, I will take great care. Do let me go, father,' said the boy, as they stretched themselves out to sleep.

At sunrise the boy got up and led his sheep out to feed, and for some reason he did not feel tempted to cross into the grassy meadows belonging to the elves, but let his flock pick up what pasture they could on Mogarzea's dry ground.

On the third day he was sitting under the shadow of a tree, playing on his flute—and there was nobody in the world who could play a flute better—when one of his sheep strayed across the fence into the flowery fields of the elves, and another and another followed it. But the boy was so absorbed in his flute that he noticed nothing till half the flock were on the other side.

He jumped up, still playing on his flute, and went after the sheep, meaning to drive them back to their own side of the border, when suddenly he saw before him three beautiful maidens who stopped in front of him, and began to dance. The boy understood what he must do, and played with all his might, but the maidens danced on till evening.

'Now let me go,' he cried at last, 'for poor Mogarzea must be dying of hunger. I will come and play for you to morrow.'

'Well, you may go!' they said, 'but remember that even if you break your promise you will not escape us.'

So they both agreed that the next day he should come straight there with the sheep, and play to them till the sun went down. This being settled, they each returned home.

Mogarzea was surprised to find that his sheep gave so much more milk than usual, but as the boy declared he had never crossed the border the big man did not trouble his head further, and ate his supper heartily.

With the earliest gleams of light, the boy was off with his sheep to the elfin meadow, and at the first notes of his flute the maidens appeared before him and danced and danced and danced till evening came. Then the boy let the flute slip through his fingers, and trod on it, as if by accident.

If you had heard the noise he made, and how he wrung his hands and wept and cried that he had lost his only companion, you would have been sorry for him. The hearts of the elves were quite melted, and they did all they could to comfort him.

'I shall never find another flute like that, moaned he. 'I have never heard one whose tone was as sweet as mine! It was cut from the centre of a seven-year-old cherry tree!'

'There is a cherry tree in our garden that is exactly seven years old,' said they. 'Come with us, and you shall make yourself another flute.'

So they all went to the cherry tree, and when they were standing round it the youth explained that if he tried to cut it down with an axe he might very likely split open the heart of the tree, which was needed for the flute. In order to prevent this, he would make a little cut in the bark, just large enough for them to put their fingers in, and with this help he could manage to tear the tree in two, so that the heart should run no risk of damage. The elves did as he told them without a

• MOGARZEA • & • HIS • SON • RETURN • HOME •

thought; then he quickly drew out the axe, which had been sticking into the cleft, and behold! all their fingers were imprisoned tight in the tree.

It was in vain that they shrieked with pain and tried to free themselves. They could do nothing, and the young man remained cold as marble to all their entreaties.

Then he demanded of them Mogarzea's soul.

'Oh, well, if you must have it, it is in a bottle on the window sill,' said they, hoping that they might obtain their freedom at once. But they were mistaken.

'You have made so many men suffer,' answered he sternly, 'that it is but just you should suffer yourselves, but to-morrow I will let you go.' And he turned towards home, taking his sheep and the soul of Mogarzea with him.

Mogarzea was waiting at the door, and as the boy drew near he began scolding him for being so late. But at the first word of explanation the man became beside himself with joy, and he sprang so high into the air that the false soul which the elves had given him flew out of his mouth, and his own, which had been shut tightly into the flask of water, took its place.

When his excitement had somewhat calmed down, he cried to the boy, 'Whether you are really my son matters nothing to me; tell me, how can I repay you for what you have done for me?'

'By showing me where the Milk Lake is, and how I can get one of the three fairies who lives there to wife, and by letting me remain your son for ever.'

The night was passed by Mogarzea and his son in songs and feasting, for both were too happy to sleep, and when day dawned they set out together to free the elves from the tree. When they reached the place of their imprisonment, Mogarzea took the cherry tree and all the elves with it on his back, and carried them off to his father's kingdom, where everyone rejoiced to see him home again. But all he did was to point to the boy who had saved him, and had followed him with his flock.

For three days the boy stayed in the palace, receiving the thanks and praises of the whole court. Then he said to Mogarzea :

'The time has come for me to go hence, but tell me, I pray you, how to find the Sweet Milk Lake, and I will return, and will bring my wife back with me.'

Mogarzea tried in vain to make him stay, but, finding it was useless, he told him all he knew, for he himself had never seen the lake.

For three summer days the boy and his flute journeyed on, till one evening he reached the lake, which lay in the kingdom of a powerful fairy. The next morning had scarcely dawned when the youth went down to the shore, and began to play on his flute, and the first notes had hardly sounded when he saw a beautiful fairy standing before him, with hair and robes that shone like gold. He gazed at her in wonder, when suddenly she began to dance. Her movements were so graceful that he forgot to play, and as soon as the notes of his flute ceased she vanished from his sight. The next day the same thing happened, but on the third he took courage, and drew a little nearer, playing on his flute all the while. Suddenly he sprang forward, seized her in his arms and kissed her, and plucked a rose from her hair.

The fairy gave a cry, and begged him to give her back her rose, but he would not. He only stuck the rose in his hat, and turned a deaf ear to all her prayers.

At last she saw that her entreaties were vain, and agreed to marry him, as he wished. And they went together to the palace, where Mogarzea was still waiting for him, and the marriage was celebrated by the emperor himself. But every May they returned to the Milk Lake, they and their children, and bathed in its waters.

[Oltümänische Märchen.]